The End of the Road

Rosaline Riley

Published by: Braxted Books

12 Braxted Park, London SW16 3DW, UK

Copyright © 2015 Rosaline Riley

A CIP catalogue record for this book is available from the British Library

ISBN: 978-0-9932122-0-8

For Kevin

Contents

'The stupid neither forgive nor forget; the naïve forgive and forget; the wise forgive but do not forget.' (Thomas Szasz)

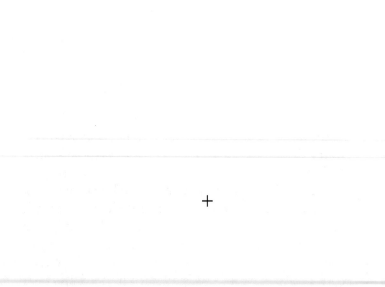

MISSING

1

'There's not a lot to tell, really,' Jane said. 'Frances was up here for the weekend. I picked her up from the station at about half past five . . .'

She paused. The policewoman, seated on the sofa opposite her, was scribbling this down and she wondered if she was speaking too fast. 'It was raining really hard,' she went on, more slowly now, 'so when we got back here we just dashed straight inside and left her case in the boot of the car.'

She paused again, but the policewoman glanced up at her impatiently, so obviously dictation speed was not required. 'Later on,' she continued briskly, 'she said she might as well go and bring it in because the rain was showing no sign of stopping. So I said there was an old cagoule of mine hanging up by the front door that she could put on. And off she went. Well . . . she'd been gone for ages and I was waiting to dish up our evening meal, so I went to see what was taking so long. But she wasn't there. . . . and it was absolutely pouring down.'

Jane had been telling this story all evening: first to her neighbours who had helped her search outside; then several panic-stricken times over the phone to her daughter, Lucy; next – and more calmly – to Fran's daughter, Emer; and finally, just over an hour ago, to the policeman who had answered her frantic call to the police station. The same story over and over again. Except that when she'd spoken to Emer, she'd said that it was 'pissing down'. She knew that if she'd said this when speaking to Lucy, her daughter would have sighed and murmured her disapproval. It wasn't the language as such that Lucy objected to, though. She never minded when Fran said things like that. It just seemed that there was one rule for mothers, another for mothers-in-law.

Jane looked away from the policewoman and stared out of the large lounge window into the darkness beyond. She could still hear the rain but it wasn't lashing the windows with the same ferocity as it had been doing earlier in the evening. There was another police officer – a young man – out there with a flashlight. She could see its powerful beam sweeping to and fro across the drive and front garden. But he wouldn't find anything. She and her neighbours had already done this earlier – albeit with a much more modest torch.

She turned her attention back to the policewoman. 'There was no sign of her anywhere,' she said. 'I looked all over the garden, and along the road, but she wasn't there. She'd just disappeared.'

Gone, vanished into the night.

'So this was when?' asked the policewoman, looking at her watch.

'Just after seven,' said Jane. The radio had been on for the News. And when The Archers signature tune had begun playing, she had turned it off. Fran, a fan of The Archers, would have said leave it on – but Fran was outside.

'About four hours ago then. That really isn't very long, you know. Not for an adult. We usually wait twenty-four hours before we decide that an adult is a missing person.'

This was what the policeman on the phone had said too, but the thought of waiting twenty-four hours before any action was taken had reduced her to near hysterics and he had taken pity on her and promised to send someone round as soon as possible.

'Yes, I appreciate that,' said Jane, carefully, 'but don't you think these are unusual circumstances? She just went outside and disappeared.' She glanced sideways through the open door into the hall where Fran's small black suitcase was standing. 'Her case was still in the car. Her handbag's here. So is her phone. She had no money on her, as far as I know . . .'

'As far as you know. . .?'

'Yes, as far as I know. What are you implying? That she's disappeared of her own accord? Why would she do that? Like this? No! It's all very odd. Something must have happened to her. Surely you can see that?'

The house phone, which Jane was clutching in her hand, began to ring. She answered it quickly, half hoping it wasn't Fran corroborating the policewoman's contention that she wasn't yet a 'missing person'.

'Hello?' she said. It was Emer. 'No, nothing. . . I've got the police here with me now . . . I'll call you back.' She rang off and put the phone down on the coffee table in front of her. 'That was Frances's daughter,' she said.

The policeman was coming back into the house. They heard the front door closing followed by the sound of wiping feet. When he appeared in the doorway of the lounge the policewoman looked at him inquiringly but he shook his head. 'No sign, I'm afraid,' he said, turning apologetically to Jane.

'Well, that's no great surprise, is it?' she said. 'I did search outside before I called you, you know!' She didn't want to antagonise them . . . but they were so patronising (and so dismayingly young!).

'This might sound like a stupid question,' said the policewoman, 'but did you actually see her go out? Have you searched the house?' Her eyes, like the flashlight had done outside, swept around the spacious room. 'Have you had a really good look round inside?'

Jane hadn't. 'Well the cagoule isn't there,' she said, 'and the front door was open, so she must have gone outside.'

'She could have come back in again. Have you looked

upstairs?'

Again, Jane hadn't. It had never occurred to her that Fran might be upstairs. And anyway, what would she have been doing up there all this time? Sleeping? Hiding under a bed? No, it was ridiculous! She wasn't anywhere in the house. She'd gone outside – into the pissing-down rain.

'Would you mind if I had a look round?'

'Be my guest.' But the policewoman wasn't her guest; Fran was her guest, and Fran was missing.

Jane didn't mind this inspection, though. Everywhere was in good viewing order, upstairs and down, because Fran, for all her laid back attitude, kept a remarkably clean and tidy house and Jane had had no intention of being found wanting in this respect – especially as she had a cleaner and Fran didn't.

The policewoman returned, thankfully without Fran in tow. Jane felt mildly ashamed of her feeling of relief, but somehow her dignity was at stake here. She needed to prove to them – and to herself – that she was capable of handling this situation. If Neil had been here, he would have been the one to deal with it. But then, he would have been the one to go out and get the suitcase in the first place and none of this would have happened. None of what? What had happened?

The policewoman sat down again and returned to her notebook. 'So,' she said, flipping back the pages and consulting what she had written earlier. 'Frances Delaney, female, white. Age?' Her pen hovered over the page.

'Fifty-five,' said Jane. She hesitated and then added: 'But she looks younger.'

'Do you have a recent photo of her?'

Jane shook her head. 'Only group ones. Probably not the sort of thing you'd want.'

'Could you give me a detailed description of her, Mrs Lord?'

Jane could. A very detailed description. But she restricted herself to generalities. 'Tall, slim, attractive. Short reddish-brown hair, green eyes,' she dictated, watching the policewoman's pen move accordingly.

'Can you remember what she was wearing?'

Yes, she could. Every last detail. 'Well, like I said, she had my old green cagoule on and . . .'

The phone rang again. She snatched it up and glanced at the screen. 'Lucy,' she said. 'No, no news . . . The police are here now . . . No, you mustn't even think about coming up tonight . . . especially in this weather. Tomorrow . . . yes. Unless she's turned up by then. No, no . . . Quite, there's nothing you can do. Yes, first thing . . . I will, I promise. Oh, and can you find a photo of Fran and bring it with you? Yes . . . OK . . . Goodnight.' She rang off. 'That was my daughter,' she said. 'She lives in London too. Frances is her mother-in-law.'

The policewoman nodded, pausing for a moment to digest this information. Then, pen poised again, she asked: 'What else was she wearing?'

'Well . . .' said Jane, pretending to think. 'Black jeans, black ankle boots, green sweater.' The sweater, she had noted earlier, was cashmere.

Green eyes, green cagoule, green sweater. How very co-ordinated it all sounded!

Also, on a waxed cord around her neck, Fran had been wearing a pendant – a Maori greenstone fishhook she had brought back from a visit to New Zealand a few years ago – which she always wore whenever she was travelling. It was her lucky charm. 'It keeps me safe,' she would say, and then laugh because she didn't believe a word of it. She always wore it, though. Was it keeping her safe now, Jane wondered?

'Was she well?' the policewoman asked. 'Not depressed or upset in any way? You hadn't quarrelled or anything, had you?'

'No! Of course we hadn't! She seemed perfectly well and happy . . . she *was* perfectly well and happy.'

'And, as far as you know, she had no money with her?'

'Look,' said Jane. 'Her bag's here with her purse in it. She went outside with nothing but my car keys – and I found them on the drive by the car.'

'Was the car locked?'

'No.'

'But the case was still in the boot?'

'Yes.'

'And is the case locked?'

Jane nodded. She had examined it earlier. The zip ends were secure in their little slots and the number code was scrambled. 'The main part of it is,' she said. 'The top compartment isn't, but there's only a newspaper in there.'

'Is it possible that she had some money in there – or in her pockets, perhaps?'

Jane sighed. 'Not as far as I know,' she said. 'Are you thinking that she planned this? That's just ridiculous. If she'd wanted to disappear why would she have come up here, to Solihull, to do it?' (And she would never have willingly disappeared wearing that old green cagoule.) Jane shook her head. 'No. Something's happened to her,' she said. 'I don't know why you can't see that, why you're not taking this seriously? Is it because she's an adult and not a child?' She could feel herself becoming hysterical again.

'We are taking it seriously, Mrs Lord, I can assure you. We'll circulate this description and all our patrols will be keeping an eye out for her. We'll check with the hospitals, too, just in case . . . Now, are you going to be all right on your own here tonight?'

Jane nodded.

The policewoman closed her notebook. 'Try not to worry,' she said, tucking it into her pocket. She picked up the hat she had taken off earlier and arranged it carefully on her head before standing up. 'Most missing persons show up of their own volition sooner or later, you know. And there's usually some simple, rational explanation.'

'Well, I can't wait to hear what it is!' said Jane.

'Try not to worry,' the policewoman repeated, obviously anxious to leave now. 'Someone will be in touch with you tomorrow. And if she does show up in the meantime just let us know on this number.' She held out a card.

Jane closed the front door after them, double locked it and slid the security chain into place. She put the card on the hall table – next to a soft toy, a cat belonging to her grandson Daniel that Bronia, her cleaner, had found under a bed that morning. She picked it up and smoothed its fur. Several weeks ago, after one of their visits, Lucy had asked if they'd left it behind, but Jane had only conducted a cursory search for it at the time because Felix wasn't a must-have toy. All the same, she thought, Daniel would be pleased to get it back tomorrow. She took it with her into the lounge and put it on the sofa where the policewoman had been sitting.

She felt very alone now, and very exposed in here with the curtains open and the lights on. Walking towards her own reflection in the glass, she went over to the large bay window and peered out. It was still raining and the branches of the trees which lined the road were bending and swaying in the wind, casting sinister shadows over the garden. Someone out there had taken Fran. She drew the curtains carefully and stepped back into the room. Picking up the phone, she sat on the edge of the sofa and rang Emer back.

Emer answered instantly. 'This is so typical of my mother,' she said, sounding annoyed at the lack of news.

'Surely you can't think she's done this deliberately?'

'I wouldn't be surprised,' said Emer, slightly defensive now. 'I'm sure she'll turn up soon.'

'Are you?'

There was a long silence which Emer broke by asking: 'Have you checked her phone? For recent calls . . . messages . . . anything that might give us a clue?'

'Yes,' said Jane, wondering why the policewoman hadn't asked her this, 'but there's nothing there.' She didn't mention how long it had taken her to navigate her way around Fran's phone which was a much more up-to-date one than her own.

'OK,' said Emer. 'Well, I'm going to come up with John and Lucy in the morning – assuming she hasn't turned up by then. If that's all right with you? So . . . I'll see you tomorrow.'

'Right,' said Jane and then, to her dismay, heard herself saying what the policewoman had said to her earlier: 'Try not to worry.'

Emer hung up.

Try not to worry. What a stupid thing to say! God, what a nightmare all this was! She went into the kitchen where the table was still set and the chilli which she and Fran had been about to eat was still in its pan on the hob. She hadn't eaten since lunch time and suddenly felt very hungry, but she put the chilli in the fridge and made herself a cheese sandwich instead. She sat down at the table to eat it, listening to the rain pattering lightly now on the skylights in the extension.

'There's usually some rational explanation,' the policewoman had said. But how could there be a 'rational explanation' for disappearing off the face of the earth like this? And what a strange expression that was! To disappear off the face of the earth. As if Fran had been abducted by aliens.

She poured herself a glass of wine and drank half of it in one gulp.

And now, she said, *we can go over to the news teams where you are.*

Frances Delaney, 55, from Streatham in South London, was abducted by aliens this evening while visiting an old friend in Solihull in the West Midlands. Mrs Jane Lord, also 55, and recently widowed, said: 'She just went outside to get her suitcase from the boot of my car and she never came back.

Jane topped up her glass, warming to her imaginary broadcast.

It was pissing cats and dogs at the time and she was wearing my old green cagoule. So, if she has been abducted by little green men, she'll blend in nicely. Especially if she had the hood up and the drawstring pulled tight - as no doubt she did considering the strength of the rain at the time.

But it wasn't funny. The police thought (and Emer seemed to think so, too) that Fran might have gone off –

what was their expression? – 'of her own volition'. But that was ridiculous. So if it wasn't aliens, then someone else must have taken her. Kidnapped her. Was that the right word to use for an adult? But why would anyone want to kidnap Fran? Surely not for a ransom. And why here – in Solihull? It made no sense. The only possible 'rational' explanation was that someone . . . some nutter . . . had . . .

She drank the rest of her wine and sat staring into the empty glass, reflecting on how arbitrary life could be sometimes. One minute she and Fran had been on course for a pleasant weekend, and then . . . this. Just like that day, three months ago. Neil's afternoon off. He'd been playing golf. 'Hello?' she'd said, answering the phone, her tone bright and routine as usual. 'Mrs Lord?' a female voice had replied. 'I'm afraid your husband has been taken ill.' By the time she'd got to the hospital he was dead. And he'd seemed perfectly all right when he'd left home earlier.

She got up and put her plate and glass in the dishwasher, wondering how long she should stay up in case Fran did come back. But there was no point going to bed yet, anyway. She wouldn't sleep. She hadn't been sleeping properly for months. And now, with this as well . . .

At a loss what to do – it seemed inappropriate to watch television and reading was out of the question – she wandered into the dining-room and switched her computer on. It wasn't working properly. It was taking longer and longer to boot itself up – or whatever the correct terminology was – and she had no idea how to remedy this. She would have to ask John to look at it tomorrow. She sighed. It really didn't do to be always relying on one man or another. She needed to be more independent. Perhaps she should do a computer course.

In the seventies, she mused, women used to go to car maintenance classes to assert their independence. The ability to maintain their own cars had seemed very important back then. She hadn't been one of those women, of course, but car maintenance was the least of her worries now. For many years, anyway, the only maintenance Neil had carried out on their cars had been to make periodic appointments for them to go to the garage. This was something she could do herself, no problem.

The computer, however, was another matter. 'What've you done to it now?' Neil would say when it misbehaved. On many of those occasions he'd offered to show her how to sort it out for herself, but she hadn't listened – either because she'd been in a hurry just then or because he'd annoyed her so much with his smugness that she hadn't felt in the right frame of mind for learning new skills.

She knew, though, that he'd never really wanted to enlighten her. He'd enjoyed having this hold over her. And now, as she was waiting for her computer to complete its litany of whirring and chugging, she could feel herself getting annoyed with him all over again. He had gone and died – suddenly – like that. Gone and left her, knowing that she was virtually computer illiterate.

She sat staring at her desktop wallpaper, a green extravaganza of bamboo, which she'd chosen because it complemented the dining-room décor. 'God, you're so sad, Mum!' Lucy had said when she'd first seen it. 'Well, I like it,' Jane had insisted. But she was sad. So very sad.

At last, the computer was ready to use. She opened her email account. Perhaps Fran had sent her a message with rational explanation in the subject box. And yes, there was one new email in her inbox . . . but it was untitled and from a slight acquaintance who had only recently heard about Neil's death. It was the usual thing – *couldn't believe it . . . lovely man . . . . must be missing him terribly . . . in our thoughts.*

Jane sighed. She should reply to it straightaway, otherwise it would become another nagging irritation. She disapproved of using emails for this purpose, it seemed impolite, but she would answer like with like. *Thank you for your kind words,* she typed, *slowly coming to terms . . . the girls, of course, have been a great comfort.* She clicked 'Send' and then moved the email and her reply into a folder marked

Condolences.

Underneath this folder was another one entitled Frances Delaney. It contained all the emails which she and Fran had exchanged over the years. She hesitated a moment then opened it and scrolled down to the first one, dated 10 September 2001, written shortly after she had found Fran on FriendsReunited.

Dear Frances, it said. *I wonder if you remember me? My daughters introduced me to this website and I have been having a wonderful time tripping down Memory Lane. It was great to see your name here. How are you? I would really love to hear more about what you have been up to all these years, if you can spare the time. With very best wishes, Jane Maxwell.*

She brought FriendsReunited up on the screen. She hadn't visited this website for a long time. It had changed a lot since its early days and held little appeal for her now, but back in 2001 she had spent many hours on it in a frenzy of nostalgia and curiosity. She clicked on her school year and the list of familiar names appeared, among them (thrillingly, that first time) Fran's, whose brief profile note read: *I live in London. I teach in a local sixth form. I have two daughters, a son and a step-daughter.*

Frances Delaney! The beautiful and popular class-mate whom, as a schoolgirl, Jane had so admired. At the centre of a dominant group of girls (a group that, needless to say, hadn't included Jane), Frances had been the life and soul of the class – naughty when younger, provocative and funny as she got older. And always clever. Always full of life.

Jane had felt instantly compelled to contact her. But it had taken her ages to compose her little email, and then ages again to pluck up the courage to send it. Because that was all that Frances Delaney had been – an old classmate, not really a friend.

And here was her own, slightly more detailed, profile note, unchanged and out of date now: *I've been living in Solihull in the West Midlands for over twenty years. I am happily married to Neil and we have two beautiful daughters - Lucy 19 and Sarah nearly*

15. I work part-time as a teaching assistant in a local primary school.

How dull it sounded. No wonder Fran had taken her time answering the email. So much time, in fact, that Jane had abandoned all hope of ever receiving a reply. *She probably doesn't even remember me,* she'd thought. *She's probably thinking, Jane Maxwell, which one was she?* Because there had been two Janes in their class – two plain Janes – and it was unlikely that either of them would have left any lasting impression on a girl like Frances Delaney.

Months later, however, a reply had arrived. Jane returned to her email account now and re-read it. *Hello, Yes, I do remember you. At least I think I do. Yes, of course I do! There were two Janes weren't there and you were the pretty one. I live in South London – in Streatham (near the Common) – with Patrick and our two younger kids. My eldest daughter lives nearby, and my son is at Warwick Uni which I see is not far from Solihull. We should meet up sometime when I'm up there transporting his stuff. How are you? Married? Children? Frances.*

She remembered how her initial delight on receiving this had been tinged with displeasure. Frances had obviously read her profile note otherwise how else would she have known that she lived in Solihull? So why these questions about marriage and children? There was a casual carelessness here (something to which the beautiful and the popular seemed to think they were entitled) which was vaguely familiar from schooldays. *Frances,* she'd replied tersely a few days later. *Good to hear from you. Yes, do let me know when you're going to be up here and we can arrange to meet. I'll look forward to that. Jane.*

She was forty-eight years old, she'd told herself at the time. Not an admiring schoolgirl any more. Any further dealings with Frances Delaney would have to be on more equal terms from then on.

The next email from Fran was dated 15 March 2002, over three months later. *Hi,* it began, completely ignoring this time gap. *I'm picking John up from university tomorrow (Sat) and I wondered if you'd like to meet up? At the university Arts' Centre, say? Mid afternoon? Frances x.*

Jane had been greatly alarmed at the suddenness of this casual suggestion. There was no time to prepare properly. What would she wear? Her hair needed cutting. Should she make an excuse, invent a prior engagement, maybe – what a pity . . . perhaps next time . . . But, in spite of all her reservations, she had wanted to go. She had wanted to see Frances again. *Hi,* she'd replied, *great to hear from you again. Yes, I'd love to meet up. I'll go over to the Arts' Centre after lunch and mooch about in the Book Shop. Give me a call when you arrive. Jane.* She had added her mobile phone number and, without pausing to consider further, had pressed 'Send'. Too late then to change her mind.

She smiled, remembering now how ridiculously nervous she'd been that Saturday afternoon, over six years ago.

~

The car park nearest to the Arts' Centre had been full and she'd had to drive round and round the campus for ages searching for a parking space. When at last she did find one, she drove into it at such an awkward angle that she had to perform some very tricky physical contortions in order to get out of her car. All of which did nothing to calm her nerves.

Once inside the Arts' Centre she made straight for the Ladies. While she was washing her hands she scrutinised all the other women milling about in there, in case one of them was Frances. There were such a lot of comings and goings, though, and so many mirrors through which to observe them that she began to feel quite dizzy. Holding her hands under the running tap, she shifted the focus of her attention on to her own reflection. Was she at all recognisable now, she wondered, as the 'pretty' Jane of Frances's memory? Probably not.

She didn't go to 'mooch about' in the book shop like she'd said she would. She'd decided that this would be too risky; Frances might pounce on her unawares in there. Instead, she went to the café by the box office where she bought a coffee and sat down at a suitably positioned table to watch and wait.

Eventually her phone rang. She answered it with shaking hands.

'Hi, I'm here – outside the book shop,' said Frances, with just the merest trace of a Lancashire accent in her voice.

'Hi,' Jane replied, rising to her feet. 'I'm in the café by the box office.'

She recognised Frances instantly. Her red hair was shorter, her face a little thinner, perhaps, but she was almost exactly as Jane remembered her. Green-eyed, and still beautiful.

Frances took a moment to identify Jane, and then flung out her arms. They embraced like long-lost friends.

'Wow!' said Frances, oblivious to the stares of people around them. 'How long has it been? Nearly thirty years!' She glanced at Jane's empty coffee cup. 'I've got to eat,' she proclaimed. 'I haven't had any lunch yet and I'm absolutely starving. What can I get you? Another . . . what? Tea? Coffee? Have a cake or something.'

Jane sat down again and studied Frances as she stood in the short queue at the counter. She wasn't wearing anything out of the ordinary – black jeans with a white shirt and a charcoal grey cardigan – but she was very striking, nonetheless. And she seemed so friendly. There really had been no need to have been so worried about this meeting.

Jane felt herself beginning to relax. It was going to be all right.

~

It's not all right now though, is it? she thought with a shiver. The central heating had turned itself off for the night some time ago and she was getting very cold. Her cursor hovered over the next email on the list. But she shouldn't look at any more now. She should go to bed and try to get some sleep – prepare herself for whatever the hours, or days, ahead had in store for them all.

She shut the computer down and sat staring at the blank screen, wishing she could shut her mind down in the same way. Blank out all the disturbing images that kept flitting across it.

On her way to bed she passed Fran's suitcase in the hall. She had noticed earlier that Fran had done the Sudoku and half of the Quick Crossword in the G2 section of The Guardian. She bent down, took the newspaper out of the top compartment of the case and put it on the hall table next to the police card. She would keep it safe, she decided. Volition permitting, Fran might want to finish that crossword.

She lay in bed, not even trying to go to sleep, her mind still full of that first meeting with Fran.

~

They'd sat chatting for over two hours. At first they talked about school and some of the other people who had appeared on FriendsReunited. Do you remember this girl . . . that teacher . . . when this happened . . . when we did that? This re-visiting of a shared past – even though they hadn't shared it closely at the time – was very pleasurable. Jane felt really glad that she had come.

By her third cup of coffee they had moved on to their lives after school. Frances had gone to university – to Bristol; Jane had trained as a nurse in Manchester.

'I thought you were a teacher?'

'A teaching assistant. I gave up nursing when Lucy came along. And then later, when both girls were at school, I used to help out and just kind of fell into the job. I never went back to nursing.'

Jane was aware how pathetic this must sound to Frances. A teaching assistant, not a proper teacher. Years ago, she'd thought about doing an education degree and becoming fully fledged, but Neil hadn't been keen so she'd dropped the idea.

'Manchester was where I met my husband, Neil,' she said, steering the conversation on. 'He was doing his dentistry degree there.'

'He's a dentist?' said Frances, pulling a face. 'Well, I suppose teeth are no worse than feet. My brother – do you remember Paul? No? Well he lives in New Zealand now and he's a chiropodist. I just couldn't imagine spending my working days fiddling around with people's feet, or in their mouths, could you?'

'What does your husband do?'

'Patrick? He's an academic. An economics lecturer. And that's what John's doing here – economics. He's going to do a Master's degree next year so he'll probably end up lecturing too.

'Following in his father's footsteps, then.'

'Yeah, except that Patrick's not his father. He's Charlotte's father – she's my youngest – but not John's or Emer's. Emerald is my eldest.'

'Right,' said Jane. (Emerald!) 'And you said you had a step-daughter?'

'Yeah, Hannah. She came with Patrick.' Frances laughed. 'We're a very mixed bunch.'

When it was time to go, Jane said: 'It's been so great to see you. We must do this again when you're up here next.'

Frances sighed. 'Actually,' she said, 'I'll probably be going past here a lot in the foreseeable future. My mother's not at all well and there's only me to look after her.' She shook her head. 'I've been in Lancashire for the last few days, in fact, trying to sort some things out for her. I've come from there today.'

'Well, next time you go up – or come down – you must stop off and have dinner with us,' said Jane.

'It's all a bit of a drag, really,' was the somewhat ambiguous response. 'But there you go. Mothers!'

'I've had a really good time,' Jane said when she got home. 'She's really nice.'

'Good,' said Neil, who had cautioned her earlier against having too high expectations of the meeting.

'She's hardly changed at all. It's amazing really. She's still got that lovely hair. And she's still very . . .' Jane hesitated, trying to find the right words to describe Frances. But it didn't matter; she could see that Neil wasn't really listening. 'Anyway,' she said, 'I'm going to invite her here – sometime soon. I think you'll like her.'

~

Since then, and especially since Lucy and John had got together, all their lives had become intertwined in ways they couldn't have foreseen. And they had all been happy. Until Neil's death. And now, when they'd already had their fair share of sorrow recently, this had to go and happen. This – because she couldn't help but think the worst now. Fran had been gone too long.

She was still awake at four o'clock, and beginning to panic. She wouldn't be able to cope unless she got some sleep. But her mind was on a tread wheel, going round and round – over the past, over the events of the previous evening, over all the possible scenarios to come.

2

The insistent ringing of the phone woke Jane from the deep sleep which had only descended upon her as dawn was breaking. She sat up in bed, her heart thumping, waves of dread rolling over her.

It was Lucy. 'It's only me. Any news?'

'No, nothing,' said Jane. She cleared her throat.

'Did I wake you?'

'No, no.' She squinted at the clock on the bedside table. Seven fifty-four.

'Oh my God!' said Lucy. 'Something awful's happened to her, hasn't it?' Jane said nothing.

'Are you all right, Mum?'

Jane didn't reply to this either. What could she say? Yes, I'm fine? No, I'm going mad here?

'Anyway, said Lucy, 'we're going to leave in about an hour. We're picking Emer up on the way. You do know that she's insisted on coming too, don't you? We should be with you about half past eleven, if the traffic's OK. But ring me if you hear anything. Even if it's bad news.'

Which, of course, I won't, thought Jane, as she put the phone down. You don't transmit bad news to people who are speeding along a motorway.

She got out of bed and went to the window. Holding the curtain aside she looked out over the back garden. The rain had stopped at last and it was a fresh autumn morning. In the centre of the lawn, the silver birch's dying, golden leaves were glowing brightly in the sunshine. It was going to be a lovely day. She put her dressing gown on and went downstairs.

Fran's suitcase was still there in the hall; the newspaper was still on the table.

She wondered whether she should ring Sarah, at university in Sheffield, and tell her what had happened, but she decided that it was probably too early on a Saturday morning for this. And it wasn't urgent; Sarah hardly knew Fran.

Shortly after eleven, a small team of police officers arrived with dogs and sticks. Standard procedure, one of the policemen told Jane. They would conduct a search of her garden and a few neighbouring ones, front and back, and have a look up and down the road and on the sports field to the rear of the houses. Jane nodded. She fetched her keys and unlocked the garage and the side gate so that they could get through to the back of the house, then she hovered outside for a few minutes, watching as they set to work. There were leaves everywhere, all over the front garden, the drive, the pavement, and in the gutter. And here and there they had blown into piles – which could be hiding . . . anything.

She had spoken earlier, on the phone, to another female police officer – Detective Sergeant Something-or-other (she really must make an effort to remember their names) – who had repeated the policewoman last night's assertion that they didn't normally regard an adult as missing until at least twenty-four hours had elapsed. But, because there had been a series of vicious attacks, some of them fatal, on women in the south Birmingham area over the past few months, they couldn't rule out the possibility that Frances might be the latest victim.

Jane closed her eyes. Her fingers tightened around the phone. She knew about these attacks, these murders. They had been all over the news. Women walking alone at night, an attacker, still at large, who kept striking, again and again. She hadn't associated any of this with Fran's disappearance though. Until now.

'It's only a slight possibility,' the detective sergeant went on. 'For one thing, your friend is considerably older than the other women were.'

This comment failed to reassure Jane. Fran might have been the exception, she thought. And anyway, how would a killer have known how old she was, swathed as she'd been in the green cagoule?

She went back indoors and stood watching through the front bedroom window as the search got under way. And, although the police officers had long since moved out of sight, she was still there half an hour later when Lucy and John's car pulled into the drive and parked behind hers. She went downstairs and out to greet them.

Emer was first out of the car. She was wearing dark denims, a close fitting purple tunic and had a long multi-coloured scarf draped around her neck. Her long, red hair was loose and her eyes were rather dramatically made up – possibly too much so, under the circumstances, Jane thought. Although she was in her thirties now, she reminded Jane very much of the schoolgirl Fran. She was, if anything, more beautiful than Fran – but perhaps not quite as attractive as Fran had been back then? And still was, Jane told herself, trying not to think about how those other women – those younger women – might have looked after they'd been attacked.

She went over to Emer, not sure whether it was appropriate to smile or not. They exchanged greetings, leaning towards each other rather awkwardly and almost-but-not-quite touching cheeks. Then Jane turned to John and gave him a warm, slightly clinging hug. 'Here you all are,' she said unnecessarily.

While Lucy was extricating herself from the back of the car, Jane went round to the other door and began releasing Daniel from his baby seat. He watched her guardedly as she struggled to undo the belt. He doesn't know who I am, she thought. He doesn't see enough of me. She gathered him up carefully and lifted him out of the car.

'Let's get inside, out of the way,' she said, glancing at a policeman who had just hovered into view.

Lucy was busy loading herself up with quantities of baby paraphernalia from the car boot and John went to help her. Emer, however, set off towards the house carrying only her coat and a small overnight bag.

After depositing their luggage in the hall – around Fran's suitcase – they assembled in the kitchen. Jane switched the kettle on and began to make coffee.

'No coffee for me,' said Lucy, pouring herself a glass of water from the filter jug and sitting down at the table. She looked pale and drawn. She had no make-up on, her hair was scraped back in an untidy ponytail, and she was wearing a long grey jersey top over grey leggings. She was all monochrome next to Emer.

'How long have they been out there?' John asked, speaking loudly over the noise of the boiling kettle.

'About half an hour,' said Jane.

The kettle came to the boil and then switched itself off. There was an awkward silence.

'Hey,' said Emer to Daniel, who was standing on the floor clutching the handle of one of the cupboard doors. 'Show Grandma Jane how you can walk now.' She crouched down and held out her arms to him.

'Oh! He's walking now, is he?' Jane asked, handing round the mugs of coffee. She felt another pang of regret. Everyone else, it would seem, had witnessed this achievement; everyone except her. 'When did this happen?'

'Only a couple of days ago,' said Lucy. 'I was going to tell you.'

'Come on, Daniel,' Emer coaxed him. 'Show Grandma Jane what a big boy you are.' But Daniel refused to oblige and remained clinging resolutely to his handle.

'Oh, God! This is awful, isn't it?' said Lucy. 'I didn't get a wink of sleep last night for worrying.'

'Me, neither,' said Jane.

Emer stood up. 'I did, I'm afraid,' she said with a shrug. 'I tried not to, but I must have drifted off. Does this mean I'm a very bad person?'

Something in the exaggerated way she'd said 'very bad person' amused Daniel and he began to laugh.

'Very bad person,' she repeated, dropping to her knees again. He shrieked with delight. 'Auntie Em's a very bad person.' He let go of the handle and staggered a few steps towards her, pointing at her mouth. She continued saying very bad person over and over until his chuckles became forced and faded away.

Lucy covered her face with her hands. 'Something awful's happened to her, hasn't it?' she said.

'We don't know that,' said Jane, deciding not to mention the serial attacker yet.

'Well where the hell is she then?'

'Emer thinks she might have gone off of her own . . . accord,' said Jane, sidestepping the word 'volition'.

'What? How stupid is that!' Lucy exclaimed.

'OK,' Emer conceded. 'I did think that for a bit, last night, at first, but obviously I don't think so now.'

'How could you have thought it at all?'

'Maybe,' suggested Emer, 'because I know my mother a lot better than you do.'

'I don't suppose she could've gone back to London, could she?' Jane asked, stepping in to defuse the situation. 'Have you checked?'

John nodded. 'She's not at the house.'

'Of course she's not,' cried Lucy. 'She wouldn't have gone home just like that without telling you! And not wearing that old cag!' She rounded on her mother. 'I really don't know why you've still got that bloody thing. It's a disgrace!'

'No it isn't,' Jane protested. 'And anyway, I only wear it for putting the bins out . . . and things like that . . . when it's raining.'

'You should've thrown it out years ago.'

'Oh, should I? And then none of this would have happened, I suppose?'

Her daughter leapt up and, just for a second, Jane, recoiling slightly, thought she was about to be attacked. But

Lucy rushed past her and over to the sink where she bent forward and leant her forehead on the mixer tap.

'Oh dear! Are you all right?' Jane asked, trying to show concern.

Lucy moaned. 'It's the smell of the coffee,' she said, retching. Jane glanced at John, but he appeared unperturbed. Lucy retched again, more loudly this time.

'Nice!' said Emer, raising her eyebrows. 'Can't you do that somewhere else? It's not very hygienic, is it, throwing up in the kitchen sink?'

'I'm not actually throwing up,' Lucy gasped. She turned the tap on and splashed water over her face. 'As you've probably guessed,' she said, straightening up, 'I'm pregnant. But this isn't quite how I was planning to tell you all!'

'Oh!' Jane touched John on the shoulder and went to give Lucy a hug. 'Congratulations!' she said, and felt slightly taken aback to realise that she wasn't as pleased as she sounded. Because didn't they have enough to contend with at the moment? Even without Fran's disappearance, she wasn't sure that she was ready yet to look forward to a new life – not in this literal sense, at least.

'Yes, congratulations, I suppose,' said Emer. 'What do you think of that, then, Daniel? A new little brother or sister. Or couldn't you care less?'

'So, all her things are here, then?' said John, steering the conversation back to his mother.

'Yes,' said Jane. 'Her phone's here. And her handbag, but there's nothing in it – of any significance, I mean. And her case is out there. It's locked, though.'

John got up and brought it in from the hall and placed it on the table.

'Here, let me have a look,' said Emer.

She began twiddling with the combination lock and at the third attempt the zip ends sprang from their slots and she was able to open the case. She smiled and held up her hands in triumph. But there was nothing enlightening in the case, either; just a couple of tops, a wash bag, a red nightdress, and some underwear.

Jane glanced at the black, maxi Sloggis. 'I've got to have comfy knickers,' she remembered Fran saying once. 'I couldn't be doing with those thongs the girls wear – not with my episiotomy scars!' And they'd laughed. But it wasn't funny now. Because if . . . ?

Emer closed the case. 'I don't know what we think we're looking for,' she said.

The door bell rang and they all froze.

'Oh, God!' said Lucy putting her hands over her ears.

Jane glanced at John and took a deep breath. He rose and followed her to the door. But the police had found nothing. No Fran, no clues, no answers.

'Oh God! This is awful,' said Lucy again.

'I think we've established that,' said Emer.

'Oh, shut up! Stop pretending you're not as frantic as the rest of us.' Lucy was getting tearful now.

'Let's all calm down,' said John. 'This isn't helping.'

Jane nodded. 'John's right,' she said. 'Look, someone's coming round from the police station this afternoon. So why don't you give Daniel his lunch and put him down for his nap? And then we should all have some lunch, too. There's some chilli from last night in the fridge, if that's all right? Or,' turning to Lucy, 'you can have a sandwich if you don't fancy that.'

Lucy nodded and began unloading jars and sachets of infant food from one of the bags she'd brought in with her. John took Fran's case back into the hall and then went upstairs with the travel cot.

Emer turned to Daniel. 'Let's go for a little walk while we're waiting, shall we?' she said. He grasped her hand and they toddled out of the room together.

'She's very good with him,' said Jane, watching them go.

'Oh yeah! She's a wonderful auntie, when she wants to be!'

'You need to stop all this sniping, Lucy. It's not doing you or anyone else any good, you know.'

'I can't help it. She drives me mad.'

There was a short pause before Jane asked: 'So, how many weeks are you, then?'

'Twelve.'

'Right.' (Twelve weeks! It was just over twelve weeks since her father had died. But life must go on.)

'I was going to tell you.'

'Does Fran know?'

'Yeah. I told her a couple of days ago.'

'Right,' said Jane again. Would Fran have passed this news on to her this weekend, she wondered? Or had Lucy asked her not to say anything until she herself had told her mother? Or was Lucy totally unaware that her mother might be offended by the order of this telling? Offended . . . and hurt.

'OK,' said Lucy, putting a bright blue plastic bowl into the microwave. 'This is nearly ready. Can you get the highchair, please?'

Putting aside her resentment for the moment, Jane walked over to the far corner of the kitchen where the highchair was parked. She had bought this from IKEA a while back because she'd thought it would be useful – and it looked smart and went well with the kitchen units. It had become a bit of a family joke though. It had splayed legs and, whenever it was out of its corner, people kept falling over it, in spite of her repeated warnings for them to be careful. Neil, in particular, had found it impossible to walk past it without tripping over one or other of these legs. 'I'm going to break my neck on this damn thing one of these days,' he'd grumbled.

Daniel came back into the kitchen followed by Emer. He was clutching Felix the cat and shouting 'Fix, Fix'. He staggered towards Lucy and thrust it at her.

'Oh, my goodness!' said Lucy. 'It's Felix. Where did you find him?'

'He was sitting on the sofa,' said Emer.

'I thought you said he wasn't here,' said Lucy to her

mother.

'He's been under the bed in your old room, all this time,' said Jane. 'Bronia found him yesterday.'

Lucy put the cat on the table and scooped Daniel up and deposited him in the highchair. 'Auntie Emer'll feed you, won't you, Auntie Emer?' she said, offering Emer the bowl of greyish-brown baby food. 'Ooops! Do mind the highchair, though,' she added, smiling. 'It's got lethal legs.'

Just after three o'clock the doorbell rang, heralding the arrival of two plain clothes police officers.

'Mrs Lord?' said one of them, flashing her ID badge at Jane. 'I'm Detective Sergeant Hooper – we spoke on the phone this morning – and this is Detective Constable Mason.'

'Yes, hello,' said Jane. Then: 'I'm sorry. . . Detective Sergeant . . . ?'

'Hooper. Karen Hooper,' said the detective sergeant, slowly this time, as though she were speaking to a child.

Jane ushered them into the lounge and introduced them to John and Emer. Lucy was upstairs getting Daniel up from his nap.

'Would you like a cup of tea . . . or coffee?' she asked them.

'No thank you,' said DS Hooper, declining the offer for both of them. 'This shouldn't take long.' She slipped off her stylish trenchcoat and sat down. She was very smartly dressed – grey suit, navy blouse – and quite heavily made up. She's probably going out somewhere after this visit, thought Jane – somewhere nice on a Saturday night.

'O.K. Let's just get some details sorted out, shall we?' DS Hooper settled herself more comfortably on the sofa and placed her phone on the coffee table in front of her. 'And could I ask you all,' she said, looking from one to another of them, 'to switch your phones to silent for the duration of this interview, please?'

Emer glanced at Jane and raised an eyebrow.

DC Mason – much less sartorially elegant in black

trousers and a black padded blouson jacket – took a notebook from her briefcase and began writing down their contact details.

'Emer Cartwright,' said Emer when it was her turn. And then, in a resigned tone: 'That's Emer – E-m-e-r.' DC Mason crossed out what she had already written and re-wrote the name.

'Short for Emerald,' said Lucy, coming into the room with a sleep-flushed Daniel in her arms.

Emer gave her a long level look before continuing with her address and phone number.

'And your mother, is she married?' asked DS Hooper, looking around the room as if she thought there might be a husband lurking in a corner somewhere .

'She is,' said John. 'But her husband's in California – working.'

'So she lives alone, in London?'

'Yes, at the moment she does,' said John. 'Our younger sister and step-sister are abroad too.'

'Do they know about your mother's . . . disappearance?'

'No, not yet.'

'And does your father know?

'Step-father. No. We decided not to tell him last night and we haven't contacted him today because it's the middle of the night over there now.' John consulted his watch as if to verify this fact.

'Forgive me for asking this,' DS Hooper said, in a far from apologetic tone, 'but does your mother have any other . . . relationships?'

'No,' said John, and Lucy echoed this.

But Emer shrugged and said: 'Who knows?' She looked round at each of them in turn. 'Well, I mean, it's not unthinkable, is it?'

'Do you have a recent photo of her?' DS Hooper asked.

John handed over the one they had brought with them. DS Hooper studied it for a moment, glanced up at Emer, and then passed it to DC Mason.

Fran's handbag and suitcase were searched again, and her phone was put in a clear plastic bag and deposited in DC Mason's briefcase. And then the questioning began. As far as they were aware, might Fran have had any relationship problems? Work problems? Financial problems? Was she in good health? Physically? Mentally? Had there been any quarrels, any disagreements? No? So none of them thought that her disappearance could be the result of a breakdown of some sort? Or of an argument?

It suddenly occurred to Jane that she might be a suspect. Were they thinking that she and Fran had argued, and that she had killed her and then . . . what? . . . disposed of her body? Had that been what the policewoman last night had gone upstairs to look for? No, she was being silly, she told herself. Why would they think such a thing? What possible motive could she have had for murdering her friend?

'OK,' said DS Hooper, changing tack. 'Mrs Lord, you said that you picked Mrs Delaney up from the station?'

'Ms,' interrupted Emer. 'Ms Delaney.'

DS Hooper paused for a moment and stared into space. Then, turning back to Jane, she asked: 'Did you park in the car park there?'

'No, I pulled in just outside the entrance. You know . . . where the taxis park.'

'And you stayed in your car?'

'Yes. It was . . . pouring down.'

'So when she came out of the station she came straight to your car?'

'Yes.'

DS Hooper turned to her colleague. 'We'll check CCTV,' she said, and DC Mason wrote something in her notebook.

'She came out of the station, looked round, then came straight to my car,' said Jane. She was beginning to panic. Did they think she was lying? Did they think that Fran hadn't come at all? That she was making all this up? No, of course they couldn't be thinking that because Fran's phone, her handbag, her suitcase were all here. She was being silly again;

she needed to calm down.

'There might have been someone watching her. Or watching both of you,' said DS Hooper. 'Maybe someone followed you home.'

'Oh, God!' said Lucy, putting Daniel down on the floor.

But Jane felt a surge of relief. Now, at last, they seemed to be accepting the possibility that Fran had been abducted. Of course they were. It was the only possible – the only rational – explanation for her disappearance.

'And you heard nothing yesterday evening when she went outside?' said DS Hooper. 'No shouts or anything?'

'No. I was in the kitchen – at the back of the house. And I had the radio on.' Jane hesitated. 'Do you still think,' she said, 'that your . . . serial attacker might be responsible for her disappearance?'

'Serial attacker! What serial attacker?' cried Lucy, in such an agitated manner that Daniel, thinking perhaps that she was shouting at him, began to scream. Jane tried to pick him up but he struggled out of her grasp and John took him instead.

'We haven't ruled it out as a possibility, yet,' said DS Hooper, her tone brisk and evasive. 'As I told Mrs Lord this morning, there have been a number of attacks on women in this area over the past few months, and so, while this person is at large, we're taking every female disappearance very seriously.'

'Oh, my God!' Lucy was close to tears. 'Mum, why didn't you tell us about this before?'

Jane shook her head.

'There's nothing specific to suggest that Ms Delaney might be another victim,' said DS Hooper. 'She doesn't fit the profile of the other victims. They've all been much younger women. And the fact that she hasn't been found yet has to be a good sign.'

'How many women has he attacked?' asked John.

'Five – in the last six months.'

'Did he kill them?' Emer asked, her tone serious. She was, Jane noted, almost as pale as Lucy now.

'He killed two. The others survived.'

'What did he do to them?'

('The badly mutilated body . . .')

'No! No! Don't tell us. I don't want to know,' said Lucy. She was crying now.

'Like I said,' DS Hooper was beginning to sound impatient, 'there's nothing to suggest that he has attacked Ms Delaney. We just have to be aware of the possibility, that's all.' She stood up, indicating that the interview was coming to an end. 'We'll continue to make routine enquiries,' she said, 'and we might want to speak to you all again. And if you do think of anything else that might be relevant then please let us know immediately. DC Mason here will be your liaison officer.'

DC Mason stood up too and handed Jane her card. After she had shown them out, Jane put it on the hall table with the other one from last night. Fran's newspaper was still there too. She hesitated a moment, then picked it up and took it to the recycling bin.

Saturday evening was awkward. They ordered an Indian takeaway which Lucy insisted she wanted, but when it came she hardly touched hers. They sat in the kitchen, eating in near silence. They'd been talking all day about Fran's disappearance but now they'd come to a full stop.

It was also the night the clocks went back, the end of summer time. They would have forgotten all about this had not John and Emer been working out the best time to ring Patrick in California to tell him what had happened. In spite of the prospect of an extra hour, Lucy went to bed early. 'Daniel'll be up at his usual time,' she said. 'Clocks mean nothing to him.' And shortly afterwards, after speaking to Patrick for the second time, John and Emer went upstairs too.

Jane had discreetly recorded Strictly Come Dancing earlier but felt that it would be insensitive to watch it now. So, after she had cleared away, she sat in the kitchen for a while, listening to the faraway sound of fireworks going off, even though it was still nearly two weeks to November the fifth. Then she went up to bed too. It was going to be a very long night. She knew she wouldn't get much sleep; but at least tonight she wasn't alone in the house.

3

As they were finishing breakfast the next morning, the phone rang. Jane rushed to answer it, her hands shaking and her heart pounding. But it was only DC Mason asking if there had been any 'developments' overnight.

'This is awful,' said Jane, replacing the receiver. 'This waiting's going to drive us all mad.'

She decided that she and Lucy should take Daniel for a walk. She invited Emer to join them but Emer declined. Indicating the laptop she'd brought downstairs with her, she said she was going to email Charlotte (who was in Australia) and Hannah (who was in New York) and tell them what had happened.

John was going to stay behind too, to do some of the jobs that had been accumulating in the house, which Jane didn't feel able to do herself. It wasn't the big things requiring professional attention that caused her problems. It was all the little plumbing, electrical and carpentry jobs which Neil, with a twirl of his screwdriver or a turn of his spanner, used to do himself that left her at a loss. 'I have no DIY skills whatsoever,' she'd wailed to Fran. 'And I'm useless up a ladder. I don't know how I'm going to manage.' Trying not to appear too needy, she had confined her list for John to three things: replacing a too-high-up light bulb on the landing; sorting out the airing-cupboard door which was coming off its hinges; and, of course, her computer.

With Jane pushing Daniel in his buggy and Lucy walking alongside, they set off for the town centre where Lucy bought some extra nappies and some more baby food. It had been decided that John and Emer would go home that evening – assuming there had been no 'developments' in the meantime – but that Lucy and Daniel would stay on for a few more days.

They continued along the pedestrianised High Street with its trees and wooden plant boxes, its quaint lamp-posts and its timber-framed Manor House. In the morning sunshine, Solihull was looking its Sunday best. All bright and beautiful, thought Jane, as they crossed the road by the Parish Church and continued on into the park.

'It's so nice here,' sighed Lucy, echoing her thought. 'So nice – after Tooting.'

They put Daniel on one of the little swings in the children's playground. As Jane pushed him to and fro, gently at first and then a little higher, he shrieked with delight. What a lovely picture they must be making, she thought. No-one watching them would ever guess that this child's other grandmother was missing. Missing, presumed . . .

Daniel protested loudly when they took him off the swing. Lucy bundled him back into his buggy and they walked away from the playground as quickly as they could in an effort to distract him. As they passed the verdigris-coated bronze statue of the Prancing Horse and Man, mounted on its stone plinth, Jane knew that Lucy would be thinking about her father. If he had been with them now he would undoubtedly have been telling them how this coating had come to form on the statue. When they were small, Lucy and Sarah had been fascinated by this, but as they'd got older they'd become progressively less so. 'Yeah, Dad, we know,' they'd say in bored tones, but this had never deterred him.

They hurried on, ploughing through the wet leaves which were strewn over the path. The park was large – two parks really, which had merged seamlessly into one. Only when Daniel began to quieten down did they slow to a more leisurely pace as they made their way to the lake at the far end.

'It's so nice here,' Lucy said again, looking at the trees in all their autumn finery.

When they reached the lake they stopped so that Daniel could look at the ducks and all the other waterfowl swimming around on it. He sat in his buggy with his arm extended and his finger pointing, laughing at all the squawking and quacking that was going on. It was an idyllic spot, marred only by the dull roar of traffic from the nearby motorway and the occasional drone of planes passing overhead.

'What I miss about Solihull,' said Lucy, throwing herself on to a bench, 'is how pretty it is . . . and how clean.'

'And how boring,' said Jane, sitting down beside her. 'You're always saying how boring it is.'

'Yes, I know. And it is. And I do really love living in London. It's just that sometimes . . .' She sighed. 'I'm probably just being hormonal. Anyway,' she turned to look at her mother, 'have you given any more thought to moving?'

It was Jane's turn to sigh now. 'I don't know what I want to do,' she said. 'Sometimes I think I'd like to sell up and move to a smaller house – or a flat, maybe. And sometimes I think I'd like to move right away from here altogether. But I have friends here . . . and my job . . . and my literature class.'

She'd been trying to think about this for a few weeks now. The house was where Neil had grown up, where they had lived nearly all their married life. They had always assumed, in a vague kind of way, that one day it would go to Lucy or Sarah. But she couldn't imagine either of them wanting to come back and live in Solihull. Most likely, when the time came, they would just sell the house and share the proceeds. So why shouldn't she sell it now? It was too big for her (obscenely big for one person, Fran would say).

She had thought about taking in lodgers (what an old-fashioned word that was). Students, maybe. But was that what she wanted? Sometimes the idea appealed; other times it didn't. Moving away from Solihull was an attractive idea too. A new life. By the sea, perhaps. Or in London, which she knew was what Lucy wanted her to do.

'You should come to London,' said Lucy. 'You could get

another job, find another class. You'd have us and . . .' She stopped abruptly. She had been going to say 'and Fran'.

They sat staring into the murky water, listening to the mournful cry of a moorhen coming from the island in the middle of the lake.

'It's too soon,' said Jane. 'I can't make any big decisions. Not yet. And not now.'

They sat in silence for a while before Lucy said: 'God, I'm knackered. I can't walk all that way back. I'll ring John and tell him to come and get us in the car. I wonder if they've heard anything.'

But when she spoke to John he said they hadn't.

While Lucy was giving Daniel his tea, Jane slipped into the lounge and set the DVD player to record the Strictly Come Dancing results. Lucy might go to bed early again tonight, and then she could watch last night's show followed by this one.

A few years ago, she and Neil had started going to a ballroom dancing class, once a week, in the leisure complex. At first, he had been a very reluctant participant, but had quickly become an enthusiast. It had been great fun. But now that she was without a partner she would probably never go again. She did enjoy the television programme, though.

Later that evening, however, when she sat down to watch it, she found she couldn't concentrate on the dancing. It all seemed too frivolous, too trivial. She fast-forwarded to the part where one of the couples was eliminated. As happened every week, the reprieved celebrity went into pretend shock while the rest of the contestants showered the ousted one with condolences and a few obligatory tears. Jane's eyes started to fill with tears too.

She could hear fireworks again, outside somewhere. She went over to the window, parted the curtains slightly and looked out. They sounded very close but she couldn't see anything. She hoped the noise wouldn't wake Daniel up. Lucy needed her rest. Even as she was thinking this, she heard

Daniel let out a loud cry of protest upstairs. She held her breath, but it was all right; he had only been momentarily disturbed. She switched the television off and crept up to bed.

But yet again, she couldn't sleep. Just after three o'clock she got up and, putting a sweater on under her dressing-gown, went downstairs. She switched the computer on before going into the kitchen to make a cup of the herbal tea which was supposed to help her sleep. It never did, but what else was she supposed to drink at this hour of the morning? She took it into the dining-room and sat down at the computer.

'It should run better now,' John had said earlier. 'I've tidied up your files and cleaned it up a bit for you.' 'Thank you,' she'd said, feeling like a computer slut. Where had all this untidiness and uncleanness come from? Apparently, it was something to do with the fact that she had used up too much memory. But how could that be? She only used it for emails. And to check Facebook. For photos too, of course, and OK, for the occasional Google-fest. But even so.

She sighed. It could do with a good clean on the outside, too, she thought, running her finger along the top of the keyboard and peering into the gaps between the keys where the almost-impossible-to reach dust had gathered. (Bronia, her cleaner, refused to go anywhere near the computer.) And the screen always seemed to be covered in smudges and fingerprints. She used to blame Lucy and Sarah for this when they were younger, but she was the only one who used it now and the marks kept returning.

She opened her email account and watched as the cursor arrow changed into a little hand. (Could it be this that was leaving fingerprints all over her screen?) She returned to the Frances Delaney folder.

18 June 2002: Jane, Thank you for the lovely meal last week. Sorry again that I wasn't the best of company. This whole situation with my mother is really getting me down. I've just got off the phone to her now. More problems! I'm going up there again next weekend to have a look at some residential homes. What fun! I won't have time to call on you on the way back this time - my last appointment is at 5.30 and I've got work the next day. But we must meet up again soon. Keep in touch. Fran x.

Yes, well . . . Thank you for the lovely meal last week!

'I'm going to invite her here,' she'd said to Neil after their first meeting.

But it had been nearly three months later before Frances – on her way back from visiting her mother – had finally agreed to come for dinner.

~

It had been a Sunday evening in early June. Jane had been waiting anxiously for Frances's arrival and when she'd heard the car pull up on the drive she'd hurried out to greet her, feeling even more nervous than she'd been at their first meeting.

'Nice house,' murmured Frances as she followed Jane into the hall.

Nice house – what did that mean? Could Jane hear thinly-disguised disapproval in the tone of this remark? She led the way through to the kitchen and introduced Frances to Neil. They shook hands, each casting an appraising eye over the other. *Nice husband?* thought Jane, looking critically at Neil and wondering what Patrick looked like.

Frances, very casual in jeans and a long-sleeved white t-shirt, was making Jane feel somewhat over-dressed in her new skirt and blue silk top. She had set the table in the dining-room as well, which also seemed a bit too formal now, but there was nothing she could do about it. She could hardly say: 'I see you're not dressed for the dining-room. Let's eat in the kitchen instead, shall we?'

Neil had wine at the ready but Frances wasn't drinking. She had a long drive home later.

'You must stay overnight next time,' Jane said.

Frances shrugged. 'Work, you know.'

'How's your mother?'

'Not good. It's all a bit of a nightmare, really. She's crippled with arthritis. She can't see very well. She can't look after herself properly. She has carers going in several times a day but things keep going wrong. She needs to be in residential care but she's resisting the idea. And it's so difficult for me to keep an eye on things from this distance. Anyway . . .' she smiled, 'enough of that. Let's talk about something more cheerful.' She turned to Neil. 'I hear you're a dentist. Not that that's a cheerful subject! It must be hard being an object of fear and loathing.'

Neil was not amused. Jane's heart sank.

It was a subdued evening. Every topic of conversation proved controversial. From the traffic on the M6 all the way to more weighty political matters, there seemed to be nothing that Neil and Frances could agree upon. It was almost as if they had signed a pact to contradict each other at every available opportunity. Jane didn't know which of them she was most displeased with.

'That was lovely,' Frances said, putting her knife and fork down. 'But you shouldn't have gone to so much trouble on my behalf.'

'It was no trouble,' said Jane, avoiding Neil's eye.

'I'm sorry I've been a bit of a misery,' Frances said later as she was about to get into her car. 'It's been a difficult week-end.'

'She's had a very difficult week-end,' Jane said to Neil when she came back into the house.

'She's too full of herself.'

'Well she's not the only one, is she? Could you have been any more confrontational? If I'd been like that with one of your friends . . .'

The evening had been a great disappointment to her. She had wanted Neil to like Frances, had wanted him to see what it was that she herself found so attractive in her.

~

Jane was about to move on to the next email in the list when Lucy appeared in the doorway.

'Mum! What are you doing? It's half-past three in the morning!'

Jane closed her email account. 'Nothing,' she said. 'I couldn't sleep.'

'Go back to bed.'

Jane shook her head. 'I won't sleep. I know I won't. At least – not until it's nearly time to get up. That's my usual pattern these days. Since your father died.'

'I wish John hadn't gone back,' said Lucy, perching on the edge of the dining table. 'He should be here, in case there's any news.'

'There's nothing he could do here. Nothing any of us can do except wait. And we might be waiting for a very long time. She might never be found, you know. It happens.'

'That would be the worst thing, wouldn't it?' said Lucy. 'Not ever knowing would be worse than knowing she was dead.'

Jane nodded.

'I still think John and Emer should be here, though,' Lucy said. 'For a few more days, at least. I know John would've stayed if she hadn't wanted to get back. If it'd been you who was missing, I wouldn't just carry on as usual. But that's Emer for you.'

Jane shook her head. 'She had appointments, patients to see.'

'She's a bloody physiotherapist, not a heart surgeon.'

'Oh, Lucy!' Jane couldn't keep the exasperation out of her voice. 'Fran's her mother. She's going through hell just the same as we are, so don't be so judgemental.'

Lucy sniffed.

'Go back to bed,' said Jane. 'You need your sleep. I won't be long.'

Alone again, she sat for a while staring at the green bamboo on her computer screen. She found this mutual animosity between Lucy and Emer very strange. What exactly was it all about? Something to do with Fran, obviously. As if they were in competition for . . . what? Her attention, her approval?

Lucy's admiration of Fran had always bordered on the

excessive it seemed to Jane. Her mother-in-law was perfection personified – so beautiful, so youthful, so funny! In marked contrast to her mother who was ordinary beyond belief! 'She won't have a word said against Fran,' she'd complained once to Neil. 'She gets that from you,' he'd replied. And Jane had been outraged. 'I like her,' she'd said. 'I like her a lot. But, contrary to what you might think, I'm not blind to her shortcomings. I never have been. You, on the other hand, are totally blind to her good points. So Lucy must get her lack of proportion from you!'

Yes, that was the problem, Jane told herself – a lack of proportion. Both Neil and Lucy had an over-simplistic – an immature – approach to Fran. It was all black or white for them whereas for her it was much more complicated. There was something about Fran's edgy vitality that she found very attractive, very life-enhancing. And, in return for a share in whatever that something was, she was prepared to make allowances for all the little faults and failings she – so clearly – saw in her friend.

Jane rather liked Emer, too, for much the same reason. It always struck her as odd that Lucy could idolise Fran while being barely able to tolerate Emer, when mother and daughter were alike in so many ways.

And there were things about Emer that Lucy knew nothing about – at least, Jane assumed that she didn't. Things that she herself had been told in confidence, one Friday evening a few years ago, when she had been staying overnight with Fran in Streatham.

~

They had spent a tiring day in the West End shopping for outfits for Lucy and John's wedding. After dinner they'd taken their second bottle of wine into Fran's sitting room and had been half watching Newsnight on the television while waiting for the late night arts' review programme to start.

'Oh, no!' said Fran when it did and the panel was being introduced. She grabbed a cushion from the sofa and held it over her face. 'Not him again.'

'Who? Howard Sage?' said Jane.

Howard Sage was a professor of English Literature at Cambridge, a literary journalist and something of a media personality. Although in his sixties, he was an attractive man and Jane rather enjoyed his wit and the outrageous manner in which he expressed his opinions. 'Don't you like him?' she said. 'I do.'

Fran snorted her disapproval from behind the cushion.

'What's the matter?' Jane asked, laughing. 'He's very funny. I would've thought he was just the kind of person you'd like.'

'Oh, would you?' said Fran lowering the cushion. She cleared her throat in a theatrical manner. 'It's funny you should say that, because for your information – and your information only – he . . .' She paused. 'He just happens to be Emer's father.'

'What!' Jane could hear herself shrieking. 'What do you mean – just happens to be?'

'I mean just that. He was a lecturer when I was at Bristol. I had a very brief affair with him. He's Emer's father.'

'No!' Jane was incredulous. She had always assumed that Nick Cartwright – Fran's first husband and John's father – was Emer's father, too. She had his surname and more than once Fran had commented on how Emer had never really forgiven her for splitting up with Nick.

'Yes, I'm afraid so.' Fran shrugged. 'I was in my final year. He wasn't actually one of my lecturers. I mean I wasn't doing any of his courses. But my personal tutor was on a sabbatical and he was standing in for her. He was very attractive. All the female students fancied him.' She grinned. 'And he didn't half fancy himself, too. He was married and had two little kids, but that didn't stop him.'

It didn't stop you, either, thought Jane. 'What happened? Did he . . . take advantage of you?' she asked, thinking gross moral turpitude.

Fran snorted again. 'Don't be silly,' she said. 'I was twenty years old and way beyond being taken advantage of.

No, I set myself the challenge and he rose to the occasion – so to speak! He was a bit of a prat but, like I said, he was very attractive, and I'd just broken up with a long-standing boyfriend, and so I thought . . . why not?'

(Even though you knew he was married with children?)

'He thought it was him who was doing the seducing. He used to call me Francesca. He thought I found it romantic but really I thought it was pathetic. I'd been on the Pill, of course, but I'd just come off it. And it was just the once.'

'What did he do when he found out you were pregnant?'

Fran smiled and shook her head. 'He didn't find out,' she said. 'I never told him. It happened before Christmas and I didn't know for sure myself until after I'd gone back in January. I didn't go to see him. And he never made any effort to contact me either. He'd probably already moved on to his next conquest by then. So that was that. And I managed perfectly well without his personal tutoring.'

Jane looked away from Fran and stared at the television screen where Howard Sage was giving forth about some film or other. 'But you were pregnant,' she said, her gaze returning to Fran. 'Did you think about having an abortion?'

'Not really,' said Fran. 'Our religious background, and all that, I suppose.'

(Which didn't stop you having an affair with a married man in the first place!)

'I didn't tell my parents, either. Well, not for ages anyway. And when I did, I was left in no doubt that I was every Catholic mother's nightmare. I didn't go home again until the next Christmas, when Emer was a few months old and my mother had calmed down a bit.'

Jane was astounded. 'How did you manage?'

'Well I struggled on without anyone really noticing. And I had Nick. He looked after me. And after our finals we got a flat together and he carried on looking after me, and when Emer was born he looked after us both.'

She made it sound so straight forward but Jane suspected that it hadn't been as easy as that. Fran's reaction to Howard

Sage, now, all these years later, suggested that the whole experience must have been very distressing for her.

'And were you and Nick . . .?' she asked.

'No. Not at first. I just kind of grew into him over time. I don't think I was ever really in love with him though. Not like he was with me. But we moved to London, got married, had John, and then he adopted Emer, so she became Emerald Cartwright.'

Howard Sage was speaking again over a cacophony of protests from the other panellists. Fran grabbed the remote control and turned the sound off.

'I called her Emerald,' she said, as though some explanation had been asked for, 'because I wanted her to have an unusual name. I was just twenty-one and full of romantic ideas.' She pulled a face. 'I suppose, in a way, I was a bit of a Francesca. But I've always liked Emerald as a name. She, of course, has always hated it. She's never forgiven me for calling her that and then giving John such an ordinary name. But John was Nick's choice. If it'd been left to me I'd probably have called him Orlando or Tarquin or something.'

'And you've never seen him since – Howard Sage, I mean?'

'Nope. Not in the flesh.'

'And what about Emer? Does she know? Has she met him?'

'I don't think so. But she might've done without telling me. From the moment she found out that Nick wasn't her real father she went on and on about meeting him. But I wouldn't hear of it. In fact, I wouldn't tell her his name for a long time. But then she found out who he was and that made her worse than ever. Partly because he's famous. And because he's Imogen Sage's father. You know Imogen Sage?'

'The actress?'

'Mmm. She wanted me to help her contact him, but I wouldn't. I thought it was a really bad idea – and I still do. She was only a teenager then and I don't think she took it any further. But like I say, I don't know whether she's done

anything about it since. The last time I asked her she said she
hadn't, but she might've been lying. She might've been to see
him and been rebuffed. She wouldn't tell me that, would she?
But she won't let it rest. She's always making veiled allusions
to him. But that's Emer for you.'

'You can't blame her for wanting to meet him.'

'Yes, I can. He's never been a father to her. And let's
face it, he's probably had loads of people turning up on his
doorstep claiming to be his offspring. He'd probably deny all
knowledge of her – or of me.' Fran was angry now. She
picked up the remote control again and turned the television
off. 'The man's a fucking opinionated, narcissistic jerk,' she
said. 'And all this biological shit is rubbish.'

~

Jane had been shocked by Fran's intransigence and the
violence of her views. It seemed to her only natural that
Emer would want to meet her 'real' father. She already had an
adoptive one and a step-one. Surely she could cope with one
more?

Fran had made her promise not to say anything about
this to anyone else. And Jane, flattered that Fran had
confided in her, had been happy to do so. Nick Cartwright
knew, of course, and so did Patrick. And John knew that
Nick wasn't Emer's father, but apparently Emer hadn't
wanted him or anyone else to know about Howard Sage. And
it would seem, from Lucy's silence on the matter, that it was
still a closely guarded secret. Jane couldn't help wondering,
though, whether Lucy might be more tolerant of Emer if she
did know.

She shivered. She was developing hypothermia sitting
down here in the cold. But there was one more thing she
wanted to do before going back to bed. She reached for the
computer mouse, opened her 'My Pictures' file and scrolled
down to the folder which contained some photographs of
Lucy and John's wedding.

Here they all were: Neil, the proud father; Lucy, the
traditional bride, accompanied by her traditional, mauve-clad

bridesmaid (Jane smiled, remembering how uncomfortable Sarah had been in that role); Fran with Nick Cartwright – the mother and father of the groom; and Emer – mostly in the background, but eye-catching nonetheless – with a boyfriend who seemed to be no longer on the scene. Yes, Jane thought, they had all been happy then. She closed the folder, wiping the smiles off all their faces with a click of her mouse.

It was the third night since Fran's disappearance. It was getting less and less likely that she would be found alive now. Jane began to cry. These were the first tears she had shed for Fran; her first real acknowledgement that the worst had probably happened. Mainly for everyone else's sake – for Lucy's in particular – she had been trying to remain positive, but she knew that at any moment a body could be found and it would most likely be Fran's. At least then, she tried to console herself, this awful, awful waiting would be over. If only Neil were here to help her through this. She missed him so much. And she would miss Fran, too. How could this be happening to her all over again?

She didn't know who she was weeping for now; for Fran, for Neil – or for herself.

4

Jane woke up to the sound of Daniel screaming. The by-now-familiar feeling of dread had already settled over her before she fully realised what she was hearing. She looked at the clock. It wasn't yet seven. She waited, hoping that Lucy would manage to quieten him: she desperately needed some more sleep. And for a few minutes there was silence, but then he started crying again. He wasn't going to settle back down. Neither was she now; she might as well get up.

Lucy, her hair loose and straggly and her face very pale, was standing by the window in her old bedroom, holding Daniel in her arms. She was rocking from side to side but this motion seemed to be more for her benefit than for his.

'Sorry. Did he wake you?' she said, turning round as her mother came into the room. 'He'd thrown Felix out of his cot and was panicking.' Daniel was clutching the toy cat in his hand. 'I think he finds having both him and Teddy in bed with him stressful,' said Lucy, 'but he won't let Felix out of his sight.'

Jane smiled. She held out her arms to Daniel who responded by burrowing more deeply into his mother's shoulder.

'Don't be silly,' said Lucy. 'It's Grandma Jane.'

But Daniel gave a little moan and clung on even more tightly to his mother.

'Oh, God! Here, take him quickly,' said Lucy suddenly, thrusting him into Jane's arms and rushing out of the room.

Jane, holding on to the struggling toddler, took her place at the window. In between his cries she could hear Lucy being sick in the bathroom. She held him at arm's length and spoke to him sternly. 'You can stop this nonsense right now,' she said. 'I'm your grandmother. Get used to it.'

He looked at her warily, his chin wobbling. Then he offered her the toy cat.

'Fix,' he whispered. 'Fix.'

'I wish I could, little man,' she said, taking Felix from him. 'I wish I could.'

By seven-thirty they were in the kitchen attempting breakfast. Daniel, in the highchair, was bashing a blue plastic spoon into a bowl of porridge and making a mess all down his bib and on the table in front of him. Lucy was slumped beside him, toying with a piece of toast, and Jane was staring into a bowl of muesli which she didn't feel like eating. What she really wanted was coffee but she knew that the smell would upset Lucy.

'Did you hear those bloody fireworks again, last night?' Lucy said. 'It shouldn't be allowed. Morons!'

'It's kids,' said Jane. 'Probably in the park.'

'It wasn't kids on Saturday. That was someone having a fireworks party or something. I don't know why they can't just wait till the proper night.'

Daniel gave a great slap with his spoon and porridge splattered all over the table and some of it on to Lucy's pyjamas. 'For God's sake, Daniel,' she cried. 'Do you have to make such a mess?'

Jane fetched a cloth and wiped the table. She took the spoon from him and began scraping porridge off his face, like a barber shaving his client. Then she scraped up the remnants of porridge still in the bowl and offered it to him. He shut his mouth firmly and shook his head. Jane made an exaggerated taken aback movement and raised her eyebrows. Daniel watched her carefully and then opened his mouth.

'That's better,' she said, pleased. 'All gone!'

'Aw gone,' he agreed.

Lucy's mobile phone was on the table beside her. She

had just finished speaking to John but there hadn't been much to say. No news. Nothing to report. It rang again.

'Oh, no. It's Emer,' she said, glancing at the screen. 'Here, you speak to her.' She pushed the phone over to Jane who gazed at it blankly, uncertain as to the procedure for answering it. Lucy made a tutting noise as she snatched it up, gave it a few little strokes and then slid it back across the table to her mother.

'Hello, Emer,' Jane said, glaring at Lucy. 'It's Jane here.' No. No news. Nothing to report. 'We're going to have this all the time,' she said, handing the phone back to Lucy. 'People ringing up to see what's happening. You'll have to speak to them if they ring you.'

'No-one else'll ring me,' said Lucy. 'John'll keep his father informed and Emer can deal with Patrick. It's the very least she can do.'

'Don't be so hard on her,' Jane snapped. 'She's suffering too. We all are. It's not just you.'

Lucy, her elbows resting on the table, covered her face with her hands.

'I know you're feeling rotten,' said Jane, relenting slightly. 'Why don't you go back to bed for a bit? I'll look after Daniel.'

Daniel, thinking that Lucy was playing a game with him, dropped his spoon on the floor and put his own hands over his eyes and began to chuckle.

'He thinks you're playing Boo,' said Jane, retrieving the spoon. She went over to the sink and rinsed it under the tap.

'Boo!' shrieked Daniel, removing his hands.

'Boo!' said Lucy. 'There's no point going back to bed. I won't sleep. Why don't we hear something? I can't bear this uncertainty.'

'I'm sorry but I'm going to have to make some coffee,' said Jane, who couldn't bear it either.

Lucy gave Daniel a piece of her toast. 'Oh no! I think I'm going to be sick again,' she said, rising hurriedly from the table and leaving the room.

Jane turned the radio on. Daniel was just messing about with the toast so she wiped his face and hands and lifted him out of the highchair which she then put back in its corner. They didn't want any accidents. She made her coffee and sat down to drink it. Daniel opened one of the kitchen cupboards and stood gazing at its contents.

'No,' she said as he reached inside it. He withdrew his hand and studied her face. He pointed back in the cupboard. 'No,' she said again. 'Close the door. That's a good boy.' He hesitated a moment and then obeyed, but right at the last moment he got his fingers caught and began to cry.

'Oh, dear,' said Jane, rising and picking him up. 'Poor fingers.' She kissed them. 'All better now.' He stopped crying, the hurt quickly forgotten. She put him back down on the floor and began to clear away the breakfast things.

Just after nine o'clock, DC Mason rang. 'Hello, Jane?' she said. 'Debbie Mason here.'

Jane? Debbie? The sudden use of first names was alarming. But there was no news, nothing to report. She's being friendly because she thinks we're in this for the long haul, thought Jane. These phone calls could go on for days, weeks . . .

'We're going to put something on the local news,' said DC Mason. 'They'll probably send a television crew round later. But don't worry, you won't have to do or say anything. They'll just film outside. State the facts, ask the public for information. That kind of thing. Sometimes we get leads like this. It's always worth a try.'

'Right,' said Jane, trying not to think about her old green cagoule getting a mention on television.

'In the meantime,' DC Mason continued, 'keep your phones on and keep checking all your messages – voice mail, emails, Facebook, things like that.'

Jane put the phone down, shaking her head. Was this all the police could suggest? Futile little gestures like checking their emails? But then, what else could they do?

'Why don't you get dressed and then take Daniel for a

little walk?' she said to Lucy.

'I can't face going out.'

'Don't be silly. We have to keep going; we have to stay positive.'

It was the kind of fatuous thing people said at times like this, she thought. Stay positive. Life goes on. Be strong.

She had spent the past three months, since Neil's death, trying to be strong. Trying to keep the full extent of her grief hidden – even from Fran who had been the one person she had felt able to talk to – because she hadn't wanted to embarrass anyone with the depth and messiness of it all. She had read the pamphlets she'd been given and had familiarised herself with the various stages of mourning she could expect to go through.

It hadn't been easy. But she had been making progress. The days when she didn't bother to get dressed, didn't keep to proper mealtimes, failed to answer the phone, were rare now. She had reintroduced routine into her life. After a few weeks absence she had gone back to school – to her 'little part-time job'. And she had forced herself to attend her literature class which had started again in October. She had had Lucy, John and Daniel to stay a couple of times, and she had driven up to Sheffield on Sarah's birthday and they'd had lunch together. It was, she had read, a matter of achieving that all-important balance between keeping busy and giving herself time to grieve.

She had made conscious efforts to keep talking to Lucy and Sarah about their father, hoping that this would be helpful for them as well as for her. She had been working on her memories, too, keeping them alive as advised, and finding that the happy ones (of which there were so many) were often the saddest ones to recall.

And, slowly and painfully, she had come to accept the fact and the finality of what had happened. Neil was gone; he was never coming back.

On the whole, she had been coping. She had even begun to feel that she might be entering the next stage of mourning

– the 'moving on' stage. And the fact that she had been really looking forward to Fran coming to stay for the weekend had seemed to confirm this.

Fran, who had listened to her; who had kept things in perspective for her; who had occasionally made her laugh through her tears. Fran, who had been 'there for her', as they said. But who wasn't here for her now.

At quarter to ten Jane's cleaner, arrived. She came every Monday and Friday morning but with all that was going on Jane had forgotten all about her. She tried to explain what had happened but Bronia's command of English didn't quite stretch to words like abducted. She looked concerned but confused and took refuge in smiling and cooing at Daniel.

'I don't think I need you this morning,' said Jane. 'I'll pay you, of course. And I'll let you know about Friday.'

'She come back I'm sure,' said Bronia.

Jane smiled and nodded. 'Yes, I'm sure she will,' she lied, her job, as usual, to reassure others.

She showed Bronia out and then phoned her school to tell them about Fran and to say that she wouldn't be in tomorrow, or possibly for the rest of the week, depending on what happened in the meantime. It was all very well telling Lucy that life went on, she reflected, but how could she go to school with all this uncertainty hanging over them? She wondered how John and Emer were getting on this morning, and whether their routines were helping them or not.

After lunch, when Lucy and Daniel were both upstairs having naps, Jane went to the front window to see if there was any sign of the TV crew. It occurred to her, though, that they might already have been and gone. She couldn't stand there all afternoon on the off chance. She would obey DC Mason's command and go and check her emails. Not that she thought for one moment there would be one from Fran. But there were still the old emails to be revisited, so, placing all their phones on the computer desk, she settled down to her task.

Throughout 2002 and 2003 Fran's emails had been dominated by the subject of her mother. They were full of accounts of medical emergencies, accidents, hospital stays, searches for an acceptable residential home. Most of them were comic in tone, but Jane wasn't fooled by Fran's flippancy. She knew that it was a stressful time for her. The constant journeying up to Lancashire alone was arduous enough without all the other problems.

Often, on these Saturday mornings, Fran would break her journey in Solihull and Jane would spend an hour or so doling out refreshments and sympathy. She had little practical advice to offer as neither her nor Neil's parents had lingered long in ill health, or had even reached a proper old age. But she would listen to Fran's outpourings and then wave her off to brave the M6 one more time.

Neil soon made it his business to be absent on these Saturday mornings and, as Fran kept turning down Jane's invitations to stop off for dinner on her way back to London on Sunday evenings, he saw little of her. Early in 2003, though, Fran finally managed to get her mother into a care home and things got better for a while. And so one Sunday evening towards the end of February, to Jane's delight, she did agree to come for dinner again. *O.K.,* she wrote. *See you about 7. Thanks. Fran x.*

This was another dinner Jane remembered well.

~

This time they had eaten in the kitchen. And this time it was Jane who was casually dressed while Fran turned up wearing a skirt and a rather elaborate green and gold velvet top. Why do I feel under-dressed, Jane wondered as she took Fran's coat? Why doesn't she feel over-dressed? Because she was sure that Fran didn't.

'How was the motorway this evening?' asked Neil, who had been instructed to be on his very best behaviour.

'Oh, you know, fair to middling,' said Fran, amusing herself by lapsing into Lancashire speak.

Jane gave a little smile of recognition. That was what her

54

father used to say whenever anyone enquired about his health. 'How are you, Jack?' 'Fair to middlin'.'

'I know you won't be drinking,' said Neil, holding up a bottle of wine. 'But you won't mind if we have a drink, will you?'

Fran grinned. 'Go for it,' she said.

And for some reason this throwaway remark seemed to annoy him. Jane gave him a warning look. Honestly! she thought. What is the matter with him? But Fran, pleased with her mother's care home, and pleased with the way her weekend had gone, was relaxed and charming. And so they were more than halfway through the meal before the convivial atmosphere began to change.

Fran announced that she wouldn't be heading northwards on the weekend of 15th of March. 'It's the anti-war demo that Saturday,' she said. 'I don't want to miss that.' She turned to Neil. 'What are your views on Iraq – I wonder?' she asked, smiling.

'Well, you obviously think you know what they are,' he replied, refilling his glass.

'Surprise me,' she countered. She turned her head slightly and Jane saw her glance at The Sunday Telegraph stacked neatly on the edge of a worktop. Her smile widened.

Goaded, Neil launched into a vigorous defence of Tony Blair and George Bush. The argument raged. Weapons of mass destruction, dossiers, genocide. Fran was impressively well informed and articulate in her views. And when Jane began to take her side in the discussion, Neil became even more angry.

He opened another bottle of wine.

But Jane was getting angry too. It wasn't only his arguments that were annoying her, it was also the incredibly pompous way in which he was expressing them. Ignoring his raised eyebrows, she reached over and helped herself to her third glass of wine.

'If either of you think that a few thousand people taking to the streets of London will make any difference, then you're being very naïve,' Neil sneered.

Fran, totally sober, was the only one not angry. She was enjoying herself. 'You're right,' she said, 'I don't think it will make much difference. But I want to stand up and be counted. I think that's important. And anyway,' she grinned, knowing just how much she was irritating him, 'it's been a while since I last "took to the streets" and I do like a good demo from time to time.' She turned to Jane. 'Why don't you come too, if you feel this strongly about it?'

Jane was flustered. Yes, she did feel strongly. So why not go? Although she had never been on a demonstration before. 'I might just do that,' she declared, staring defiantly at her husband.

After Fran left they had a huge row.

'I don't know why you let her influence you so much,' Neil said.

'No-one is influencing me! I'm perfectly capable of forming my own opinions.'

~

She'd been wiping a work surface as she spoke and, with a violent swipe of her cloth, she'd sent The Sunday Telegraph flying off the edge of it. Its various sections had scattered all over the floor, but neither of them had made a move to pick them up. Later, on her way to bed, she'd gathered them up and thrown them into the recycling bin, knowing full well that Neil hadn't finished with them yet.

It was amusing to look back on now, but at the time she'd been furious with him. He'd seemed so determined to undermine her friendship with Fran. Well thank goodness he hadn't succeeded.

She hadn't gone on the march, though.

The doorbell rang, not once but three times and with increasing intensity, shocking her back to the present moment. She leapt up and hurried to answer it, but Daniel was already yelling upstairs.

It was the television people. A young woman, clipboard in hand, was standing on the doorstep. Further down the drive, a group of other people were waiting around, ready for action. Among them Jane could see a middle-aged man with a large, hand-held camera, and another woman in big, shaggy boots with a matching furry microphone.

'Hello, Mrs . . . Lord,' said the young woman, consulting her clipboard. 'Midlands Today. I believe you're expecting us.'

Jane nodded.

'We'd just like to verify a few facts with you if we may.' And without a hint of concern or sympathy she proceeded to read out the information she had been given by the police.

'Yes, that's right,' said Jane, wincing slightly at the mention of the 'old green cagoule'.

She went back inside to watch out of the lounge window. There wasn't much to see, though. They just seemed to be doing the same take over and over and over again.

Lucy, carrying Daniel, came in to join her. 'Do you think this'll do any good?' she asked.

Jane shrugged. 'It can't do any harm. Someone, somewhere might have seen her.' (In my old cag.)

Lucy went to retrieve her phone. 'I've got a message,' she said, handing Daniel to Jane. 'It's from John . . . Patrick's on his way home. He's arriving at Heathrow early tomorrow morning . . . God, I hope he doesn't come up here. We can't cope with him on top of everything else. What can he do, anyway?'

Jane tended to agree, but it did sound harsh. He was Fran's husband; he was suffering too. But what would they do with him if he did come up? She hardly knew him. For most of the time she'd known Fran, he'd been in America. She'd only met him twice: the first time at Lucy and John's wedding; the second time just after Daniel was born.

'Perhaps . . . when this news item goes out . . . there'll be some developments,' she said. She wasn't sure exactly what she meant by this though. The only 'development' could be that Fran would be found. Dead or alive. But anything would be better than this interminable waiting.

Lucy went upstairs to change Daniel's nappy and Jane

went into the kitchen and put the kettle on. Then she wandered back into the lounge and went to the window. It was getting dark outside. The television people had gone. She wondered what they'd said that had required so many takes. She decided to record the news broadcast. John and Emer would want to see it – and Patrick too if he did come up.

At six-thirty they settled down to watch the Midlands Today programme. Daniel, all ready for bed in his sleeping bag, was sitting on Jane's knee drinking his milk from a spouted cup.

Lucy was on the phone to John. 'We're watching it now,' she said. 'I bet we're not on till the end.'

Jane sat listening to them arguing about what to do about Patrick.

'What's the point in bringing him up here?' Lucy was saying. 'There's nothing he can do. All we're doing is sitting here waiting. Nothing's happening. It's awful.'

Now John was doing the talking. Jane kissed Daniel's head and stared at the television screen.

'Yes, I know . . . ,' Lucy said. 'I know, but . . . Well, I'm sorry but that's not our problem. And it's not fair on Mum, either. She's stressed out enough as it is. And she doesn't really know him, does she? Neither do I for that matter.' A pause. 'I know he is. Yes . . . No . . . OK.' A longer pause. 'He'll be jet-lagged anyway. OK. We'll see what happens after this thing on the news. OK. Don't keep going on about it.'

'Oh! Here we go,' cried Jane, grabbing the remote control and turning the sound up on the television.

'It's on now,' Lucy said into her phone. She held it out towards the television so that John could hear.

There was a shot of the female reporter standing outside the house, talking into her microphone. *Police are investigating the disappearance of a 55 year old woman from outside this house in Solihull at seven o'clock last Friday evening.* (The photo of Fran appeared on the screen and Daniel, recognising his grandmother, thrust out his arm and pointed at it while continuing to drink his milk.) *Frances Delaney, from South*

London, was visiting her friend, Mrs Jane Lord. (Back to the reporter). *Mrs Delaney went outside to get her suitcase from the boot of Mrs Lord's car (a shot of the car on the drive) and hasn't been seen since. It was raining very heavily at the time.*

There have been a series of attacks, two of them fatal, on women in the south Birmingham area over the past few months and the killer is still at large. A police spokesperson, however, told us that it was impossible to say at this stage whether this disappearance is related to those attacks.

Mrs Delaney was wearing an old green cagoule over black trousers. (The photo of Fran came up again). *Police are appealing for witnesses.* (The camera panned along the tree-lined road where there were leaves everywhere but not a potential witness in sight.) *If you saw anything suspicious or have any information which might help them with their inquiries, then ring this number* (a number appeared on the screen). *This is* (the reporter gave her name and then intoned: *in Solihull,* as though she were on a foreign assignment).

And that was it. What an anti-climax! What good would that do? No-one had seen anything: no-one had been about. They knew that already. But what else had they been expecting? What else was there to be said?

Lucy put the phone back to her ear and burst into tears.

Over dinner they talked about Patrick. His first wife had been killed in a car crash when their daughter Hannah was only seven months old. How must he be feeling now, they wondered, now that another tragedy seemed to be looming? And they speculated, as they had done many times before, on the state of his and Fran's marriage.

It had always seemed odd to Jane that Patrick was away in America for most of the time, but it had been like this for over four years now and Fran seemed happy enough with the arrangement. She'd told Jane that Patrick had wanted her to go to California with him but that she'd refused. 'My life's here in London,' she'd said. 'What would I do with myself over there? Anyway, he didn't absolutely have to go – he chose to go. And I chose to stay.'

Jane had often wondered about the whys and wherefores of Fran's transition from Nick Cartwright to Patrick. She knew what Fran had told her – 'Me and Patrick – Patrick and I – were only friends when I broke up with Nick.' But she also knew that Emer had a different version of the order of events. 'Well, she would think the worst of me, wouldn't she?' Fran had said dismissively. 'The truth is, I should probably never have married Nick in the first place. I loved him – I still do – but I wasn't in love with him. And I kept thinking, what if I never fall in love? What if I grow old and die without ever experiencing all that head over heels stuff? And once I started thinking like that, well . . .'

Poor Nick, Jane had thought.

'And did you fall head over heels in love with Patrick?' she'd asked.

'Do you know, it was such a long time ago I can't remember,' Fran had replied, and Jane hadn't known whether she was joking or not.

'He's supposed to be coming back in March, for good,' said Lucy. 'So we'll see how they get on then.'

There was a short silence as they realised they were contemplating a possible future for Fran.

'I think I'll give DC Mason a call,' said Jane. 'See if there's been any response yet.'

But when she rang the mobile number she'd been given it went straight to voicemail. 'She's probably off duty,' she said. 'Shall I ring the police station?'

'They'll ring us if there's any news,' said Lucy. 'Oh God! This is so awful, isn't it?' She was close to tears again.

'Go and watch the telly,' said Jane. 'Try and take your mind off it. (As if that were possible!) I've recorded Coronation Street and EastEnders.'

Jane cleared away the dishes and wandered back into the dining room. The computer was sleeping. She woke it up and went back to her archive.

In the summer of 2003, Fran had had to sell her

mother's house in order to fund the nursing home fees. Jane had offered to help her clear it out but Fran had said that Emer would do that. As her mother's condition deteriorated, the tone of Fran's emails changed. *My poor mother is in a terrible state now. I don't think she knows who I am anymore. She can't walk, can't see properly, isn't eating. All very harrowing. Oh, how I wish this was all over and done with.*

Finally, at the beginning of December, it was.

Her brother came home for the funeral and stayed over for Christmas. And then Fran made a spontaneous decision to go back with him to New Zealand where she stayed for two months. The emails stopped for the duration of this trip. When she returned home, she sent a short group message to all her family and friends informing them of the fact. Jane replied: *I'm so glad to hear that you're back safely. I'm really looking forward to hearing all about your Antipodean adventures. Hope to see you soon. Love, Jane xx*

This had been followed by a long silence. Jane recalled how hurt and puzzled she'd been. She'd wondered whether she should write to Fran again to see if anything was the matter but Neil had advised against this. 'Don't go running after her,' he'd said. 'She obviously has no need for you now, so just forget about her.' But then, he would say that.

When, at last, an email did come – dated 10 June 2004 – Fran made light of this long gap, hardly bothering to make an excuse for it. And, re-reading this email now, Jane was taken aback to realise that it had been in this gap that Lucy and John had got together . . . *my son and your daughter! How about that?* At the time, she'd been so pleased to hear from Fran again that it hadn't occurred to her that this might have been the reason – the only reason – she was rekindling the friendship.

Had it always been a friendship of convenience, she asked herself now? Had she been fooling herself all this time, thinking that she and Fran had something special? If John Cartwright hadn't married Lucy would she and Fran still be friends? Perhaps Neil had been right all along. 'You invest too much in her,' he'd said. But she'd ignored him. Because who was he to make such a judgement? He'd never liked Fran. Well anyway, she consoled herself, even if it had started out like that, it was different now. She and Fran were close, and especially so since Neil's death.

She turned the computer off. She didn't know why she was bothering with all these old emails anyway. She should just concentrate on the here and now. Get through this ordeal – get them all through it – as best she could.

She went and joined Lucy in the lounge and they watched the rest of Coronation Street together. It had nearly finished when the phone rang. Yet again, they looked at each other in alarm.

It was DC Mason. 'I missed your call, Jane,' she said. 'Has something happened?'

'No. I was ringing to see if anything was happening at your end – after the news item?'

'Well, I've rung the station and there have been one or two calls. There always are when there's been something on the telly. But I have to say they don't sound very useful. We'll follow them up, though. You never know . . . I'll update you in the morning.'

In the morning! Fran would have been missing for four whole nights by then. Three nights already, four nights soon, and then five . . . It was what she would keep on doing – counting out the time like this. It was a pointless thing to do, she knew that, but she wouldn't be able to help herself. It was what she had been doing ever since Neil's death; counting out the days, and then the months – before and after it had happened – as if all this numerical data could make sense of it.

'You should go to bed,' she said to Lucy. 'And tomorrow we should definitely go out – go for a walk, do some shopping or something. And if there're no further . . . developments . . . then you should think about going back to London. On Wednesday, perhaps.'

'I can't leave you here on your own.'

'Yes you can. You can't stay here for ever.'

'Come back with me then. Come and stay for a bit.'

'I can't do that yet. It's too soon,' Jane said, but she didn't quite know what she meant by this. It was what she had said yesterday, referring to the fact that it was too soon after Neil's death to make life-changing decisions. But Fran's disappearance was different. In this neither-dead-nor-alive limbo, how long should they wait before resuming 'normal life'? Was there an etiquette to these things, she wondered?

Lucy went upstairs and Jane was thinking about going to bed herself when the phone rang again.

'Hello?' she said, clutching the receiver with both hands.

'Mrs Lord?' It was a man's voice.

'Yes?' said Jane, her heart contracting. She beckoned to Lucy who had reappeared at the top of the stairs.

'Solihull Police station here. It's Frances. We've found her.'

THE COTTAGE

1

Fran took Jane's keys and went to the alcove by the front door where the coats were hanging. The old cagoule which Jane had mentioned was hidden away underneath another jacket. She held it up for inspection. It'd seen better days but it was waterproof and long, and thankfully not one of those you had to put on over your head.

Still with the keys in her hand, she tried to thrust her arm into one of its green sleeves but couldn't get her closed fist past the cuff at the bottom. Impatiently, she pulled her arm out, put the keys down on the window sill, and tried again. With some difficulty she managed to engage the zip and pull it half way up. Then she raised the hood, picked up the keys and opened the door.

'Whoa!' she said, closing it again quickly. It was bucketing down outside. She pulled the zip up as far as it would go and carefully tucked her hair inside the hood. She pulled the drawstrings tight under her chin and tied them in a bow. Ready now for the elements, she opened the door again and slipped out, pulling it almost closed behind her so that the driving rain wouldn't get into the house.

The security lights came on as soon as she stepped outside. Pools of water had collected on the path and as she navigated her way round them she pointed the key fob at the car and pressed what she thought was the right button to open the boot. But nothing happened. She tried again and heard the central locking system go into action but still the boot remained shut. The rain was blowing into her face and her hands were cold and wet. She was fumbling now. 'Come on, come on,' she muttered, pressing one button after the other. 'Stupid bloody thing!'

The door of the boot sprang open suddenly and a light came on inside. Her case had slipped right to the back and she leaned in and pulled it towards her. Then, taking advantage of this extra light, she paused to study the key fob. She couldn't see the markings properly without her reading glasses but she located what she hoped would be the right button to lock the car again and placed her thumb over it in readiness.

She was about to heave her case out of the boot with her left hand when, seemingly from nowhere, a hand touched her other arm. With a cry of alarm she straightened up and turned round. The keys slipped from her grasp and fell to the ground. Her first fleeting impression of the man who was standing there beside her was of someone young, bareheaded and very wet.

'Sorry,' he said. 'Are you going somewhere?' And something else she couldn't make out because of the noise of the rain and the muffling effect of her hood.

'What?' she said leaning closer and peering at him. 'What's the matter?' He seemed distressed, but that could have been the effect of the rain running down his face like tears.

He started speaking again but it was hard to make out what he was on about. He was pointing towards the end of the drive where Fran could see a van parked on the road.

'I can't hear what you're saying,' she shouted.

'I just want to talk to you, to show you . . .' he said turning away from her and gesturing towards the van.

Perhaps there had been an accident or a breakdown or

something, she thought. Aware that the rain was blowing into the car boot, she reached up and slammed the door shut before splashing down the drive after him. The road was deserted. There was no-one around, no other vehicle on the road apart from this old, dark blue van. The man opened the passenger door and Fran, thinking that there might be someone inside in need of help, bent down to look in.

'I just want to talk to you,' he was saying. 'I just want to show you . . .' Seeing that the van was empty, it began to occur to Fran that something wasn't right. She tried to back away but he grabbed her arm.

'What are you doing? Let go of me!' she said, trying to disengage herself from his grasp.

'It's all right,' he said. 'I'm not going to hurt you.'

But she continued to struggle.

'Keep still will you! Keep still you crazy woman!' He was using both hands to hold her now.

Fuck! she thought, as his grip tightened, what's happening here? 'Let go of me!' she shouted. 'Let go! Help!' She tried to scream, but the pathetic noise she was making was totally inadequate. No-one would hear her, especially not in this wind and rain.

Nevertheless, he was taking no chances. With one restraining arm around her, he put his other hand across her mouth to silence her, and then began steering her towards the back of the van. Pinioned like this, it was difficult to keep her footing and she stumbled as they went.

No, no, no! This couldn't be happening! Not to her! No!

She continued struggling as he opened one of the back doors.

'No! Get off me! Let me go!' she tried to shout from behind his hand.

But it was no use. He was far too strong for her. He began to force her into the van. He pushed her into a sitting position and, before she could wriggle out again, he lifted her legs and rolled her inside.

'It's all right. I'm not going to hurt you,' he said again,

and then slammed the door shut.

Fran's heart was pounding with such terrifying violence that she thought she was going to die. It was too dark to see anything inside the van. On her hands and knees she crawled and groped her way around, exploring the limits of her confinement. There was something on the floor along one side. Tins – of paint, she thought, locating a handle. She lifted one up, and then another. They were very light, so they must be empty. Could she defend herself, knock him out with one of these, she wondered? But there was a partition between her and the driver's seat. She tried to get up on to her knees but banged her head on the roof of the van and sat back down again. And all the time she was whimpering: 'No, no, no!' This couldn't be happening! It couldn't!

She heard more doors slam and then the engine starting up. It spluttered noisily a few times before it got going properly and the van began to move. She hammered on the partition with her fist. Where was he taking her? What was he going to do with her? 'Let me out. Let me out,' she tried to shout, but she was gasping for breath. There were no windows. She was going to suffocate. There wasn't enough air. Shouting would use it all up. She felt panic threatening to overwhelm her. She loosened the drawstring under her chin and tried to calm herself down by taking slower breaths.

The van began to pick up speed; they must be out on the main road now. It felt to her as if they were going very fast. She tried to brace herself against all the bumps and jolts, but her discomfort was extreme. I'm going to get bruised to death in here, she thought.

Whenever the van slowed to a halt, she began beating on the sides and roof as hard as she could. But the stops were short – for traffic lights, or a roundabout, probably – and no-one seemed to hear her. On and on they went.

She couldn't believe she'd let this happen to her. What an idiot she'd been. She should have run back into the house when he'd first appeared. Had she thought that bad things didn't happen in respectable Solihull? If she'd been in

Streatham she'd have been a lot more streetwise.

She tried to think how best to deal with the situation. Her heart began pounding again. What should she do when he eventually stopped and got her out? Should she hit him with a paint tin, or might this make matters worse? Should she try to reason with him? Who the hell was he, anyway? And what did he want? I'm not going to hurt you – that's what he'd said. Well, he was hurting her. The bastard! I'll kill him, she thought. I'll scratch his fucking eyes out. I'll . . . But fear overcame her anger. It was much more likely that he would be the one to do the killing. He would rape her, and then kill her. 'No, no, no,' she moaned. 'Please God, no.'

The road they were travelling along now seemed to be very winding and she placed her hands on the floor of the van to steady herself. After a while, she felt it slow down then turn sharply to the right. It bounced along for a few more minutes and then stopped. She heard a door slam – and then nothing. She waited, straining to hear what was going on, but all she could hear was the sound of the rain beating on the van roof. She wondered what the hell he was doing.

She thought she could hear footsteps on gravel. Then the door opened and she could just make out his shadowy form as he stood there in the rain waiting for her to struggle towards him. She swung her legs out of the door and felt uneven ground beneath her feet.

'Mind your head,' he said, taking her arm in an almost gentlemanly manner and helping her to stand up.

'Where are we?' she asked, staggering slightly. She shook his hand away and peered through the rain. It was very, very dark. They must be out in the countryside somewhere. There was a building – a house, possibly – and a light in an open doorway. This must be where he was taking her.

'What do you want?' she said. 'Let go of me!' She tried to move away from him but her legs weren't working properly.

He took hold of her arm again and began to steer her towards the light. 'It's all right,' he said. 'I'm not going to hurt you. I just want to talk to you.'

They crossed the threshold of the building, stepping on a scattering of letters on the floor as they did so.

'It's all right, it's all right,' he kept repeating.

'No! It's not all right,' she cried. 'What the hell's going on?'

The light was coming from a small lamp on a console table just inside the door, but it was doing little to illuminate the room they were standing in.

'Where are we? Why have you brought me here?' she asked, turning to look at him. But as he let go of her arm and closed and locked the door, Fran wasn't so sure she wanted to know the answer to her last question.

Brushing past her, he strode across the room and switched the main light on. It took a few seconds for her eyes to become accustomed to the sudden brightness but when they did her heart gave a violent lurch.

She saw the window first, with the solid blue shutters. Then the brick fireplace. And, as if to confirm what she was seeing, her eyes flew up to the framed watercolour which was hanging above it. She glanced at the blue two-seater sofa and the matching armchair, and out of the corner of her eye she registered the staircase rising up along one side of the room.

At the top of this staircase there were two bedrooms. She knew this because she had been here before. One weekend a few years ago. With Neil Lord. It had been a secret then, and now that he was dead, a secret she had thought was safe for ever.

Her hands flew up to her throat; she couldn't breathe again. She clawed at the drawstring under her chin, undid it and flung back the hood of the cagoule. Whirling round, she stared hard at her abductor.

He was younger than she'd initially thought – and quite good looking. He was wearing a black leather jacket over a grey sweatshirt. His denim jeans were rain-sodden. His hair, too, was soaking wet, and water was dripping down his face so that he still looked as if he might be crying. But his appearance – slightly reassuring though it was – told her nothing.

'What are we doing here?' she said. 'Who are you?'

But something wasn't right. He was staring back at her, looking shocked and dismayed.

'Who are you?' she repeated.

'Shit,' he said quietly.

And slowly it began to dawn on her. Now that he could see her properly he didn't know who she was either. He'd got the wrong person!

'Oh, my God!' she said. 'You thought I was someone else, didn't you?'

He didn't reply, just kept on staring at her.

'You thought I was Jane, didn't you?' she said. 'Jane Lord. It was her house. You thought I was her.'

Again, he didn't respond. He sat down on the window seat and ran his hand over his wet hair.

Fran's mind was racing. He'd thought she was Jane. But why had he wanted to bring Jane here, of all places? I just want to talk to you, he'd kept saying. But what about? And why here? Neil had told her that the cottage belonged to some friends of his; it was their weekend retreat, he'd said. And Fran had imagined them to be a middle class, middle aged couple. Her abductor was much too young to be one of them. But he did have the keys. So who was he?

'I think you should just take me back,' she said. 'Before things get any more out of hand.' She moved towards the door. 'Just unlock this and let's go.'

'Shut up!' he said. 'Shut up and let me think.'

It was very cold. Fran wrapped her arms around herself to warm up a bit but the cagoule was wet and uncomfortable. She watched him carefully. He was wet through and must be feeling the cold too. And he obviously didn't want to be there anymore.

'Let's just go back,' she said, persuasively now, 'before Jane calls the police? Because she will, you know. If we go now you can drop me off somewhere nearby and no-one will know you did this. You can just drive away. It'll be all right.'

There was a short silence, and then he stood up and said: 'Yeah, OK. Let's go.'

On his way to the door, he was momentarily distracted by the letters on the floor. He picked them up and shoved them into the drawer of the console table.

'Come on,' he said, unlocking the door. He went to turn the light off, but it was too dark to see anything outside now so he put it back on and ran out to the van and switched the headlights on. He came back, turned the light off again, and gestured to Fran to step out into the rain. She tipped her hood back up and waited while he locked the door and pocketed the keys.

'I'm not going in the back again,' she said as she followed him to the van. He opened the passenger door and she got in. It was going to be all right, she told herself, fastening her seat belt, he was going to take her back. God! What a thing to have happened!

He put the key in the ignition and tried to start the engine. It spluttered a couple of times, like it had done before, and then cut out. He tried again. The same thing happened. And again.

'You're probably flooding it,' said Fran, calling on her meagre knowledge of engines. 'Leave it for a minute.'

He seemed visibly annoyed by this advice, but did as she said. To no avail, though, because the van still wouldn't start. Swearing, he got out and fiddled under the bonnet for a while. Fran's optimism began to fade. Back in the driver's seat, he tried again to coax the engine into life, but it was no use. It gave one last splutter before dying completely. They were going nowhere.

'Get out,' he said, obeying his own command. He slammed his door shut, slammed the bonnet down and came round to her side of the van.

He took her by the arm again but she shrugged him off. 'I can walk by myself,' she muttered.

They went back inside.

'What are we going to do now, then?' Fran asked. 'Have

you got a phone with you? Ring for a taxi.'

But he wouldn't. 'I don't want anyone coming here,' he said.

'Well let's walk then,' said Fran. 'There must be a village, or a pub or something nearby.' She knew perfectly well there was a pub because she had been there. It was quite a distance away, though, and it would be difficult to walk there in the dark. But what else could they do? 'We could get a taxi to come to the pub – if there is one,' she suggested. 'Or I could go there on my own and you can do whatever you want.'

'No,' he said. 'I can't risk that. Not with the van still here.'

He took his mobile phone out of his pocket and sat down on the window seat. He began typing a text. It was a long one, and when he'd finished he kept the phone in his hand, ready and waiting for a reply.

'What was that about?' Fran asked, sitting on the arm of the sofa.

He shook his head. They sat in silence for a few minutes and when his phone rang – with a particularly strident ringtone – both of them jumped. He glanced at the screen and then rejected the call.

'What are you doing?' Fran said. 'Why didn't you answer that?'

He shook his head again and continued staring at his phone.

Fran watched him intently. He seemed harmless enough – helpless even – but he was confused and worried. He could easily do something stupid. And she had no idea who he was, or what he wanted.

Eventually the text message he'd been waiting for arrived. He read it carefully, but it obviously didn't contain a solution to their problem. 'Shit!' he murmured and put the phone back in his pocket. Fran's heart sank.

'We'll have to stay here tonight,' he said, 'and I'll try and fix the van in the morning.'

'What! Are you mad?' she said, standing up. 'We can't

stay here all night.'

'Yes, we can. I'll sort it out in the morning. Then I'll take you back.'

'Jane will have called the police. They'll be looking for me now, you know.'

He got up and locked the door. 'They won't find you here,' he said putting the keys back in his jacket pocket. He crossed the room into the adjoining kitchen. Fran followed and watched in dismay as he checked that the back door was locked too.

'This is stupid,' she said. 'You can't keep me here against my will. It's freezing cold, and . . .' She turned to the fridge. There was a folded tea towel over the top of its door to stop it from closing properly. It was switched off and empty. 'There's nothing to eat here.'

'We'll manage till morning,' he said. He opened a cupboard. 'There's tea and coffee.'

'But no milk.'

'We'll manage.'

He filled the kettle and took two mugs from an adjoining cupboard. He knows his way round, thought Fran. Who the hell was he? And if he knew Jane, had he also known Neil? But she wasn't going to ask him that. She wasn't going to mention Neil.

She went back into the living room. The wind was making a mournful sound in the chimney. The shutters on the window were locked. The upstairs windows, she knew, were shuttered too and would also be locked. There was no obvious means of escape.

She was shivering with cold. They could do with lighting a fire but the log basket by the fireplace was empty. And even if it hadn't been, her captor probably wouldn't want to light a fire. He wouldn't want any smoke signals to be seen.

She took the wet cagoule off and sat down on the sofa. Her thin cashmere sweater, elegant though it was, wasn't nearly warm enough for here. She fingered the greenstone pendant around her neck. The cord had become a bit skewed in her struggles and she readjusted it now, feeling the need to keep her lucky charm in good working order.

He came in and handed her a mug of black coffee.

'Thanks,' she murmured, and then added: 'I hope this won't keep me awake tonight!'

The coffee tasted awful but it was hot and the mug was warming to her hands. He sat down in the armchair and Fran scrutinised him again. He must be feeling the cold, too, she thought. He still had his jacket on, but his jeans were soaked through.

'Who are you?' she said. 'What did you want with Jane? Why did you want to bring her here?' She thought he was going to ignore all her questions but the last one seemed to goad him into speech.

'I wasn't going to bring her here,' he said. 'I just wanted to talk to her. But then I saw her leaving . . . saw you leaving. . . and I . . . I . . .'

'You panicked,' said Fran. 'And just for the record, I wasn't leaving, I was arriving. But if you hadn't seen me, what were you going to do? Ring on the doorbell? Does she know you?'

He didn't answer.

'She doesn't, does she? So what do you want to talk to her about?' She hesitated for a moment. 'And why here? Where is here, by the way? Where exactly are we?'

'Why don't you just fucking shut up?' he said.

'Why don't you just fucking tell me what's going on?' she retaliated. But she knew it wasn't a good idea to make him angry.

'I need the loo,' she said, getting up and heading towards the kitchen. She stopped abruptly and looked enquiringly at him. 'Where is it?' she asked, hoping he hadn't noticed that she'd appeared to know where she was going.

'On the left through the kitchen.' He hadn't noticed. He was much too preoccupied with his own thoughts.

Fran groped for the pull-cord to turn the light on. There were two pull-cords, one for the light, one for the extractor fan, and inevitably she tugged on the wrong one first. She remembered this bathroom. With its distinctive yellow suite and yellow tiles, it was hard to forget. It had once been an outhouse on the side of the cottage but now was part of the interior. Its heavy door was the original outdoor one and it had a huge key in the lock. The bathroom window, high up over the bottom end of the bath, was little more than a slit – too small for anyone to get through. There was, she noticed, no shower curtain here now like there had been before, and no fluffy bathmat on the grey flagstone floor.

She locked the door. She was shivering more than ever now. The bathroom, so tiny that it could barely accommodate the bathroom suite, was even colder than the rest of the house. She glanced around. There was a grey hand towel hanging on the back of the door, and a partly filled soap dispenser on the washbasin. The toilet roll, uncomfortably close to the loo on a holder on the wall, was more than half used up. There were no other toiletries anywhere. Remembering the empty fridge, too, she wondered when the cottage had last been occupied.

She turned the hot tap on and washed her hands under the running water. It stayed cold. She stepped into the bath as she was drying her hands and tried to look out of the little window. But the glass was streaked with rain and it was too dark outside to see anything. She knew what was out there anyway – a garden hedge and beyond that, fields. There were no other houses to be seen, out of this or any of the other windows in the cottage. The lane came to a dead end here too, so there would be no cars passing by. It was a perfect little hideaway.

Fran squinted at her watch – twenty to nine. What now? It was too early to go to bed, or was that a silly thing to think, under the circumstances?

'It's freezing in here,' she said, returning to the living room. 'Isn't there an electric fire or something?'

He shrugged. She began to prowl around, looking for one.

'Perhaps there's something upstairs?' she suggested. He gave an exaggerated sigh, got up out of the armchair and ran up the stairs. A few moments later he reappeared with a duvet and threw it towards her. It was a single one, blue with large black and white footballs all over it. She hadn't seen this before. It must have been in the other bedroom. She draped it round her shoulders and sat down on the sofa again.

It was obviously a child's duvet. So Neil's friends must have had a child, she thought. Could this young man be that child? Was this his parents' cottage? He had the keys. It was a possibility. But she'd imagined them as being 'posh' like Neil. This young man had a definite Brummie accent. He didn't sound like the offspring of second home owners.

'So,' she said. 'You'll be able to fix your van in the morning, will you?'

He didn't bother to reply.

'Who are you?' she said, undeterred. 'Why don't you tell me what you want to talk to Jane about?'

'Mind your own fucking business,' he snapped.

'I think you've made it my business, haven't you?' she snapped back. 'I didn't ask to be brought here, you know. I think you owe me an explanation.'

Again, there was no reply.

'The police'll be involved now,' she persisted 'So, whatever it is you wanted to talk to Jane about, you can't now. You've made a right mess of things, haven't you?' She stopped, feeling that she wasn't doing her cause any good talking like this. He needed to be helped out of his predicament, not ridiculed because of it. 'If you tell me what this is all about,' she said, altering her tone, 'I might be able to help you.'

He stared at her, and for a moment she thought he was going to explain himself. But then he gave a short laugh and looked away. 'Fuck you,' he said. 'And fuck her.'

It was probably best to keep quiet, she decided. Best not to upset him anymore. Just get safely through the night and then get out of there in the morning. And then maybe Jane would be able to cast some light on the mystery – although, somehow, this didn't seem very likely. Jane would probably be as mystified as she was – possibly even more so. She wondered what Jane was doing now. She would have called John and Lucy, and Emer too, and told them what had happened. They would all be going out of their minds with worry, wondering what on earth could have happened to her. And would they have contacted Patrick yet?

She sat, swathed in the duvet, and studied her captor. He was obviously very cold and confused. And as she began to warm up a little she began to feel sorry for him.

'I suppose we may as well go to bed,' she said after a while. 'That's not an invitation, by the way,' she added, attempting levity again, but he was not to be amused.

He got up and went upstairs again. She could hear him moving about. Was he going to bed, leaving her downstairs on her own? But, no. A few moments later, he came back down with two pillows under his arm. Both of them had plain blue pillow-cases on.

'Leave that here,' he said, gesturing towards the football duvet. 'You can sleep upstairs. I'll sleep down here.'

Obediently, Fran unwrapped herself and rose to her feet. 'Well good night, then,' she said, heading for the stairs.

He didn't reply.

There were two doors at the top of the stairs, both of which were open. The door into the smaller bedroom over the kitchen had been closed when she was here before and she hadn't been sufficiently interested to open it and look inside. She stood in the doorway now and peered in. There was a small pine chest-of-drawers in there and a single bed – devoid now of its duvet and pillows.

The other, much bigger room was where she and Neil had slept. She switched the light on. It was, as it had been then, very sparsely furnished. There was a double bed, fully made up with the same pale green pillow-cases and the darker green patterned duvet cover; a bedside table with a small brass lamp on it; a wooden chair, and another pine chest-of-drawers – a larger version of the one in the room next door. She opened the top drawer; it was empty. The shutters on the window were locked like the ones downstairs. There was no escape.

She closed the bedroom door. The wood was swollen and she had to exert quite a bit of pressure to get it to shut properly. This meant she would hear him if he tried to get in during the night. But of course he wouldn't. That wasn't what he was about. For which small mercy she should be thankful. Count her blessings. Take refuge in platitudes. Fuck off, she told herself.

She sat on the edge of the bed and took her boots off. It was freezing up here but she didn't really want to get into bed wearing her cashmere sweater. She decided not to take it off, though, because being partially undressed might put her at a disadvantage. She removed her greenstone pendant and placed it on the bedside table. It wouldn't do to inadvertently strangle herself with it in the night. What would the young man downstairs do then? Bury her in the garden?

She lifted the duvet and examined the sheet, wondering if it was clean. But it hardly mattered whether it was or not. This was her bed for the night; she had no choice but to lie in it. She tried to switch on the bedside lamp but it wouldn't come on. The light bulb must have gone. She went over to the door and flicked off the light switch but the darkness was total – thick, heavy, unnerving. And in the dark the wind in the chimney up here sounded so much louder. She switched the light back on again.

The bed felt cold and damp even through all her clothes. She pulled the duvet around her and closed her eyes. It would be all right, she reassured herself. It was only for one night. In the morning he would sort the van out and take her back to Solihull.

And then what? The police would be involved now. There would be questions to be answered. But all they needed to know was what had happened. She wouldn't say that she had been here before. They need never find out about that.

In fact, they need never find the cottage either. She would be vague in her description of the place and its whereabouts – although this could be tricky because if she said that he had driven her back she would have to give some details. Had they been in the town or the countryside? From which direction had they returned? She could say that she'd been in the back of the van again – but if they ever caught him, he might contradict that.

No, the best thing – for both her and the young man downstairs – would be for the police never to catch him and never to locate the cottage. But what if they did – catch him and discover the cottage? Would they be able to link it to her affair with Neil? She didn't think so. Her abductor showed no signs of knowing that she had been here before, so she was safe there. But what was his connection to Jane? And why had he brought her here of all places? Who was this young man who had the keys and was familiar with the place? God! What a fucking mess it all was!

Fran turned over on to her back. To have been abducted was bad enough, she thought, but to have ended up in this room again – in this bed! She stretched out her arm and ran her hand over the empty space by her side.

~

She had come up by train on the Friday evening and Neil had met her at Leamington station and taken her for dinner at a restaurant in a big hotel on the outskirts of the town. The cottage had been a further twenty minute drive from there, along dark minor roads, in the depths of the countryside.

She could see that he had been there earlier, preparing the place for her arrival. There was a bottle of whisky and two glasses on a side table by the sofa. Logs were stacked ready in the grate. She watched as he struck a match and applied it to the twists of folded newspaper pushed in among them. The fire took straight away. It looked like a routine he'd been through many times before. Which Fran found a curiously unwelcome thought.

'These friends of yours who own this place,' she said,

'are they friends of Jane's, too?'

'Hardly,' he replied. 'That would be asking for trouble, wouldn't it?'

Yes, she decided, he'd definitely done this before. He was probably an old hand at cheating. And he was probably thinking the same about her – erroneously, as it happened – but there was no going back now. Not that she wanted to, mind; she'd been looking forward to this.

Experienced or not, getting themselves into bed proved awkward for both of them. Fran had brought her special-occasions nightdress with her. It wasn't an overly sexy one, but it was red. She got undressed in the bathroom and then, feeling very self-conscious, she toiled up the steep stairs to where a fully-dressed Neil stood waiting for her just inside the bedroom door. Her arms were full of discarded clothes, though, so he had to wait a moment longer while she made a detour round him and deposited them on the chair, making sure that her underwear was out of sight at the bottom of the pile.

He took her in his arms and began kissing her, slipping one shoulder of the red nightdress down as he did so. What, she asked herself, feeling slightly panic-stricken, was she supposed to do now? Start ripping his clothes off in a display of middle aged passion, perhaps?

Instead, she lay in bed and watched as he undressed himself. He was in good shape – for his age – and he seemed confident enough. He was wearing boxer shorts and she couldn't help wondering – thinking of Patrick's y-fronts – whether he wore these all the time, or if they were his dirty weekend equivalent of her red nightie. He sat down on the edge of the bed to take his socks off. Then, with a rather unsettling bounce, he whipped off the boxers and rolled in beside her.

The lamp was on her side of the bed. She leaned over and switched it off.

~

It had taken them a few more awkward moments to get into

their stride, she remembered. But once they had, neither of them had been disappointed.

2

L ong before she opened her eyes, Fran was aware that she wasn't really asleep. Unwilling to acknowledge where she was and what had happened to her, she had been trying to slip back into a proper sleep, but it wasn't to be. It was a wonder she had slept at all. Surely she should have lain awake all night worrying about the predicament she was in? But she hadn't. And she hadn't dreamed either. There had been no nightmares about backs of vans or wicked abductors, just blessed oblivion.

Reluctantly, she lifted her head from under the duvet and felt the cold air on her face. It was very quiet. The wind seemed to have dropped and there was no sound of rain. The light had been on all night. She squinted at her watch. It was quarter to seven. Still dark outside, probably. Too early to get up yet. But she needed the loo, so she would have to go downstairs, and if she woke him up – well, too bad. He was lucky she hadn't had to go down in the night after drinking that coffee just before going to bed. She eased herself upright and thrust her feet into her boots.

The bedroom door was stuck and she had to yank it open, making more noise than she'd intended. With only the bedroom light to guide her, she felt her way down the stairs. The young man was stirring on the sofa so she switched the light on. He made a groaning sound as he emerged slowly from under the duvet and she half expected the footballs to roll off as he did so. She could see that he still had his sweatshirt on but his jeans were spread out over the armchair and his jacket was on the floor.

'Good morning,' she said. 'I hope you slept well.' He probably hadn't, though. The sofa was small and he was a tall young man.

He grunted.

Fran went to the bathroom. God, it was cold! She washed her hands but decided she wouldn't be washing any other parts of her anatomy; she'd freeze to death if she did. She'd have a hot bath later when she got back to Jane's. She looked at herself in the mirror. What a mess! Smudged mascara, hair all over the place. She took a piece of toilet paper and wiped under her eyes. But this only made her look more tired and worn. She raked through her hair with her fingers. What did it matter anyway?

Back in the kitchen she put the kettle on and made two mugs of coffee. The dirty mugs from last night were sitting in the sink. There were two more clean ones left in the cupboard. Enough for just one more drink, she thought – because she was damned if she was going to start washing them up.

She went back into the living room. He was standing now, zipping up his jeans and fastening his belt.

'I bet those are still damp,' she said. 'You're going to catch your death of cold.' She could see that she was irritating him so, trying to lighten the mood, she added: 'Not that I'm suggesting you should walk around in your underwear, mind.'

He shook his head as if to clear it of her stupid remarks and bent down to pick up his jacket. Fran glanced at the duvet. She wanted to drape it around herself again but he had just come out from under it and it felt a bit too intimate.

'It's not properly light yet,' she said, handing him his coffee, 'but when it is, you should get out there and get that van fixed and then we can get out of here before we both die of cold. Not to mention starvation.'

She studied him. His hair, now that it was dry, was fairer than it had looked last night. And, slouched in the armchair, avoiding eye contact, he looked even younger than he had then, too. She was aware that she was speaking to him as if he were one of her sixth-form students, but he probably wasn't much older than them. And he needed telling.

She sat down on the sofa and put her mug on the floor. Enough time had elapsed since he'd vacated the duvet, she decided, wrapping herself in it. And it was too bloody cold for niceties, anyway. She picked up the coffee mug and cradled it in her hands.

'Have you thought about where you'll drop me off when we get back to Solihull?' she asked.

A long silence. Was he thinking about this, or just not talking to her?

'Say something, for Christ's sake.'

He turned his head and looked at her. 'Have you thought about what you're going to say? To . . . to everybody? About where you've been all night?'

'Well, obviously, I can't say I was out clubbing, can I?' she said. 'I'll just tell them the truth – that you brought me here . . . somewhere . . . I don't know where, and kept me overnight because your van broke down. I'll say I don't know why you did this, which, of course, I don't.'

'Will you tell them it was Jane Lord I wanted to talk to, and not you?'

'Would it make any difference if I did?' Fran said. She had been asking herself this same question. If she could get him to tell her who he was, and what he wanted to talk to Jane about, then she could assess how much information she could provide without incriminating herself.

'I don't know. But . . .' his tone became defiant, 'I'm not going to get caught. I'm not going down for kidnapping you or something.'

'I'm sure it won't come to that,' she said trying to sound reassuring. 'I'm not bothered about having you arrested or anything. I just want you to take me back.'

He stood up. 'I'll have a look at it now,' he said, moving towards the door.

Fran stood up too, but he said: 'No, you stay here. I don't want you seeing the number plates.'

He was about to unlock the door when a thought seemed to strike him and he turned to the console table and took the letters out of its drawer. He opened the front door, letting in a shaft of bright sunshine for a moment, and then locked it again behind him.

Fran gave a little groan. Those letters would have had the name of the owner of the cottage on them. She should have thought of this before and tried to get her hands on them, or at least get a look at them – although, without her glasses this might not have been that easy. Well anyway, it was too fucking late now.

She thought about what he had just said about the number plates. How could they go back now without her seeing them when he dropped her off? What was he going to do about that? She could see that it mightn't be as straightforward as she'd been hoping.

Still wrapped in the duvet, she began to wander around. She was sure that when she'd been here before there'd been more things around: more pictures on the walls, perhaps; cushions; candlesticks on the mantelpiece; vases - of dried flowers? And yes, there had been a cream coloured rug on the floor in front of the fireplace. The house had definitely felt lived in then. But it didn't now. A thought struck her. Perhaps it was for sale. Perhaps her young man was an estate agent with access to the keys.

She went into the kitchen. Things were missing from in here too. There had definitely been a toaster and a microwave before. She opened the cupboards and found a few pans, some plates, some bowls, the two remaining mugs. There were no tins, no cans, no packets. No food at all except for half a jar of instant coffee – less than half a jar now – and a box of teabags. She opened a drawer. Inside was a handful of cutlery, some wooden spoons, a tin opener. And three kitchen knives.

She took the largest one of these out and stared at it, thinking that if this were a film she would slip it into her boot now and use it later if she had to. But she would probably stab herself in the foot if she tried this, or ruin her boots, or both. And anyway, she wasn't going to stab him. There was no need. He'd been an idiot but he didn't deserve to die (even if he was an estate agent). She put the knife back in the drawer.

She was feeling very hungry now – she hadn't eaten since lunch time yesterday. She went and curled up on the sofa and thought about the huge breakfast she would demand when she got back to Jane's. Scrambled eggs would be the main feature of this, she decided. No doubt Jane would want answers to her questions but Fran would insist on eating first in order to satisfy this fierce craving which was engulfing her now.

When she heard the key in the door, she stood up and reached for the green cagoule. The duvet fell in a heap on the floor.

But the news wasn't good. 'I can't fix it here,' he said. 'I need to get it to a garage.'

Fran was dismayed. 'Well OK,' she said, thrusting an arm into a sleeve of the cagoule and heading for the door. 'Let's walk to the nearest village and then we can go our separate ways.'

He shook his head. 'No,' he said, blocking her way. 'I've told you. I can't let you go while the van's still here.'

'Of course you can,' she said trying to get past him, but he pushed her aside and locked the door again.

Fran thrust her other arm into the cagoule and then lunged at him. 'Give me those keys!' she said. 'Give them to me now. This has gone on long enough.'

He pushed her away. She lost her footing in the heaped up duvet on the floor and fell against the sofa. He made a move to help her up but she waved him away and struggled to her feet.

'Just let me out,' she shouted, frantic now. 'You can't keep me here. I won't stay any longer.'

She rushed over to the window and began clawing and tugging at the shutters. He pulled her away. Breaking away from him she rushed into the kitchen and opened the knife drawer.

'Open the fucking door or I'll kill you,' she screamed, pointing the knife at him.

'Don't be stupid,' he said, backing away.

'Stupid! It's you who's stupid, you fucking maniac.' She advanced towards him. 'Now open that door and let me out.'

He just stood there staring at her. He wasn't going to do as she said and common sense told her that one of them was going to get hurt if she didn't stop behaving in this hysterical fashion. She gave a howl of frustration and threw the knife down on the floor. He picked it up and went over to the drawer and removed the other two knives. Fran followed him into the living-room and threw herself down on the sofa.

'Listen,' he said, taking his mobile phone out of his pocket, 'it'll be all right. I've got a mate who works in a garage. I'll ring him and see if I can borrow their pick-up truck to tow the van away. Then I'll borrow my . . . a car . . . and come and take you back to Solihull.'

Fran sat and watched him, trying to make sense of what he had just said. Was this a good plan or not? But she couldn't think properly. She needed to take deep breaths, to calm down.

'Fuck!' he said, glaring at his phone. 'My battery's dead.'

She covered her face with her hands.

'Look, it doesn't matter,' he said, 'I can go home and sort out the pick-up truck. It'll only take a bit longer. But I'll go and get some food first, yeah?' He hesitated. 'I'll have to lock you in the bathroom while I'm gone, though.'

'What?' She uncovered her face, incredulous. 'Why?'

'I can't leave you out here. I can't trust you.'

'Trust me! You can't trust me? What the hell are you talking about?'

'You'll try and get out. I know you will. I'm sorry but . . .' He reached out, grabbed her arm and pulled her to her feet.

She thought about fighting again but decided against it. He was young and strong. He'd get the better of her. And it was humiliating, all this screaming and struggling. She snatched up the duvet with her free hand and let him lead her into the bathroom.

'I'll be as quick as I can,' he said, taking the key out of the lock.

Fran listened as he locked the door on the outside. Near to tears now, she lowered the toilet lid and sat down. She took the cagoule off and draped herself in the duvet again. She mustn't panic, she told herself. She was the adult here. He wasn't much more than a boy – a miserable, confused boy. So when he came back she needed to take charge of the situation. She could see now that threatening to kill him with a kitchen knife had been a bad idea. She needed to assure him that she wasn't interested in retribution, that she meant him no harm. She needed to convince him that the best course of action was to let her go – after she'd eaten, though, because she was starving. Which was probably why she was shaking so much. Her strength was low.

She reached out, turned on the tap and cupped her hand underneath it. She should drink, stay hydrated, be sensible from now on. She stood up and dried her hand on the damp towel. Then she stepped into the bath and stood on tiptoe to peer out of the slit of window. All she could see, across fields, was a line of trees in the distance, their bare branches outlined against an expanse of blue sky. That must be where the road is, she thought. She measured her head against the window to see if it would fit through were she to smash the glass. But she already knew that it was too narrow. And anyway, what would she use to break the window, her bare hands?

She returned to the toilet seat, but it was uncomfortable, and she felt rather foolish enthroned there in her football-festooned cocoon, so she transferred herself to the bath instead. She stretched out, facing the shower attachment, and tried to compose her thoughts.

What would everyone be thinking, she wondered? Would John and Lucy be on their way to Jane's now? Poor Jane. She didn't need all this on top of everything else she'd been through recently. She would be thinking the worst. They all would. And Patrick – would they have contacted him now? He would be in a state too, all those miles away in LA. But it would all be resolved soon. She wasn't in any danger. It was just a really ridiculous situation she had got herself into. They'd all have a good laugh about it in the future.

Unless, of course, they were to find out about her previous visit here. There would be no laughing then.

Fran eased herself on to her side and closed her eyes. What if it did all come out? What would happen then? Well, everyone would be shocked, of course – and hurt. John would be embarrassed, too. And Lucy, who had hitherto been such a fan of hers . . . ? Fran could live without Lucy's adulation, but she was the mother of her grandchild – grandchildren soon – so it would be very awkward. And then there was Emer. Fran could just imagine her saying: 'I don't know why you're all so shocked. She's done it before, hasn't she?' (Yes, it would be a prime opportunity for Emer to remind her mother about that fucking prick, Howard Sage.) 'Let's face it,' she would say, 'she's never been bothered about consequences.'

That just shows how much you know, little Miss Judgemental, Fran thought defensively. The accusatory words had riled her – even though they were ones that she herself had put into Emer's mouth.

As for Patrick . . . Well, she could probably handle him. After all, he'd chosen to go away and leave her alone. It must have occurred to him that something like this might happen. (Although probably not quite so quickly! He'd hardly landed in America before she'd embarked on this affair.) She had often wondered whether he had been unfaithful during all this time in California. She thought not, but couldn't be sure. And would it matter anyway, as long as it made no difference to their status quo?

But . . . the more she thought about it, as she lay there in the yellow bath, the less sure she was that Patrick would feel the same way. It was one thing approaching infidelity from a hypothetical standpoint, quite another to deal with the reality of an actual affair – and one so close to home, too.

Which brought her to Jane. How would she react? Stupid bloody question. She would be devastated. It hardly bore thinking about. It was, after all, a double betrayal – her husband and her friend. And seeing that her husband was no longer around, it would be her friend who would have to face the consequences.

Maybe Emer was right. As far as Neil Lord was concerned, she certainly hadn't considered the consequences at the start of the affair.

~

It was Easter 2004, and Patrick, against her wishes, had just left for California.

This was something he'd been talking about doing for a while, but, as he'd always assumed that Fran would go with him, it had only become a viable proposition once her mother had died. When it became clear, however, that he would be spending five years there, she'd thought that he was asking too much of her.

And they'd been arguing about it ever since she'd come back from her trip to New Zealand. (In fact, one of the reasons she'd gone there in the first place – and why she had stayed so long – was to evade the issue.) Right up until the last moment she had thought that he wouldn't go without her. But he had. And if he was hoping she would change her mind at some point in the future, he was deluding himself. Because she wouldn't.

She hadn't contacted Jane since she'd been back from New Zealand. When she'd first met her, that Saturday afternoon at Warwick Arts' Centre, she'd thought her pleasant enough, and it'd felt good reminiscing about old times and old places with someone from a similar background, but she'd never intended their relationship to develop much beyond a few more meetings like that. Meetings which, when they did take place, had done little to change her mind. Jane, in her big, anonymous house in conservative Solihull, with her pompous, Telegraph-reading husband and her two predictable daughters. What really did they have in common? Now that Fran wouldn't be going up and down to Lancashire anymore, did she honestly want to be bothered to stay in touch?

There was no getting away from the fact, though, that Jane had been a good friend to her during those last horrible months of her mother's life. She had been persistently kind, inviting Fran into her home, feeding her and listening to her woes. And Fran, who had been vulnerable at the time, had been touched by this. Feeling ever so slightly guilty, she kept telling herself that she should send an email. Soon.

When Neil texted, suggesting that they meet – In London for conference. Wondering would you be free for lunch tomorrow? Neil Lord – it crossed her mind that he wanted to tell her off in person for her lack of consideration towards Jane. On further reflection, however, this seemed very unlikely. So what was this invitation all about? She wondered how he had got her number. Had he asked Jane for it, or had he got it from her phone without her knowledge? In which case, was he propositioning her? Did she want him to be? He was a pain in the arse, but . . . Possibly, she texted back.

A few hours later he rang her. He said he was attending a conference in Bloomsbury. He should be finished by twelve o'clock the next day but couldn't be absolutely certain of the exact time, so why didn't they meet in the Great Court at the British Museum? And if by any chance he was delayed – or it was raining – she could keep herself amused – and dry – while she was waiting for him.

His studiedly off-hand manner was already amusing her. 'Fine,' she said. 'I'll see you then'

The next day, due to a freakish combination of favourable travel conditions, she arrived early at the British Museum. (She hated it when this happened. It reminded her of a time when she was fifteen and had been stood up, in a shop doorway, by some stupid boy who obviously hadn't realised how lucky he'd been that she'd consented to meet him in the first place.) Picking up a random leaflet from the Information Desk, she went to sit down near the entrance to wait for him. Peering over the top of her reading glasses, she took in the spectacle before her. The place was heaving with visitors, nearly all in groups of varying sizes and nearly all casually dressed. It would be easy enough to spot Neil when he did arrive – a single man, smartly attired.

At ten to twelve she saw him walking briskly through the doors. She lifted the leaflet up to her face and watched him over the top of it. In his dark suit, shirt and tie he looked more impressive than she remembered him being – handsome, even. He stood still for a moment and looked around, but he didn't see her. He consulted his watch. He, too, was early. He walked over to a display stand, studied it for a moment and then turned and began walking across the domed Court, weaving in and out of the crowds as he went. Fran leapt up and began following him.

He stopped at one of the shops and began to take a great interest in the jewellery on sale there, leaning in closer to get a better look at one of the items. Was he thinking of buying something? For her? No, much more likely, it would be for Jane.

He looked at his watch again. Fran moved further away and took her phone out of her bag. Sorry, running late. Shouldn't be long, she typed, and a few moments later watched him reading her text. It was funny – and exciting – to have him at her disposal like this.

He wandered off into the gallery of Egyptian sculptures and she followed, being careful not to lose him in the crowd. He didn't stay in there but walked straight through to the Greek and Roman Sculptures room where the walls were lined with statues of men and boys, many of them naked. In the centre of the room was a statue of the goddess Aphrodite, crouching and also naked. Neil stood for some time, studying this attentively. When at last he moved away, Fran went over to have a closer look at the crouching female figure. Aphrodite, the Goddess of Love. What had Neil been thinking as he looked at her, she wondered? And a tremor of desire took her quite by surprise.

Back in the Great Court, assuming that Neil had returned to the entrance, she walked a semicircle round the dome and went into the Ladies. Yes, he's a prat, she thought, surveying herself in the mirror. But he wouldn't be the first prat she'd got herself involved with. And if this turned out to be just an innocent lunch, she knew now that she would be disappointed. She took her phone out and texted: I'm here. Then she took off her glasses, put them back in her bag and went out to meet him.

~

Less than two months later she had called a halt to the proceedings (the sum total of which had consisted of the weekend at the cottage shortly after their first lunch meeting, and three other occasions in London hotel rooms.) She'd ended the affair when she'd heard that John and Lucy had become an 'item'. Or at least that was the excuse she'd given Neil. But she wouldn't have carried on with it much longer anyway. Aphrodite's powers had not been unlimited.

It was also because of John and Lucy that she'd re-established contact with Jane. It'd been a bit awkward, after so many silent months, but expediency had required it. And she was glad of this now because, in spite of her earlier misgivings – and misdeeds! – something solid had developed between them.

This had surprised Fran. She had always been effortlessly popular, never short of friends and admirers – even if they did tend to come and go – but she had never had a close friend before. A 'best' friend. Not a female one, anyway. Not until Jane came along and, little by little, began assuming that role. And, little by little, Fran had come to value this friendship. She didn't want to lose it now.

She opened her eyes and gazed up at the bathroom ceiling which had once been white but had faded badly. One thing was clear. She must do all she could to safeguard her secret. Which shouldn't be that difficult, she reassured herself, because whatever her abductor wanted had nothing to do with her.

But who was he and what did he want with Jane? She sighed loudly. She didn't want to start going over all this again. It was too exhausting. And right at this moment, if she was honest, all she really cared about was getting something to eat. She fumbled with the duvet to free her arm and have a look at her watch. He must have been gone long enough now. And hopefully he would bring back something substantial. Not just crisps or chocolate. She tried not to think about scrambled eggs on toast.

The yellowness of the bathroom was beginning to irritate her. 'God! I can't believe that someone actually went out and chose that colour!' she'd said to Neil when she'd first seen it. 'They probably wanted a warm colour,' he'd said. And she'd recognised the familiar, barely-suppressed note of annoyance in his voice. He'd obviously forgotten – momentarily – that they were about to become lovers. 'And don't forget, bathrooms were all coloured in the eighties.' 'That's no excuse,' she'd said, amused that he was defending his friends against her scorn. 'Bad taste is bad taste whatever the decade.' But she'd changed the subject then, because she, too, needed to remember that on this occasion she wasn't there to spar with Neil.

When Fran heard the young man coming back into the cottage she struggled out of the bath with some haste. She wanted to be vertical when he opened the bathroom door. He let her out and she stood in the kitchen doorway watching him unpack the carrier bag he'd brought back with him. He placed three packets of sandwiches, a packet of chocolate biscuits, a small container of milk, two cans of Diet Coke and a glossy magazine on the worktop. Her spirits rose when she saw the sandwiches.

He put the kettle on and took the two remaining clean

mugs out of the cupboard.

'I'll just have a sandwich and a cuppa,' he said, 'then I'll go.'

He took one of the packs of sandwiches and gestured towards the rest of the things on the worktop. 'Those are all for you. I've been eating on the way back.'

Fran picked up her mug of coffee and the two remaining packs of sandwiches. One was egg and mayo on brown bread, the other ham salad on white. She allowed herself a small smile. And the magazine – Cosmopolitan. How thoughtful of him. A pity she didn't have her reading glasses with her, but it would be churlish to point this out.

'Thank you,' she said.

They sat in the living room and ate their breakfast. Fran tried not to wolf the sandwiches down too quickly.

'You don't need to lock me in that bathroom again,' she said when they'd finished eating. 'I won't try and escape. It'd be pointless, anyway. I'd only get lost, so I might just as well wait for you to come back and get me.'

He seemed to be thinking about this, but after a few moments he stood up and shook his head. 'No,' he said. 'I can't risk it.'

'I'll freeze to death in there,' Fran protested. 'At least in here I could walk about to keep warm.'

He shook his head again. 'I'll get the other duvet as well,' he said, making for the stairs. He came back down with his arms full of the green duvet and the pillows.

'Oh, for fuck's sake . . .' Fran muttered, trying to keep her temper. 'This is so stupid.'

He carried them into the bathroom and threw them into the bath. Then he got the cans of coke, the chocolate biscuits and the copy of Cosmopolitan and deposited them on the toilet lid.

'How long do you think you'll be?' she asked.

He shrugged. 'Two, two and half hours or so, depending on the trains, to get home and back with the pick-up truck. Then I'll tow it to the garage and come back for you.'

Fran glanced at the packet of biscuits, wishing now that she'd saved one of the packets of sandwiches for later.

He locked her in again and she heard the front door slam behind him. She checked her watch. Quarter to twelve. It would be teatime before she got back to Solihull. Looking on the bright side, though, it would be dark by then which might make it easier for him to drop her off.

It was already getting dark in the bathroom. The sun had moved around the house, taking with it much of the daylight and, presumably, the modicum of warmth it had provided. Fran pulled the light cord and set about arranging the duvets and the pillows in the bath. She put the single duvet down as a mattress and doubled up the larger one and placed it on top. Then, making sure that the cans of Coke and chocolate biscuits were within arm's reach, she picked up the magazine, stepped into the bath and slipped under the top duvet. She propped herself up against the pillows and pulled her knees up to rest the magazine against them. Braving the cold, she kept one shoulder and arm outside of the duvet so that she could flick through its pages.

It was interesting that he had bought this magazine for her. She tried to visualise the shelves in the shop to imagine what other choices he might have made. At some point he must have decided that she was a brown bread and Cosmo kind of girl. She gazed at the cover. *Learn to love your body*, she read, scanning the large banner headlines surrounding a picture of Angelina Jolie. *How normal is your sex life?* Without her glasses, though, the magazine was of limited use. She couldn't read any of the articles; she could only look at the pictures. She sighed deeply and reached for a chocolate biscuit.

She kept getting in and out of the bath, trying to ward off the stiffness she was feeling. She tried not to keep looking at her watch. Prufrock might have measured out his life with coffee spoons, she mused, but she was measuring out her afternoon with nibbles of chocolate biscuit and sips of Diet Coke. The literary thought inevitably made her think of

Howard Sage. Who had written a book about T.S. Eliot. Which she had never read. And for the umpteenth time she found herself wondering whether Emer had read it – or any of the other things he had written. But why was she thinking about Emer and Howard Sage now, for Christ's sake? Here she was, a prisoner in a yellow bathroom in a freezing cold house in the middle of nowhere. They should be the least of her worries.

The afternoon wore on and she began to get anxious. Her young man should have been back ages ago with the pick-up truck. Perhaps he had been back, she thought, but hadn't bothered coming into the house. Would she have heard him if he had? She listened carefully and could just make out the sound of motorway traffic in the distance – a faint but constant whooshing noise. The bathroom was at the back of the house but if she could hear the motorway surely she would have heard a truck at the front? Anyway, it was so late now that he must have been and gone. He would be back again soon to get her.

But as the afternoon slipped into evening she began to think that he wasn't going to come back for her at all. Once he had taken his van away there would be nothing to connect him to this house, or with her disappearance, so why bother? He could just leave her here and forget all about her. She got out of the bath again, sat on the toilet seat and leant her head on the wash basin. She mustn't let panic overwhelm her. She would be all right, she told herself. She could survive for quite a while on the remaining biscuits. And there was always water in the tap. That was the most important thing.

But no-one knew where she was. No-one seemed to come here anymore. She would never be found. At least, not until it was too late. She was going to die – slowly but surely. She couldn't breathe. Her hand went to her throat and she realised that she wasn't wearing her pendant; she'd left it on the bedside table upstairs. And this discovery reinforced her sense of doom.

For the first time since being in the back of the van, real

fear gripped her. She didn't know this young man. She had no idea what he wanted. She had been stupid to believe him. She should have fought more, refused to be incarcerated in this cold, horrible bathroom. She should have stabbed him with the knife when she'd had the chance, and made her escape. But it was too late now. He wasn't going to come back for her. She was going to die.

She could hear herself moaning out loud. She must stop this and think. There had to be something she could do. She lifted her head and turned to look at the window again. Should she try to break it and shout for help? But the cottage was too far away from anywhere. There wouldn't be anyone within earshot.

No, she needed to attract attention in some other way. What about the light? Morse code? She stood up and stepped to the light cord. What was SOS in Morse code? Was it three short, three long, three short – or was it the other way round? Oh, God! She couldn't think straight. She tried both, standing there pulling on the cord like a lonely bell ringer. But it didn't matter whether she was doing it right or not. No-one would see her signal. And even if they did they wouldn't recognise it as an SOS call. They'd think it was car headlights in the distance, or a low-flying aircraft – after all the airport wasn't far away. It was no fucking use. No-one was going to find her. She was going to die.

Leaving the light off, she slid down on to the cold, flagstoned floor and, with her eyes closed and her head on her knees, rocked gently to and fro. After a while she began to feel a bit calmer.

She was still sitting on the floor in the dark when she heard the key turning in the lock. The door opened and the light went on. She sat there, blinking, for a moment and then struggled to her feet, all semblance of calmness deserting her now. Letting the duvet fall to the floor she launched herself at him and began beating him with her fists.

'Where the hell have you been?' she shouted. 'Where the fucking hell have you been? I thought you were never coming back.'

As her shouts turned to sobs he stopped defending himself against her blows and took hold of her arms.

'I'm sorry,' he said. 'I didn't mean to be so long.'

She dropped her head, almost resting it on his shoulder.

'I'm sorry,' he kept repeating as she strove to control herself.

'Let's go then,' she said at last, stepping out of their half-embrace. She caught sight of herself in the mirror. She was a mess – hair all over the place, face streaked with tears – but it didn't matter. All that mattered was getting out of there.

'I'm sorry,' he said again. 'We can't do that.'

Fran followed him into the kitchen, trying to concentrate on what he was telling her. Something about how long it had taken him to get home because the train had been delayed, and then how he hadn't been able to get the car he'd been intending to borrow and so had had to come back by train too, and it was a long walk from the station. What she did hear clearly, though, were his next comments. The van was still outside. Monday morning was the earliest he could get the pick-up truck, so she would have to stay there till then.

'What? No! No way!'

'But I've brought you some things,' he said, nodding towards a plastic carrier bag on the floor. 'And I've got us a takeaway too. Indian . . . I hope that's all right.' He indicated a cluster of brown paper bags on the worktop. 'We'd better eat it straightaway while it's still hot.'

Fran stared at him in disbelief. 'What? Are you mad?' she said. But the smell of the curry was distracting her. They should eat first and argue later.

The carrier bag contained a grey sweatshirt and a navy fleece. She put both on over her cashmere sweater. He was dressed more warmly now, too, she noticed. He had on a thick, black woollen jumper under his leather jacket.

He took two plates from the cupboard and two forks from the drawer, gathered up the food and took it into the living room. Stopping only to retrieve the green duvet from the bathroom floor, Fran followed him.

There was a small coffee table in one of the fireplace alcoves and he pulled this in front of the sofa and spread the food containers out on it. He had brought some cans of lager too. They ate in silence for a while. But Fran was thinking hard. What could she say to get him to see reason?

'Look,' she ventured at last. 'Why don't we just leave now . . . after we've eaten this, I mean? We can get a train to Birmingham or somewhere and then go our separate ways. I don't know where this place is. I don't know this area at all. So even if I tried to tell the police where I've been, I wouldn't be able to. And honestly, I'm not bothered about having you caught. I just want to get out of here.'

'And how could we get a train without you seeing the name of the station?' he said. 'No, sorry, but we're going nowhere till I get the van away from here on Monday morning.'

'Monday morning! Come on, you know that's ridiculous. You have to let me go before then. You're not thinking straight.'

'I am thinking straight,' he said. 'I'm sorry, but like I said, we have to stay here till then.'

We! So he wasn't going to lock her in the bathroom again. He was planning to stay too. But what an absolutely ridiculous situation this was. What on earth were they going to do till Monday morning?

'Won't there be someone missing you, too?' she asked. 'Like your girlfriend, or your parents, or your flatmate? Won't they be wondering where you are and what you've been doing all weekend?'

'It's all taken care of,' he said, taking his newly charged phone out of his pocket. He studied it for a moment and then put it back.

Fran mopped up her curry sauce with her last bit of naan bread. 'Well, that was delicious,' she said. 'Now, tell me, what else do you have planned for this evening? Not to mention all day tomorrow.'

'Look,' he said. 'I'm sorry about all this. I really am. I know it was a mad thing to do, bringing you here. And I don't know why I did it. But it's done now and you'll just have to make the best of it.'

'Oh, really! And how, may I ask, do I do that?'

He didn't answer.

'The least you can do is tell me what you wanted with Jane?'

He shook his head.

'You do know, don't you,' she said, watching him carefully, 'that you can't possibly talk to her now? You won't be able to say whatever it was you wanted to say to her, so all this will have been a waste of time – for you as well as for me.'

He remained silent.

'When I tell her about you, will she have any idea what this is all about?'

He shrugged.

'Is that a "no", a "don't know" or an "I'm not telling you"?'

With just a suspicion of a smile, he shrugged again.

'Tell me whose place this is then. You've got the keys. Is it yours? Yes? No? Well OK, if we're going to be stuck here together, at least tell me your name.'

'As if!'

She sighed. 'Well . . . Asif . . . I'm Fran – in case you're interested.'

When they had both finished eating, Fran gathered up the empty containers and lager cans and stuffed them into the carrier bags. She put their plates together, with their forks arranged neatly on top.

'You can do the washing-up,' she said, pushing them towards him. 'I'm the guest here.'

He took the plates and the rubbish into the kitchen.

'You'll need some hot water,' she called after him. 'Isn't there an immersion heater somewhere?'

He reappeared looking bemused.

'Come on, you know this place. Where's the hot water cylinder? There must be an airing cupboard somewhere?'

There was – upstairs in the smaller bedroom. He bounded up and switched the immersion heater on.

Good, Fran thought. Hot water. She would be able to have a quick shower in the morning now. It was a pity there were no proper towels, though, but she could use pillow cases or something to dry herself with. If she didn't freeze to death in the process, it would make her feel better. If it wasn't so bloody cold she could have had a bath tonight. When she was a kid, Saturday night had always been bath night. And this inconsequential thought gave rise to such an unexpected pang of nostalgia that for a brief moment she thought she was going to cry.

'I'll have to wait for it to heat up,' he said, coming back into the room. He took his phone out of his pocket again and spent a few minutes fiddling with it. He seemed to be reading and sending texts, giving Fran the impression that perhaps things weren't as 'taken care of' as he'd said. Someone – his girlfriend, his mother – obviously needed more information.

When he'd finished he reached into the carrier bag at his feet and extracted a can of lager. 'Do you want another one?' he asked, holding it out to her.

Fran took it from him. 'Yeah, why not, Asif,' she said. 'It's Saturday night. Let's get legless.'

The sleeping arrangements were the same as for the previous night. Despite Fran's efforts to lighten the mood he obviously didn't trust her enough to sleep upstairs too. Well, that was his choice, she thought as she removed her cashmere sweater and draped it over the chair to air off. She put the grey sweatshirt back on and, turning out the light, clambered into bed. The darkness didn't seem to be a problem tonight.

But, unlike last night, tonight she couldn't get to sleep. She lay awake for hours going over and over things in her mind. It would be all right, she kept telling herself. He would take her back to Solihull on Monday morning and, in a week or so, it would all blow over. It had been an ordeal – for all of them – but no real harm would have been done. In fact, her young man would be the one who would come out of this the worst because, even if he didn't get arrested, he'd failed in whatever it was he'd been intending to do.

She had a vague, uneasy feeling that all wouldn't be well. It was the cottage that was the problem. Whatever it was he'd wanted to talk to Jane about must have had something to do with this cottage. Or was it purely coincidental that they'd come here? The bloody place! If only she'd never come here with Neil. But there was no point regretting this now. She had been here before. But no-one knew that. Her young man had given no indication whatsoever that he knew anything about her previous visit.

It would definitely be best for her if he didn't get caught and if the cottage was never located. Also . . . if she didn't tell anyone that he'd abducted her by mistake, there would be nothing to connect him to Jane. But . . . if the police were to catch him, he was bound to say that he'd never meant to kidnap Fran, that he'd only meant to talk to Jane. Then it would seem very suspicious that she hadn't told them this in the first place.

No, she would have to tell them the truth – about this weekend, not the other one – and hope that all would be well.

3

The next morning, before going downstairs, Fran went into the other bedroom and switched the immersion heater back on. Her young man was still asleep on the sofa, almost completely hidden under the duvet. She went into the kitchen and saw that he had washed the dishes last night; it was the carrier bags of empty food containers that were responsible for the strong smell of curry in there.

She went back into the living-room, carrying two mugs of coffee. He hadn't stirred. She looked around for his jacket. The keys would be in its pocket. She could make her escape. But he hadn't been that careless; the jacket was tucked safely under his pillow. Disappointed, she was turning away when she noticed his phone on the floor by his head. Very quietly, she put the mugs on the coffee table and bent down and picked it up.

Her heart was pounding as she crept out of the room and locked herself in the bathroom. She sat on the toilet lid and examined the phone. Who should she call? 999? But how would she explain where she was? In a cottage with a van parked outside, somewhere in the countryside, about a twenty minute drive from Leamington Spa? Would that get her anywhere? The only other number she knew by heart was her own – and her phone was in her handbag at Jane's. She could ring that and perhaps Jane would answer. She still wouldn't be able to say exactly where she was but she could tell her that she was all right and that she would be back tomorrow. And Jane would pass on this information to everyone else – including the police.

With shaking hands she tapped in her number. She held the phone to her ear and waited, but all she could hear was the thumping of her own heart. She squinted at the screen. No! The fucking battery was dead again! But he'd been playing with it yesterday evening. How could it have run out again so soon? She fought back tears of frustration. Fuck, shit, fuck, she thought, raising her hand to throw the phone on to the floor. But she stopped herself. She mustn't do that. It wasn't a good idea to let him know what she'd done. She should put it back where she'd found it.

'Rise and shine!' she said, sitting down in the armchair and picking up her coffee. 'We've got an exciting day ahead of us.'

Just before he went out in search of food for the day, he produced his phone charger from his jacket pocket and plugged it into a socket at the side of the chimney breast.

'I'll get some newspapers too,' he said, his arms full of duvets and pillows, as he ushered her into the bathroom. 'What would you like? The Sunday Telegraph?'

Fran gave an exaggerated groan. 'Are you trying to torture me even more?' she said.

'What would you like then?'

'Apart from my freedom – and my reading glasses, you mean?'

He stared at her with what looked almost like dismay.

'And get rid of that rubbish in the kitchen,' she said, trying not to feel sorry for him. 'It stinks of curry in there.'

When he had gone she took the pillowcases off the pillows and got undressed. She had a very quick shower, using up almost all of the soap in the dispenser. The pillowcases made very poor towels and she felt uncomfortably damp as she struggled back into the same underwear, socks, jeans and cashmere sweater that she'd been wearing for days. The bath was wet now; she couldn't lie down in it. So, huddled in both duvets, she sat on the toilet lid, listening to the whirring of the extractor fan, and hoping that he wouldn't be gone long.

After about an hour he returned and let her out of the bathroom. Fran put the kettle on and examined his purchases. He had bought more sandwiches – seven packets of them, all on white bread this time – more biscuits, two tins of soup, two pork pies, a carton of milk and the Sunday Mirror and Sunday Express.

'There wasn't much choice,' he said. 'The shop wasn't open so I had to go to a petrol station and these were all the sandwiches they had.' He groped in his pocket and produced a pack of cards. 'And I got these for you. Something for you to do if you can't see to read.'

She was touched. 'Thank you,' she said, taking the cards from him.

'Oh and by the way, the clocks changed last night, so its only quarter past nine now, not quarter past ten.'

'Oh great!' she said. 'Just what we need. An extra hour.'

After they had breakfasted on two of the packets of sandwiches, Fran suggested that she be allowed outside for some fresh air.

'I haven't seen daylight for nearly two days,' she said. 'I won't try and run away.'

He seemed to be entertaining the idea.

'You can come with me. No-one will see us here (careful! She mustn't reveal too much knowledge about their location.) . . . will they?'

He was still thinking.

'You can cover up the bloody number plates, if that's what's bothering you,' she persisted. 'Use the pillow cases in the bathroom.'

It was a crisp, sunny morning and Fran, wearing the green cagoule, took deep breaths of the fresh, autumn air. It was good to be outside – good to be alive, she thought. She took a surreptitious look at the dark blue van, trying to ascertain what make it was but she wasn't very good at that sort of thing and couldn't see any badges or writing on it to give her a clue. The green pillowcases, looking as though they'd been laundered and were hanging out to dry, were draped over the number plates.

They walked along the lane a little way, awkwardly and in silence, and then returned and went round to the back of the cottage. Fran stood in the long grass and surveyed the scene before them. On the Sunday morning she'd been there with Neil, she'd watched him mow this grass. She could picture him now, pulling an old- fashioned lawn mower out of the small shed at the side of the house. 'It's the least I can do,' he'd said, his face red with effort as he shoved the heavy machine over the rough ground. She knew there was a gardener who tended the lawn at the house in Solihull, so doing this was probably a novelty for him. And when he'd finished they'd driven down to the village pub for lunch.

Resisting the temptation to take her young man's arm and begin promenading with him, Fran walked on alone to the low fence which separated the garden from the fields beyond. She stood there in the autumn sunshine and gazed at the rather melancholic scene. The trees were nearly all bare now and the fields were empty, save for the newly ploughed ones on to which squawking flocks of birds kept swooping in search of food.

It had been spring the last time she was here. The trees had been coming into leaf. There had been lambs with their mothers in some of the fields, and cows in others. Clusters of daffodils had littered the garden, and there had been an abundance of wild flowers – blue and yellow and white ones, whose names she didn't know – bordering the fields and encircling the trees. On the Saturday afternoon, Neil had taken her for a walk in a nearby wood where the ground had been thick with bluebells. *('Bluebells I'll gather,'* her father used to sing to her when she was a little girl.) And she remembered how, a couple of years later, Jane had mentioned a favourite April walk of hers in what must have been that same bluebell wood. Fran shivered and wrapped her arms around her cagoule-clad self.

(*'Bluebells I'll gather / Take them and be true.'*) The song was in her head now, along with the memory of her father. Yes, he'd thought the world of her when she was a little girl. But when she became a big girl she'd been much too complicated for him. She would never forget how, when her mother had reacted so violently to her pregnancy, he'd just stood by and said very little. And how, when things had calmed down, the little red-haired, green-eyed, infant Emer had become his new little girl.

Fran gave a slight sniff. What, she wondered, would he make of the grown up Emer now, if he were still alive?

She moved on along the fence. She could hear the muffled roar of traffic on the motorway quite clearly now – and also, somewhere in the distance, the sound of a train thundering by. Overhead, a plane was descending noisily – like the birds – as it prepared to land at the airport. Although there were no houses or people to be seen, civilisation was not that far away.

People always thought the countryside was so much quieter than the city, yet it was noisier here than in her garden in Streatham. There, the traffic noise was muted and, except when there was an event on the Common, or one of her neighbours was having a barbecue, only the sound of birdsong and the intermittent wailing of sirens disturbed the peace. She wouldn't be hearing any sirens here, though, she reflected, unless the emergency services were suddenly to converge on the cottage to rescue her. But how likely was that?

She walked on further, followed closely by her captor.

'Let's walk across the field a bit,' she suggested.

But he shook his head. 'Too risky,' he said. 'Someone might see us.'

Too risky – that's what he kept saying. How cautious he was. Neil, on the other hand, hadn't been at all risk averse. He'd taken her to the pub and out for walks where they could easily have been seen by people who might recognise him.

They spent the rest of the morning perusing the newspapers. Fran screwed up her eyes and scanned the headlines, first in one paper then, when he had finished with it, in the other. Apart from the usual dross, there were articles on the American presidential election which was just over a week away. Patrick would normally be very involved with this. Her disappearance must be proving very inconvenient for him.

She glanced up and saw that her young man was looking at her. 'Isn't this cosy?' she said, readjusting her duvet. 'A really nice, restful Sunday.'

He ignored the remark, but then, a moment later, blurted out: 'Are you a relation of Jane Lord's?'

The question took her by surprise.

'No,' she said. 'I'm just a friend. Although . . . I suppose in a way we are related. My son's married to her daughter.'

He looked interested. 'Which one?' he asked.

Fran pounced. 'Which what? Which daughter?' He looked flustered. 'You know that Jane has daughters then?'

He shrugged. 'So?'

'It's the older one – Lucy. Do you know her?' (And more to the point, did you know her father? But don't ask this. Don't.)

He didn't reply. And before she could question him further his phone, which was still plugged into its charger, emitted a bleep. He reached over and removed it from the cable which he left plugged in the wall. The incoming message took some time to read and then a long session of texting followed. Hopefully, things were being sorted out.

'Is everything all right?' she asked. 'Is Plan A still in operation for tomorrow?'

He grunted.

'Shouldn't you be at work in the morning?'

'I'll tell them I'm going to be late,' he said.

Was he an estate agent, Fran wondered again? She rather hoped he wasn't because she was beginning to feel quite fond of him. There would be no point asking him, though, because undoubtedly he would consider it too risky to say.

She was also wondering what John or Emer would tell her Sixth Form College about her absence tomorrow morning. 'I'm afraid Frances Delaney won't be in today, and probably not for the rest of the week. She's been kidnapped.' Original, yes, but somehow not very convincing.

Lunch was one of the tins of soup – vegetable – and another sandwich. They decided they would keep the pork pies for later. And Fran was looking forward to this. She hadn't eaten a pork pie in years. She'd loved them when she was young – when she seemed to be hungry all the time and they were satisfyingly filling. It would be a real retro pleasure, she thought.

When they had finished eating, she stood up and collected their empty bowls and plates together.

'Just so you know,' she said, 'I'm definitely not going to do any washing up. But can I tempt you to a cup of tea? There's only a bit of coffee left and we should save that for the morning.'

The long afternoon stretched out before them. If she'd had her glasses with her she could have done the crosswords in the papers. She could probably see well enough to do the sudokus, though. But when she asked her companion if he had a pen on him, he looked up from his phone, on which he appeared to be playing a game of some kind, and said 'no, sorry'.

She tried to remember if there had been a television there before. She thought there might have been, but couldn't be sure. But more to the point there definitely wasn't one there now.

Then she remembered the cards. She peeled the cellophane wrapper off the pack and tipped them into her hand. She moved their mugs off the coffee table and, pausing only to rewrap herself in the duvet, slid on to the floor. She had, she noticed, attracted his attention, but only for a moment. She began to shuffle the cards. She didn't know many card games and anyway it was most unlikely that he'd want to play Snap with her, so – with only the prospect of incoming text messages to relieve the monotony – she would have to entertain herself.

She began to lay out a game of Patience. She hadn't played this for aeons – not since she was twenty-one years old and living in a tiny flat in Bristol with Nick Cartwright. In fact, it'd been Nick who'd shown her how to play it.

Another wave of nostalgia swept over her. And something else, too, that she couldn't easily put a name to. Poor Nick, she thought. She had certainly tried his patience over the years.

Poor Nick. And poor Jane.

4

It was nearly eight o'clock on Monday morning and Fran was back in the bathroom, sitting on a pillow on the floor with the double duvet wrapped around her. Her young man had just left. He had told her that there was a train to Birmingham at eight twenty-four and that he would be back with the pick-up truck in approximately one-and-a-half to two hours. So with a bit of luck she should be back in Solihull for a late lunch.

Laid out on the toilet seat, within easy reach, were the last of the sandwiches (cheese and pickle), a mug of coffee and slightly less than half the packet of biscuits from yesterday. Also, the pack of cards. She would eat first, then wash, then play Patience.

She ate the rather soggy sandwich and drank the coffee. Then she stood up and stripped to the waist. She wasn't going to have a shower today as that would make the bathroom too damp and steamy for comfort. There was hardly any soap left anyway, and the pillowcases were still adorning the van's number plates outside. She washed as best she could and dried herself on the small damp towel before putting her clothes back on. She slipped her pendant over her head and, looking in the mirror, adjusted the cord. What a sight she was. And what a sight she'd be when she turned up on Jane's doorstep later. She'd be wearing the rather fetching green cagoule then, too.

She wondered who would be there to welcome her back. John and Lucy and Emer? But perhaps they had all been at Jane's over the weekend but had gone home now. Perhaps they had given up hope of ever seeing her again. Alive. This was, indeed, a chilling thought. She hadn't really considered what her family and Jane must have been going through. This whole thing would've been much more horrendous for them than it'd been for her. They hadn't known what she'd known – that she'd never been in any real danger, that it'd all been a stupid, but essentially harmless, mistake.

But she was all right. And soon all the worry and upset would be over. And she knew exactly what she was going to tell them. She was going to say that her young man had mistaken her for Jane, but that he wouldn't tell her why he'd wanted to take Jane to an empty cottage somewhere – she'd no idea where – in the middle of the countryside. She would describe his physical appearance and hope that Jane might be able to enlighten them as to his identity. She would tell them about the problems he had had with the van. She would, basically, tell them the truth. Not quite the whole truth, but the truth nevertheless. Everything was going to be all right.

When her young man returned, she was playing Patience on the bathroom floor. He unlocked the door and handed her a mug of tea. The coffee was all gone now.

'The van's all hooked up and ready to go,' he announced. 'I'll be back in about an hour.'

'And where will you drop me off?' she asked.

'I've got that all worked out,' he said. 'Don't worry.'

'As if I would,' she said.

She drank the tea and ate two of the biscuits, thinking how strange it was to be so looking forward to brushing her teeth. She felt light-hearted and slightly light-headed – excited even.

Her enthusiasm for Patience, though, seemed to have faded. Her neck was stiff and she was aching all over from crouching on the floor. She put the cards away and made herself as comfortable as she could in the bath. He would be back soon. There was nothing to worry about . . .

When she woke up it was so dark she couldn't see her

watch. What time was it? She scrambled out of the bath and groped for the light switch. She pulled and pulled but nothing happened. This bulb must have gone, too, like the one upstairs, she thought. Or there might have been a power cut or something. She groped around for the other cord – the one for the extractor fan – and pulled on this too, but again nothing. Yes, it must be a power cut, she told herself. It would come on again soon. Unless it wasn't a power cut. Perhaps the electricity had been cut off. What was going on? Where was he? Why hadn't he come back for her?

It was like Saturday afternoon all over again; the same thoughts and fears racing around in her mind. He wasn't going to come for her. He'd never intended to. Now that he'd taken his van away he had no need to. She'd been a fool to think that he would. She'd been a fool to like him. What did she know about him? Nothing. He had to be unstable to do what he'd done in the first place. Why had she trusted him? He hadn't trusted her.

She tried to be rational. Surely he'd been intending to come back? She couldn't have got him that wrong. So perhaps something had happened to delay him. Perhaps he was on his way right now. He would walk in any minute. Or perhaps something had happened to him – he might have had an accident. He could be in hospital . . . and if he was, would he tell someone about her? Or would he think that would be 'too risky' – even if it meant she might die? No, he had brought her brown bread and a pack of cards. He wouldn't wilfully leave her to die. But perhaps he was dead himself. He could have been driving too fast. He could have been killed on one of these country roads.

Irrationally, this thought brought tears to her eyes. She sat down on the toilet seat and reached for the toilet paper, but there was none left; she had used it all up earlier, with no thought for the future. And she had been eating the biscuits in the same abandoned way too. She had been stupid, stupid, stupid.

She sat down on the floor and began to rock back and

forth. There were still a few biscuits left, she told herself, and there was plenty of water in the tap. She wasn't going to die. Not yet. But eventually she would. She would starve to death, slowly and agonisingly. Because no-one knew she was here. No-one except him. And he wasn't going to come back for her.

She was crying properly now, but there were no tears, only a loud wailing sound which echoed round the small dark bathroom. She clutched at the greenstone pendant around her neck, feeling that her luck had finally run out.

QUESTIONS

1

Jane put the phone down. 'They've found her,' she said to Lucy who was standing at the bottom of the stairs now, clutching the newel post. 'She's OK.'

Lucy sank into a sitting position and burst into tears.

'She's OK,' Jane repeated. 'They're going to get a doctor to check her over. Then they'll need to get a statement from her before they can bring her back here.'

She went to reset the central heating control. The house would need to be warm when Fran returned. 'It'll be ages before she gets here,' she said to Lucy. 'You should go back to bed – after we've rung John and Emer.'

But Lucy was dismissive. 'Don't be silly! As if I could possibly sleep now.' She picked up the house phone. 'I'll ring John. You ring Emer on your mobile.'

While they were waiting, they puzzled over what little information Jane had been given. Fran had been found, locked in a house, somewhere in the countryside out towards Medworth. Someone – a woman who had seen the news item – had tipped them off as to its location. Fran was all right – just cold and hungry.

'All right,' said Lucy. 'What does that mean? Do you think she's been . . . harmed?'

'Raped, you mean?' said Jane. She shared Lucy's concern. It was what they were bound to wonder.

When Fran finally arrived, however, she wasted no time in dispelling their fears. 'It's all right,' she said, standing in the hall, wrapped in a police blanket. 'I'm fine. Absolutely fine.' She handed the blanket to the policeman who was accompanying her and gave Lucy, who had burst into tears again, a brief hug.

'I'm fine,' she repeated. 'I really am.' Turning to embrace Jane, she added: 'Now don't you start crying too.'

Jane stepped back and looked at her. She was, of course, still in the same clothes she'd been wearing on Friday evening. Her pendant was round her neck. Her hair was a mess. Her face was red and blotchy as though she too had been crying recently. She looked tired and strained. She looked her age. But she didn't look violated.

The policeman left and Fran held up her hands to stop them asking their questions. 'I have to get out of these clothes and have a shower first,' she said. 'And then I need something proper to eat. They gave me some biscuits at the police station, but I'm starving.'

Later, sitting at the kitchen table in Jane's warm but unflattering winter dressing-gown, and tucking into scrambled eggs on toast, she told them what had happened.

She described how her 'young man' had bundled her into the back of his van and driven her to some house, at the end of a track, in the countryside somewhere. And then how, once they were inside, he had discovered his mistake.

'He'd thought I was you,' she said to Jane. 'It was you he wanted, not me.'

'Me!' Jane was astounded. 'He thought you were me?'

'Yeah, I was wearing that cagoule, remember. I had the hood up. I could have been you. It wasn't till I put the hood down and he got a good look at me that he realised I wasn't.'

At the mention of her cagoule, Jane gave Lucy a forbidding look. 'But what on earth did he want with me?' she said.

Fran shook her head. 'I don't know. He said he'd come to talk to you. He hadn't meant to kidnap you – me. He thought you were going away somewhere when he saw me – who he thought was you – putting my – your – case in the car, and he just panicked. But I haven't a clue what he wanted with you. I kept asking him, all weekend, but he wouldn't say.' She shrugged. 'He must be someone you know. He knows you – or at least he knows what you look like.'

'What does he look like?' Jane asked.

Fran gave them a brief description.

Jane shook her head. She didn't know many young men. But then a thought occurred to her. 'Oh, wait a minute,' she said. 'I think he might've been here before. A couple of weeks ago someone like that came to the door.'

'You never mentioned that before,' said Lucy.

'Well, why would I? I opened the door. There was this person standing there. He asked if . . . someone or other – I can't remember what name he said – lived here. I said no, and off he went. It didn't seem significant at the time. But it could have been him, couldn't it?'

'You should tell the police,' said Lucy.

Fran paused for another mouthful of food and then resumed her story. She told them about the problems with the van. And about how he kept locking her in the bathroom. But she'd never thought he meant her any harm. Until he hadn't come back for her. Then she'd thought she was going to die. Which was horrendous. But she'd been rescued. So all was well. She was here now. Crisis over.

'I'll make some more toast,' said Jane, rising from her chair. 'Would you like some, too, Lucy?'

She kept her back turned to them as she placed the bread in the toaster. Her hands were shaking. Crisis over, indeed! Someone – some unhinged individual – wanted something from her. He'd been desperate enough to . . . kidnap . . . to get whatever it was he wanted. He was still out there somewhere. And Fran thought the crisis was over!

Daniel woke up at seven thirty and began to cry. Jane dragged herself out of bed and went in to him. She didn't want him waking Fran who needed to sleep after her ordeal.

Her grandson seemed quite pleased to see her. He was standing up in the travel cot, holding on with one hand and dangling Felix over the side with the other. His teddy was on the floor. Overnight, he seemed to have switched his allegiance from bear to cat. She changed his nappy and then took him into her bedroom. Fran still had her dressing-gown, and it was too chilly to be wearing only her nightie, so she sat Daniel on the bed and began to get dressed. He watched her with great interest.

'Where's Grandma Jane?' she said, hiding in her sweatshirt. She heard him make an excited little sound. 'Boo!' she cried, pulling it down over her head. He laughed with delight and rolled over on to his back. Smiling, she picked him up and took him downstairs.

Some time later, Fran, encased in the grey fleece dressing-gown, came down for breakfast. Jane and Daniel were sitting on the kitchen floor, building towers with the extra large Lego bricks Lucy had brought with them. As soon as he saw Fran, Daniel abandoned the bricks and forgetting that he could walk now crawled over to her with great speed and agility, shrieking with delight as he went.

'Hey, Danny boy,' said Fran, crouching down and taking him in her arms. 'How are you doing?'

'We've made a great big tower, haven't we, Daniel?' said Jane. But he had lost interest. She heaved herself up from the floor, staggering slightly before she attained an upright stance. 'Breakfast?' she said to Fran. 'Scrambled eggs again, or would you like something else?'

'Ooh, yes please,' said Fran, rising (smoothly) to her feet. 'I seem to have developed an insatiable craving for scrambled eggs on toast.'

All morning, one or other of them seemed to be either making or receiving phone calls. The police still had Fran's mobile so she had to use the landline. First, she made a quick call to Emer. And then Lucy, who had been speaking to John at the same time, handed her phone over so that Fran could have a quick word with him too. This done, Fran then had a long conversation with Patrick who had just got in from Heathrow.

While all this was going on, Jane decided to ring her school on her mobile. She told them what had transpired and said that she was hoping to return later in the week. Hearing her say this, Lucy, who was speaking to John again, waved a warning finger at her mother and shook her head vigorously. Jane chose to ignore this. 'I'll let you know,' she said to the school secretary and rang off.

'I'll speak to you later,' Lucy said into her phone to John. She turned to Jane. 'You can't go back to work yet,' she said. 'You should take the rest of the week off. You've had a shock.'

'We'll see how it goes,' said Jane, thinking how everything seemed so provisional these days, but that it would be her decision to make, not Lucy's.

'Patrick's going to drive up tomorrow to take me home,' Fran announced, handing the house phone to Jane. She turned to Lucy. 'You can come back with us too, if you want.'

'You can't leave till the police have spoken to you again,' said Jane, affronted that Fran should think it was all right for them to up and go just like that, as if nothing had happened. Leaving her to cope with the aftermath alone.

'Yes, I know. But they'll do that today,' said Fran.

'And they might need you . . . for identification purposes or something . . . if they catch him.'

'They won't,' said Fran. 'Catch him, I mean. They don't have a lot to go on.'

'I certainly hope they do catch him,' said Jane. She could hear her voice rising. She was getting upset. 'Because I, for one, would really like to know what this is all about.'

'Well so would I,' said Fran, 'but I'm just being realistic. Like I said, they've only got what I've told them – and that isn't much, is it?'

'You said last night that they were going to look at CCTV footage at the petrol station where he went shopping.'

'And what will that show? A blurred image. Probably not as good as the physical description I've given them. Or the one you could give them if he is the same person who came here before.'

'There's fingerprints and DNA.'

'Only useful if he's on their data base. Which isn't very likely. He didn't seem like the criminal type to me.'

'You're beginning to sound as though you don't care whether he's caught or not,' said Jane. And then, ignoring Fran's snort of protest: 'It might be over for you, but it's not for me.'

'I think I'll stay a bit longer,' said Lucy.

'You don't have to,' said Jane, looking at Daniel who had gone back to playing with his bricks. 'You go back with Fran. I'll be fine.'

'He won't come back here, if that's what's worrying you,' said Fran.

'I'm not worrying.' (Of course she was worrying! Who wouldn't be worrying under the circumstances?)

'I honestly don't think he will,' said Fran.

'He might,' said Lucy. 'He's been before. We don't know what he'll do.'

'No. He'd think it was too risky.'

'I wish he would,' said Jane, 'then I'd know what this is all about.'

'Well, even if he does, I don't think he's dangerous or anything,' said Fran. 'He left you to die, don't forget,' said Lucy.

'No, I don't think he did. It must've been him who told that woman where I was – the woman who rang the police station. It must've been him. No-one else knew.'

Well that's all right, then, thought Jane. Nothing to worry about. Silly me!

Not long after lunch, when both Daniel and Lucy were

having naps upstairs, DS Hooper and DC Mason arrived. They had brought Jane's cagoule and Fran's mobile phone with them. Jane bundled up the cagoule and put it on the hall table. DS Hooper unbuttoned her trenchcoat and sat down on the sofa in exactly the same place she'd sat on Saturday afternoon. She was wearing a different suit today, though, a black one, and a white, businesslike blouse. She was also wearing much less make-up.

'How are you today, Ms Delaney?' she asked.

Jane half hoped Fran would answer 'fair to middling' but she said: 'I'm well, thank you. I'm just glad this is all over.'

DS Hooper gave her a long, serious look. 'Oh, but it's not over,' she said. 'We've yet to find your abductor, haven't we?'

She turned to Jane and the seriousness of her expression intensified. Somewhat alarmed, Jane turned to Debbie Mason and gave her a small smile.

But DC Mason didn't smile back. Instead, she said: 'Mrs Lord,' (so, no more 'Jane' and 'Debbie'!) 'it would appear, from information we've just received, that the cottage where Ms Delaney spent the weekend belonged to your late husband.'

There was a loud gasp – Jane couldn't tell whether it had come from her or from Fran – and then a long silence. She stared uncomprehendingly at the policewoman.

She could hear Fran repeating what they had just been told. 'Neil!' she was saying. 'The cottage was Neil's?'

Both policewomen were staring intently at Jane now.

She shook her head. 'No, that can't be right,' she said.

'I'm afraid it is.' It was DS Hooper speaking now. 'Are you saying, Mrs Lord, that you have no knowledge of this cottage – in Fieldend Lane East, near Medworth?'

'Fieldend Lane . . . ?' Jane said slowly. She frowned. 'Well yes . . . he did own a cottage out there somewhere, once. In fact, there were three cottages. His aunt . . .' She shook her head, confused. 'No, it was his great-aunt, I think . . . she left them to him. But that was a long time ago. He sold them years ago.'

'How many years ago?' DS Hooper asked.

'I don't know . . . years and years ago. Not long after we were married.' Jane was struggling to remember. 'There were three cottages. Two of them were together near the farmhouse which I think used to be his grandfather's. Those were empty and he sold them straight away. The other one was further away, all by itself at the end of . . . a track . . .' She trailed off and put her hand to her mouth.

'Yes, Fieldend Lane,' said DS Hooper.

'It was a tied cottage,' said Jane, 'and there was an old man still living in it. Neil had to wait till he died before he could sell it . . . Which he did, a few years later. Die, I mean. And then Neil sold it.'

'Well not according to the Land Registry,' said DS Hooper. 'It would seem that he's still the owner.'

Jane shook her head. 'No, that can't be right. There must be some mistake.' She turned to Fran who seemed as shocked as she was. 'He sold it,' she said. 'Years ago. At least, that's what he told me.'

'Exactly when did he tell you that?' asked DS Hooper.

'I don't know *exactly* when. Years ago. It was for sale for a long time, if I remember rightly, and then finally someone bought it. That's what he told me.' She was trying to hold DS Hooper's interrogative gaze. 'It was over twenty years ago.'

'So you've never been there yourself?'

'No. Well . . . yes . . . when he first inherited the cottages, we did go for a drive out there to have a look at them. But we didn't go inside any of them.'

'And you've definitely never been there since?'

Jane was very aware that both policewomen were watching her closely. 'No, of course I haven't,' she said. 'Why would I?' But it was obvious they didn't believe her. They thought she had something to do with Fran's abduction!

'So . . .' DS Hooper said, 'as far as you were aware, your late husband sold the last of the cottages over twenty years ago?'

'Yes. It was old and run down. They all were. He just wanted to get rid of them.'

'Well, Mrs Lord, I can tell you that this particular cottage isn't that rundown now. It's been renovated. And it looks as though it's been lived in – until fairly recently, I should say.' DS Hooper turned to Fran. 'I think Ms Delaney can testify to that?' she said.

Fran gave an almost imperceptible nod of her head.

'Well I can testify that I know nothing about any of that,' said Jane, stung by the note of triumph in DS Hooper's voice. 'I thought it'd been sold years ago.'

'This information, together with what Ms Delaney has already told us – that her abductor mistook her for you – throws up a whole new line of inquiry,' said DS Hooper, standing up. 'We'll ask around the village,' she went on. 'See if anyone knows who might have been living there. Also, there'll be an update on Midlands Today, this evening, saying where and when Ms Delaney was found. That might also throw up some more information. We'll keep you informed.'

'I . . . I think this . . . young man . . . might have been here once before,' Jane said. She didn't know whether telling them this was going to make her seem more or less suspicious. 'Someone answering his description came to the door a few weeks ago. One evening . . . He said he was looking for someone whose name meant nothing to me. That could be how he knew who I was, how he knew that Frances wasn't me when he saw her properly . . . don't you think?'

DC Mason wrote this down in her notebook.

'We'll be asking a lot more questions, Mrs Lord,' DS Hooper said, rising to her feet. She shot a look at her colleague. 'DC Mason will be talking to you at length, very shortly. In the meantime, it would be useful if you could trawl through your memories and see what else you can come up with.' She turned to Fran. 'And if you think of anything else, please let us know.'

'I'm going back to London tomorrow,' Fran said.

'You have our phone number, don't you?' DS Hooper

replied, belting herself into her trenchcoat.

'I do, indeed,' said Fran, looking askance at Jane and raising an eyebrow.

'The cottage is a crime scene at the moment,' DC Mason said to Jane, a little less coldly now, 'but I'll let you know when you can have access to it.'

'I can't think properly,' said Jane when they had gone. She pressed her fingertips to her temples. 'I don't understand any of this. If it's true, then why didn't he sell it? And why did he tell me he had? And he had it renovated! Christ, Fran, what's he been doing there?'

'There'll be a simple explanation,' said Fran.

'Oh I'm sure there will be. It's not going to be a nice one, though, is it?'

'I don't know what to think.'

'That's Daniel crying,' said Jane. 'They'll be down in a minute. Don't say anything to Lucy about this. Not yet. Not till I've had a chance to think about it.'

'OK.'

'Promise me you won't,' insisted Jane, only aware that she was sounding like a schoolgirl when Fran began to trace the shape of a cross over her heart.

Lucy appeared in the doorway with Daniel in her arms. 'I see you've got your cag back,' she said to her mother. 'I hope you're going to throw it out now.' She handed Daniel to Fran. 'Did the police have anything new to say?'

'They're still investigating,' said Fran.

The news item was very brief.

Following last night's report on the disappearance of Frances Delaney (the picture of Fran again*) from outside a house in Solihull last Friday evening, a tip off by a member of the public led police to this isolated, uninhabited cottage* (a rather picturesque shot of the cottage*) near Medworth in Warwickshire, where Mrs Delaney was found, locked up, cold and hungry, but otherwise unharmed. Police are appealing for information about her captor who forced her into his dark blue van (possibly a Ford Escort) and drove her to this remote spot. He* *is described as white, in his early twenties, tall, and fair-haired. If you have any information – about the abduction or the cottage* (the shot of the cottage again) *– then ring this number.*

'Well, *Mrs* Delaney, let's see if that evokes any response,' said Jane.

But Fran was dismissive. 'It won't,' she said. 'Apart from a possible round up of every blue van owner in the Midlands. There're only two people with any real information – my young man and the woman who rang the police. And they're not likely to come forward, are they?'

'Someone else might have some information. You never know. So I'm not giving up hope yet,' said Jane.

Fran really doesn't care whether he's caught or not, she thought. But she did. Because the more she thought about it, the more she realised that she was as desperate to talk to this young man now as he'd been to talk to her last Friday evening. But she didn't want him to approach her privately. She wanted their conversation to take place in the presence of the police.

2

Patrick arrived at noon the next day. When she heard his car pull into the drive, Jane went out to meet him.

'Jane!' he said, embracing her. 'How is she?'

'Oh! You know Fran. She's bouncing back.'

'And how are you?'

'Me? I'm fine.'

Fine. We're all just fine, she thought as she led him into the house.

She stood back discreetly while Patrick and Fran greeted each other. It was obviously a great relief to him that Fran was unharmed. Also, Jane reminded herself, it had been nearly two months since they'd last seen each other, so it wasn't surprising that the greeting was . . . she searched for the right word . . . fulsome. Under other circumstances, witnessing this little scene, she would have felt a pang of longing for Neil. But what she was feeling now was quite a different kind of pang.

'I'm perfectly fine, really I am,' Fran laughed, extricating herself from Patrick's embrace. 'It all sounds so much worse than it actually was.'

'Hi Patrick, it's so good to see you,' said Lucy, offering a cheek to be kissed. 'But I don't think she's as fine as she'd have us believe. She's just putting a brave face on it. I happen to know that she didn't sleep well last night.' She turned to Fran. 'No, you didn't. I had to get up with Daniel and I saw your light on.'

Jane, who hadn't been sleeping well for months, busied herself with the lunch.

'Are you sure you're going to be O.K.?' Fran asked Jane later as they were about to depart. She was holding Daniel while Lucy, leaning awkwardly into the back of the car, was struggling to install his car seat.

Jane reached out to stroke Daniel's head. 'I'll be fine,' she said, trying not to feel like she was being abandoned. After all, it'd been her who'd persuaded Lucy to go too. She wanted to be alone. She couldn't think properly with them around, and she had a lot of thinking to do. She also wanted to go and visit the cottage, as soon as she could, and she wanted to do that alone too.

Lucy straightened up and gave her mother a hug. 'I'll ring you when we get back,' she said. 'You'll be all right, won't you?'

Jane, feeling tearful all of a sudden, confined herself to a nod of the head.

'I'll ring you this evening,' said Fran, handing Daniel to his mother. She gave Jane a meaningful look. They hadn't had a chance to talk properly yet without Lucy being present. 'Take care now,' she added, slipping into the passenger seat beside Patrick and reaching for her seatbelt.

'You too,' said Jane, recovering herself. 'You're the one who's had the traumatic experience. You need to look after yourself.'

'I'll see that she does,' said Patrick, starting the engine.

'I'm absolutely fine,' said Fran, shaking her head. 'There's no need for all this fuss. To be honest, I feel a bit of a cheat.'

Jane stood waving goodbye until the car disappeared from sight. She closed the front door and – just in case – slipped the chain into place. Back in the kitchen she started clearing away the lunch things. What a mess small children make, she thought as she wiped the table where Daniel had been sitting. She carried the high chair back to its corner, trying not to think about Neil tripping over its legs. That had been a fond memory. But could any memories be described as fond ones from now on, she wondered?

All the previous night she had lain awake, trying to dredge up other memories. Of things that hadn't seemed particularly important at the time and had left only faint traces behind. What she could remember was how delighted she and Neil had been when they'd heard about the cottages. Neil's mother had died not long before and he'd inherited the house. The money they would get from selling the cottages would help with all the improvements they'd been planning for it.

She had a vague memory of driving down country lanes to go and see the cottages, but she had been new to the area then and everywhere was unfamiliar. She wouldn't know how to get there now. She could just about picture the properties. All three of them had looked very rundown. The one that was causing all this bother now had been at the end of a track. It had had wisps of smoke coming from its chimney and they hadn't wanted to stay parked outside for too long in case someone came out to see what they wanted. The legal work hadn't been completed; the cottages weren't actually theirs yet.

She also remembered Neil executing a very bad five point turn on the narrow, uneven road. (Had they been in their dark blue Triumph Herald, she wondered? Or had that been replaced with the white Renault by then? And why did this matter?)

She sat down at the kitchen table and put her head in her hands. Why had he lied to her? Why had he been deceiving her all these years? He must've had another woman. Or women. It was the obvious – the only – conclusion to be drawn. He'd been using the cottage to conduct at least one extra-marital affair. Their marriage had been a sham. And she'd never suspected a thing. And, worst of all, she'd spent the past three months grieving for this man.

Propelled by anger, she leapt to her feet and went into the hall. She would phone the police station to see if they had found out anything more. She hesitated a moment and then dialled DC Mason's number. 'Debbie' sounded friendly today. Yes, she would take Jane to the cottage tomorrow, she said. The electricity had been cut off so it would be best to go in the morning, before it started getting dark. There would be someone there repairing the back door lock where the police had broken in on Monday night. This person, she said, would also change the other locks if Jane agreed to foot the bill. 'And,' she added, 'I'd like you to compile a list of your late husband's friends, acquaintances, colleagues – anyone who might know something about this cottage – so that we can question them.'

Jane put the phone back on the hall table and sat down on the stairs. So, it's my cottage now, she thought. Unless, of course, he'd left it to someone else. In another will, perhaps. Could he have done that? There must be some legal records somewhere – solicitor's documents from when he'd sold the first two cottages, and, if he hadn't sold this one, there must be deeds or something, too. Why hadn't their solicitor mentioned these things when he'd been sorting out Neil's affairs (his financial affairs, that was)? Then she remembered that they'd had another solicitor back then – some old guy who had been his parents' solicitor. The one they had now wouldn't have had anything to do with the cottages. And the old one was probably long dead, so where would the deeds be now? She shook her head. She could do without this, she really could. She had more than enough things to sort out as it was.

She stood up. She needed to get out of the house. She would go to the shops. Her food stocks were low after all the visitors she'd had. More eggs were definitely needed. She went to get her coat, and the sight of the green cagoule hanging up beside it gave her a momentary surge of satisfaction. It was her cag, she thought: she would decide, in her own time, what she was going to do with it.

Just after six, Lucy rang to say that they'd got back safely. The traffic had been an absolute nightmare, though; there had been an accident on the motorway which had delayed them for forty minutes, and then it had taken them nearly another hour to get across London!

'Anyway, I can't chat now,' she said. 'Daniel needs seeing to. I just wanted to check that you're all right.'

'I'm fine,' said Jane.

Fran, however, did have time to chat when she rang later that evening. 'You must be going out of your mind,' she said. 'Tell me what you've been thinking.'

Jane, sitting in the kitchen with her third glass of wine, seemed to find this question amusing. 'What've I been thinking?' she said. 'What do you think I've been thinking?' She paused, but Fran remained silent. 'Well . . . I've been thinking what you've probably been thinking,' she went on. 'He must have had another woman. Maybe lots of other women. A whole string of mistresses. Isn't 'mistress' a funny word, by the way?'

'He might not have been using the place himself,' Fran said. 'He could've been letting it out or something.'

'Oh, come on! If he'd been doing that he would've told me. He wouldn't have said that he'd sold it.'

There was another short pause and then Jane asked: 'What does Patrick think about all this?'

'I haven't told him yet.'

'Oh? You can, you know. But perhaps not Emer; not till I've told Lucy.'

'OK.'

'It would put his mind at rest – knowing that this whole thing is about me and not you.'

'He knows that already. Anyway, what are you going to do now?' Fran asked, changing the subject.

Jane gave a harsh little laugh. 'I'm going to wait and see what the police come up with.'

'Which might be nothing.'

'Well then, I'll do it myself; I'll become a private investigator. And if I'm successful I might have a career change and take it up professionally.' She refilled her glass and raised it in a mock toast. 'And if your young man does coming knocking on my door I'm going to invite him in and listen to what he has to say, because he knows something about all this.' She took a long drink of wine. 'Do you think he might be the wronged husband of one of Neil's mistresses?'

'Hardly,' said Fran. 'He's too young.'

'Perhaps Neil liked them young. Or . . . another possibility. You'll like this one. Per-haps your young man was his lover. Per-haps my dear departed husband was gay.'

'I don't think so,' said Fran. 'Jane, how much have you had to drink?'

'Not nearly enough. But I'm getting there.'

Fran gave a loud sigh. 'Just go easy,' she said.

'What I don't understand,' said Jane, ignoring this admonition, 'is how I could've thought we were happily married all these years.'

'Because you were.'

'I wouldn't have been if I'd known.'

'But you didn't know.'

'No, but I do now.'

'You think you know, but you can't be sure.'

'Yes I can. I know something was very wrong – and it cancels out all that happiness. And I'm talking over twenty years here. How could all this have been going on, all this time, without me knowing a thing about it? Was I that easy to deceive? Well, yes, obviously I was.'

How had he managed it, she'd been wondering? Surely he hadn't been away from home enough times to make good economic use of this cottage? But there had been courses and conferences. And the emergency dental service that his practice participated in had involved night-time and weekend work from time to time. And then there had been the bloody football matches, especially those oh-so-important cup tie games which had sometimes required overnight stays in far flung corners of the country. Allegedly. And there had been a time – a while ago now, admittedly – when he'd started playing an excessive amount of golf on Sundays. But was all this enough to merit the expense and bother of a second abode? Well, he must have thought so.

'I'm going to go and have a look at it tomorrow – the cottage,' she said. 'Debbie dear is taking me. And the police have been making inquiries in the village, to see if anyone knew who had been living there. So, watch this space, as they say.'

'Why don't you come and stay with us – or Lucy – when you've done that?' said Fran. 'You shouldn't be on your own right now.'

(Oh, shouldn't I?) 'No. I've got things to do here. I'm going to go through all Neil's stuff. He must've left some evidence behind. There's no such thing as the perfect crime. Isn't that what they say? Whoever *they* are.'

'Don't go jumping to conclusions,' said Fran. 'The fact that he didn't tell you about the cottage doesn't necessarily mean that he was . . . unfaithful to you.'

'What else was he using it for then? A drugs den? A safe house for spies? Come on, give me a break! Anyway, the point is he lied to me. And it wasn't just the one lie, was it? It was – what's the expression? – the lie that went on lying. For years and years.'

'I don't know what else to say.'

'There is nothing else to say. Go to bed Fran. I'll speak to you tomorrow.'

Jane rang off. She felt annoyed with Fran and wasn't quite sure why. She thought it might have something to do with that stupid email she'd been reading on Monday evening, the one that had caused her to question their friendship – or, at least, the depth of their friendship. On the other hand, it might have nothing at all to do with the email. It could just be that Fran was being especially annoying since she'd come back from . . . captivity. Cap-tiv-ity. Since her release from . . .

Out of nowhere the word 'bondage' sprang into Jane's mind. 'Out of the house of bondage,' she said out loud. But bondage meant something a bit different these days, she thought, knocking back the rest of her wine. The cottage hadn't been a house of bondage for Fran in the modern sense. But perhaps it had been for Neil. 'I am the Lord thy God,' she said, out loud again, 'who brought thee out of the land of Egypt, and out of the house of bondage.' Yes! Who knew what her Lord and God had been using it for?

Any road up, she said to herself in a Birmingham accent, what she should do now was try and get a good night's sleep. Or did she mean a night's good sleep? No, the quality of the sleep was immaterial (Mr Worthing!). Any old sleep would do, as long as it lasted all night. A full night's sleep was what she meant. And what a novelty that would be. Perhaps another drink would do the trick. But not more wine. Wine was useless. She got up and went to the drinks cabinet in the dining-room. After a careful examination of its contents she selected a bottle of Neil's whisky and took it back with her into the kitchen.

3

Fran put the phone down, feeling very uneasy. She was worried about Jane, of course she was, but she was worried for herself too. If discoveries were going to be made, and Jane seemed hell bent on making them, was she – as one of Neil's 'other' women – in any danger of being found out? No, she told herself, she couldn't possibly be. She'd only been to the cottage with Neil that one time.

'Is everything all right?' asked Patrick when she went back into the kitchen where he and Emer were sitting.

'Yeah. I'm just a bit worried about Jane, that's all,' said Fran. 'She sounded drunk, which isn't like her. All this is very hard for her on top of everything else.'

'Yes, but you were the one who was kidnapped,' said Emer. 'You need to think about yourself, too. Jane was coping very well over the weekend. She's stronger than you think.'

'And that's your considered opinion, is it?' said Fran, and instantly regretted her tone. She needed to keep reminding herself how awful the past few days had been for everyone. Her family hadn't known, as she had, that she'd been safe and well. They'd been thinking the worst.

Emer stood up. 'I'm going now,' she said, 'but I might call round tomorrow evening to see how you are.' She walked out of the room before Fran could say anything more.

'We all need to put this behind us and get back to normal,' Fran heard Patrick say as he walked Emer to the front door.

'She sounds as though she's already back to normal,' she

heard Emer reply. 'But that's just my considered opinion, you understand.'

Fran sighed.

'Yes, I know, I know,' she said when Patrick came back into the room.

'We should get an early night,' he said. 'We're both tired.'

'Have you decided when you're going back?' Fran asked.

'I thought I'd try and get a flight on Monday,' he said. 'I'd really like to be back for the election. I've got several things lined up that I really don't want to cancel.'

'What a good job I was found then,' said Fran. 'And that I'm not dead. That would have been inconvenient for you.'

'Come on, Fran. You know I don't like leaving you. Why don't you take some time off and come back with me?'

'Why don't you – take some time off, I mean – and stay with me?'

'I will if you really want me to . . .'

Fran shook her head in disbelief. 'I'm just trying to make a point,' she said. 'I have commitments too, you know. I can't take time off, just like that. Not in the middle of term and not when I'm already having this week off.'

'For a very good reason.'

'Look, it was you who just said we should all get back to normal. Running away from things isn't getting back to normal, is it?'

'You wouldn't be running away, you'd be recovering – from a dreadful experience.'

'I can do that here.'

'And being with your husband is hardly running away, is it?'

'It's not being with my husband that I'm objecting to. It's having to go to California to do it.'

'Well if you really think that from a work point of view you can't come, OK. But . . .'

'But what?'

But before he could say anything further Fran shook her head and held her hands up in the air. 'No! she said. 'Don't

answer that. We've been over this so many times. I'm not
going to have yet another discussion on the subject. I don't
want to go back with you now and that's that.' And then
(even though she wasn't going to discuss it any further): 'It's
just as much your choice as mine that we're apart. More
yours, in fact. So don't go blaming me. There were always
going to be consequences.'

Fran woke up in the middle of the night – just as she had
done last night at Jane's – in a state of panic. Then, she
couldn't remember what, if anything, she had been dreaming
about. But her dream tonight had been very vivid. She had
been walking alone across the bottom of the Common in the
dark. Someone had come up from behind and grabbed hold
of her. Thinking that it was her young man, she had twisted
round to give him a piece of her mind, only to see, to her
horror, that it was someone else. Someone much older,
someone much more threatening. And her efforts to free
herself from his grasp had woken her up.

She eased herself on to her back and lay listening to the
reassuring rhythm of Patrick's breathing. Might this dream be
an early symptom of post-traumatic stress disorder, she
wondered? The police in Solihull had recommended that she
get some counselling. She had smiled and nodded, but she
had no intention of doing so. There was no need. She was
fine. It had all been a stupid misunderstanding. Her young
man had been harmless, and she wasn't going to let the
experience – bizarre as it had been – affect her.

What was affecting her, though, was this whole business
of Neil and the cottage. He'd lied to her when he'd told her it
belonged to friends of his. She wasn't sure why this was
bothering her, but it was. She felt annoyed and . . . something
else. Diminished, maybe? Which was stupid because she'd
wondered at the time whether he'd used it before for other
assignations. But she hadn't dwelt on the thought, preferring
instead to think that she was a special aberration. Now,
however, it was beginning to look like she'd been just another

of his 'other women'.

She heaved on to her side with her back to Patrick. Why on earth did this matter, she asked herself? She hadn't wanted any commitment from Neil. Just as she hadn't wanted him to make any demands on her. It had been a bit of excitement, a bit of fun, that was all. One weekend; a handful of nights. All quite . . . harmless. But he'd lied to her. And OK, she conceded, it wasn't a lie of the same magnitude as those he'd been telling Jane, but she felt slighted nonetheless. So how must poor Jane be feeling?

Poor Jane, for whom, while the affair was in progress, she hadn't felt any sympathy at all. But then, why should she have? Jane hadn't known anything about it. What she hadn't known hadn't hurt her. And once the affair was over, that was that as far as she was concerned. Only on those few occasions when she and Neil had been forced into close proximity had she given it much thought. Around the time of the wedding, mainly, and when Daniel was born. And on those occasions she'd found it quite amusing because their naughty little secret seemed to worry him far more than it did her.

But, if Jane were to find out about it now . . ? There was absolutely no reason why she should, but if she did . . . ? And, of course, that was what this gnawing anxiety was all about. She might have been dreaming about being abducted again but Fran knew that what she was really afraid of was being found out.

She turned over again and rearranged herself in the bed.

4

'You think I had something to do with this, don't you?' Jane said to DC Mason in the car next morning. Her head was throbbing and she felt slightly sick.

'Well . . .' said DC Mason, easing the car out on to the main road, 'it certainly did seem a bit suspicious at first. But you genuinely didn't seem to know anything about this place, so no, we don't think so now.'

Jane stared out of the window. She wanted to ask the policewoman to drive more slowly; she really did feel awful – in spite of an unusually lengthy sleep. Under the guise of a sigh, she took a deep breath.

The policewoman gave her a quick glance. 'All this must be a terrible shock for you,' she said.

Jane made a little noise of assent.

'And Frances. How is she feeling now?'

Jane closed her eyes and willed herself not to say 'fine'. 'She's being very laid back about it,' she said. 'She seems to think that her "young man" as she calls him, is harmless and that he just had a moment of madness.'

They were crossing the motorway now, heading towards Knowle.

'People often establish a rapport with their captors,' said DC Mason, sounding to Jane as though she were quoting from some training manual. 'It's a form of self preservation. But we can't assume that he is harmless. You should be very careful, Jane. Be on your guard. This isn't over for you.'

No, it definitely isn't, Jane thought. It's only just beginning.

'The woman who gave you the tip off,' she said. 'Was she old, young? Did she have an accent – local, perhaps?' (Fran had said that her young man had a Birmingham accent.)

'It's hard to say,' DC Mason replied. 'It was a very short phone conversation.'

'Who do you think she might've been?'

'She could've been anyone – his mother, his sister, his girl-friend, or none of the above.'

'You think this has something to do with my husband, don't you? Of course, you do. I do. Whatever he was using this place for has got to have something to do with this.'

'It is our main line of inquiry, yes. And now that we have your list of his friends and colleagues we'll do our best to find out more about it. And it goes without saying that if you find out anything yourself, you should let us know straight away.'

The route they were taking was the one Jane used to go to the Arts' Centre at the university. As DC Mason accelerated through the familiar bends and turns on the country road, Jane felt her stomach clenching and unclenching. And then there it was – the flashback. She was sitting in the passenger seat of the Triumph Herald (!) driving along a similar road. They were going to look at the cottages. She was holding her stomach and telling Neil to slow down, to drive more carefully. She was pregnant – with Lucy. So it must have been 1982. But really, what difference did it make, knowing the exact year?

They came to a junction and instead of going straight across turned right along a straight stretch of main road.

'You said you were going to ask round the village,' Jane said. 'Did you find out anything?'

'Not a lot. The people who own the shop have only been there a short while and the people who run the pub have only just taken it over. We did manage to speak to some of the locals but they couldn't tell us much. It looks like it was only used as a holiday, or a weekend, cottage. But this is a popular area for visitors – walkers, people fishing, that sort of thing – and there're always lots of strangers about, especially in the summer. So whoever was using the cottage wouldn't have stood out in any way.'

Jane gazed out of the car window. Although it wasn't yet midday, the sun was quite low in the sky, casting a wistful light over the empty fields and the bare trees. It is lovely out here, she thought. But did one really need a weekend cottage in order to enjoy this countryside? It was practically on their doorstep, for God's sake!

They drove through the village of Medworth, over the canal bridge and then right on to a very minor side road. This quickly deteriorated into a track that came to an end just a few yards beyond the cottage. The track was as Jane remembered it. The cottage looked different though – less stark somehow. The front door and the window frames were painted white now. They had been a dark colour – brown, possibly – before. And the old dilapidated roof had been replaced, she noticed, looking up at the chimney which had no smoke coming out of it now.

There was a white van parked outside and a workman was testing the new lock he had just put on the front door.

'All done,' he said to DC Mason, slipping the key on to a key ring which already had other keys on it. He took a piece of paper out of the pocket of his overalls and handed this and the keys to her. He turned to Jane. 'The locks on some of the shutters have been broken off,' he said. 'If you want me to replace those too, I could come back. My number's on the invoice.'

He picked up his bag of tools and made for his van.

DC Mason unlocked the door and handed Jane the key ring and the invoice. It was very gloomy inside, once they had closed the door behind them. DC Mason opened the shutters and Jane stood looking at the place. It must have been the words 'holiday' and 'weekend' which had been leading her to expect something more luxurious than what she saw before her now. It was dated, and much more Argos than Habitat. He'd spent money on it, but he hadn't been profligate.

She went into the kitchen and opened and closed a few

drawers and cupboards. She ran her finger along the speckled worktop. Where had he got this from, she wondered? B&Q? Wickes? And the pine table, she noted with something approaching annoyance, was a smaller version of the one they used to have in their kitchen at home, before they'd had the extension built.

There was a little pile of sawdust by the back door and she almost caught herself looking for a dustpan and brush to sweep it up with. What was she thinking! It didn't matter what the place looked like. It could go to wrack and ruin for all she cared!

'This is where we found Frances,' DC Mason was saying.

She stood back to let Jane enter the very small, very cold, and very yellow bathroom. What on earth had possessed Neil to choose a bathroom suite in such a bilious shade? Even allowing for changing fashions . . . Poor Fran, she thought, stuck in here all that time. Well at least there'd been no danger of her suffering from sensory deprivation.

She went upstairs on her own. This must be the bedroom where Fran slept, she thought, pushing the door open wider. The bedroom where Neil must have slept too. The shutters up here were locked but there was just enough light for her to see what she needed to see. A double bed with a creased sheet. A folded duvet at the foot of it.

She put her head round the door of the other bedroom. There was a folded duvet in there too – on a single bed. A single duvet, covered in large footballs. Fran hadn't said anything about footballs.

What she was looking at, she realised with a shock, was a child's bedroom.

'You didn't tell me that one of the duvets had footballs all over it,' she said to Fran on the phone that evening.

She was sitting in the kitchen with a glass of whisky on the table in front of her. She didn't intend to get drunk again tonight, only to let the whisky blur her edges, which it seemed to be doing very nicely.

'I didn't realise you required a detailed description of all the furnishings and fittings,' Fran replied.

Jane smiled. 'Only the relevant ones,' she said.

'And how is that relevant?'

'Well it is, isn't it? There's a child's bedroom there. I've been imagining that he used the cottage to entertain a succession of mistresses, but what I'm thinking now is that there might've only been one woman – who had a kid who loved football. Neil would have liked that, wouldn't he? The football bit, I mean. And I think that boy grew up to be your young man.'

It was, she thought, an elegant theory. But there was a long silence on the other end of the phone.

'Think about it,' she urged. 'Why would he have bothered to keep the cottage just for random affairs? He could've gone to hotels for those. But this would make some sort of sense, wouldn't it?'

The more she thought about it, the more sense it seemed to make.

'OK,' said Fran. 'I'll go with the bit about my young man being the child in the bedroom. He did know his way round the place. But . . . are you saying that Neil kept the cottage and did it up just because he was having an affair with a woman who happened to have a kid? How would he have known that the relationship was going to last? It would've been a bit of a gamble, wouldn't it? All that just for this one woman?'

It was a fair point, forcing Jane to concede that her assessment of the situation was by no means conclusive. 'So you think the woman with the child came along later?' she said.

'Don't ask me,' said Fran.

Jane sighed. 'Well anyway,' she said. 'The football duvet does seem to indicate that there must have been a long-term mistress somewhere along the line. 'And what I need to do now, is find out who she was.'

The next morning, Jane decided to drive out to the cottage again. The police didn't seem to be making any headway at all. But they were concentrating on Fran's abductor: she was more interested in the woman whom she'd now convinced herself was his mother. Perhaps she would find something at the cottage that they'd missed. So while Bronia was doing the cleaning she set off, hoping that she would remember the way.

She unlocked the front door and stepped into the semi-darkness of the living room. Mindful of DC Mason's exhortation to be on her guard, she locked the door behind her. She opened the shutters and stood there, uncertain what to do next. She opened the drawer of the console table. It was empty. She went into the kitchen and opened and closed a few drawers and cupboards in there too, but found nothing of any significance in them. She went upstairs and did the same. She was wasting her time; there was nothing there. All personal belongings had been removed.

She lingered in each bedroom in turn. The green duvet cover had a distinctly nineteen-eighties British Home Stores look about it. Both it and the football one were well washed. They had been in use for a long time. So the child who had slept in that bed would be grown up now. In his early twenties as Fran had said. It must have been her young man.

Back downstairs, she was having one last look round when her attention was caught by the framed watercolour hanging over the mantelpiece. It was a pleasant enough picture – green fields under a blue sky, with a line of leafy trees on the horizon. She went over to the fireplace and peered at it closely. It looked like an amateur painting which had been rather carelessly framed. It had slipped a bit in its homemade mount. She lifted it down and turned it over. Perhaps if she took it out of the frame she might find something written on the back.

She carried it into the kitchen and took a knife out of the drawer. With some difficulty she managed to remove the painting from the frame, chipping the wood in the process.

But that didn't matter; it belonged to her now. There was something written on the back, in pencil, but it had faded badly. There wasn't much daylight in the kitchen so she unlocked the back door and went out into the sunlit garden. She could see better out here but it was the handwriting that was the problem now. She couldn't make out what it said.

She raised her eyes from the painting and looked around. It was a lovely garden – overgrown, but charming nonetheless. She took a few steps further into the long grass and stopped to admire the view of the surrounding countryside. She glanced down at the painting in her hands and then held it up and compared it to the scene in front of her. It was the same. Except that it was autumn now, and it had been high summer then. Someone (and it most certainly wouldn't have been Neil) had sat out here in the summer sunshine and painted this picture. And then someone (and this time it might have been Neil) had framed it and hung it over the fireplace.

Jane's eyes filled with tears, blurring both the real landscape out there and the representation of it in her hands. She went back into the house and put the painting back into the damaged frame. She didn't try to hang it up again but propped it up on the mantelpiece instead.

She arrived home to a clean and tidy house. Bronia had had plenty to do that morning after all the visitors there had been over the past week. But, as a general rule, she knew that she didn't need Bronia twice a week anymore. Perhaps after Christmas she would reduce her hours. Perhaps, after Christmas, she would sell the house and say goodbye to Bronia altogether.

Poor hardworking Bronia, who lived alone in a bedsit over a shop on the Stratford Road and sent what little spare money she had to her old and ailing father back home in Poland. With her pale skin, light blue eyes and almost colourless hair, she always looked as though a permanent layer of dust had settled over her. As though her life as a cleaner, here in England, had taken the shine off her.

Each of Bronia's predecessors had left of their own accord; there had never been any need for Jane to sack anyone before. And although she felt sure that Bronia would have no trouble getting other cleaning jobs, she did pay her more than the going rate and couldn't help worrying that other employers might not be as generous.

Who had done the cleaning at the cottage, she wondered? It definitely wouldn't have been Neil. It must have been the watercolourist who'd rolled up her sleeves and got stuck in.

Jane made a sandwich for her lunch and sat down to eat it with a pen and paper to hand. She would make a list of things to do and then she would make sure that she got on and did them. First, she would call her solicitor and get him to sort out whatever it was that needed sorting out so that she could sell the cottage as quickly as possible. Then she would contact school and tell them that she would be back in next week as usual. She paused, pen poised over the paper. Should she bother replacing the locks on the shutters? Did she care whether the cottage got broken into? 'Locks??' she wrote, and then finally: Search N's office.

She made the phone calls straightaway and crossed them off the list. With the phone still in her hand, she debated with herself about whether to call some of the people on the list she'd given to Debbie Mason that morning. Was it only polite to warn them that the police wanted to speak to them, or, from an investigative point of view, would this be counter-productive?

Immediately after the news items on the television, a few of these people had contacted her – out of concern maybe, but also curiosity. None, however, had given any indication that they knew anything about the cottage. Was this because they didn't know, she wondered, or because they weren't going to say? But once they'd been interviewed by the police, once they knew that she knew about the cottage, there would no longer be any need to cover up for him.

One of those who had been in touch was Martin Williams, Neil's practice partner of the longest standing. He and his wife Kay could, she supposed, be described as old friends of theirs, but she had only seen them once since the funeral and not at all since the abduction. If anyone had known what Neil had been up to it would have been Martin. But she would wait and see what the police managed to find out before she spoke to anyone herself, she decided, putting the phone down.

She glanced at her list. Item three could wait. And item four was going to be a big project.

She wasn't quite sure what she would be looking for in Neil's office. Something to indicate that he owned the cottage. Some financial evidence, perhaps? He had obviously spent money on renovating and furbishing the place so there might be invoices and receipts somewhere. But, if she were to find any, wouldn't that only confirm and illustrate what she already knew?

What she really wanted to discover was the identity of the 'other woman'. But would he have left any evidence of this lying around at home? Letters perhaps? She had never come across any. In all these years. He had been exceptionally careful. Would they have even corresponded by letter, she wondered? Back in the nineteen-eighties, possibly. More recently though it would have been by text or email.

After Neil's death, she had dealt with some of the recent voice mail messages and texts on his mobile phone. Then, when calls kept coming in, John had taken temporary charge of it to spare her the pain of answering them. She had examined his contact list. It was very long and included many professional people whom he could hardly have known, and even some random dental patients. The woman's name might be on this list. But there had been a lot of women's names on it – too many for her to pursue individually. And the phone wasn't working anymore; she had cancelled the contract.

She had dealt with his emails, too. His password – Beatrice21 (his mother's name and birth year) – hadn't been a secret. But there had been no unexpected messages there; no-one who was a stranger to Jane, unaware that he had died, asking why he hadn't been in touch. He could easily have had other accounts, though. Ones she knew nothing about.

Nevertheless, she thought, there might be something in his office – some little thing he had failed to hide. She went upstairs and surveyed the room. It was full of bookcases and filing cabinets and shelf upon shelf of folders. His desk was still the same untidy mess it had been the day he left home and never came back again. It all needed sorting out, but she hadn't been able to work up any enthusiasm for the task. Now, however, she had a motivation.

First, she would get rid of all the things that weren't relevant to her and in the process extricate all the documents and paperwork that were. The football memorabilia, for example, would be the first to go. And then there were the dentistry textbooks and periodicals. Martin or one of the other practice partners could advise her what to do with those. Once the police had spoken to them.

At half past five she was still at work when the doorbell rang, peal after insistent peal. Her first thought was that it was him. She hovered at the top of the stairs, hoping that whoever it was would go away, but the bell kept on ringing. She went down and opened the door as far as the chain would allow. There were three children standing there, draped in red-paint-splattered sheets, who, as soon as they saw her through the gap, began to shout: 'Trick or treat? Trick or treat?'

Oh God, she'd forgotten that it was bloody Hallowe'en! She wanted to shut the door in their faces but instead she reached for her handbag on the hall table and groped inside it for her purse.

'I have no treats,' she said, slipping the chain off the door and offering them a pound coin. The biggest of the three grabbed it off her and they all went running and banshee-wailing down the drive. An adult waiting for them on the pavement raised his hand in acknowledgement of her participation. But Jane didn't return the salute. She felt no good will towards them – and she certainly wasn't going to answer the door to any more horrible children that evening. She turned the hall light off and retreated into the kitchen.

'It's fucking Hallowe'en,' said Fran on the phone, later. 'I've been repelling kids all evening.'

'I've been lucky,' said Jane, taking a sip of the whisky she'd poured earlier in anticipation of Fran's call. 'I've only had one visit.'

'We never did all this commercialised, ghoulish stuff when we were kids, did we?' said Fran.

No, thought Jane, we didn't. At this time of year, in their childhood church-going days, they had observed the feasts of All Saints and All Souls. The former had been about honouring the heaven dwelling dead. All Souls, the day after, was for remembering the dead who were not yet in heaven. Those who were languishing in purgatory, atoning for their sins. Like Neil.

'Christ, I sound like a grumpy old sod, don't I?' Fran was saying.

'Yes, you do,' agreed Jane, and then, before Fran could ask her the same question, added: 'But how are you – otherwise?' Fran had had an awful experience, she reminded herself. She mustn't become too obsessed with her own problems.

'I'm fine. So what's been happening at your end?' Fran asked, batting the ball straight back into Jane's court.

'Nothing much. Nothing from the police. I did go back to the cottage again this morning. And I've been dealing with paperwork all afternoon.'

'When are you going to tell Lucy about the cottage?'

This was a question Jane had been pondering too. She'd decided that she would wait until Christmas when she could tell both her daughters face to face. And she might have something more concrete to tell them then, too. They would be upset, of course – especially Lucy who had always been her daddy's girl – so she would probably wait until Boxing Day so as not to spoil the festivities for them.

'Not yet,' she replied. 'After Christmas probably, when she'll be feeling much better. And Sarah will be here, too, so I can tell them together. And I can take them to see it too. So please don't forget that you promised not to say anything to her till I do.'

She was aware how kind and considerate this must make her sound. The good mother looking out for her children. But a part of her couldn't wait to tell Lucy and Sarah about their father – their lying, cheating, bastard of a father.

When the phone call ended, Jane took her glass of whisky into the dining-room. She switched her computer on, telling herself that she hadn't checked her emails since Monday evening – not that there would be many, if indeed any, but she would check anyway.

There was one from her bank informing her that her online statement was ready, and another from Birmingham Rep. advertising their upcoming Christmas programme. She emptied her junk folder and then hesitated, moving the cursor up and down the list of her other folders. She was only going through the motions of being undecided, though. She knew she was going to re-read the email which had caused her so much disquiet the other night. She brought the cursor to rest on 'Frances Delaney' and clicked it open.

Long time no write. 10/06/2004.

Hi Jane, Here I am at last. I've been in such a whirl since I came back from NZ. Patrick is working in LA now. He's been there since just after Easter. He wanted/still wants me to join him but after a lot of thought I've decided not to. What would I do, stuck out there with no job? So I'm staying here. We'll see each other in the holidays of course – in fact I'm going out to California for a few weeks in the summer, as soon as term ends. We must meet up in September when I get back. There's lots to talk about, not least my son and your daughter! How about that? It's beginning to look like we're going to be related! Hope all is well with you and yours, Fran x

Jane read this through a couple of times. It was so

typically Fran, but was it really that damning? Did it matter that Fran hadn't written to her for months? Did it matter why she had written again at that precise time? They were friends now; that was the important thing. Since Neil's death they had become very close. And it was Fran who was here now to help her through this present nightmare.

Good old Fran, she thought, raising her glass

5

It had been decided that when Patrick went back to LA. Emer would come and stay with Fran for a while, until she had fully recovered from her ordeal – which, she insisted, she already had. She grumbled about being treated like a child but didn't object too strongly to the plan. It was quite unnecessary, but it would do no harm to have some company in the evenings and someone else in the house at night.

She went back to college on the following Monday morning. No-one there knew about her ordeal – she'd told them that she'd had a severe bout of food poisoning but was feeling much better now. Later that afternoon, straight after she'd finished teaching for the day, she drove Patrick to Heathrow. Or rather, he drove there; she would drive herself back.

He had offered to get a cab, to save her the hassle because she might be tired after her first day back at work, but she wouldn't hear of it.

'I always take you to the airport,' she said. 'There's nothing wrong with me. For Christ's sake stop fussing!'

A few minutes into the journey, she came to a sudden decision. She should have told him before so she had to be careful what she said. 'I spoke to Jane at lunchtime,' she said. 'And you're not going to believe this . . . It turns out that that place I was taken to – that cottage – was Neil's! Apparently, he inherited it years ago and he told poor old Jane that he'd sold it, but he hadn't. You can imagine the state she's in now.'

The ensuing conversation kept them going for the rest of the way.

The traffic was heavy as usual and by the time they got to the airport they had to say their goodbyes as soon as Patrick had checked in.

'It won't be long till Christmas,' he said, holding her close. 'Look after yourself.'

'You, too,' she replied.

'And don't go spending any more weekends in cottages with strange men while I'm away.'

Fran gave a weak smile. 'Very funny,' she said. 'Text me when you land.'

She stood and watched as he made his way towards the security gate. At the last moment he turned, just as he always did, gave her his customary soulful look and raised his hand in farewell. Today, this didn't amuse her as much as it usually did. Nevertheless, she waved back jauntily and began inching away . . . very slowly. Only when he had quite disappeared from view would she walk away properly. This was a little game she played – forcing him to be the one to make the decisive final move. It could be a time consuming procedure and right now he seemed to be going for the record. But she held her ground, and at last he was gone. This was always a poignant moment but today her sadness was almost instantly replaced by relief. Now she could get back to her ordinary, everyday routines and put this weird episode right behind her.

She walked back to the car park and took the lift up to the second floor. But as she stepped out of it she realised that she wasn't at all sure she was on the right level. She stood still and tried to think. It wasn't the first time this had happened to her but it was the first time she had felt so panicked by it. For Christ's sake, she told herself, get a grip. You'll find it.

She pressed her key fob and looked round, hoping to see some flashing lights, but none appeared. It reminded her of the night on Jane's driveway; she'd been pressing buttons then, to no effect.

She was definitely on the wrong floor. Think! They'd parked less than an hour ago, for fuck's sake. But one visit to the airport was like every other and no clear picture was emerging. They must have parked higher up. Patrick had this infuriating habit of always wanting to go up high even when the signs said there were empty spaces lower down. Usually she remonstrated with him about this, but she mustn't have done so today and he'd taken advantage of her silence. How could he have done this to her – after her recent ordeal? Her fucking ordeal!

She went back to the lift and went up another floor. But the car didn't seem to be there either. For the third time, she entered the lift and pressed the button. There was a long delay. She stabbed at it again, and just as the doors were closing a young man leapt in to join her. As the lift began ascending he suddenly lunged across, almost touching her, to press a button for another floor. Visibly shaken, she got out at Level 4 and thankfully, this time, there was the car.

She should have waited a few minutes, to collect herself, but she just wanted to get out of the car park as quickly as possible. Driving slightly faster than was advisable, she went down the circular exit ramp, round and round, holding tightly on to the steering wheel as if it were a lifebelt and she were on one of those helter skelter slides in a swimming pool.

It took a further ten minutes for her to calm down and by then she was driving on the inside lane of the motorway, doing forty miles an hour. 'What the hell's the matter with you?' she said out loud, 'Why are you being so fucking pathetic?' She looked in the rear view mirror. The traffic was heavy and there were unbroken lines of vehicles behind her. She indicated, and at the first available opportunity muscled her way out, accelerating as she did so, first into the middle, and then the outside, lane. The driver behind her sounded his horn in protest. She raised her arm and middle finger in response.

There was no way she was giving in to this.

Wednesday, the fifth of November, brought news from America of Barack Obama's presidential victory. Patrick sent Fran a short, triumphal email from LA. In the evening, and quite coincidentally, the annual firework display was taking place on Streatham Common.

Fran was very fond of this event, which was just as well as it was practically on her doorstep and therefore impossible to ignore. She found the sight of crowds of happy people, coming in their hundreds from the High Road and all the side streets around, very uplifting. And the fireworks, as fireworks tended to be, were always spectacular.

This year, John and Lucy brought Daniel round to watch the display – in spite of Fran's misgivings. He was, in her opinion, much too young to appreciate fireworks. But would they listen? And, of course, almost as soon as the first bangs went off he started to cry. Within minutes he had worked himself up into such a state, howling in terror and refusing to be consoled by any of them, that they had to go back indoors.

It was a bit less noisy there, but he still wasn't happy so they decided to take him home. Only, of course, they couldn't because they were blocked in by a line of double-parked cars. Knowing that this would be likely to happen, Fran had warned them against parking where they had but, needless to say, yet again her advice had been ignored.

'I did warn you,' she said, directing her remarks at John although it'd been Lucy who'd insisted that they park where they had. 'It's always like this. You should have parked further away like I told you to. It'll be ages now before you can get out.'

She had been planning to go to a neighbouring house for a post-fireworks supper later and was just as anxious for them to leave as they were to go.

'It won't be that long,' said John. 'Come on Danny. Let's go upstairs and watch out of Grandma's window.'

But further explosive volley from outside convinced Daniel that he still wasn't safe. He let out another anguished howl and clung to his mother's knee.

'Oh, do shut up, Daniel,' said Lucy, picking him up. 'You're making more noise than the fireworks.'

Fran put the kettle on.

'Not for me,' said Lucy. She looked up at the clock on the wall. 'Where's Emer got to, then?'

'Probably watching the fireworks on her way here,' said Fran.

'How's it going, having her here?'

'She only came on Monday evening,' said Fran, refusing to accept Lucy's implicit invitation to criticise Emer. She found the constant sniping between her daughter and daughter-in-law tiresome. 'I really don't need anyone here, though. I'm fine.'

'Well it's good that she is here,' said John. 'Good for both of you. Right now, I think she needs your company as much as you need hers. It was a terrible weekend for her too and you should remember that.'

'It was terrible for all of us,' Lucy cut in.

'And you know what she's like,' continued John. 'Always trying to make light of things, but she's not as hard as she'd have us think. You should cut her a bit of slack – both of you.'

Fran was a bit taken aback. John rarely passed judgements, so when he did his utterances tended to sound deeper than they probably were.

Before anyone could say anything else, they heard the front door opening and a moment later Emer appeared in the kitchen. 'Why aren't you all out there?' she asked.

'This young man doesn't like the noise,' said Fran.

'Oh dear.' Emer held out her hand to Daniel. 'Why don't you come upstairs with Auntie Em and we'll watch the pretty lights through the window.'

'We've tried that,' said John.

'He won't go,' said Lucy. But even as she spoke Daniel slipped off her knee and went over to Emer.

John laughed, but Lucy couldn't hide her annoyance.

'Oh, and you're blocked in, by the way,' Emer said over her shoulder as she and Daniel left the room.

Fran went off to her supper and had an enjoyable evening.

But the walk home later unnerved her. Fireworks were still going off around and about, creating a slightly war-zone impression, and although the distance from door to door was only about fifty yards she couldn't stop herself from looking over her shoulder every few steps to check that she wasn't being followed.

Once safely inside her own front door she let out a deep breath. It wasn't a sigh of relief, though. She was feeling alarmed not relieved. All this over-reacting – just like the other evening at the airport. It was so stupid. So unlike her.

Emer was in the sitting room, stretched out on one of the sofas, watching the news. 'A good evening?' she asked, glancing away from the television.

'Yeah, very pleasant,' said Fran, sitting down on the other sofa.

'What's the matter?' Emer turned to look at her more closely. 'You look . . . flustered.'

'I'm fine.'

'You're not, though, are you? You should've called me and I'd have come and walked you home.'

'Oh *please!* As if that was necessary! I'm not a child. Stop fussing.'

'I think you should consider getting some counselling like the police advised you to. You've suffered a trauma. There're bound to be side effects. Even for someone as strong and untouchable as you think you are.'

Fran sighed. Counselling indeed. 'Look,' she said. 'Let's not make more of this than it was. I'm fine.'

'Have you heard anything else from the police?'

'No. And I don't suppose we will now.'

'But that's not good enough, is it? You should get on to them again. It's been over a week now.'

'I really don't see the point. If there was anything to report we'd have heard.'

'The point is that a crime was committed. It needs solving.'

'Lots of crimes never get solved. And it looks like this is

going to be one of them. It's not as if the police haven't made any enquiries. I know they have. But they haven't got anywhere with them. It happens. It's no use getting upset about it.'

'Well, I think it's awful – not knowing what it was all about.'

'You're beginning to sound like Lucy, do you know that?'

'No.' Emer swung herself into an upright position. 'I'm sounding like a concerned daughter. Which will never do, of course. So I'll just shut up.'

Fran, mindful of John's earlier comments, sighed again. 'I just want to forget about it,' she said. 'And I wish all of you would forget about it, too.'

'I don't understand why you're being so passive. It's not like you.'

'I'm not being passive, I'm being realistic.'

'You can't just pretend that it never happened.'

Fran reached for the remote control and turned up the volume on the television.

'Yes We Can!' the newly elected president of the USA was proclaiming. 'Yes We Can!' the people were roaring back.

'Well there you are!' said Fran. 'Yes We Can!'

John was right, of course. Everyone had been affected by Fran's missing weekend and – just possibly – she hadn't fully appreciated this.

She'd expected Lucy to over-react (after all, this was Lucy's default mode) and had forced herself to make allowances when she did. Lucy, she kept reminding herself, was pregnant and hormonal, and still grieving for her father. But she probably hadn't given sufficient consideration to Emer. Or to John, for that matter. How had he been feeling?

He always appeared outwardly calm and strong, but who knew what was going on inside? He'd always been like this – even as a little boy. She remembered how well he'd coped when she and Nick had split up. They'd told him that he would still see his daddy regularly and that Nick would always be his father and would always love him, and six-year old John had accepted this, developing a stoical attitude to life which he seemed to have retained ever since.

It had been Emer who had gone into meltdown. She had screamed and shouted and cried herself to sleep for nights on end. She had blamed her mother – not unreasonably, Fran had been forced to concede, because how could a twelve-year old possibly understand the complex reasons that had led her to end what had been a perfectly good marriage, when she could hardly understand them herself?

Emer had pleaded with Fran to let Nick come back to live with them. She had tried to enlist John in this, but all he kept saying was that Nick would always be their father and would always love them. As if that were sufficient consolation. 'You're such a stupid little boy,' Emer had raged. 'You don't love Dad as much as I do. I hate you. I hate you nearly as much as I hate Mum. I wish you would both die and then I could go and live with Dad.'

It had been during one of these particularly stormy outbursts that Fran had uttered the fateful words: 'You need to stop this now, Emer. After all, Nick's not your real father, is he?'

Emer had been six when Nick adopted her. At the time they'd kept her informed about what was going on but she hadn't been that interested. Apart from the excitement of changing her name from Delaney to Cartwright, it had meant little to her and it'd hardly been mentioned since. But the throwaway comment, Nick's not your real father, is he?' changed all that, marking as it did the beginning of Emer's campaign to establish the identity of her 'real' father.

Fran, totally contradicting herself, kept telling her that Nick was her 'real' father in every meaningful sense of the word, but Emer would have none of it. 'You said he wasn't,' she kept replying, 'so tell me who is.' Nick had thought that Fran should tell her, but Fran had disagreed. All she would say was that he had been one of her university lecturers and it didn't matter what his name was.

She'd justified this by telling herself that Howard Sage wasn't any old 'real' father. He'd been well on his way to becoming a public figure at the time and because of this – and for other rather less clear reasons – she'd wanted nothing to do with him. She certainly hadn't wanted Emer to try and contact him, which she'd felt sure Emer would have done had she known who he was.

Not too long after this, Fran had brought a step-father (and a little step-sister) into their lives. John had accepted this with his usual equanimity and, to everyone's surprise, so had Emer. Her problem had never been with Patrick; only with her mother.

6

So far, Jane's search of Neil's office was proving non-productive. Nevertheless, she resolved to continue with it. She had more or less resigned herself to the fact that she wasn't going to discover the identity of the 'other' woman in there but at the very least, she kept telling herself, there must be something relating to the running and upkeep of the cottage. She knew that if she did find anything it wouldn't advance her cause, but this seemingly total lack of evidence was driving her to distraction. OK, she reasoned, he'd had a second address where bills and things like that would have gone to – Fran had mentioned some letters that her young man had taken away with him – but even so, how uncharacteristically meticulous he'd been! But she would continue sifting and sorting. There must be something; and if there was, she would find it.

She was trying to maintain her faith in the police, although she feared they would lose interest soon. Fran's abduction would become just another unsolved case, no longer a priority for them. Every few days, she'd been ringing Debbie Mason to see if they'd made any progress with their investigations but it seemed that none of the people they'd questioned so far had been able to cast any light on Neil's connection to the cottage. 'Have you come up with anything?' Debbie Mason kept asking, as a matter of course. Jane had told her that she'd been scouring the house for clues. But: 'No, not a thing,' was her constant reply.

But someone must know something, Jane thought. Why were these people protecting him? Didn't they realise how important this was? Perhaps they thought, misguidedly, that somehow they were protecting her. Perhaps now was the time to talk to them herself, face to face. But who exactly were 'they'?

Halfway through November, Fran announced that she and Patrick had decided not to spend Christmas in New York with Hannah as had been their original intention. 'Emer's still going,' she said, 'but Patrick's coming home instead. Hannah's disappointed, but she'll get over it.'

Jane wondered whether this change of plan might be a sign that Fran wasn't coping with the aftermath of her ordeal as well as she insisted she was. Fran, however, dismissed such a suggestion as nonsense. 'I'm absolutely fine,' she said. 'I've just changed my mind, that's all. And please stop calling it my ordeal. If anything, it was more of an ordeal for you lot than it was for me. I was never in any real danger, and I knew that all along.'

Jane said nothing.

'Anyway, why don't you come down for a weekend?' Fran said. 'It'd do you good.'

Jane suspected that it would do Fran good too, but she couldn't always be thinking of other people. 'No,' she said, 'I need to be here . . . just in case.'

'Just in case what? My young man won't come calling on you now, if that's what you're still thinking.'

It wasn't. Jane knew that with each passing day it was less and less likely that he would put in an appearance. 'No, but someone else might,' she said.

She was thinking of the woman who had provided the tip off. She must have been close to him. If she'd phoned the police to help him out of the mess he'd got himself into, as Fran thought she had, then she might help now – by contacting Jane on his behalf. So while there was unfinished business all round she would continue to hope.

But some of this business, she knew, was hope-less. Some of it would have to remain unfinished for ever. Neil would never come back, would never have to explain himself or face her wrath. In many ways, this was the hardest thing of all to bear.

It had taken her a long time to accept that he had died and left her. How much more time was it going to take now to come to terms with the fact that he had died and left her with all these unanswered questions? Her overwhelming emotion was one of anger. Anger not only because of his betrayal – although, goodness knew, that in itself was more than enough to justify the magnitude of her feelings – but also because of the innocent months she had just spent mourning him. All that pain; all that yearning! Oh yes, she still wanted him to come back to her. But if he were to walk through that door right now, what a confrontation there would be!

But he wasn't going to come back. He had escaped the consequences of his actions. He had got away with it, whatever 'it' was. And the only retaliation available to her was to sully his memory in the minds and hearts of their daughters – which she would do, with some satisfaction, when the time was right.

'Look what you've done to me,' she screamed at him in her head. 'Look what you've reduced me to, you bastard . . . You fucking bastard!'

She had begun to notice that apart from her sessions in Neil's office and the occasional foray into the dining-room to use her computer she was spending all her time in the kitchen these days. There was a small television set in there that she had taken to watching in the evenings, seated either at the kitchen table or in the old rocking chair she had appropriated from her mother's house many years ago. It would have been much more comfortable to sit in the lounge but she seemed reluctant to go in there now.

This strange behaviour seemed to have started at Hallowe'en. But she'd had a specific reason for taking refuge in the kitchen that evening. What was her reason now? Was she afraid of being at the front of the house after dark? Did she still think that he might be lurking outside – maybe even trying to look in through the window? No, Fran had been right all along. Her young man would be too afraid to show up on the doorstep.

So what's keeping me out of here, Jane asked herself one evening, as she stood on the threshold, looking into her lounge? It'd been in this room, all those years ago, that she'd had her first meeting with Neil's mother. Although the older woman had been pleasant enough, Jane had been overawed. She'd been glad that Neil had already met her parents – had already visited their modest council house – because she might never have had the nerve to take him there had she seen his home first. But that was silly, she'd told herself. She'd always known that he was posh; and he'd always known that she wasn't.

(Her own mother, needless to say, had been overjoyed with her prospective son-in-law. 'Our Jane's done very well for herself,' she would say whenever an opportunity presented itself – never failing to incense Jane's older sister who, by implication, had done less well.)

If Neil's mother had found her wanting, though, she had kept it well hidden. Shortly after they were married, all three of them had lived together in this house, in relative harmony, until her rather sudden death the year before Lucy was born.

The house, of course, had looked very different in those days. It had been re-decorated several times since then, and a lot of the old furniture had gone. But not all of it. The dark oak bookcases and occasional tables were still in here; the oak dining table and chairs, and the sideboard and drinks cabinet, were still in the dining-room, as was the console table in the hall. All of these were things it would have been foolish to part with – solid substantial things, verging on the antique.

Since the senior Mrs Lord's death, Jane had always considered this house to be her home. Looking round now, though, she began to wonder. Yes, she had been responsible for the replacement wallpapers and carpets and curtains, but they had all been chosen to complement this old furniture. These family heirlooms. Neil's family heirlooms. Had the house ever really been hers in the way that it had been his? Or had she just been a lodger here all these years, a bit like the 'other' woman at the cottage?

If she were to sell up and move away (and how could she not, now?) what would she do with all this furniture? She didn't want it any more. She wanted new things. Lucy and Sarah could have it, or dispose of it as they saw fit.

She wandered back into the kitchen and poured herself a glass of whisky from the bottle which had its own designated place on one of the work tops now. The rest of the house might be Neil's, she thought, but this room was hers. Years ago, they had had a large extension added to it, and quite recently it had been refitted for the second time – all to Jane's specifications. Her mother-in-law wouldn't recognise it now.

She switched the television on and sat down in the rocking chair which, at the time of the second refit, had been sanded down, stained and re-varnished so that it would 'go' with its new surroundings. This was something she would take with her when she went, she thought. It was hers.

She had told Lucy, that Sunday morning in the park when Fran was missing, that she wasn't ready to make a decision about selling the house. Well now, it seemed, she had made it. Or rather, it had been made for her, which might or might not be regarded as progress. And perhaps she should move to London. That would certainly please Lucy.

So . . . even though she wasn't planning to do anything about it just yet, it wouldn't do any harm to start exploring the possibilities. Tomorrow she might go online and do some preliminary research to see what she could afford down there. Which would be that little bit more now, once she had sold the cottage.

It occurred to her that if Neil were still alive, and she had found out about his . . . misdemeanours, and they had got divorced, then she would have been entitled to only half his worldly goods. Now she had them all. It was a small consolation, but she would extract what grim satisfaction she could from it.

She paused in her rocking and took another sip of whisky. She held the glass out in front of her and gazed at the amber liquid. Although she was intending to ditch the drinks cabinet when she did move, she would definitely be taking all of its remaining contents with her.

The more blanks Jane drew in Neil's office, the angrier she became. It felt like a game of hide-and-seek that he was winning hands down. There had to be something there relating to the wretched cottage. For instance, he must have had keys for it. Where were they now? Not anywhere here, so where else could he have kept them? Where did men keep their keys?

Since his death she'd been putting off dealing with his clothes, imagining that it would be a difficult and painful task. Now, more in anger than in sorrow, she started clearing out his wardrobe and drawers, conducting a thorough search of all his pockets as she did so. She found nothing; but on the positive side, it'd been a job that needing doing.

It wouldn't have been a major breakthrough if she had found the keys, though. Their discovery wouldn't have told her anything she didn't already know; they wouldn't have opened any doors she hadn't already been through. But it was so infuriating. He seemed to be getting the better of her at every turn. Had he really needed to be so pathologically careful about a set of unidentifiable keys? Even if she had accidentally stumbled across them at any stage over the years, she would hardly have jumped to the right conclusion about what they were for, would she?

He'd been playing golf when he'd collapsed and been taken to hospital. Was it possible, she wondered, that his golfing partner – someone in the know – had removed the incriminating keys before the ambulance had arrived? No, that was too far-fetched! And anyway, that afternoon he'd been playing with some elderly, retired guy whom he'd hardly known.

The missing keys, she could see, were becoming an obsession.

A few days later, to her surprise, she got a phone call from Kay Williams who was hosting a coffee morning for a local charity and was wondering if Jane would like to go along and support it. It was on one of Jane's school days, however, so she had to decline – regretfully, but with some relief.

'That's a shame,' said Kay. 'It's been ages since I've seen you. I was just saying to Martin the other evening, we must have Jane round for dinner one of these days. How are you, by the way?'

'I'm fine,' said Jane, wondering what else Kay and Martin had been saying to each other in the wake of their visit from the police. 'Yes, that would be lovely.'

It was hardly a serious invitation, though, was it? One of these days! Clearly, without Neil, their friendship wasn't going to survive. It was sad, really. Or was it? Because if she did find out that they had known about his . . . activities . . . all along?

As she was mulling this over, she recalled something. Shortly after Neil's funeral, Martin had called round to sort out some financial matters relating to the dental practice and the partnership. She had signed some papers and then handed him a bunch of Neil's surgery keys. The keys to the cottage could have been – must have been! – on that bunch. So why had he never returned them? It could only be because he'd known what they were and he'd been covering up for Neil!

That evening, she braced herself and rang him at home. After the usual exchange of pleasantries, she said: 'I was wondering – do you remember those keys I gave you? Were there any there that didn't belong to the surgery? I seem to be missing some.'

'I don't think so,' he said. 'I gave them to Liz. She didn't say anything about any spare ones but I can ask her if you like.'

Liz was one of the receptionists at the surgery – the chief one, the office manager or whatever they were called these days. She had been with the practice for as long as Jane could remember. She had known Neil for a very long time.

'If you would,' said Jane. 'I'd really like to find them. Oh . . . by the way, I've got a pile of textbooks and papers here that I'm not sure how to dispose of. Do you think you might take them off my hands? Find a suitable home for them? The Dental School maybe?'

'Yes, of course,' he said. 'Give me a shout when you're ready and I'll come round and get them.' (Was she just imagining that he sounded happier talking about books than he did about keys?) 'Anyway Jane,' he went on. 'How are you doing . . . after that dreadful kidnapping business?'

'Well, you know . . .' she said. 'The major shock was finding out about that cottage. I have no idea why he kept it or what he was using it for. And the police don't seem to have come up with anything yet. I expect they've been to see you?'

'They have,' Martin said, 'but we weren't able to be of much help, I'm afraid.'

'That's the thing,' said Jane. 'No-one seems to know anything. Or if they do they're not saying. It's all very . . . puzzling, isn't it?' She paused. 'I know what I think he was using it for . . .'

'It must be very distressing for you. If there's anything else we can help you with, just say the word,' he said, and the conversation was over.

Jane went upstairs to Neil's office and surveyed the tower of textbooks on the floor. If she were to take them round to the surgery herself, she could have a few words with Liz. She could ask her about the keys, and about the visit from the police. She might be able to probe wider and deeper than they had. Yes, she would do that tomorrow afternoon after school.

But she would need something to put them in. She went down to the utility room where she kept empty boxes that might come in useful but couldn't find one that was anywhere near big enough. Damn! she thought, feeling her resolve beginning to weaken. Then she remembered the parcel which had arrived by post that morning. She hadn't opened it yet because she knew what was in it. It was the tricycle that Lucy had suggested as a possible Christmas present for Daniel. She tore the wrapping paper off and took it out of its box. He'll love it, she thought, gazing with pleasure at the chunky, multi-coloured toy. He would probably love the box too, but that couldn't be helped. She took it upstairs and began filling it with books and magazines and papers.

She parked on the shopping parade, a few yards away from the surgery. The large cardboard box was on the back seat, its colourful exterior at odds with its contents. She had had quite a struggle getting it down the stairs and into her car; someone else would have to carry it in for her now.

She hadn't been to the surgery for a while. Why hadn't she been sent a reminder, she wondered, running her tongue over her teeth? She must be more than due for a check up. She took a deep breath and opened the door. The reception area, she noticed at once, had been repainted since her last visit. There was a new carpet on the floor too.

When Neil first came to work here, the surgery had been upstairs. Where Jane was standing now had been a ladies' clothes shop. There had only been Neil and Martin back then, but over the years others had joined them as the practice had grown. They had bought the shop – never a viable enterprise – and gradually other extensions had been added to the building.

There were two women seated behind the reception desk; Liz and a young woman whom Jane had never seen before.

'Jane!' said Liz. 'This is a surprise! How are you?' She glanced at her computer screen.

'Hello,' said Jane, forcing a wide smile on to her face. 'It's all right, I'm not here for any dentistry. I've just come to drop off some things for Martin. Is he in?'

Liz picked up one of the phones in front of her and spoke softly into it. 'He'll be out in five minutes,' she said, 'if you'd like to take a seat.'

Jane stayed where she was, her smile still in place. 'I hear the police paid you a visit,' she said, 'so you'll know all about the little hoo-ha we had a couple of weeks ago.'

The other receptionist, who must only just have realised who Jane was, was listening in with great interest now.

'Yes,' said Liz – awkwardly, Jane thought. 'That must have been so awful for you. I hope your friend is OK now.'

'She's fine,' said Jane. 'But the really awful thing was finding out that Neil owned the cottage she was taken to. That was a huge shock, I can tell you.' She gave little laugh. 'I had no idea that he owned a country residence.' She laughed again, hoping to indicate that it wasn't sympathy she was looking for but information. 'Did you know anything about that?'

She thought she saw Liz stiffen slightly.

'Me? No,' said Liz, shaking her head.

'Did anyone here?' Jane had to raise her voice over the low, humming sound of a drill coming from a nearby room.

'I don't think so. But I wasn't there when the police spoke to the partners.'

One of the phones began to ring. 'Williams, Lord and Coleclough?' the other receptionist sang into its receiver.

'Gosh (gosh!) this place has changed over the years, hasn't it?' Jane said in a conversational tone, looking around as she spoke. 'I remember when it was just three pokey rooms upstairs. You were here then, weren't you Liz?"

'Oh yes. I've been here nearly twenty-five years now, would you believe? I was only part time when I started, mind. I did mornings and Grace did afternoons. Do you remember Grace?'

Jane smiled uncertainly. Did she remember Grace? She didn't think so.

'It was all pen, paper and filing cabinets in those days.'

Liz waved her hand over all the computer equipment in front of her. 'I'm only just managing to keep up with all this, I can tell you.' She seemed more comfortable now, talking about herself.

A door opened and an elderly man emerged from one of the treatment rooms. At the same moment another phone buzzed.

'Excuse me,' Liz said to Jane, picking it up with one hand and taking a piece of paper from the man with the other.

Jane stepped back and studied her. She had put on quite a bit of weight over the last few years but obviously hadn't yet accepted that she needed a larger clothes size; the seams on her burgundy coloured suit were stretched to their limit. She was very smart though, with her red, manicured nails and her matching lipstick.

She'd been here nearly twenty-five years, she'd said. So she must have been here when Neil had decided to keep the cottage? Could she be the 'other' woman? Might she have been a sufficiently attractive proposition back then? No, it couldn't have been Liz. She had three children who would probably have been . . . what? . . . almost teenagers at the time. They couldn't all have slept in that one bed. And they were all girls, so the football duvet would hardly have been appropriate.

What about this Grace, though? Might she have been the one? Jane couldn't bring any Grace to mind. So many receptionists had come and gone over the years. Only Liz had been a permanent fixture.

Another door opened and a mother with two small children came tumbling out. A moment later they were followed by Martin.

'Jane!' he said, advancing towards her with his arms outstretched. He sounded pleased to see her, out of all proportion to the fact that they'd only spoken to each other the previous evening.

Jane walked into his brief embrace. 'I was passing,' she

said, 'so I thought I'd drop those books in – save you the trouble.'

He seemed relieved that this was the reason for her visit. Why was she making him so uneasy, she wondered? And Liz, too? Was it just general embarrassment in the presence of the bereaved – the wronged bereaved – or were they feeling guilty?

She delved into her handbag for her keys. 'Shall we get them?'

Martin followed her outside.

She unlocked her car. 'Careful now,' she said. 'This box is very unwieldy and very heavy.'

She trotted along beside him as he staggered with impressive speed back towards the surgery.

When the box was safely inside, she murmured: 'Did you ask Liz about those keys?'

'Oh, sorry,' he said. 'I forgot.' He turned to the reception desk. 'Liz, do you remember when I gave you that bunch of Neil's keys? You didn't come across any that weren't for here, did you?'

Liz frowned in concentration and then shook her head. 'No,' she said, 'I don't think I did.'

'Right,' said Jane. 'Well, not to worry. I'll just have to keep on searching.'

'I went round to Neil's surgery today,' she told Fran that evening, 'to see if I could find out anything.'

'I thought the police'd already done that.'

'They have, but listen . . . you know how I've been looking for Neil's cottage keys and haven't been able to find them anywhere?'

'I do indeed!'

'Well, I remembered that I'd given a whole lot of keys back to Neil's partner, Martin, straight after he died. Keys for the surgery. So I was thinking that the cottage keys must have been among them. But when I asked if they'd found any that didn't belong to them, they said they hadn't. I think they're lying. Either Martin, or the receptionist – her name's Liz – or both of them. And I think they lied to the police too, when they said they knew nothing about the cottage. One or other of them. Or both.'

'Oh, come on. This is all supposition. You can't know for sure that the keys were . . .'

'Yes, I can! The bloody things must have been somewhere! It all makes sense. They didn't give them back to me at the time because they were covering up for Neil. But the really interesting question is, why are they still covering up for him now, when they know that I – and the police – know about the cottage?'

'And the really interesting answer is . . . ?'

'Well, like I said, there's not much point them covering up for Neil now, so they must be protecting someone else. Someone like your young man and his mother! Martin, or Liz, or both of them, must know who they are.'

There was a short silence while Fran processed this. 'OK,' she said. 'If we ignore the extreme shakiness of your initial premise, it could be plausible. But even if you're right – and it's a big if – they're not going to admit it, so none of this gets you anywhere, does it?'

Jane hadn't told Fran all her suspicions, though – and wasn't about to yet. When the call was over she went to her computer and signed in to Neil's email account. She scrolled down his list of contacts . . . E, F, G. But, to her disappointment, there was no Grace there. If she wanted to speak to this woman she would have to make further inquiries. But who could she ask? Certainly not Martin or Liz who, if Grace had been Neil's mistress, were doing all they could to safeguard her identity.

There was always Debbie Mason. She could ask whether the police had thought to question past receptionists – specifically ones who had been around at the time Neil had decided to keep the cottage. If they hadn't, she could point them in that direction – starting with Grace.

When Jane got home from school the following afternoon there was a message on her answering machine.

'Jane? It's Kay again. We were wondering if you'd like to come round for something to eat tomorrow evening? Nothing formal, just the three of us. Say 7.30? Let me know. Bye.'

Jane's first reaction was one of dismay. She listened to the message again. Following her visit to the surgery yesterday, had Martin imposed this upon his reluctant wife, she wondered? Had the invitation been extended out of guilt for prior neglect, or guilt because they knew they'd been deceiving her? On the other hand, it could just be a kind (if rather belated) invitation from both of them. She might have been wrong thinking this was a friendship that had come to an end.

She sat down on the stairs to think. It was time she started going out again and this would be a good place to start. It would also, she thought with a flicker of excitement, be an opportunity to find out more about this Grace person before she mentioned her to Debbie Mason.

Conversation around the Williams's dining table had stalled for the third time. Jane picked up her wine glass and then put it down again. She had drunk all of the one small measure she was allowing herself (she was driving); she would have to find her courage elsewhere.

'It's all right,' she said, glancing at the place where Neil would have been sitting had he been there with them. 'There's no need for us to keep skirting round the subject. I want to talk about it, and I think you do too.' This last remark was directed specifically at Kay who immediately nodded her agreement. 'Neil must have had a mistress,' Jane went on, 'and the cottage must have been where he entertained her. And I – I knew absolutely nothing about it. But I'd really like to know whether you did – either of you. Because if you did, you can tell me now. I'll understand why you kept silent before.'

She looked from one to the other of them, trying to gauge their reactions.

'Well I certainly didn't know,' said Kay turning to give Martin an almost accusatory look.

'Neither did I,' he said. 'Not about the cottage, anyway. But . . . I wouldn't be totally surprised if there was a woman involved. Don't ask me why. It's just a feeling I got from time to time.'

Jane stared at him. How come he had been so intuitive? She had never had that feeling. 'Are you sure you knew nothing about the cottage?' she persisted, trying to get him to look her in the eye. 'I'm pretty sure that the keys for it were among those I gave back to you, and yet no-one returned them, which makes it look as though someone knew what they were for but didn't want me to know.'

Martin shook his head. 'It was Liz who dealt with the keys,' he said, still not meeting her gaze.

'Oooh!' interrupted Kay. 'You don't think Liz could've been . . . ?'

Jane smiled. 'That did cross my mind, too,' she said, 'but on reflection I don't think so. What I do think, though, is that she might well know who was.'

'I'm not clear how this ties in with your friend being kidnapped,' said Martin.

'Well, the kidnapper was obviously connected to the cottage in some way. The police think that if they can establish who was using it then they'll find their man. But I'm more interested in finding Neil's 'other' woman. I think the kidnapper might be her son, and I think he wants something from me. He kidnapped Frances by mistake, remember. He thought she was me.'

'How intriguing!' said Kay. 'Well it is,' she said to Martin who had given her a sidelong look. 'So why haven't the police found him?'

'Well, all the people they've questioned so far claim to know nothing about the cottage or another woman,' said Jane. 'But they haven't finished with their inquiries yet, so we'll have to wait and see.' She smiled at each of them in turn. Kay knew nothing; Martin she was less sure about – much less sure. 'I was talking to Liz yesterday,' she said, watching him closely, 'about the "olden days". She mentioned someone called Grace who used to be one of your receptionists years ago. I couldn't remember her, though.'

'Grace! Oh I remember Grace,' said Kay. 'She was a character.' She turned to Martin. 'I wonder if she's still alive? She must be well into her eighties now, wouldn't you say?'

Jane reached for her wine glass again, forgetting that it was empty. She knew that when she related this little story to Fran she would do so with a comedic touch. They would laugh about it. But right now, she wanted to weep.

'Well there you are,' said Fran. 'I think you can definitely rule her out. Unless, of course, you think my young man might have been her grandson?'

Jane sighed. 'I'm going to speak to Debbie Mason on Monday and ask her to check up on past receptionists,' she said.

'Don't you think they'll have done that already? They are detectives, for Christ's sake.'

'Not very good ones, though. They'd have come up with something by now, if they were.'

When she did speak to DC Mason, however, she was told that the police had indeed questioned previous receptionists. The surgery had been very cooperative in providing the names and, where possible, the addresses of these women. All the relevant ones had now been eliminated from their inquiries.

Jane's only hope now was the woman who had tipped off the police. The phrase 'unfinished business' kept going round and round in her head. As long as Fran's young man had unfinished business with her, she argued with herself – and with Fran – there was still a possibility that this woman would contact her on his behalf.

But Fran was dismissive. 'That's just wishful thinking,' she said. 'It's much more likely that nothing further will happen and you'll never find out what my young man wanted. You should resign yourself to that. Forget about Neil's speculative mistress. Let it go and move on.'

Jane moved the phone away from her ear and glared at it. She didn't trust herself to speak. *Speculative mistress! Let it go!* If their positions had been reversed, would Fran have ever let it go? Of course she wouldn't.

'Why don't you come down here for a few days?' Fran said as the silence between them lengthened. 'Take your mind off things.'

'My whole life has been turned upside down,' said Jane. 'I need to face up to that, not have my mind taken off it. You know, sometimes I think your 'weekend in the country' has affected your brain. You never used to make such fatuous comments.'

She heard Fran sigh loudly. 'OK,' she said. 'Point taken.'

7

Fran put the phone down and gave a little yelp of annoyance. She knew she shouldn't have used the words 'speculative mistress'. No wonder Jane had been incensed. And telling her to 'move on', too! As if that were possible. Jane wouldn't rest until she'd found out what Neil had been using the cottage for. Who, in her position, would?

She was finding all this talk about the cottage and Neil's mistresses very unsettling. She kept reassuring herself that her secret was safe. Her young man – whatever else he might know – had known nothing about her previous visit there. There was no reason at all why this should ever come to light, even if he did get caught. And there was every reason to hope that he never would – if only Jane would leave things to the police.

But something else was troubling her. Her little affair with Neil had never been a big deal. He'd meant nothing to her, and she obviously hadn't meant much to him either. She had, after all, only played a tiny part in his shenanigans. But perversely this was the problem. The realisation that she'd been just one of his 'other' women was intensely unpleasant.

It was like with Howard Sage, all those years ago. She'd probably been just one of many for him, too. She remembered how hurt she'd been when he hadn't sought her out after that Christmas vacation. It had been a blow to both her vanity and her pride, but she'd protected herself by proclaiming that she'd never liked him anyway, and that she wanted nothing more to do with him.

But that had been then and this was now, and she

certainly wasn't going to waste time thinking about Howard Sage. As far as Neil Lord was concerned, if all she was suffering from was hurt pride, then she was being pathetic. The only person entitled to feel hurt by his behaviour was poor Jane – who would also be hurt by Fran's behaviour were she ever to find out about the affair. Which she must never do. And she wouldn't, because there was no reason why she should.

Fran was still having the dreams about walking across the Common. Not every night, but sufficiently often for them to be a bit of a nuisance.

They followed the same pattern every time, always featuring the path which, within the family, had become affectionately known as the hypotenuse. (Once, many years ago, Emer had been telling her mother about some incident which had taken place on one of the several paths at the bottom of the Common and Fran had been trying to ascertain exactly which one she meant. John, who had just started doing geometry at school, had piped up saying: 'She means the hypotenuse one.' This hadn't helped as there were several contenders for this description depending on which triangular configuration you were looking at. A fierce argument had broken out involving disputes over right angles and accusations of nerdiness, but eventually the path had been identified and the description had stuck.)

During the day the hypotenuse was a much used path. Leaving aside the dangers of being mown down by children on bikes and scooters, or of being bitten by one of the ever-increasing number of ugly, dangerous dogs being exercised on the Common, it was totally unthreatening. At night, however, it could seem much less so. It was totally visible from the High Road and was well lit. But this lighting had a disturbing effect. When walking in a homeward direction your own elongated shadow was cast on to the path in front of you and if anyone happened to be walking behind you, you could see their elongated shadow creeping up on yours.

In Fran's dreams there always was someone following behind her as she walked along this path. Someone waiting to pounce. But she knew that the dreams weren't really about this particular path, or about being physically assaulted. Neither were they about her young man. The threatening figure in them was much too old to be him.

She'd thought she knew who it was. You didn't have to be a psychoanalyst to work that one out, she'd told herself mockingly. But, such being the improbability of dreams, she woke up one morning with the disconcerting feeling that it mightn't be Neil Lord, after all. It could just as easily be Howard Sage.

What with one thing and another, it wasn't escaping her notice that Howard Sage was on her mind a lot these days. This was funny because generally she only thought about him whenever Emer made some oblique reference to him, or when she saw him on the television, or read an article by him – or about him – in a newspaper or magazine. And none of these things seemed to have happened recently. He didn't seem to be in the public eye much anymore.

She wondered, briefly, whether he might have died – whether this might be why he was haunting her dreams (if, indeed, he was the hypotenuse man) – but it didn't seem likely. She would have heard or read about it somewhere if he had. But just to make sure, she would Google him. No, she confirmed, scrolling down the entries, he was still alive and kicking. And still writing. And being written about, too, she could see, skimming through a magazine interview given by his daughter, Imogen.

Poor Imogen, whose marriage to another actor had ended in divorce last year. He'd cheated on her, apparently. But even though he'd apologised, profusely and publicly, she hadn't been able to forgive him. She had spent her childhood, she said, watching her mother put up with her father's repeated indiscretions, time and time again, and had vowed that she herself would never do the same. Men could be such bastards. She was dating someone else now though who she was hoping might be the exception.

Fran sat back and stared at the computer screen. That was what she had been, one of Howard Sage's 'repeated indiscretions'. She wondered whether Emer had read this article, too. She must have. She had spent half her life devouring everything she could find about her famous 'real' father and her famous half sister. Fran checked the date of the interview. It was over a year old. It could explain why Emer hadn't alluded to him for a while. Perhaps she could see now that Fran had been right about him all along.

The article, though, could have come too late. Emer might already have contacted Howard Sage, sometime in the past. And if she had, he must have rebuffed her, which was what Fran had always been afraid of. 'God! Not another one!' she'd imagined him saying. Now, she could hear Imogen and her mother saying it too. Which was precisely why she had been right to want to keep his identity secret.

Emer had been nearly seventeen when she'd found out that Howard Sage was her father. And then it had been by accident. Patrick, of course, had known that Nick wasn't her biological father. That honour, Fran had told him, belonged to one of her university lecturers. She hadn't given him a name and Patrick hadn't asked for one. A name wouldn't have meant anything anyway – unless, of course, it was a famous name, and that hadn't been the case at the time. So the revelation, when it came, had been a shock for him as well as for Emer.

~

Fran and Patrick had been out for dinner and Emer had been coerced into babysitting. When they returned home she was lying on the sofa watching something on Channel 4. There was a glass of wine on the coffee table in front of her.

'I hope that's all you've had,' said Fran. 'You shouldn't be drinking.'

'It's Friday night,' said Emer. 'I shouldn't even be here.'

'What is this you're watching?' said Patrick, lifting Emer's legs off the sofa and sitting down beside her.

Fran went into the kitchen and looked round for signs that Emer had had other people in the house while they'd been out. She found none, but that wasn't conclusive; she would cross-question John in the morning. When she returned to the sitting room, Patrick had changed television channels and Emer was complaining loudly about how unfair it was that they'd made her stay in and babysit and now they wouldn't even let her finish watching her programme. Fran sat down on the other sofa and glanced at the screen. And there he was! Howard fucking Sage!

She had heard him on the radio and seen pictures of him in the papers but she hadn't seen him 'live', so to speak, since Bristol. For a moment she sat there fascinated, then, aware of the danger, became alarmed. 'Let her watch that other thing if she wants,' she said.

'Yeah,' grumbled Emer. 'You can't just come in and start laying down the law.' She reached for the remote control, pointed it at the television, and then paused. 'Hey,' she cried, animated all of a sudden. 'You know who that is, don't you?'

Fran sat very still, staring at Howard Sage who was momentarily occupying the whole screen.

Emer turned to her. 'That's Imogen Sage's father,' she said. 'You know, the one on EastEnders.'

Fran made a little non-committal noise.

'Yes, it's Howard Sage,' said Patrick. He turned to look at Fran too. 'He used to be at Bristol. Was he there when you were?'

Fran shrugged and made another strange little noise.

'No, he looks a lot older than Mum,' said Emer.

'No, I mean he was a lecturer there, not a student,' said Patrick.

'A lecturer. Really?' Emer let the remote control fall into her lap. 'Do you think he might have known my father then?'

She said this playfully but Fran was unnerved. 'For Christ's sake, just put your programme back on, will you?' she snapped.

But Emer wasn't to be diverted. 'Did you know him?' she asked. 'This Howard Sage guy, I mean, not my father, who you very obviously did "know".' She waited for a reply, and when none came, said: 'I'll take it that you did, then.'

'Give me that,' said Fran, reaching for the remote control.

But Emer got to it first. 'No, let's leave this on,' she said. 'Patrick wants to watch it, so we'll all watch it.'

Fran made another grab for it but Emer moved her hand away. 'What's the matter with you?' she said. 'What're you getting so upset about? You like this stupid bloody programme.'

Another close-up of Howard Sage was filling the television screen. Having just made some witty comment, he was sitting there looking very pleased with himself. Fran looked across at Emer and saw the same smug expression on her face. It was the first time she had ever seen any likeness to him in her daughter, and it shook her badly. But even as she was looking at her, Emer's expression was beginning to change. It was as if she, too, was noticing the similarity. She leaned in towards the television set and when Howard Sage started speaking again she began turning up the volume. Up and up and up it went until his voice was filling every corner of the room.

Patrick snatched the controls off her and pressed the mute button. 'What the hell are you playing at?' he said.

Emer leapt to her feet and took a few steps across the room towards where Fran was sitting. 'Oh, my God!' she was screaming. 'It's him! It is, isn't it? It's him! Answer me!'

'For Christ's sake, Emer!' said Fran. She closed her eyes and shook her head. But it was too late.

~

8

A few days after she'd had dinner with Martin and Kay, Jane got a call from the dental surgery. It was from Martin. He'd asked Liz about the keys again, he told her, and it turned out that when she'd had another think and a good look round she'd found some that couldn't be accounted for.

'Really?' said Jane, who was standing in the hall watching Bronia polishing the banister.

'I think it was a genuine oversight on her part,' Martin said.

'Really?' she said again, making no effort to hide her incredulity. Someone was lying. One of them – maybe both of them – definitely knew something.

He offered to drop them round but she said that she didn't actually need them anymore; the locks at the cottage had been replaced.

'But the police'll be interested in them,' she said, wishing that she could see his face. 'Frances's abductor had keys for that cottage, and now you're saying there've been some keys lying around in your surgery for months which might have been them.'

She put the phone down and gave Bronia a big smile before going into the kitchen and closing the door behind her. Someone definitely knew something. It didn't really matter who – although she would prefer it to be Liz. Now the police would question everyone at the surgery again. They would find out who Neil's mistress was. How right she had been to concentrate on the keys.

She picked up her mobile phone and rang Debbie

Mason.

Bronia was in the kitchen, cleaning the fridge in preparation for the Christmas food onslaught, when DC Mason came round the following Monday morning. Jane made coffee for all three of them and then, mugs in hand, she led the policewoman into the lounge.

DC Mason put her mug down on the coffee table and reached into her briefcase. She extracted two old deadlock keys on a plain key ring and placed these on the coffee table too. They both sat and stared at them for a moment. 'If these are the keys to the cottage . . .' she began.

Jane's high hopes plummeted. 'What do you mean "if"?' she cried. 'They are. They must be.'

'They could be yours – for somewhere in this house. Maybe old ones for locks you no longer have?'

It was possible, but Jane shook her head. 'No,' she said. 'They must be for the cottage.'

'Well, unfortunately, we haven't been able to verify that. The old locks that were there have gone now. But even if we were to establish that these are the cottage keys, the receptionist maintains that she thought they were old ones from the surgery, and that she'd forgotten all about them until Martin Williams pressed her to remember. She denies any knowledge of the cottage.'

'She's lying,' said Jane.

'Even if she did know what they were for,' the policewoman said, shaking her head, 'it doesn't follow that she knows anything about Frances's abduction. The two things aren't necessarily connected.'

'She's withholding information. I know she is.'

'We've no proof of that. We've questioned her extensively but she insists she knows nothing.'

Jane was fighting back tears of frustration. 'She's lying,' she said again.

'I know this is hard for you,' Debbie Mason said, 'but you mustn't go around making unsubstantiated accusations.'

Jane could see that they weren't on the same mission. The police were only interested in catching the abductor; she was desperate to find Neil's mistress. And she was convinced that Liz knew more than she was saying.

But what could she do about it? Nothing, it would seem.

She had come to a full-stop in Neil's office, too. Fran's right, she thought reluctantly, there might never be any answers to my questions. Perhaps she should just resign herself to this fact. *Let it go. Move on.* So easy to say, but how did one let go of something like this?

She was so angry, so full of rage. And if Neil had been alive she would have had some outlet for her feelings. He would have had to explain himself. And she would have shouted and screamed at him; made him suffer; exacted her revenge. But as it was, all she could do now was go on about it to Fran. On and on. Fran could only listen, though; she couldn't share the pain. Only Lucy and Sarah would be able to do that – when she told them.

But . . . Jane paused, not liking where her thoughts were heading. If she wasn't going to find out anything more . . . ever . . . was there any real need to tell them about the cottage? What good would it do inflicting this upon them? A pain shared wouldn't be a pain halved, it would be a pain trebled. But even as this thought was formulating in her mind, she found herself rebelling against it. Of course she should tell them. They had a right to know. Why should she be the only one to suffer? And why on earth should she protect and preserve Neil's memory?

Justification and indignation – yes. But revenge? Would this make her feel any better in the long run? 'Something else to worry about now,' she said out loud. She gave a harsh little laugh. Had Neil tortured himself with questions like this over the years, she wondered? No, of course he hadn't. The bastard!

On the phone to Fran that evening, she heard herself saying: 'I think I will come down. Next weekend, maybe?'

This spur of the moment decision took her by surprise, but she needed to talk to someone about this and Fran was the only person she could turn to. 'If the offer's still open,' she added.

'Of course it is!' Fran sounded almost too pleased, making Jane wonder, yet again, whether her friend had fully recovered from her ordeal.

'I'll make it a long weekend then,' she said. Long enough for both of them to benefit from it.

She would get to see Daniel – and Lucy and John, too, of course. And while she was down there, she might also get a chance to look at the outsides of one or two of the properties she'd seen advertised on the internet. But that would mean telling Fran and Lucy what she was thinking, and since she hadn't made any definite decision about moving yet, the last thing she wanted at this stage was for either of them to get involved.

'Great. Will you drive or come by train?' Fran asked.

'Train,' said Jane.

She didn't feel confident enough to drive there by herself. It wasn't the motorway that was the problem; it was getting across London once the motorway ended. Whenever they'd been to visit Lucy in Tooting, Neil had always driven that last bit of the journey. John had shown them a really useful rat run but it involved a great deal of weaving and turning and she wasn't sure she could manage it by herself without someone to do the navigating. And the alternative – staying on the A40 all the way to Hyde Park and then undergoing the white-knuckle drive along Park Lane before crossing the river at Vauxhall Bridge – was unthinkable.

As Jane would be away all weekend, she cancelled Bronia's Monday morning cleaning session, assuring her that she would still get paid, of course. She wasn't looking forward to telling Bronia that she would be reducing her hours soon, but she'd resolved not to say anything about that until after Christmas.

On Friday morning she set off, trundling her suitcase down to Solihull Station to catch the Chiltern Line train to Marylebone. She kept looking round to check she wasn't being watched or followed – after all, Fran's young man had panicked at the sight of a suitcase before – but she wasn't seriously expecting to see him.

As Fran would be working, Lucy had offered to pick her up from Balham station and drive her over to Streatham later in the afternoon. She'd issued instructions as to how her mother should get to Balham from Marylebone but Jane hadn't really been listening. She was quite capable of finding her own way. She wasn't a child.

On the way down on the train, though, she did find herself worrying about the Underground which she hadn't been on since the 7/7 bombings. But it was silly to be so apprehensive, she told herself sternly. It was perfectly safe. And even if it wasn't, she couldn't not go on the tube if she was seriously intending to become a Londoner.

When she got to Marylebone she studied the Underground map carefully. It looked as though her best option would be to take the Bakerloo line to Elephant and Castle and then the Northern line south to Balham . . . although she vaguely remembered Lucy mentioning Oxford Circus. But that would mean two changes, so perhaps she'd misheard.

Trying not to think about the depth of the descent, she struggled down the escalator with her case and got on to a train. She sat down with her case wedged awkwardly against her leg. It was very hot. She undid the top two buttons of her coat, thinking that maybe she was overheating because she was panicking. No-one else around her seemed to be too hot, but then, they probably weren't thinking about bombs. Feeling the need to distract herself, she focussed on the linear map above the seats opposite her, and began counting the number of stops to her destination. It seemed that as well as going all the way to Elephant and Castle she also had the option of changing on to the Northern line at Charing Cross,

Embankment or Waterloo. Four possibilities. Which one to choose?

The train eased into Oxford Circus where the platform was crowded with people. A large number of them piled into her carriage and Jane undid another button on her coat. She thought that she'd decided to stick to her original plan and go to Elephant and Castle, but as the train pulled into Charing Cross she found herself forcing her way to the doors to get off. This was a big mistake. Hauling her case behind her, she had to walk for what seemed like miles before she got to the Northern line, and once there she saw to her dismay that she would have to change again at Kennington. She should have listened to Lucy's instructions. By the time she arrived at Balham she was exhausted.

She made her way on to the street and rang Lucy as pre-arranged.

'We're in the car park,' Lucy said. 'I'll wave to you.'

Jane crossed the road and walked the few yards to Sainsbury's car park where she saw Lucy standing by her car. They embraced.

'So, you got here all right?' said Lucy, putting Jane's case into the boot.

'Yeah, no problem.'

'Coming via Oxford Circus is definitely the best way.'

'Mmm.'

Jane climbed into the back seat next to Daniel who was all big brown eyes beneath a Fair Isle hat with ear flaps. 'Hello little man!' she said, leaning over and kissing him on the cheek.

He surveyed her solemnly for a few seconds and then turned away to look out of his window. Disregarding all her attempts at communication, he kept his eyes averted all the way home.

For the past two years Lucy and John had been living in Tooting. Neil had always found their three-bedroom terraced house very small and poky. He'd never been able to understand why they'd chosen to live in London, where this was all they could afford, when they could have had a much better house – with a decent garden – elsewhere. Jane had to keep warning him not to say this to Lucy as it would undoubtedly have offended her. The house, she'd insisted, was perfectly adequate for them, and in time they would be able to afford something bigger.

With another baby on the way now, though, Jane had been wondering whether they might already be considering a house move. If they were, it would make sense for her to wait and see where they moved to before she herself chose an area. London was such a huge place. It could take nearly as long to get from one end of it to another as it took her now to get from Solihull to Tooting. She didn't want to move just to be near them, though – or Fran. She wanted to move because she wanted to make a new life for herself. And London might just be the place for doing that. But she wasn't sure yet. There were so many things to take into account.

Lucy gave Daniel his lunch and then put him down for his nap.

'You could have stayed here, you know,' she said when she came back downstairs.

'I know. But I thought Fran could do with the company.'

'Don't you think she's coping, then?'

'No, she's coping . . . but I just think this whole thing has shaken her up more than she's letting on.'

'She's not going to New York for Christmas now. Did you know that?'

'Yes, that's what I mean. Little things like that.'

'She should've had some counselling. We kept telling her but she wouldn't listen.'

'Yes, well . . .' Why were they going on about Fran? Fran was all right. Jane turned her attention to Lucy. 'Anyway, how are you? You're looking much better than you were a few weeks ago.'

'Yeah, I'm feeling much better, thank goodness. I think the worst is over now.'

'You'll be blooming by Christmas.'

'Yeah, Christmas . . .' said Lucy glancing at her mother. 'It'll be strange this year without Dad, won't it?'

Jane nodded.

'I was wondering . . .' Lucy paused, and Jane tensed. When Lucy used that tone of voice there was usually something controversial in the offing. 'I was wondering whether it wouldn't be better . . . instead of us coming home . . . if you came down here for Christmas.'

'No! I want you to come home.'

'But now that Fran and Patrick are going to be here . . .'

'What difference does that make?'

'I just thought that if you came down here we could all have Christmas dinner at theirs.'

'And what about Sarah? She wouldn't want to spend Christmas Day at Fran's. She hardly knows them.'

Lucy shrugged. 'I'm sure she wouldn't mind.'

'And there isn't enough room here for both of us to stay.'

'We could manage. Daniel could come in with us and Sarah could have his room. Or you could stay at Fran's. I'm sure she wouldn't mind.'

'No! Absolutely not! I've planned our own family Christmas. I've already ordered the turkey.'

'Well, at least think about it,' said Lucy.

'No!' Jane was angry now.

'OK, don't go getting all upset. I just thought it would be easier for everyone, that's all.'

'Well if it's too much trouble for you to come home . . .'

Lucy gave a loud sigh. 'Don't be silly,' she said. 'I was only thinking about you.'

'Were you? Well, I really want you and Sarah to come home for Christmas.'

It would seem that her dilemma had resolved itself. She was obviously still intending to tell her daughters about the cottage.

'I've been wondering whether there's any point telling Lucy and Sarah about the cottage,' she said to Fran as they were eating dinner that evening.

Fran looked surprised. 'I thought you were going to tell them at Christmas,' she said. 'Why the change of mind?'

'I'm not saying I have changed it. I've just been wondering whether it's really necessary, that's all. Whether it would achieve anything?'

'It'd make you feel better,' said Fran.

'That's not very noble, though, is it?'

'Yeah, well,' Fran laughed. 'Do we really care about nobility?'

'The thing is,' said Jane, launching into the argument she'd been rehearsing for days, 'if I'm not going to find out anything else, shouldn't I just do as you said and let it go? It'll carry on driving me mad, of course, not knowing why he kept the wretched place, but is it really necessary for the girls to go through the same pain and uncertainty about their father?'

'But they're adults,' said Fran, 'They should be able to deal with it. And if it affects the way they think about Neil, well that's his doing, not yours.'

Jane thought about this for a moment. 'Well, yes and no,' she said. 'If I tell them, then won't it be my doing?'

'If you don't tell them now, and they find out later, will they thank you for keeping it from them?' Fran asked, refilling their wine glasses.

She's thinking about Emer and Howard Sage, Jane thought. 'If I keep it from them,' she said, 'I suppose, I'll be deceiving them in much the same way as Neil did me.'

'Exactly.'

'Perhaps he thought that he was being noble, protecting me from whatever it was he was doing wrong,' said Jane.

'For Christ's sake! What are you saying now?'

Jane took a long drink from her glass. 'I don't know what I'm saying,' she said. 'It's all quite beyond me. I thought I had a happy marriage . . .'

'We've been through this before,' said Fran. 'You did

have.'

'I thought I had.'

'It's the same thing.'

'No, it's not. I had a happy delusional marriage. The question is . . . did Lucy and Sarah have a happy childhood, or was that delusional too?'

'Well that's something they'll have to decide for themselves,' said Fran, pouring more wine into Jane's glass. 'But . . . it's up to you.'

This wasn't quite what Jane wanted to hear. She wanted Fran to talk her out of her uncertainty, to tell her that she was being unnecessarily sensitive and self-sacrificing. 'I know it's up to me,' she said. 'And I probably will end up telling them. After all, why shouldn't I? You're right. It's all his fault, not mine. And protecting them would mean protecting his reputation. Why should I do that? I'll never forgive him for this. Never.'

'The thing is, though,' said Fran, 'you don't really know what it is that you can't forgive him for.' She shook her head at the warning look coming from Jane. 'I know you don't like me saying this, but you're only speculating about what he might have been up to at that cottage.'

'Yes but it's not idle speculation, is it? And it's not just that he owned some cottage or other that none of us knew about. It's the fact that it was the cottage, the one you were taken to.'

Fran sighed. 'OK,' she said. 'But until – unless – you have more information, it might not be such a bad idea to leave things alone.'

Jane felt slightly confused. Fran seemed to be contradicting herself. 'No, I can't do that,' she said. She felt decisive now. 'I have to tell them. There's got to be some pay back.'

While Fran was making breakfast next morning, Jane stood at the kitchen window and looked out at the garden. It was much smaller than hers in Solihull, but for a London garden, she supposed, it was quite large – especially when compared to Lucy's few feet of outdoor space. If she were to move down here would she need, or indeed want, a garden? Somewhere where she could sit outside in the summer would be nice – a balcony or a terrace, perhaps – with a few plant pots and containers. But she certainly didn't need acres of lawn and whole dormitories of flower beds anymore. And there were plenty of parks and Commons around here for grass and trees.

She turned away from the window and looked round the kitchen. This too was smaller than hers, but it would be more than adequate for her requirements. She was beginning to sound like an estate agent. 'What are your requirements, Mrs Lord?' one had asked her the other day when she'd phoned to inquire about a property not too far away from here. She'd murmured something about three bedrooms and somewhere that didn't need any work doing to it. But what exactly were her requirements, she wondered? Not anything that an estate agent could satisfy, she suspected.

She began considering Fran's house from the point of view of a prospective buyer. It was beautiful; she had always admired it. It was older than hers and had retained many of its 'period features' – stained glass, cornices, original Edwardian fireplaces. But a house like this, here in London, might be too expensive for her. She needed to do some more research.

'Have you thought any more about moving?' Lucy had asked her yesterday. 'No, not really,' she'd replied.

It would be a big decision; one she had to get right. And she wasn't used to making big decisions on her own. And, irrespective of interfering family and friends, that was what she was now – on her own.

Fran had decided that Jane needed 'taking out of herself' and had planned a busy day for them. It involved a morning trip to Tate Modern to see the Rothko exhibition, followed by lunch and a walk along the South Bank to Waterloo Bridge (for one of the best views in London, of which you could never see too much).

As they were leaving the house, Jane noticed a 'For Sale' board outside another house further along Fran's road. She hadn't seen this property on the internet so it must only just have gone on the market. She wondered what the asking price was, but she would have to wait until she got home to find out because she couldn't use Fran's computer to do so without revealing her intentions.

It was a grey and bitterly cold day. They set off at a brisk pace. Once they'd left the Common behind, the journey to the station did little to persuade Jane that Streatham was a part of London she might want to live in. As if reading her critical thoughts, Fran pointed towards the other side of the High Road. 'There's going to be a massive redevelopment there,' she said.

'Really?' said Jane, glancing across at the pink and purple Art Deco Ice Rink which had undoubtedly seen better days.

They crossed the road at the traffic lights and went into the station where the electronic sign on the platform informed them that their train was going to be fourteen minutes late. Jane folded her arms and hunched her shoulders against the nasty wind blowing down the railway line towards them. It was an exceptionally ugly station. Everyone, on both its platforms, looked exceedingly miserable. But it was a grey and miserable day. She should reserve judgement and not rush to cross Streatham off her list of potential places to move to just because of the weather, a delayed train and a dingy station.

The train took them to London Bridge and from there they walked along by the river to Tate Modern. As its gigantic brick tower rose up improbably before them and St Paul's appeared majestically on the opposite bank, Jane began to feel re-energised.

The Rothko exhibition was crowded and they wove their way laboriously through its many rooms without speaking. Jane, who wasn't always appreciative of abstract art, found the paintings peculiarly satisfying. She liked the red ones but spent quite some time looking at the brown, grey and black ones, too. Fran moved on but she loitered, losing herself in the sombre shades. She wondered whether it was the quality of the art or her own emotional state which was responsible for the strange resonances she was experiencing. She would like to come back on her own and see it all over again. If she lived in London, she could do that.

Fran was a member of the Tate and so they toiled up the stairs to the Members' Room for lunch. It was very crowded in there, too. They had to hover for quite a while, holding on to their laden trays, before a small table near the window became available. From there, the view of the London skyline across the river, with St Paul's in the centre, was magnificent.

'Wow!' said Jane, pausing to gaze at it before placing her tray on the table.

'Well, what did you think of Rothko then?' said Fran, taking a huge bite of her chicken and avocado wrap.

'Surprisingly,' said Jane, 'I liked it a lot.'

'Why surprisingly?'

'Because I'm usually ambivalent about abstract stuff.'

'Me too,' said Fran. 'In fact, I have been known to be positively antagonistic.' She took another bite and carried on talking with her mouth full. 'I liked this though. I think I might buy a print.' She paused to chew and swallow. 'I think a big red one would go well in my sitting-room. Which isn't as philistine as it might sound, given that it's Rothko we're talking about.'

They stayed there, drinking coffee and talking, well into the afternoon. (It reminded Jane of the afternoon at Warwick Arts' Centre.) Not once did they mention Neil, death, abduction or the cottage. Both of them, it would seem, had been successfully 'taken out of themselves'.

They went down to the gallery shop to buy Fran's print.

'I'm going to get it framed,' she said when she'd chosen one. 'It's a bit more expensive to do it here, but if I don't I know I'll never get round to doing it myself.'

Jane was tempted to buy one too. But she could see that Fran knew exactly where she was going to hang her bold red painting, and what colour frame she wanted for it, whereas she couldn't imagine a Rothko on any of the walls in the house in Solihull. No, she decided, she would wait until she'd moved before she bought anything new. And she had a brief vision of a large room, empty except for a rocking chair, its white walls bare, except for a sombre brown and grey painting.

They retrieved their coats from the cloakroom.

'Wrap up warm,' Fran ordered, pulling on her dark green woollen hat and winding her scarf several times around her neck. 'We're going to Waterloo Bridge and it'll be freezing by the river.'

Jane did as she was told and they set off. The clouds had lifted while they'd been inside, making it even colder than it'd been before. It was dark now and all the buildings, on both banks of the river, were lit up, creating golden and red and blue reflections in the dark, fast moving water. It was an exhilarating sight.

They arrived at Waterloo and Fran led the way on to the bridge. 'This is my very favourite bridge,' she announced, setting off along its length.

Jane followed, bracing herself against the bitingly cold air rising up from the river below. The views from the bridge were indeed glorious. Down river St Paul's and the City skyline – tall cranes rising up decoratively above and between the skyscrapers – and all the way past Tower Bridge to Canary Wharf. Arrested by the sound of waves slapping against the piers beneath them, Jane looked down into the dark swirling river water and shivered. It was all so beautiful, and – of a sudden – all so sad.

'And now the other way,' said Fran. They crossed the road and looked up river, to Big Ben and the Houses of Parliament on one side, the London Eye on the other – an electric blue circle soaring cleanly above its smudged image on the shimmering surface of the water below.

But it was too cold to linger and they walked briskly along the Embankment to the tube station. Jane's euphoria began to dissipate when the train pulled in to the platform and she saw how crowded it was. They pushed their way on and groped for handrails to cling on to. She wondered what would happen were she to faint now. She absolutely mustn't, of course. Not if she was contemplating moving to London. She caught Fran's eye and managed a smile.

'Fucking nightmare,' Fran murmured as the train slowed into Waterloo and lots of people elbowed their way off before even more forced their way on. They moved further down into the carriage.

'We'll get off at Stockwell and go to Brixton,' said Fran.

Jane studied the map. Only three more stops. She could just about cope with that. Thankfully, the train from Stockwell was comparatively empty and she began to regain her composure. She could do this, she told herself. It just needed getting used to.

As would Brixton, she thought, as they emerged from underground on to a street heaving with humanity. Music was blaring out from some unseen quarter, there was a strong smell of illegal substances in the air, and an immaculately-suited black man, in a state of great agitation, was telling passers-by that their salvation lay with Jesus. No-one was listening to him. They fought their way on to a bus and hauled themselves up the stairs. Surrounded by unfamiliar languages and strange accents, Jane felt as though she was in a foreign country. The only English voices she could hear belonged to Fran and the insistent woman on the recording who kept telling them, again and again, that they were on the 1-0-9 – To – Croydon Town Centre.

'Do you think you'll always live in London?' she asked Fran, once they were off the bus and walking along the path at the bottom of Streatham Common.

'I can't imagine living anywhere else,' Fran said. 'Mind you, if I won the lottery or something, I'd move somewhere more central. Somewhere on a bloody tube line, for example.

I do love the Common though.' They both turned their heads slightly to admire the stately expanse of grass rolling downhill towards them, beautifully lit at this moment by a half-moon that had just emerged from behind the clouds. 'I'd miss it if I ever did move away.'

Could Jane say that about any part of Solihull now? At one time – during the delusional years – she'd loved everything about it. The parks were great; the shops were wonderful; the streets were pleasant; the town centre was picturesque and pleasing (in the daytime, at least). But now?

They walked along in silence for a few moments. Halfway along the path Fran said suddenly: 'Ever since that weekend, I keep having dreams about being attacked while I'm walking along here.'

'Do you?' said Jane, surprised not by what Fran had said but by the fact that she'd said it.

But Fran's confessional moment had passed. 'Not all the time. Just now and then. Nothing to worry about.'

They ate dinner that evening in Fran's dining-room.

'It's only something quick,' she said, wrapping salmon fillets in foil, 'but I can offer you three courses and it's Saturday night so we might as well eat in style.'

The first course was soup.

'I've been thinking . . .' Jane said slowly, trying to balance her spoon across the top of her empty bowl. 'I've been thinking about selling the house.'

'Good idea,' said Fran, getting up and disappearing into the kitchen. She raised her voice: 'It's much too big for one person. I keep telling you that. Sell it and buy somewhere smaller.'

'It's not so much the size that's bothering me,' said Jane. She put the spoon down and cradled her wine glass in both hands. 'It's the fact that it's Neil's house. He grew up there, it's always been his home. But I don't feel that it's mine anymore.' She waited for a response from Fran, but none came. 'I've been thinking about moving out of Solihull altogether,' she ventured. 'Making a completely fresh start somewhere else.' She paused again. 'Maybe move down here to London?'

'Yeah?' said Fran, returning with the salmon and busying herself unwrapping the foil parcels. 'But you don't want to live too near Lucy. You'd spend your life babysitting if you did. I've had to establish clear ground rules on that front already. And when number two comes along . . .'

Jane forced a smile. 'Not too near Lucy,' Fran had said, but what she had also heard was, 'or me, either'. It wasn't the reaction she'd been looking for. She'd thought that Fran would be enthusiastic about the idea. But it seemed she was only interested in getting Jane into a smaller dwelling – a widow's pad somewhere. Anywhere. As long as it wasn't nearby.

Jane felt deeply hurt, and rather foolish. How could she have got this so wrong? 'You invest too much in her,' Neil had said. And he was right. Well, no – he hadn't been right when he'd said it, but it was possible that he was right now. She was expecting far too much from her friendship with Fran. She took a long drink of wine. What was the matter with her? Fran wasn't hostile to the idea of her moving to London, just indifferent. But was indifference any better? She was getting this out of all proportion, especially seeing that she wasn't even sure about moving herself. She would drop the subject. She'd been silly to bring it up in the first place after she'd resolved not to say anything to either Fran or Lucy just yet.

'Shall I open another bottle?' Fran asked, refilling Jane's glass and oblivious to the distress she'd just caused.

'Why not?" said Jane. 'I'm drinking too much these days but I feel I have just cause.'

'I think we both do,' said Fran.

9

They got up late the next morning, a little bit the worse for wear. After breakfast Fran suggested they go for a walk to clear their heads. John and Lucy would be bringing Daniel over in the afternoon so they wanted to be on form by then.

They walked up to the Rookery – the formal garden tucked away, unexpectedly, at the top of the Common. Jane had never been there before but she'd heard its praises sung many times. And justifiably so, she thought, as they went through the gates. An impressive terrace afforded a wonderful view, all the way over some splendid fir trees, to the 'skyscrapers' of Croydon. And a slight frost, lingering in spite of the bright sunshine, was adding a fairy tale quality to the beauty of the place.

'Mind you don't slip,' Fran warned as they began walking down the steps which descended to a series of small gardens below. As they strolled along the paths, each leading to hidden and fresh delights, she informed Jane that the Rookery was another reason why she loved Streatham Common so much.

Given the chance, Jane felt she could get to love it too.

'I didn't know that house along the road was for sale,' Lucy said, as soon as she arrived later that afternoon. She hung her coat up in the hall and turned to her mother. 'You should go and have a look at it while you're here.'

The directness of the remark took Jane aback. 'Should I?' she said.

'Mum's been thinking about moving,' Lucy said to Fran.

She took Daniel's coat and hat off and handed them to John. 'I'm trying to persuade her to come and live down here.'

'I'm only in the very preliminary stages of thinking about it,' said Jane. Lucy should know better than to embarrass her like this. 'It's probably outside my price range, anyway.'

'Well let's see then, shall we?' said Lucy. She turned to Fran. 'Can we use your computer?'

John emptied some toys from a bag they'd brought with them and set them out on the kitchen floor for Daniel to play with. The three women crowded round Fran's laptop. Lucy tapped away knowledgeably on the keyboard, and soon the house in question appeared on the screen. Fran leaned in closer. She's not looking at it as a potential home for me, though, Jane thought. She's just interested in the asking price; she's calculating her assets.

Lucy, too, had homed in on the price and seemed to find it encouraging. 'You could easily afford that, couldn't you?' she said to her mother. 'The house in Solihull must be worth a fortune now.'

'It'd need a lot of money spending on it, on top of that,' said Fran. 'It belonged to a really old couple. It's not had anything done to it for years – for decades, probably. Look at that kitchen. And see – there's no photo of the bathroom, so you can imagine what that's like!'

'She could have it renovated,' said Lucy.

'Oh, could she?' said Jane. 'And what if she didn't want to be bothered with all that?' But, in spite of the fact that she'd specifically told the estate agent that she wasn't interested in anything that needed work doing to it, she was beginning to think that it might be exciting to renovate somewhere like that. Then she could have everything exactly as she wanted it. She could turn it into something like Fran's house – only better.

She moved closer to the laptop and instructed Lucy to go through the photos again. She wanted Fran to summon up more interest, too. But Fran was already moving away to put the kettle on.

'Ring up in the morning and we can go and have a look at it before you go,' said Lucy.

For a moment, Jane was tempted to agree to this, but: 'No,' she said. 'I couldn't face all that work.' Neither, she thought, could she impose herself where she wasn't wanted.

'Well that's a pity,' said Lucy. 'I think it could be just right for you. It'll get sold and then you'll be wishing you'd listened to me.'

Jane laughed. 'No I won't,' she said. 'I haven't decided yet that I want to move. And I certainly haven't decided that I want to move to London.'

'Of course you do,' said Lucy. 'If you leave Solihull where else would you go? Down here would be perfect.'

Fran caught Jane's eye and raised an eyebrow.

'Don't bully your mother,' John said to Lucy. 'It's a big decision and she's right to take her time over it.'

Jane smiled at him, grateful for his intervention – although she couldn't rule out the possibility that he might only be saying this because he too, like Fran, wasn't overjoyed at the prospect of having her practically on his doorstep.

Fran had made a large pot of tea and taken a cake out of the fridge. She loaded everything on to a tray and they all trooped into the dining-room. John fastened a portable child seat on to one of the dining chairs and deposited Daniel in it. There was, Jane noted, no resident highchair in Fran's house.

'Put this on him, Mum,' said Lucy, passing a bib over to her. Daniel was already reaching out for the cake and Jane had to struggle to get his arms into the bib's long blue sleeves and to fix the Velcro fastening at the back of his neck.

They had only just sat down when they heard the front door opening and a voice called out: 'It's only me.'

Jane caught Lucy's look of annoyance.

'It's Emer,' said Fran, getting up to fetch another cup and saucer from the kitchen. 'She said she might drop in.'

Emer bounced into the room. 'Hi everyone!' she beamed.

She was wearing a dark green cardigan over a black

dress. Her long red hair was held off her face by two plaits that were fastened at the back of her head. She had small gold hoops dangling from her ears. Once again she reminded Jane of Fran as she'd looked back in their sixth form days.

But Fran now was several shades less vibrant than Emer. And that was how it would go on, Jane thought, for Fran and for her. A slow, steady fading; a paling into insignificance. Not for Neil, though, he would never get any older now. Which was something else to feel aggrieved about.

Emer pulled out a chair next to Jane and sat down. 'Hi, how are you?'

'I'm well,' said Jane.

'And how's Daniel? Eating yummy cake, I see.' Emer leaned across the table and pretended to take some off his plate. Daniel squealed in protest then waited in delighted anticipation for her to try again, which she did. Then: 'Oh look. Here's some for Auntie Em,' she said showing him the piece of cake Fran had just handed her. Daniel reached out for it, not wanting the game to end, but Lucy placed a restraining hand on his.

'That's enough now,' she said. 'Eat your own cake, nicely, like a good boy.'

'This is just a flying visit,' said Emer. 'I have to be at Victoria at half past five,' (Jane caught John and Lucy exchanging glances. Who was she meeting?) 'but I thought I'd just come by and say hello to you.'

This last remark was directed at Jane who felt rather foolishly flattered.

'Have you heard anything more from the police?' Emer asked. 'About the kidnapping?'

Jane glanced at Fran. 'No,' she said. 'Their investigations don't seem to have led anywhere.'

'Which you already know,' said Fran.

'And there have been no repercussions for you?' Emer said, ignoring her mother. 'I mean . . . seeing that it was you he thought he was dealing with.'

'No. I've not seen or heard anything from him.'

'Which you also already know,' said Fran.

Again Emer ignored her. 'It must be very unsettling for you,' she said. 'I don't know about you two,' she looked first at John and then at Lucy, 'but I think it's weird the police haven't come up with anything. They must know whose cottage it was, at least.'

'For Christ's sake!' said Fran, her voice rising in exasperation. 'I've already told you this. They do know who owned it but it hasn't got them anywhere. The owner didn't live there. It'd been unoccupied for a very long time. Anyone could have broken in and used it. Which my young man obviously did.'

'Except he didn't break in, did he? He had a key. And,' Emer gave an exaggerated groan, 'I do wish you'd stop calling him your young man. I'm beginning to think you've got Munchausen's Syndrome or something.'

'You don't mean Munchausen's,' said John.

'No, you don't.' Lucy's laugh had a triumphant tinge to it. 'Isn't that when you pretend to be ill when you're not?'

'OK. But you know what I mean. The one where you get too close to your captors. What's it called? Stockhausen Syndrome?'

'Stockhausen's a composer,' said Fran.

'Oh, for fuck's sake!'

'Oh! Auntie Emer! Little ears!' said Lucy, pointing at Daniel.

'Uhh . . . sorry,' said Emer pulling a guilty face. 'What the . . . is it called then?'

'Stockholm,' said Jane. 'Stockholm Syndrome.'

Fran snorted. 'Well I'm certainly not suffering from that. Or any other syndrome, for that matter,' she said. 'I can honestly say, hand on heart,' she placed both hands, palms down, on her chest, 'that I've never, not even for one moment, thought that my young man was either Swedish or a musician.'

Daniel joined in the laughter that followed this remark, provoking even more hilarity.

'OK, I give up,' said Emer, rising to her feet. 'I'm out of here.' She smiled at Jane. 'It was good to see you again. Take care, won't you?'

'I will. And you, too,' said Jane. They're laughing, she thought, but Emer could well be right. Fran had consistently defended her 'young man'. She wasn't at all bothered that he'd never been caught. Perhaps she had been too emotionally involved.

The front door slammed behind Emer and Fran got up and went into the kitchen to make some more tea.

'So Emer won't be here for Christmas?' Lucy called out to her.

Jane flashed her a warning look across the table.

'No,' Fran called back. 'She's still going to New York.'

'I've already told you that,' John said to Lucy.

Fran came back into the room.

'I've been trying to persuade Mum to come to us for Christmas,' said Lucy, avoiding Jane's eye.

Jane sat very still and stared into the middle distance.

'And?' Fran said, looking quizzically at Jane.

'And I made it quite clear that that wasn't going to happen.'

There was an awkward silence. Fran poured more tea into their cups.

'I'm sorry,' said Lucy, her tone totally unrepentant. 'I just thought . . .' She sniffed, once, twice, the tears threatening to start. 'It's going to be so awful at home, at Christmas, without Dad. I don't think I can bear it.' She looked from John to Fran but neither of them responded to this plea for sympathy. She sniffed again. 'But I can see,' she said turning to her mother, 'that you're not going to change your mind. Not after you've ordered the turkey.'

The temptation to tell Lucy, there and then, about the cottage was almost overwhelming. 'If you must know . . .' Jane began, and then, thinking better of it, changed course. 'It's got nothing to do with the fucking turkey!'

They all shot quick glances at Daniel. Lucy gave a gasp –

but more of surprise than disapproval. 'OK,' she said. 'If it means that much to you . . .'

'It does,' said Jane, returning Fran's look.

The train was crowded. There was no window seat available, depriving Jane of the opportunity to turn her attention away from her fellow passengers. Everyone in the carriage seemed to be attached to some electronic device or other, most of which were emitting annoying little noises. Trivial mobile phone conversations were another source of irritation. It was going to be a long, tedious journey.

She had Mrs Dalloway in her handbag. She had read it several times before but had brought it with her because it was about London. But she hadn't opened it all weekend; and she wasn't going to now.

When the train slowed into High Wycombe station, a handful of people got off and Jane changed seats. Now, trying to block out everything going on around her, she could stare out of the window and think her thoughts against the moving backdrop of Chiltern Line countryside. She'd had enough of London with all its pendulum swings of emotion. She would be glad to get home.

Home is where the heart is, she thought ruefully. But where was her heart now? Long after she'd married and had children, she'd still referred to the house she'd grown up in as 'home'. 'I'm coming home,' she would say to her mother. And 'home' was Lancashire, too, where she came 'from'.

Solihull was where she lived now, in a house which, until recently, she'd thought of as 'home'. But it wasn't where she was 'from'. It was where Lucy and Sarah were 'from', though. And they would keep returning there until . . . well, until she got rid of the house. They would continue to visit her in her new abode – wherever that might be – but it wouldn't be 'home' for them. Would it become home for her, she wondered? Or was she destined to feel homeless for ever?

Oh God! she thought. She must stop thinking like this. The physical moving could wait. It was the psychological 'moving on' she needed to concentrate on. Tomorrow she would go to school; on Friday she would go to her class; she would carry on with her preparations for Christmas. And once she'd told Lucy and Sarah about their father's cottage, then she could begin to 'let it go.'

When the train reached Leamington Spa she found herself thinking, nearly home now. Home, that is, where I hang my hat; not home where my (broken) heart is.

ANSWERS

1

With just over two weeks to go, Jane was trying to focus on her preparations for Christmas. She had bought or ordered most of her presents and had just started writing her cards. She was keeping this simple – no chatty little news messages in them this year – but already she had had to rewrite one or two after automatically signing them 'from Jane and Neil'.

What was really preoccupying her, though, was how she was going to tell Lucy and Sarah about their father and the cottage. How would they react, she wondered? And, more interestingly, how did she want them to react? Did she want them to feel the same hurt and anger she herself had felt when she'd first found out, or did she want to protect them from some of that pain? She knew that, to a large extent, it would depend on how she presented the whole thing. She kept rehearsing how she might go about it, experimenting with a range of possible scenarios: different times of day; various stage settings; alternative scripts. It was an absorbing past-time.

A few days after she'd returned from her trip to London, she was upstairs, about to change out of the clothes she'd been wearing to school, when the doorbell rang. She went down, noting with approval as she did so that she was no longer apprehensive about answering the door. She had stopped thinking that it might be Fran's young man.

She looked inquiringly at the middle-aged woman who was standing on the doorstep.

'Jane,' the woman said. (*Jane!* And a statement not a question.) 'I'm Sylvia Ashworth. We did meet once, a very long time ago, but you probably don't remember me.'

Jane didn't, but her heart began to beat faster. This must be it then.

'I used to be a receptionist – at the Warwick Road practice.'

'You'd better come in.' Jane opened the door wider. I've been expecting you, or at least someone like you, she thought, her accelerating heartbeats thundering in her ears.

They stood in the hall looking at each other. This woman, with her grey hair and glasses, was much older and much more ordinary looking than Jane had been imagining her to be.

'Shall I take your coat?' she heard herself saying.

The woman removed her gloves and fumbled her way out of her long, heavy, camel coloured coat. Underneath it she was wearing a charcoal trouser suit and a red blouse. She was probably on her way home from work, Jane thought, feeling momentarily relieved that she herself was still smartly dressed from her day at school. If this woman had arrived a few minutes later she would have been in her old tracksuit. She took the coat and hung it up in the alcove (on top of the green cagoule, the fate of which was still undecided), then turned and led the way into the kitchen.

She had been waiting for this encounter. She had known that it would happen sometime – in spite of what Fran kept saying about her speculations. She felt suddenly and unexpectedly calm, her heart rate almost back to normal. The other woman, though, looked very uncomfortable. She glanced, almost furtively, round the large room and then stood there, twisting her gloves in her hands.

Jane had no intention of putting her at ease. 'I'm sorry,' she said, her tone neutral, her expression impassive. 'What did you say your name was?'

'Sylvia – Sylvia Ashworth.'

'Sylvia . . . ?' Did she remember a Sylvia?

'I was Broadhurst back then,' the woman offered.

Ashworth, Broadhurst – neither name meant anything to Jane. Who is Silvia? / What is she? she thought. But she knew who this Sylvia was. There were more interesting questions to be asked now.

She flung out her hand, indicating that they should sit down. When they were facing each other across the kitchen table, she said: 'Well anyway, what can I do for you . . . Sylvia?'

'You know why I'm here, don't you?' the woman said. Her accent was decidedly Brummie. She reminded Jane of Liz.

'I have a good idea.'

'I thought I'd come and . . . explain about the cottage. You do know now that Neil still owned it?'

Jane nodded, flinching at this woman's casual use of her husband's name.

'And your . . . friend. How is she?'

'She's fine,' said Jane. 'So you know about the . . . abduction?'

Sylvia nodded.

'It was you who told the police where she was, wasn't it?'

Sylvia nodded again.

'So you know who abducted her?'

'That's why I'm here.' Sylvia paused. 'It was my son.'

It was Jane's turn to nod her head now, which she did slowly and at length, hoping that she was conveying her lack of surprise. Because she wasn't surprised; it was what she'd been thinking ever since she'd seen the football duvet in the small bedroom at the cottage. What was surprising, though, was that this woman was admitting it so openly. Did she not think that Jane would go straight to the police with this information once she had left?

'OK . . . ?'

But Sylvia hadn't finished speaking. 'My son – and Neil's,' she said.

Jane sat very still as this piece of information seeped into her consciousness.

He was Neil's son! Of course he was! It made perfect sense. It had been there as a possibility all along only she hadn't been able – or willing – to see it. Neil hadn't kept the cottage because of this Sylvia woman; he'd kept it because he'd had another child – a son. He'd had two families, and the main one had known nothing about the other. You heard about things like that. About how the second family only came to light when the man (because it was always the man) died. Her mind flashed back to Neil's funeral. Had Sylvia been there at the crematorium, lurking in the background, grieving separately from the rest of them? Had her son been with her? But even if she'd seen them, she wouldn't have had any idea who they were.

The silence lengthened. Jane thought she was presenting a picture of outward calm but Sylvia said: 'Perhaps we should have this conversation another time, when you've got over the shock.'

'No!' This came out louder than Jane had intended. 'No,' she repeated more quietly. 'I want you to tell me everything.'

She got up and put the kettle on, then, realising what she was doing, switched it off and sat down again. What was she thinking? This wasn't a social visit. She was under no obligation to be hospitable.

'His name's Mark,' said Sylvia. 'I know – and he knows, too – that what he did that weekend was really crazy. But he would never have harmed your . . . friend. He's a good boy; he always has been.'

He doesn't take after his father, then, thought Jane. 'How old is he?' she asked, noting Sylvia's use of the word 'boy'. Fran had said that he was in his early twenties.

'He was twenty two last week. A little bit younger than your Sarah.'

Your Sarah! – whose twenty-second birthday had been in early October. They could almost be twins, for God's sake! Jane gave a harsh laugh. 'Well, you seem to know all about us,' she said. 'So go on and tell me all about you and Neil. And Mark.'

'Well like I said, I used to be a receptionist at the Warwick Road surgery,' Sylvia said, settling into her story. 'I was married then, that's why I was Broadhurst. Ashworth's my maiden name. Well I say married, but we'd just split up. I wanted children, you see, and he decided he didn't. So that was that as far as the marriage was concerned. I was in a bit of a state and Neil was very kind to me. I was flattered, I suppose, and I . . . I made myself very available.'

Jane stared hard at the middle-aged woman sitting opposite her, trying to imagine what she might have looked like twenty-two years ago. Even without the grey hair and glasses she couldn't have been much of a looker. So what was the attraction? And Fran's words came back to her: you were the pretty one. Well yes, she'd have been prettier than this woman. But this woman had made herself 'available' and Neil had obliged. How many other such opportunities had he 'availed' himself of, over the course of their married life, she wondered?

'I told him I was still on the Pill,' Sylvia went on, avoiding Jane's eye, 'but I wasn't. I wanted to get pregnant. I felt time was slipping by and I had to seize the chance while I had it. That's what it was all about really. I wanted a baby. Neil was a bit incidental, I'm afraid. I liked him but I wasn't in love with him or anything. Anyway, then he told me that you were pregnant . . .'

Jane's eyes filled with tears and she turned her head aside so that Sylvia wouldn't see them. She was remembering how excited they'd been when this pregnancy was confirmed. They'd been trying for over two years and were beginning to think it would never happen. They had been overjoyed. Both of them. But how overjoyed would she have been had she known that her husband was impregnating another woman at the same time?

Sylvia didn't seem to notice Jane's distress. 'He said we had to stop seeing each other,' she said. 'I was disappointed. But like I said I wasn't in love with him.' She shrugged. 'Then a few weeks later I discovered that I was pregnant too. I couldn't believe my luck. But I didn't tell him because I thought he'd probably ask me to get rid of it and that was the last thing I wanted to do. I handed in my notice before I started to show. I let him think it was because I was finding it too upsetting to stay there. I told him I'd got another job but I hadn't.'

She stopped talking and waited until Jane looked directly at her again.

'I never meant for him to find out' she said. 'I didn't want to make any claims on him. I was going to do it all on my own.'

Jane gave a strained, twisted smile.

'No, honestly,' Sylvia insisted. 'I'd got what I wanted and I thought that was the end of it as far as Neil was concerned. When Mark was born I moved in with my mother. I couldn't really afford my own place anymore and I needed someone to help look after him when I did go back to work. She only had a two-bedroom council flat and it was very overcrowded, but . . .' She trailed off and took a long, panoramic look round the large kitchen.

'And Neil knew nothing about it – about him?' said Jane.

'No.'

'So how did he find out?'

'When Mark was about six months old I got a part-time job at another practice. Neil knew one of the dentists, and it came up in conversation that I was working there, and that I'd got a young baby. He came round to see me. He was very agitated. I told him I'd got back with my husband and the baby was his, but he didn't believe me. The maths didn't really work out. I told him I didn't want anything from him but he said he couldn't just walk away from his responsibilities. He was very upset.' She paused, waiting for Jane to react. 'He just wanted to do the right thing,' she said.

'The right thing!' Jane didn't want to let this woman see how upset she was, but she couldn't keep the bitterness out of her voice. 'Well pardon me if I'm not as impressed as you are by his moral rectitude.'

'I know this must be very upsetting for you,' said Sylvia, 'but I'm only trying to explain how it was.'

It struck Jane that this woman, who at the outset of their encounter had seemed so nervous and uncomfortable, was now firmly in control of the situation. 'Let's just stick to the facts, shall we?' she said, coldly. 'I'll make my own judgements.'

'He wanted to see Mark,' Sylvia said. She gave Jane a long look before adding: 'He couldn't help being pleased that he was a boy.'

Jane tried not to react to this. Neil had always wanted a son, and when they'd had another girl, she'd expected him to suggest that they try again. It had been a relief that he never did – two children had been quite enough for her – but she'd often wondered why. Well, now she knew.

'He started giving me money for Mark,' Sylvia went on. 'I didn't want to take it, but he insisted. Then, when Mark was about a year old, he took me to see the cottage. He said he'd inherited it and was going to get it fixed up so that I could use it whenever I wanted. He could see how cramped we were in my mother's flat. He said it would be somewhere he could come to see Mark. I asked him – I said, what about you? – and he said you thought it'd been sold, so it would be quite safe for us to use it.'

Jane shook her head and sniffed.

'I went there a lot when Mark was little. At weekends mostly. It's a bit remote, and at first I was scared of staying there on my own, but it's only a few minutes drive to the village and I got used to it. Neil would just come and spend an afternoon with us. Occasionally, a whole day.' She paused.

'He hardly ever stayed overnight.'

She wants me to ask, Jane thought, trying hard not to but unable to resist: 'So you were sleeping together again?'

'Once or twice. Not for long. Like I said before, it was never what you'd call a love affair. It really wasn't.'

'And he talked about us – about me and the girls?'

'Sometimes.'

'And what did you tell your son, when he got older?'

'That his dad lived somewhere else and came to see us when he could. At first he didn't think it was that unusual. Lots of kids in his class at school had strange family set-ups. He loved it when Neil did come to the cottage. He used to take him to football matches, too.

'But when he got to be a teenager, he didn't want to keep going there at weekends. And when he got old enough to go to the football with his mates he began to resent Neil making any demands on his time. He started asking all kinds of questions – about what his dad did and where he lived, and about you and your family. He used to get very angry. He felt he was less important to Neil than you lot were. He kept saying he was going to find out where you lived and go round to your house and tell you who he was.

'Then Neil wanted him to stay on at school and do some A-levels but he wouldn't listen. He kept saying he didn't want to be like Lucy and Sarah. He didn't know their names then, but he did know that he had two half sisters. Anyway, they had some huge rows about this. And as time went on they saw less and less of each other. Over the past few years, they hardly saw each other at all. And then we heard that he'd died. It was a massive shock. I expect it was for you, too.'

Jane gave Sylvia a stony stare. How dare she compare their two families! It was unbelievable.

'Mark was upset – and confused. I think he felt guilty because he'd been the reason their relationship had deteriorated like it did. But he was still angry. He felt he deserved some sort of recognition . . . that we both did. He wanted me to contact you but I said no. I told him I'd never made any demands before and I wasn't going to start now. So he . . . kind of lost patience with me and decided he was going to talk to you himself. That's what he was trying to do that weekend.'

'I think he came here once before that,' said Jane. 'If it was him he didn't say who he was or what he wanted. He just rang the doorbell, made something up and then went away.' (She wished now that she had paid more attention to this caller.)

'Did he? I didn't know that.' Sylvia sounded a bit annoyed.

'Then he came again . . .'

'Yes. It was a really crazy thing to do, kidnapping someone like that. He thought it was you, but that's no excuse. I don't know what he was thinking. He didn't plan it. It just sort of happened.'

'And you knew nothing about it?'

'No, of course I didn't. Not until I saw that news item on the television on that Monday evening. Then I put two and two together. He'd been acting strange all weekend, coming and going and not letting me or his girlfriend know where he was or what he was doing.

'He would've brought your friend back on the Friday evening, you know, if his van hadn't broken down. He texted me to see if he could borrow my car but it'd gone in for a service and they'd found something wrong with it. I thought it would be fixed by Saturday lunchtime but it wasn't. And then on the Monday the garage was waiting for a spare part so it still wasn't ready.'

Jane couldn't keep up with all this. 'You seem to have been exceedingly unfortunate with your vehicles,' she murmured.

'He got into such a panic when I told him he couldn't have it on the Monday either,' Sylvia continued. 'And then I saw it on the news! I heard your name mentioned, and I saw your friend's picture, and I knew straight away that Mark had something to do with her disappearance. I cross-questioned him and eventually he owned up and said she was at the cottage. We still had the keys, you see. He said he was going to let her go as soon as he could get transport. That would have been the next day, though, and I knew that . . . Well anyway, I phoned the police. He didn't want me to at first. He was scared. He didn't want there to be any connection to the cottage. But I told him that . . . I was too worried to leave her there any longer.'

There was a long silence. Jane felt drained of emotion. She knew there were lots of questions she should be asking, but for the moment she couldn't think what they might be. 'Would you like some tea?' she asked instead.

'If it's not too much trouble,' Sylvia replied.

Jane got up and switched the kettle back on. 'How did you find out that Neil had died?' she said. 'Who told you?'

'We just heard . . .'

'It was Liz Hartley, wasn't it?' Jane put three spoonsful of tea into the pot and turned round to face Sylvia. 'She's known about you and Mark all along, hasn't she? And about the cottage? She's a friend of yours, isn't she?'

Sylvia said nothing.

'Who else knew? Did Martin Williams know?'

But Sylvia wasn't going to say anything on this subject. So Jane would have to remain uncertain about Martin. But she'd been right about Liz and the bloody keys! And Liz must have left the name Sylvia Ashworth (or Broadhurst, or whatever she called herself) off the list of receptionists she'd given to the police. With or without Martin's collusion.

'Why have you come here and told me all this?' she said. 'You know I'll go straight to the police now and your son will be arrested.'

'You won't have to,' said Sylvia, 'because that's what we're going to do now – inform the police. We reckon it's just a matter of time before they find out about us, so we've taken some legal advice and been told that the best thing Mark can do is hand himself in.'

'I see,' said Jane. She hadn't been expecting this.

'If he pleads guilty and says how sorry he is then the police, or whoever it is who decides these things, might not press charges,' said Sylvia. 'And even if they do, well, there're a lot of mitigating circumstances to be taken into account. It wasn't pre-meditated, he's not going to do anything like it again, he has no previous convictions . . .'

'But it was a serious offence,' said Jane. 'He forcibly abducted Frances, then held her against her will for three days and nights.'

'Yes, I know. But he didn't mistreat her. And if she was prepared to make a favourable statement to that effect . . .'

So that's it, thought Jane. That's why she's come here before going to the police. Not to put me out of my misery but to see if Fran might speak up on her son's behalf.

The kettle switched itself off and she poured the boiling water into the tea-pot.

'Whatever makes you think she'd do that?' Jane carried two cups and saucers over to the table and then went back for the tea-pot and milk jug. 'I wouldn't if I were her,' she said, sitting back down and staring at Sylvia.

Fran, of course, had already made a reasonably favourable statement and would, in all probability, be prepared to add to it. But Jane wasn't going to let this woman know that. Not yet, anyway.

'Mark tells me she's Lucy's mother-in-law,' said Sylvia.

'Is that relevant?'

'Well, he is Lucy's half-brother – and Sarah's. That might mean something.'

Jane gave a scornful laugh. 'It means nothing to me,' she said, busying herself with the tea things. And as for Frances . . . Well, like I said, it was a horrible thing that happened to her. She's still affected by it. If you'd gone to the police straight away instead of waiting all this time, that might have helped, but you didn't, did you? You're asking a lot.'

Sylvia bit her lip and turned her head to the side. Jane, following her gaze, was slightly discomfited to see that it had come to rest on the bottle of whisky sitting on the work-top by the sink.

Strange as it may sound, though,' she went on, relenting slightly (and hoping to regain Sylvia's attention), 'she grew quite fond of your son over that weekend. Although, I have to say, she might not have done if she'd known who his father was. There was no love lost between her and Neil.'

'Wasn't there?' Sylvia said, giving Jane a long, level look. She paused. 'Have you known her long?'

Jane frowned. What a funny thing to ask, she thought. 'We were at school together,' she said.

They drank their tea in silence for a few moments.

'You really had no idea about the cottage or any of this, did you?' Sylvia said.

Jane felt herself flushing. 'No,' she said. 'Not until the police told me that it still belonged to Neil. It was like you said – I thought he'd sold it years ago. He covered his tracks well. I never had any reason to suspect anything.'

How pathetic this sounded. As if she was seeking sympathy. As if she expected this woman to say: 'I'm so sorry Jane for all the pain I've caused you.' But she could see that Sylvia wasn't here to express any regret for the trouble she'd caused. Why, exactly was she here, though? She kept emphasising that she'd never wanted money. So did she want something else? Like . . . what was the expression she'd used – some sort of recognition? Whatever that meant.

'He was going to sell it, you know,' Sylvia said.

(No, actually, I didn't know!)

'We hardly used it anymore. I'd already cleared most of our things out, but when I heard he'd died, I thought you were bound to find out about it then – I thought it might be in his will or something – so I didn't go back again.'

His will. Was that why she was here? Did she think Neil might have left them something in his will?

Jane shook her head. 'There was no mention of it,' she said. 'If your son hadn't kidnapped Frances, I might never have found out. Although I think he'd have made sure I did, one way or another, don't you?'

Sylvia said nothing.

'The picture over the fireplace,' Jane said. 'Did you paint it?'

Sylvia looked surprised. 'Yeah, I did it years ago,' she said. 'I did lots more, but that was the only one that ever got framed.' She smiled. 'I loved going there. Even after Mark wouldn't go anymore I'd go by myself sometimes, for the odd day or just for the afternoon, and do some painting. I . . .' She stopped, possibly realising that she was revealing too much about herself. 'I used to check with Neil first, though,' she said, looking attentively at Jane again, 'just to make sure he wouldn't be there at the same time.'

Jane was momentarily puzzled by this remark. Surely she wasn't saying that Neil went there on his own sometimes? Then she realised this wasn't quite what Sylvia was implying.

'Are you saying he took other women there?' she said.

Sylvia shrugged. 'Who knows?' she said carelessly.

The thought obviously didn't bother her. But then, he hadn't been her husband; she had never, by her own admission, been in love with him, so why should she care?

She seemed keen to make the point though. 'I don't know whether I was his first,' she said, 'but I doubt if I was his last.'

Later that evening, Jane rang Fran. She wasn't quite ready to talk about all this yet, but Patrick was due home for Christmas the next day and she felt it wouldn't be appropriate to leave it until then.

'Hi, it's me,' she said, trying to keep her tone casual.

'I wasn't expecting you to ring tonight,' Fran said. 'Are you all right?'

'I'm fine. I just thought I'd let you know that I met Neil's speculative mistress this afternoon.'

There was a long silence.

'What are you talking about?'

'His mistress. She came here, to the house, would you believe? Your young man – his name's Mark, by the way – is her son, just like I said he was. And she's the woman who told the police where you were.'

'No shit! And she admitted all this?'

'Oh yes. But I've not told you the best bit yet. Neil didn't keep the cottage for her. He kept it because this Mark is his son too.'

The silence on the other end of the phone was prolonged.

'Well say something,' said Jane.

'No!'

'Yes! Your young man is Neil's son. It all makes sense now, doesn't it? She told me all about their little affair and their lives since. So now I know everything.'

She proceeded to give a summary of what Sylvia had told her. And for once she felt she had Fran's full attention.

'Wow! So what happens now?' Fran asked when she'd finished.

'She wants you, as the victim of the crime, to put in a good word for him. Say what a wonderful, kind and considerate abductor he was.'

'OK, but I've always said he was harmless, haven't I? I'd just be telling the truth.'

'Well, that's up to you. I expect we'll be hearing from the police in the morning.' She gave a mirthless laugh. 'I've really got something to tell Lucy and Sarah now, haven't I?'

They talked for a bit longer. Fran said that, all things considered, it had to be a good thing that Jane had some answers to her questions at long last. It might be painful right now, but in the long run . . . There was another silence. Then: What's she like?' she asked. 'I mean, what does she look like?'

'Well, that's the thing,' said Jane. 'I've been imagining someone very attractive, but she's very ordinary. Plain, grey hair, glasses. And she's older than us I'd say. Possibly older than Neil, even.'

'Yeah?'

When the call came to an end, Jane got up out of the rocking chair and went to put the handset back on the hall table. As she was doing so she caught sight of her tear-stained, swollen face in the mirror above it. After the Sylvia woman had left she had gone upstairs, lain down on her bed and wept. Something she hadn't done for a while – at least not with such violence and abandon.

Fran, listening to her on the phone, could have had no idea just how painful – how devastating – Sylvia's revelations had been for her.

2

Fran was right; knowing – as opposed to speculating – was better than not knowing, but this new information was very upsetting.

Jane kept going over and over what Sylvia had told her. What Neil had done had been a terrible betrayal. He'd had an affair with another woman (a very ordinary-looking woman, older than his wife). That was bad enough, but it was the timing of the affair that made it so much harder to bear. How could he have embarked on it when he did – when she'd thought they'd been concentrating all their efforts on having another baby? 'I made myself very available', this Sylvia woman had said. As if that were a good enough reason. As if no man could possibly have resisted her extreme ordinariness! And it wasn't as if I hadn't been 'very available' too, she thought angrily. No, there could be no excuse for his behaviour.

Sylvia had said that he'd called a halt to proceedings as soon as he'd found out she was pregnant. Well how very noble of him! What would have happened, she wondered, if she hadn't been pregnant? How long would the affair have lasted then? Not very long, surely, because who was she, anyway, this Sylvia? Just an ordinary-looking receptionist with whom Neil could have had nothing in common. Nothing, that is, until they'd had a son together.

Without that little complication, Jane told herself, the affair would have been short-lived, and he would have sold the cottage just as he'd always intended to. But with that little complication, he – how did Sylvia put it? – he just wanted to do the right thing. Well perhaps . . . just perhaps . . . she could understand that. Deceiving her had been a terrible thing to do, but once he had started along that path she could see that it would have been hard to backtrack. And the double life he'd led – much too slight to call double, really – had never really impinged on her life or that of her children, had it? OK, he'd been absent sometimes when otherwise he would've been present, but that hadn't bothered them at the time.

Hang on! What the hell was she saying here? That he had become a victim of circumstance? Well yes, maybe, but the circumstance was entirely of his own making. She shouldn't be making excuses for him, for God's sake!

The next morning, while Jane was at school, Debbie Mason sent her a text message. Ring me when you can re massive development. At lunchtime, Jane obeyed this command, staying behind in the classroom so that no-one would overhear the conversation.

'So . . . he has handed himself in then,' she said. 'I suppose his mother told you we had a long conversation yesterday evening?'

'She did. It must all be a terrible shock for you,' said DC Mason, echoing what she had said to Jane, weeks ago, when she'd found out about the cottage.

'It's not very pleasant,' Jane said, forcing a laugh. 'But I know now which is the main thing.

'Yes. I've spoken to Frances and she's relieved that it's all been explained, too.'

'What happens now?'

'Well, there'll be reports and statements and reviews of the case. It's a pity he didn't do this weeks ago. But still, he's done it now, and he's sorry, and seeing that he's of previous good character and there are mitigating circumstances . . . We'll need to see Frances again, of course. And soon. But if she's prepared to accept all this, he stands a good chance – of getting off lightly, at least.'

'What about DS Hooper? Will she make things difficult

for him?'

DC Mason laughed. 'I couldn't possibly comment on that,' she said. 'But at the end of the day it's up to the CPS.'

'They want me to come up to Solihull and review my statement, and things like that,' Fran said that evening. 'Next Thursday, would you believe?'

'Why don't you stay overnight?'

'I was thinking of getting Patrick to drive up with me.'

'You could both stay.'

'Yes . . . we could. If you're sure it's not too much hassle for you just before Christmas?'

'No, I've got everything under control.'

This was true at the practical level. Most of the food had been bought; Bronia was on top of all the housework-y jobs; the Christmas decorations were ready at hand. She's been wondering whether she should bother with these – under the circumstances – but Daniel was old enough to appreciate Christmas this year so she'd decided to make the effort. She would just tone things down a bit, go for a more subdued aesthetic: lots of holly and silver-frosted pine cones; white fairy lights around the dining-room walls; snowflakes on the window in his bedroom.

She had also been wondering about the Christmas tree. (Up to now, of course, this had always been Neil's responsibility – buying a suitable one and erecting it properly being a skilled job for which only he was equipped.) Maybe this year they should have a smaller one than usual as another gesture of mourning? (Or an even bigger one as an act of defiance?) In the end she'd decided to wait until John arrived. He could help her make a dispassionate choice, and do all the necessary lifting and carrying. They would muddle on somehow.

Fran and Patrick went straight to the police station when they arrived in Solihull on Thursday afternoon. It was nearly teatime when they got to Jane's house. She was home from school and had just started preparing their evening meal. Patrick brought their overnight bags straight in with him. There would be no going out to get them later, on this visit.

'All done then?' Jane asked.

'Yes, and what a rigmarole it was,' said Fran.

She'd added to her original statement, she told Jane, maintaining that all the new information now in her possession only served to reinforce her view that her abductor had been a misguided but essentially harmless young man who had constituted no real threat to her health and safety. She had then been assessed by a medical person whom she had assured that she was in good shape both physically and mentally. (She made no mention of the dreams she'd been having, Jane noted.)

She'd been given a copy of a letter from Mark, she said, in which he expressed his deep regret for what he'd done. She patted her handbag to indicate its presence. He'd offered to meet with her so that he could apologise in person if she so wished, and she'd been tempted to accept this offer – she'd have liked to have had a few words with him. But . . . she'd decided that it was probably best that she didn't see him again.

Finally, she'd been told (by the obnoxious DS Hooper) that she would be informed, in due course, of the decision of the Crown Prosecution Service, but that, in any event, it was most unlikely she would have to appear at any further hearing that might take place.

'So that's that then,' she said. 'All over and done with as far as I'm concerned.'

I wish I could say the same, thought Jane, smiling at them both. She felt a little awkward, embarrassed even, with Patrick there. She hardly knew him – yet he knew all these intimate details about her marriage.

She spent the evening watching him and Fran closely. They were a married couple, she kept reminding herself, and Patrick would be home for good in March. This was something she needed to think about. It was bound to have some effect on her relationship with Fran. Their phone calls, for instance, would have to be less frequent – and much shorter. And also, if Jane were to move to London . . .

The conversation seemed to have moved back to the abduction weekend.

'I wonder if I should've agreed to meet him?' Fran was saying.

'It might've helped,' said Patrick.

'I wasn't aware I needed help. And I'm warning you! If you say the word "closure" I'll throttle you. No, I meant it would've been interesting to talk to him.'

'What's happening with the cottage?' Patrick asked Jane. 'Is it for sale?'

'Not yet. Apparently there's still a lot of paperwork to be sorted out.'

'I'd quite like to go and see it,' he said. He turned to Fran. 'You might not think you need it, but I wouldn't mind a bit of "closure".' Then: 'Oh, I'm sorry Jane. That was insensitive, wasn't it?'

'Yes, it was!' said Fran.

'No,' said Jane. 'I think it's a good idea.'

Now that she knew about Sylvia and Mark, she would like to have another look at the cottage herself. And it would prepare her for when she took Lucy and Sarah there after Christmas. She looked at Fran. 'We could go in the morning. If you can face it . . .?'

'Of course I can "face it",' Fran said, sounding annoyed. 'If you two want to go, then let's go.'

3

'Did you sleep all right?' Jane asked at breakfast the next morning.

'Yes, thank you,' said Fran. She had, in fact, slept very badly. She suspected that she'd had the dream again, but she couldn't quite remember.

'Are you sure you want to do this?' said Patrick.

'Yeah, it's no big deal,' said Fran. It was a bit late for him to be expressing concern, for Christ's sake. There was no way she could back out now without losing face.

They decided to take two cars because Jane said it would be silly for Fran and Patrick to come all the way back to Solihull when they could get straight on to the motorway near Medworth. 'There's a nice old pub there, too,' she said, 'where we can have lunch before you go.'

'Lovely,' said Fran, her heart sinking. This trip was promising to be more of an ordeal than the fucking abduction weekend had been.

She went in the car with Jane; Patrick followed behind.

'If this is all too much for you . . .' said Jane.

'Of course it's not. In fact, I'm quite looking forward to seeing the old place again.'

When they got to Medworth, Jane pointed out the pub. 'That's it,' she said. 'The Barge Pole. It looks nice, doesn't it? And the food's supposed to be very good.'

Fran glanced at the pub where she and Neil had had Sunday lunch (the food had indeed been very good), and then, as they drove across the bridge over the canal, she saw the steps leading down to the towpath where they'd gone for a stroll afterwards.

Jane turned the car off the main road and drove down the track leading to the cottage. Fran, thinking about her bumpy ride in the back of the van, found that she could re-live that experience with equanimity. It wasn't the abduction that was the problem here.

'Are you all right?' Patrick asked as they got out of the cars.

'I'm fine,' she said.

It was a dull, overcast day, and the electricity was still off. Jane opened the shutters but the living-room was still very gloomy.

'We had the lights on all the time, so it didn't look as dark as this,' Fran said. She didn't want them getting the wrong impression.

They looked round the living room and then went into the kitchen. It was all as Fran remembered it – from the last weekend she'd spent there, that was, not from the first one which she was trying her best not to think about at all.

They carried on through to the bathroom where both Jane and Patrick spent what seemed to Fran like an inordinate length of time, standing in the doorway, gazing into the bath.

'Would you like me to lie down in it? she said. 'I could go upstairs and get the duvets so you can get the full effect?'

They moved away, but she stayed a while longer, recollecting her final few minutes in there on that last evening. She'd been sitting on the floor with her head on her knees when she'd heard the banging and shouting. Unable to account for the commotion and thinking that she was in new danger, she'd struggled to her feet. But there had been nowhere to hide. It wasn't until she'd heard voices calling her name, and the sound of the key turning in the lock on the other side of the door, that she'd realised she was being rescued.

Without thinking what she was doing, Fran followed Jane and Patrick up the stairs. Patrick confined himself to a quick glance around both bedrooms and then retreated, leaving her alone with Jane in the main one. The shutters were closed and there was barely enough light to see. Feeling very uneasy, she began backing away from the door.

But Jane wasn't ready to leave. 'I've been thinking all sorts of things this last week,' she said. 'I was even coming round to thinking that perhaps I could forgive him for the affair. You know, what with the stress of us trying to conceive and this Sylvia woman throwing herself at him. I was thinking . . . Oh, I don't know what I was thinking! But coming here again now, to this bedroom . . .' Jane shook her head and sat down heavily on the edge of the bed. 'What I absolutely can't forgive,' she went on with a catch in her voice, 'is that they went on sleeping together, here.' She thumped the mattress with her fist.

Fran made an involuntary movement, as if she had been on the receiving end of the blow.

'It was supposed to be over,' Jane went on, her voice rising. 'But as soon as he'd fixed up this place – which was supposed to be for his little son – there they were, at it again. How can I forgive that?' She thumped the bed again, more viciously this time. 'If they'd been "in love" I might be able to understand, but they weren't. She made sure I knew that – "it was never a love affair". No, the simple fact is that my husband was a cheating bastard. He's dead, anyway. He doesn't care whether I forgive him or not. I don't know why I keep on torturing myself like this.'

Fran was a loss for words. All this pain and heartache. All this . . . consequence.

Jane gave a shaky laugh. 'Sorry,' she said, trying to pull herself together. 'It's being here that's doing this to me.' She stood up.

Fran stood staring at the dent that Jane's fist had left in the mattress.

'Sorry!' Jane said again. 'I know it can't be pleasant for you either. Come on, let's go.'

She led the way downstairs.

'Are you OK?' Patrick said, putting an arm round Fran.

'Of course I am,' she murmured.

Jane went to close the shutters.

'What happened to that?' Fran asked, having a last look round and noticing the picture propped up on the mantelpiece.

'I took it down to see if there was anything written on the back,' said Jane. 'It turns out she painted it.' She went and picked it up. 'I think I'll take it home with me. I might give it back to her if I ever see her again.'

Fran raised her eyebrows. 'Will you – see her again, I mean?'

Jane shrugged. 'Who knows?' she said.

'Well don't go getting too friendly with her.'

Jane sniffed. 'Don't worry,' she said, 'I won't. I'd have to forgive her first and that's never going to happen, is it?'

The Barge Pole, all oak beams, old pictures and brass ornaments, was just as Fran remembered it. The log fire, burning fiercely in the large open fireplace, hadn't been lit then, and there had been no Christmas decorations, but nothing else had changed. It was unexpectedly busy for lunchtime, but, as Patrick pointed out, it was the Friday before Christmas. They ordered their food at the bar, and Fran and Jane went to secure a table while Patrick got their drinks.

'This is nice,' said Jane, looking appreciatively at the fire and glancing round at the Christmas tree in the corner and all the holly and tinsel everywhere.

Fran looked across at the table where she had sat with Neil. She had been enjoying herself then, delighting in the novelty of the situation. And, after two nights at the cottage, she had been looking forward to their next assignation. But now, she couldn't imagine why she had felt like that. Being here, with the husband she'd been deceiving and the friend with whose husband she'd been doing the said deceiving, made what she'd always insisted on regarding as harmless fun suddenly seem pathetically self-indulgent and . . . shameful even.

Patrick came over with their drinks and after a while the food arrived. Despite their efforts to be light-hearted, upbeat and full of Christmas cheer, the mood remained subdued. Patrick, Fran could see, was probably thinking that his exercise in trauma resolution had back-fired. And Jane, doing a great job covering up her own distress, must also be thinking that Fran was still suffering from the after effects of her abduction and imprisonment. Well, better they think that than know what was really upsetting her.

Her uncharacteristically pensive mood continued well into their journey home. She kept telling herself that it was irrational to feel . . . Exactly what was it she was feeling? Remorse? Or was that a bit over the top? Regret, then? OK, she wished now that she hadn't done it. But there was no point beating herself up over it, she told herself. She wasn't responsible for Jane's present suffering. Jane knew nothing about her affair with Neil.

But she couldn't banish from her mind the image of Jane sitting on that fucking bed, thumping that fucking mattress. An image, she feared, that would continue to haunt her.

When they got on to the motorway, Patrick, who was driving, put the radio on and switched it to Radio 3. Normally Fran would have objected to this, insisting that they talk to each other instead (at least until such time as she herself decided she wanted to listen to Radio 4), but today she was so lost in her own thoughts that his little subversive act went unchecked for quite a while.

She had been sitting still for too long. She uncrossed her legs and shifted position, beginning to take stock of her surroundings.

'Slow down!' she said, her hand going to the greenstone pendant around her neck. 'You're doing ninety.'

'I'm overtaking.'

'You're being reckless.'

Patrick moved back into the middle lane. 'Shall we stop

at this service station?' he said. 'We don't know what the traffic's going to be like in London. This is our last chance.'

'When you put it like that,' said Fran, reaching out and turning the radio off, 'what choice do we have?'

But the service station was upon them before Patrick could get into the inside lane and he missed the turn off.

'I told you not to go so fast,' said Fran. 'That was our "last chance" and we've missed it.'

She turned the radio on again and re-tuned it to Radio 4. It was dark outside now and she was only dimly aware of the landscape they were speeding through. Soon they would be in the bright lights of London, and then home, where she could put all this Neil Lord business right out of her mind.

'Remember!' she said to Patrick. 'We mustn't say anything about all this to anyone yet. Not even Emer. Not till Jane's told Lucy.'

4

Later that evening, Jane rang Fran. She'd told herself that she wasn't going to ring so often while Patrick was there, so, ostensibly, it was to check that they'd got back all right. But the visit to the cottage had unsettled her and she needed to talk.

'I'm sorry about what happened this morning,' she said. 'I don't know why I got so upset – or so angry. I honestly thought I was getting over the anger bit. I mean, only the other night I caught myself understanding why he might have thought it necessary to deceive me about the cottage all these years! How noble was that?' She gave a hollow laugh. 'Anyway,' she went on, conscious that Fran wasn't contributing to the conversation, 'you must be sick and tired of listening to me going on and on about all this.'

'I'm not sure what it is you are going on about,' said Fran. 'Are you saying you're thinking of forgiving him? Or is that just the whisky talking?'

Jane looked at the glass in her hand, turning it this way and that to admire its contents. What exactly was she saying? Perhaps her edges were too blurred for any real clarity of thought.

'I think what I'm saying,' she said slowly, 'is that I might be able to forgive him for not telling me about Mark, and about the cottage once it was ongoing. But I definitely can't forgive him for the affair, or for not telling me in the first place. About Mark and the cottage, I mean. If that makes sense?' She could almost feel Fran shaking her head. 'It's something to do with the difference between betrayal and deception,' she went on. 'If there is a difference. Do you think there is? I'm not sure now.'

'Would you like me to look them up in the dictionary?' Fran asked.

But even as Jane was laughing at this facetious suggestion, she knew that she herself would be doing just that as soon as they'd finished speaking. It might sound ridiculous to Fran but it was important to her that she sort out the emotional mess she was in.

'It's something to do with commission and omission,' she persisted.

'You don't say!' said Fran.

'Yes I do. It's like with sins.' Jane knew she could talk confidently to her convent-educated friend about sin and be understood. 'You commit sins, don't you?' she said.

'All the time,' agreed Fran.

'No, listen. Seriously. You commit sins, but there are also sins of omission. Neil committed the sin of adultery, then he omitted to tell me about the consequences. Perhaps what I'm saying is that I can forgive his *o*-missions but not his *com*-missions.'

'Not to mention his *e*-missions!' said Fran, and they began giggling like schoolgirls.

'No, concentrate,' Jane said, composing herself. 'What I think I'm saying is that I might be able to forgive him for deceiving me all those years. I might be able to understand that. But I can't forgive him for betraying me in the first place.' She paused, expecting Fran to say that she shouldn't forgive him for any of his sins. 'For me,' she continued when Fran remained silent, 'that particular betrayal might just be unforgiveable.'

Adultery, she thought later when the call had ended. She'd been going on about adultery, but was there any point trying to get Fran to understand how she felt about this when Fran herself had had an affair with a married man? That made her an adulterer – an adulteress. Or did you have to be married yourself to merit the title? Well anyway, Howard Sage had been an adulterer: adultery had been committed. Fran had sinned, however you cared to define it.

All that had been a long time ago, though . . . But, out of nowhere, Jane suddenly remembered DS Hooper asking: 'Does your mother have any other relationships?' And Emer had replied: 'Who knows? It's not unthinkable, is it?' At the time she'd thought that was just Emer being Emer. But if Emer was right, and Fran had had other affairs, then she definitely wasn't the person to talk to about the intricacies of adultery.

Jane wandered into the dining-room and reached for the dictionary on the bookshelf over the computer. Unhelpfully, it informed her that 'deception' was 'a form of betrayal'. So now she was even less sure about the distinctions she had been trying to make. She obviously hadn't yet arrived at a neat enough argument to support this newfound desire of hers to be reasonable and forgiving. She closed the dictionary and went to slip it back into its slot on the shelf. For now, she resolved, she would stop trying to make her head rule her heart. She would cling on to her anger and get what satisfaction she could from telling Lucy and Sarah about their lying, cheating, reprehensible father. She paused, her hand still on the dictionary. She slid it out again and looked up 'reprehensible', just to assure herself that it was the right word. It was.

The question of forgiveness, though, continued to exercise her. Who benefitted from it, she wondered, the forgiver or the forgivee? (If there was such a word?) If the forgivee was dead – which Neil was – it couldn't possibly matter to him whether she forgave him or not. However, it might make a difference to her. If she could bring herself to forgive him – not necessarily right away, but in time – then she might rid herself of all this destructive rage. Forgive and forget, isn't that what they say? (*Them* again.) But how hard it was to forgive. And how utterly impossible it would be to forget – regardless of the benefits of doing so.

If Sylvia hadn't got pregnant, and the affair had run its

course (its short course), and if she had found out about it (or better still, if Neil had told her about it), and if he had been sorry and begged her to forgive him, would she have? And if she had, would they have then been able to put it behind them? Or would she have spent the rest of their married life in a state of uncertainty – ever suspicious, always insecure? 'I don't know whether I was his first,' Sylvia had said, 'but I doubt if I was his last.' It was what anyone would think under the circumstances.

So even if she had been able to forgive him for the affair with Sylvia back then (and even if she could bring herself to forgive him for it now) this thought would have always been (and would always be) at the forefront of her mind. Whichever way she looked at it, she seemed doomed to spend the rest of her life dwelling, not only on his affair with Sylvia, but on these other 'speculative' affairs too.

She went into the kitchen and poured a drop more whisky into her empty glass. What I need right now, she thought ruefully, is forgetfulness. Not forgive and forget forgetfulness. Just forgetfulness.

The next afternoon, Jane drove into Birmingham to pick Sarah up from New Street station. As her daughter, tall and fair-haired, came walking towards the parked car, Jane found herself thinking about Mark. Fran had said that he was tall and fair-haired too. She herself couldn't remember what the young man who had come to her door had looked like, but now, of course, she was seeing him in her mind's eye as a young version of his father. It would seem that Neil had passed on the same genes to both Sarah and Mark. They might even be mistaken for twins, conceived as they'd been only a few months apart.

Back at the house, Sarah hung her coat up in the alcove and peeped into the lounge. 'No tree yet?' she said.

'It's on my list,' said Jane. She didn't say she was waiting for John. It sounded so feeble.

'When are Lucy and John coming?'

'Tomorrow morning,' said Jane, thinking how nice it would be to have Sarah to herself for one evening.

Sarah would keep talking about the abduction, though. The fact that the abductor had mistaken Fran for Jane was a continual puzzle. What could he have wanted with her? Did she think – did the police think – he might still try to contact her? Did they think he still posed a threat? Was she safe?

'I'm sure there's nothing to worry about,' said Jane, seeking to reassure Sarah whilst simultaneously thinking that, touching though her concern was, it had been rather a long time coming. The abduction had been weeks ago now.

She felt uncomfortable, knowing that she was withholding vital information, but she had made a firm decision that she wasn't going to say anything until Boxing Day. They would have as happy a Christmas Day as they could manage, and then she would tell them.

The Cartwrights arrived at lunchtime the next day. Within seconds of the car pulling up on the drive the hall was awash with their belongings: suitcases; carrier bags full of presents; Daniel's pushchair and travel cot; his changing mat and a giant pack of nappies; a box of baby food, and a wicker basket full of toys.

'Oh my goodness,' laughed Jane. 'All this for one little boy!'

They all embraced. Daniel, Jane was pleased to see, seemed less wary of her than he'd been before. He allowed her to take his coat off without protesting and then let Sarah take him into the kitchen. Lucy gathered all their coats together and turned to hang them up in the alcove. Too late, Jane remembered that she'd been meaning to remove the green cagoule and put it away somewhere out of sight. She braced herself for its discovery but Lucy, busy piling coats on hooks, didn't notice it.

She did, however, notice the absence of a tree.

'I thought perhaps John could come with me to get one this afternoon, and then Daniel can help decorate it,' said

Jane.

'Are you going to put any more decorations up?' Lucy asked, surveying the pine cones and the holly.

'I thought we'd tone things down a bit this year,' said Jane, 'but if you want to put more up, you can. You know where they're kept.'

Lucy sniffed but said nothing, leaving Jane uncertain as to whether she approved or disapproved of the present state of the house.

After lunch Jane and John went out in search of a tree.

'It's going to be a difficult Christmas, isn't it?' she said to him as they drove to the garden centre.

'It is,' he said. 'For all of you. But we'll get through it. And you mustn't let Lucy get you to do things you don't want to do. She's all over the place at the moment, but she needs to consider other people as well as herself.'

Jane turned and flashed him a grateful smile. She had always felt fortunate in her son-in-law. 'If I hadn't got in touch with Fran when I did,' she'd said to Neil on more than one occasion, 'then we'd never have had a son-in-law as lovely as John. I think you should thank me for that.'

They ended up buying a much larger tree than what Jane had been envisioning. She wasn't sure whether this was her choice or (in spite of what John had said) a concession to Lucy's expectations. It took some manhandling to get it into the back seat of the car, and then out again and into the house. They set it up in the lounge, in the wide bay window, but as it was already Daniel's teatime they decided not to decorate it until the next day. A pleasure deferred, thought Jane who was looking forward to seeing the expression on Daniel's face when they turned the lights on. It would be a magical moment.

One, no doubt, that would cause Lucy and Sarah to mourn the fact that Neil wasn't there to see it too. His absence was already haunting them more than she'd anticipated it would; it seemed to be a theme running through everything they said and did. Knowing what she knew, it was beginning to annoy her. She hadn't told them yet because she thought it would spoil their Christmas. Now she was beginning to think that the opposite might be the case.

After they had all gone up to bed that night, Jane, in the process of locking up and turning out the lights, stood on the threshold of the lounge and stared at the undecorated tree looming in the semi-darkness, ominous and forbidding. For a second, she thought she saw its bare branches swaying and was reminded of the night of Fran's disappearance when she'd stood at that same window and looked out at the wind-bending trees in the darkness beyond.

She closed the door and after a short detour to the alcove walked slowly and quietly up the stairs with the green cagoule over her arm.

The next few days passed quickly enough in the usual pre-Christmas flurry of activity. Sarah divided her time between catching up with old school friends and playing with Daniel. Lucy and John went into Birmingham one afternoon, without him, to do some last minute Christmas shopping. And Jane cooked and shopped and facilitated all their comings and goings, fretting all the while over the revelation to come.

On Christmas Eve, once Daniel was in bed – a big red stocking hanging from the end of his cot – John rang his mother. It was just a routine call; an exchange of seasonal platitudes. From the one-sided snatches of conversation Jane could hear, it sounded as though Fran was saying something about being sad that she wouldn't see Daniel in the morning when he opened his presents. But if that was what she was saying, Jane doubted that she really meant it. Fran was neither that sentimental nor that great a fan of Christmas.

'She wants a word with you,' John said, holding out his phone to Jane.

Jane hadn't spoken to Fran for days. 'Hello,' she said. 'Are you all ready, then?'

Fran gave one of her snorts. 'Why does everyone keep saying that?' she said. 'It's only a meal, for fuck's sake.'

Jane smiled.

'I just wanted to check that everything's all right,' Fran said. 'With . . . you know? You haven't told them yet, I take it.'

'No. Boxing Day,' said Jane. John was still in the room.

'OK. Good. Well let me know how it goes.'

'I will.'

'OK. Well, Happy Christmas then!'

5

Christmas Day had its own traditional timetable. At eight o'clock they all trooped downstairs to watch Daniel open the presents which, Lucy explained, Father Christmas had left specially for him under the tree. He listened solemnly, as though he understood what she was talking about, but what little excitement he was showing was far outweighed by theirs.

His largest present was the multi-coloured tricycle which, being boxless, Jane hadn't even tried to wrap. Daniel rushed straight over to it. John picked him up, sat him on its red saddle and placed his feet on the green pedals.

'Push! Push with your feet!' they urged him, and after several attempts to do just that he did manage to travel a few yards across the carpet before coming to a standstill.

'It'll go better on the kitchen floor,' said John.

'Come and open your other presents,' said Lucy sitting on the floor by the tree and offering him a parcel. He took it from her and gazed at it solemnly.

'Let's open it,' said Sarah sitting down beside Lucy. She began tearing the wrapping paper off. Daniel crouched down and began tearing at it too. And for the next few minutes he devoted himself to repeating this activity – tearing off the paper, glancing briefly at what was revealed and then moving on to the next ripping experience.

He's still too young, thought Jane with a fixed smile on her face. 'Let's have some breakfast now, shall we?' she said, leading the way into the kitchen.

'I wish Dad was here to see him with his presents,' said

Lucy.

John and Sarah nodded their solemn agreement. But, Jane reflected with a hardening of her heart, Daniel wasn't the first little boy Neil had missed seeing on Christmas morning.

Jane and Sarah were attending to the Christmas dinner and Daniel came to join them in the kitchen.

'Aren't you going to play with your new toys?' Jane said. 'Where's your tricycle? Go and have a ride.'

But the contents of her kitchen cupboards were of greater interest to him than his Christmas presents.

Jane sighed. 'Grandma's trying to cook a special dinner here,' she said, 'and you're getting under her feet.'

Sarah steered him to another cupboard, away from the oven and the hob. 'Look,' she said, 'you can play with the things in here. But keep out of Grandma's way, there's a good boy.'

Daniel thought about disobeying for a moment but then changed his mind. He sat down and began pulling tins out on to the floor. Jane opened the oven door and peeled back the foil on the turkey.

After a while, John and Lucy came in. They wanted Daniel to go and talk to Grandma Fran, but he was much too engrossed with the task in hand.

'Come on. Come and tell her what Father Christmas brought you,' said John.

'No!'

'Yes! Leave those tins alone and come and talk to Grandma Fran,' insisted Lucy.

Daniel looked at the tins and gave a loud sigh. He placed the palms of his hands on the floor in front of him, pointed his bottom into the air and got to his feet. John took him out to talk to Fran while Lucy stayed behind to put the tins back in the cupboard.

There were six chairs round the table in the dining-room. Jane removed two of them and put them in the hall out of the way. She brought the high-chair in from the kitchen and placed it on the side of the table where it was least likely to cause any problems. 'I'll put this here,' she said, 'but please be careful, all of you. We don't want any accidents, do we? Not on Christmas Day.'

'This looks wonderful, Mum,' Sarah said as they all sat down.

'It does indeed,' said John. Jane had placed him at the head of the table where Neil always used to sit.

Lucy said nothing. Jane, desperately wanting this meal – and the rest of the day – to go off well, glanced at her anxiously.

They all watched in silence as John began to carve the turkey. It was a task for which he was noticeably under-qualified, but he struggled on manfully while Jane opened the wine. Last year, they'd had champagne; this year she'd thought this would be too celebratory. She leaned over the table and began filling their glasses, taking care not to get in the way of the plates of turkey that were being passed round. A few moments of purposeful activity followed as they all added the rest of the food to their plates. The usual comments about Brussels sprouts were made. There was much passing of gravy. Then there was an awkward pause. Who was going to propose a toast? Saying what?

Jane glanced at John, but he obviously hadn't recovered yet from wrestling with the turkey. She raised her glass. 'Happy Christmas!' she began.

They raised their glasses in the air and waited for her to say more. But there was nothing more to be said. They clinked their glasses, trying hard to look one another in the eye as they did so. 'Happy Christmas!' they chorused.

Jane took a good swig from her glass and then picked up her knife and fork.

Christmas Day could be difficult at the best of times, but all things considered, Jane thought later that evening, the day had gone well. Granted, Lucy had been quieter than usual, forever hovering on the verge of tears – but she was pregnant and they'd all made allowances. Daniel had been the centre of their attention. He'd been pushed around on his tricycle; he'd been read to; he'd had puzzles done with him. But now he had gone to bed.

'Right! He's off,' said John, coming back into the lounge with Lucy.

'OK, time for some grown-up games now,' said Sarah.

Lucy flopped down on the sofa.

'Scrabble?' Jane suggested.

'Oh for Christ's sake!' Lucy grabbed a cushion and clutched it to her stomach. 'Let's not keep on pretending. This has been an awful day.'

Jane looked at John, then at Sarah. Had it really been so awful, in spite of all her efforts? 'Some of us have been trying our best to make it bearable,' she said quietly. 'But you don't have to play if you don't want to.'

Lucy began to cry.

'Go and get the Scrabble,' John said to Sarah. He began clearing a space on the coffee table. 'Are you going to play or not?' he asked Lucy when they were ready to start.

'I just miss Dad so much,' she said, burying her face in the cushion.

'I know you do,' he said. 'But this isn't helping. Come on, come and play. You know you want to beat me.'

'You're all heartless,' Lucy wailed. 'Acting as though nothing's any different.'

'Oh, come on, Lucy,' Jane said. 'That's not fair. What do you want us to do, spend the rest of the evening sitting here crying with you?'

'I just wish Dad was here, that's all.'

'We all do,' said Sarah. 'He was my dad too, you know.'

Lucy made a little deprecating noise.

'What does that mean?' Sarah said, her voice rising.

'Whatever you want it to mean.'

'Right, let's just stop this,' said Jane.

'No,' said Sarah. 'I'm sick and tired of her attitude. We've been falling over ourselves all day, making allowances for her. She's not the only one grieving. She's so bloody insensitive.'

'Insensitive! I'm fucking pregnant in case you hadn't noticed. I'm probably being too sensitive.'

'Not towards other people, you're not.'

'Let's just leave it at that,' said Jane. 'Either play Scrabble with us or go to bed.'

'Don't talk to me as if I were a child.'

'Stop behaving like one, then,' said Sarah.

'Stop it! Both of you. I've been working hard all day to make this a reasonable Christmas. Why do you have to spoil it now?' Jane could feel herself getting agitated. 'I know you're missing your father, but . . .'

'I just want him to be here so much,' sobbed Lucy. 'I thought I was getting over it a bit – but I'm not. You might be, but I'm not.'

'Don't speak to Mum like that?'

'Come on, Luce,' said John. 'You're tired and upset.' He tried to put his arm round her but she shrugged him off.

'Leave me alone. You haven't a clue how I'm feeling. None of you have.'

'Right, that's it!' Jane rose to her feet. Lucy wasn't the only one who was tired and upset. 'I've had enough of this,' she said. 'Put the Scrabble away. I've got something to tell you.'

'And you've known about this for months?' Lucy was distraught.

'About the cottage, yes. About this woman and . . . his son, only for a couple of weeks.'

'I don't believe it! She must be making it up. It can't be true? We'd have known. Wouldn't we?'

'You'd have thought so,' said Jane.

'I'm going to be sick,' said Lucy, struggling to her feet and rushing out of the room. John got up and followed her.

Jane turned to Sarah. 'You're going to need time to take all this in,' she said.

Sarah shook her head. 'This Mark,' she said quietly. 'He's only a bit younger than me.'

Jane reached across the sofa and took her daughter's hand. 'I know, love,' she whispered. 'I know.'

'So you're saying Fran's put in a good word for him?' Lucy said to her mother the next morning.

John was playing with Daniel in the dining-room. Sarah was sitting stock-still in the rocking chair.

Jane nodded.

'I just don't understand why she agreed to do that,' said Lucy. 'He kidnapped her and held her prisoner for days. He should be punished for that.'

'He's probably been punished enough already,' said Jane. 'There's nothing to be gained by being vindictive. And anyway, she hasn't said anything about him that she's not already said before.'

'And he is our brother,' said Sarah. She began rocking in the chair, gently at first, then with gathering force.

Lucy made a sneering, I-can't-believe-you-just-said-that noise. 'Oh, come on,' she protested.

'Well, he is, whether you like it or not. Our half-brother, anyway.'

'No! John's Emer's half-brother. And Charlotte's. There's no way this Mark person's related to us like that.'

'Well technically he is,' said Sarah, raising her voice above the audible creaking of the rocking chair.

'Not to me, he isn't.'

'It's not really a matter of choice, though, is it? We can't choose our family. More's the pity, sometimes.'

It occurred to Jane, listening to this exchange, that it was the existence of this half-brother that was preoccupying her daughters more than anything else. Lucy was rejecting him; Sarah was thinking of . . . what? Welcoming him into the family? For them, their father's betrayal centred on him having another, a secret child. Yes, well, she thought angrily, he's betrayed me by having a secret mistress, a secret child, and a secret bloody cottage, too!

'You're being too hard on him,' Sarah said. 'It's not his fault he's our brother. He's not to blame for Dad's . . .'

'He's to blame for what he did to Fran.'

'Well she's prepared to forgive him,' said Jane, 'so there you are.' She turned to Sarah, about to tell her that Fran called him her 'young man', but instead she said: 'You're going to break my rocking chair if you keep on like that.'

While it was still in motion, Sarah launched herself out of the chair and stomped out of the room. It continued to rock by itself, slowing down very gradually. Jane waited until it came to a standstill before she, too, left the kitchen.

She went into the dining-room where John was sitting at the table with Daniel on his knee. They were playing with a puzzle which involved inserting various jungle animals into their appropriate slots on a wooden board.

'Lucy's taking this very badly,' she said.

'I know,' John had to raise his voice above the sound of Daniel roaring like a lion. 'But it's something she'll have to accept. (Shush, Danny, I'm talking to Grandma).' He looked up from the puzzle. 'What did you make of this woman coming to see you like that?' he said. 'Do you think she wants something from you?'

'Such as?'

'I don't know. But she could have gone straight to the police without confronting you first. It sounds as though she wanted to see you for a reason. And I don't understand why she contacted the police in the first place – that Monday night. Her son could've gone back for Mum the next morning and dropped her off somewhere well away from that cottage so that no-one would've been able to locate it. But she practically handed him in, didn't she?'

'Hmm,' said Jane. 'She said that he didn't want her to call the police but that she was worried about Fran.'

'Yeah but that doesn't make sense, does it? A few more hours wouldn't have made that much difference. It looks like she wanted the cottage to be identified.'

'So you think she wanted me to find out about it because she wants something from me?'

'I don't know. But there's something not quite right about the story she's telling you. It doesn't quite stack up. If she contacts you again, I'd be very careful.'

What John had said continued to trouble her for the rest of the day. This Sylvia woman had kept on insisting that she'd never wanted anything from Neil. But perhaps she wanted something from Jane now. Otherwise, why had she informed the police that night?

And then there was Mark, the half-brother. So far, Jane hadn't considered the consequences of his existence. But she could see now that it was more than likely that Sarah (and even Lucy, given time) would want to develop a relationship with him. It was a bit like Emer and that actress – what-was-her-name? – Imogen Sage. She was Emer's half-sibling – perhaps not in the same way that John and Charlotte were (Lucy was right there), nor even Hannah who was their step-sister – and Jane knew that Fran thought Emer might have contacted her. Well . . . if she had, that was her business. And if Lucy and Sarah ever decided to forge some kind of relationship with Mark, that would be their business, too. Whatever they chose to do would have nothing to do with her. She wasn't related to him.

But . . . maybe she was. Maybe – technically – she was his bloody step-mother.

6

Jane wanted to show them the cottage. 'I think it would be good for you to see it for yourselves,' she said. 'Why don't we go on Sunday morning and then, if the weather's all right, we could go for a walk afterwards. It's in the countryside, there must be plenty of nice walks round there.'

On Sunday morning she had another suggestion to make. 'Rather than take two cars, why don't we all go in the Mercedes?' she said. Neil's car hadn't been out of the garage since his death. She should probably sell it. She would sell it. But it had been out of sight and low down on her list of things to do. 'Yes? No?' she said.

'OK,' said Lucy. 'If it'll make things easier.' She turned to Sarah. 'It's only a car.'

Sarah opened her eyes wide. 'Did I say anything?' she said.

Taking the Mercedes, however, proved to be an involved operation. Getting it out of the garage meant that their other cars had to be moved; Daniel's car seat had to be installed; decisions had to be made about who should drive and who should sit where. Lucy had to be in the front, of course, and logically, Jane and Sarah should have gone in the back with Daniel. But it also made sense for Jane to drive. She knew where they were going; she was used to the car.

'Arghh!' said Sarah, wedged between John and Daniel's car seat and struggling to fasten her seat belt.

'Ttt. It's not far. You'll be all right,' said Lucy.

'That's easy for you to say.'

'Oh, for Christ's sake! You can't expect me to squash in

the back. Stop complaining.'

'Oh, sorry. I'd forgotten that complaining was your prerogative.'

'For God's sake, both of you!' said Jane.

'Sake!' shouted Daniel.

They drove out of Solihull, across the motorway and into the Warwickshire countryside. It was a beautiful, cold, bright morning. Sunlight was flickering through the trees and Jane lowered the sun visor to stop being dazzled by it. Mindful of pregnant Lucy in the front and uncomfortable Sarah in the back, she manoeuvred the bends in the road as carefully as she could.

As they neared the cottage, conversation stopped. Jane began to wonder whether coming here was a good idea after all but she wanted Lucy and Sarah to see the cottage. It would, she felt, help them to face up to the reality of what their father had done.

'Nearly there,' she said as they approached Medworth.

There were lots of parked cars on the grass verges, and groups of walkers on the street, all heading out of the village into the open countryside. As they drove past the Barge Pole and across the bridge over the canal, she couldn't help picturing Neil and Sylvia and Mark in this setting. Pub lunches; walks along the canal bank.

A few minutes beyond the village she slowed down and turned on to Fieldend Lane East. 'Sorry,' she said to Lucy as they bounced along the track for another mile or so before coming to a halt outside the cottage.

'God, it is out of the way, isn't it?' said Lucy, unfastening her seatbelt and hauling herself out of the car.

'Yes,' said Jane. 'The road ends here. It's all very private and hidden away.'

She took the cottage keys out of her handbag and unlocked the front door. They all trooped into the dark interior.

'Well, this is it,' she said, opening the shutters.

It was a bit like a house viewing with her as the estate

agent. (This is the living-room – a good size, full of character.) They all looked around, not quite knowing what to say. Jane's eyes rested for a moment on the lighter patch on the wall over the mantelpiece where the painting had hung.

'OK,' said Sarah, moving on.

In the kitchen, Daniel toddled over to one of the cupboard doors and tried to open it. It was not as yielding as Jane's. Puzzled, he began tugging on the handle and when the door did open it threw him off balance and he sat down heavily on the floor. For a moment he contemplated crying, but then he saw the pans inside the cupboard and changed his mind.

'And here,' said Jane, leading the way through the kitchen and opening the heavy door to the left, 'is the infamous bathroom.' (Small, retro, but could easily and inexpensively be brought up to date.) They crowded into the doorway to see where Fran had been held prisoner.

'Oh wow! Look at that colour!' said Sarah. They all gazed at the bilious-yellow bathroom suite and tiles. 'Who'd choose that?'

'Your father, it would seem,' said Jane.

'Oh . . . oh, I'm going to be sick again,' said Lucy, elbowing Sarah out of the way and making a dive for the yellow toilet bowl.

Jane and Sarah backed away, leaving John to attend to his heaving and retching wife. Sarah wandered up the stairs but Jane stayed in the kitchen to supervise Daniel who had got two doors open now and was trying a third. This cupboard was empty though.

'No,' he said, turning to Jane with a disappointed expression on his face.

'Never mind,' she said.

When they had finished looking round the house they went outside into the garden. Jane closed the shutters carefully (she hadn't bothered to get the lock replaced which was a slight worry) and went to join them. They were standing looking out at the view depicted in Sylvia's painting.

253

No-one, she noted, was commenting on how beautiful it was. A plane flew overhead and they looked up to watch its noisy passing. The sun was already beginning to sink in the sky. The best part of the day was nearly over.

'Come on,' she said, walking back towards the car. 'Time to go if we want to have that walk.'

'I'm going to take some photos,' said Sarah, holding up her phone and clicking away.

'For Christ's sake!' said Lucy. 'Whatever for?'

'For posterity,' said Sarah, walking to and fro to capture the cottage from several different angles.

The cottage – its renovation, its maintenance and its usage – was the main topic of conversation at dinner that evening. Seeing it, had, indeed, made the whole thing real for Lucy and Sarah. There could be no more doubting that their father had had this secret existence. The only unbelievable thing now was that they had never known about it. They searched their memories for occasions when Neil had been away from home – for afternoons, for whole days, whole weekends. How many of these absences had been genuine; how many bogus? And all those football-match occasions. It would seem he hadn't been lying about those, but he hadn't been telling the whole truth either.

'When are you going to sell the place?' John asked.

He's probably bored to death with all this, Jane thought. His interest in the cottage was, understandably, confined to the weekend Fran had spent there.

'When all the paperwork's been sorted,' she said. 'The sooner I can get rid of it the better. But I don't know whether it'll sell easily. It's a bit of a niche property. It could take ages.'

'That house on Fran's road is still for sale, you know,' said Lucy.

'Is it?' said Jane. She knew that it was. Since her last visit to London she'd been keeping a close internet eye on it. She was familiar with all its details now. Disregarding the fact that she was fairly certain she would never consider buying it, she had even made several imaginary alterations to it.

'What house? What are you talking about?' asked Sarah.

'Mum's going to move to London and there's this house for sale near Fran's.'

'Lucy! Really!' Jane was annoyed.

'You're moving to London?'

Jane heard the dismay and disapproval in Sarah's voice. But Sarah would be graduating in the summer, she thought. It was most unlikely she would ever come back home to live. It shouldn't matter to her where her mother lived. 'It's just an option I'm thinking about,' she said. 'I certainly haven't made any decisions, and I'm not going to yet. It would be foolish to rush things.'

'But that house'd be perfect,' said Lucy, ignoring Jane's protestations. 'I would've thought that now you'd be keener than ever to move away from here.'

'Moving away won't make the pain go away,' said Jane.

The next few days passed uneventfully. Learning all these things about her father seemed to have lessened Lucy's grief, and she became a lot less tearful. She was adamant, though, that she wanted nothing to do with her newly discovered 'brother'.

Sarah went back to Sheffield on New Year's Eve. But before she left she asked Jane for Mark's surname. 'It's not Lord, is it?' she said. 'I've searched on Facebook for a Mark Lord but I can't find one.'

'His mother's name's Ashworth now. But his might be Broadhurst. I don't know.'

'If I did find him, would you mind if I contacted him?'

'I don't know,' Jane said. Would she mind? It was hard to say. 'But if you do, I'd like to know about it. I don't want there to be any more secrets.'

New Year's Eve proved to be more duty than celebration. They had dinner later than usual but after they'd finished eating there was nothing else to do other than drink and watch television until midnight. When, at long last, Big Ben chimed, they wished one another 'Happy New Year' with as much forced gaiety as they could muster. John rang Fran and for the next few minutes they repeated the process down the airwaves. This done, they took their empty glasses into the kitchen.

'We can leave 2008 behind us now,' Jane said. 'And we've got a new addition to the family to look forward to in 2009.'

She meant the new baby, of course, but Mark leapt unbidden into her mind. Annoyed by this unwelcome intrusion, she set off across the room towards the dishwasher. On the way, disregarding her own constant warnings to be careful, she tripped over a leg of Daniel's highchair and only just saved herself from falling to the floor with her glass in her hand.

The Cartwrights were leaving on Friday morning.

While Lucy and John were packing the car, Jane took Daniel into the kitchen out of their way. She sat him down in front of one of her designated cupboards and, opening its door, invited him to set to work on its contents. This had been his favourite activity over the past two weeks. None of his Christmas presents – not even the tricycle – had provided him with as much pleasure as taking tins out of cupboards and putting them back in again had. 'This boy's going to be a shelf-stacker in a supermarket when he grows up,' Jane had said on more than one occasion.

But something had changed. Daniel, clutching his toy cat Felix, just sat and gazed into the open cupboard. After some serious thought he turned to look at Jane and then leaned forward and put the cat on the bottom shelf.

'Oh, poor Felix,' said Jane, clearing the table. 'What's he doing in there?'

Daniel stood up and tried to fling the door shut. Because it had a soft-close mechanism, it took several attempts before he could get it to close with a sufficiently satisfying clunk.

When it did, he opened it again and repeated the action.

Lucy came into the kitchen. 'We're all ready to go,' she said.

'Don't go without Felix,' Jane said, opening the cupboard door and removing the toy. She handed it to Lucy. 'Your son seems to have lost interest in the tins all of a sudden.'

'Just a passing phase,' said Lucy. 'I wonder what the next one will be.'

Jane took Daniel by the hand and began to walk outside with him. That's what life is, she thought, a series of 'phases' to be grown out of or passed through. It was a pity that the transition from one to the next wasn't always as easy as this one had been.

'Give some serious thought to this moving business,' said Lucy as they were saying goodbye. 'You can come down in a week or two and we can do some house hunting.'

Jane smiled. 'I'm not going to rush things,' she said. 'You'll just have to be patient.'

'It'd be nice to know something definite before this baby arrives,' said Lucy.

Jane followed the reversing car to the end of the drive and then stood on the edge of the pavement waving until it disappeared from sight round the bend in the road. She walked slowly back into the house and looked around. Yesterday afternoon she and John had taken the Christmas tree to the garden centre to be shredded and now, with only the few decorations still in place, the lounge looked drab and bare. And the house felt very empty.

She forced herself up the stairs and began to strip the beds, wrestling breathlessly with duvet covers in the process and thinking how alarmingly unfit she'd become. She would get more exercise, she resolved. Start going for long, brisk walks; resume the gentle yoga she used to do before Neil died. In the meantime, removing duvet covers and sheets would have to suffice. She needed to get it done. Bronia would be arriving any minute and her task this morning would be to vacuum and dust the bedrooms before remaking the beds with clean bed linen. Jane sighed. She hadn't spoken to Bronia yet about reducing her hours. But she wasn't going to say anything today. There was no immediate rush.

She went to hang some clothes up in her wardrobe and her attention was caught by Sylvia's painting which she'd put in there out of the way. She'd told Fran that she might give it back to Sylvia. Would she do that, she wondered? Sylvia might interpret the gesture as some kind of olive branch.

The green cagoule was hiding in the wardrobe too, out of Lucy's sight. Jane took it out and inspected it. Should she keep it or get rid of it? Another decision she was clearly incapable of making. Leaving the painting where it was, she closed the wardrobe door, took the cagoule out on to the landing and dropped it over the banister into the hall below. She threw armfuls of bedding down on top of it and then went down the stairs herself.

She had just finished loading the washing machine when Bronia arrived. They exchanged New Year's greetings and asked each other if they'd had nice Christmases. They both said they had, but Jane had an unpleasant feeling that Bronia might have spent it all alone in her dingy little bedsit. They might both have been lying.

Before going upstairs to start on the bedrooms, Bronia picked up the cagoule and took it to the alcove by the front door where she hung it up on a hook of its own. Jane watched her do this in silence.

She hovered in the hall, uncertain what to do next. There were lots of things that needed doing . . . but they could wait. She went into the dining-room and switched on her computer. She would check her emails and then perhaps have another quick look at the house on Fran's road.

But her interest in the house seemed to have evaporated. Did she really want to move to London, she asked herself? If Fran didn't live there, would she be even considering it? Well, the answer to that was obvious. She sat back in her chair and gazed into the thicket of green bamboo that had materialised on her computer screen. She needed to get things in perspective. She had been too dependent on Neil, and now she was in danger of becoming too dependent on Fran. Patrick would be back permanently, soon. Fran had her own life to lead. Jane was – and should be – only a part of it.

As for London – well, it would always be there for her to visit. She didn't have to reside there to enjoy its attractions. She could go and stand on Waterloo Bridge whenever the fancy took her, with or without Fran.

No, the sensible thing would be to stay in Solihull, in the house where she had lived for such a long time, and where, for the most part, she had been happy. It was her home; it had been silly to think otherwise. And she could make it more so. She could redecorate, for example, and get rid of all the old furniture. She could have the downstairs floors sanded and varnished, like Fran's. She could have louvred wooden shutters on the windows too. She had always admired Fran's shutters.

And while this work was in progress there would be plenty of cleaning for Bronia to do. She could continue employing her for two days a week for quite a while yet.

7

Emer had only been home from New York a few hours when Fran rang her to fill her in on all the news.

'Oh my God!' Emer said. 'Poor Jane. How's she coping with all that?'

'Surprisingly well,' said Fran, refusing to dwell on the scene in the bedroom at the cottage. 'And see – I told you that my young man was harmless, didn't I?'

'And Lucy? I bet she took it with her usual fortitude?'

'She's upset, but then who wouldn't be?' Fran paused for a moment. 'What she and the other girl – Sarah – have to decide now is what, if anything, they're going to do about their new brother. Lucy's saying she wants absolutely nothing to do with him, but apparently Sarah's not so against the idea.'

'I can understand that,' said Emer.

'I'm sure you can.'

Another pause.

'Why didn't you tell me all this before?'

'I promised Jane I wouldn't say anything till she'd told Lucy and Sarah herself, in person, at Christmas.'

'As if I'd have said anything to Lucy if you'd asked me not to! You should've told me. I take it that you told Patrick straight away?'

'More or less. But come on, don't go over-reacting. Perhaps I could have told you, but do you tell me everything? I don't think so.'

'What the fuck's that supposed to mean?'

What did it mean? Fran wondered, trying not to think of

Howard Sage. 'Well, I'm sure there're things you've never told me that perhaps you should have,' she said. She had no idea why the conversation had taken this turn. She hadn't intended to go down this road; she just couldn't seem to help herself. 'Things about Howard Sage, for example,' she heard herself saying. (She was fucking obsessed with the man these days!)

'Oh! There're things I've never told you about Howard Sage, are there?'

'Yes, I think there are.'

'Like what?'

'Like . . . whether you've ever contacted him, for example.' (Why did she keep saying 'for example'? She wasn't teaching now, for Christ's sake!)

There was a short silence.

'I'd really like to know whether you have,' Fran said. 'Him or any of his . . . legitimate kids.'

Emer gave a disbelieving laugh. 'Well I suppose that's a *legitimate* question,' she said. 'But I'm not going to do this over the phone.'

'OK. Well why don't you come round one evening and tell me face to face?'

'Yeah, why don't I? And then we can have a proper mother/daughter heart-to-heart. Won't that be a novel experience for both of us! And you can cook dinner for me, too, while we're at it.'

Fran put the phone down and stared into the distance for a moment. Yes, she thought, she has contacted Howard Sage. And now she's going to tell me about it and I'm not going to like it.

The dining-room table was set for dinner.

'I know it's just the two of us,' said Fran. 'But still . . .'

Emer was holding a large box folder. 'Great,' she said, putting it down next to her place setting.

Fran arranged a dish of broccoli and another of spinach in the centre of the table, and eyed the box folder with apprehension. She went back into the kitchen and took a large baking dish out of the oven. It was very hot. 'God, this is heavy,' she said as she carried it to the table, wondering if its weight was the only reason her hands were shaking.

They sat down and she filled both their wine glasses to the brim.

'What's in the box?' she asked, serving Emer with a helping of fish and potatoes.

'Mmm. This smells delicious,' said Emer, ignoring the question. She began helping herself to the vegetables.

Fran bit her lip.

'The box,' said Emer, after a suitably annoying pause, 'contains my Howard Sage memorabilia collection.' She put the serving spoon back in the dish of broccoli. 'Which I'll share with you in due course.' She picked up her knife and fork. 'I know you told me to leave things alone,' she said, putting a forkful of food into her mouth and pausing to chew it, 'all those years ago, when I was a teenager. But . . .' Another pause while she swallowed this first mouthful and loaded her fork in preparation for the next. 'I couldn't do that, so . . .' She put more food into her mouth. 'I decided to contact him . . .' More chewing. 'My "real" father, Professor Howard Sage.' More swallowing.

'Oh, for Christ's sake, either eat or talk,' said Fran.

'Sorry,' said Emer, 'but I'm starving, so if it's all right with you I think I'll eat for a bit first.'

'You're enjoying this, aren't you?' said Fran.

Emer waved her fork over the food on her plate. 'Yes I am, it's delicious, thank you,' she said, smiling.

They ate in silence for a few more minutes.

'What's in your Howard Sage collection?' Fran asked, indicating the folder.

'You just need to be patient for a little while longer,' said Emer, picking up her glass and almost spilling its contents. 'Ooops!' she said. 'Cheers!'

After a few more mouthfuls she was ready to talk. 'So yeah,' she said, 'I decided to contact him. I wrote to him – at the BBC because I didn't know where he lived then. I do now, of course.'

'When was this?'

'Ohh . . . when I was at uni. 1993, I think. Or maybe '94.'

'And what did you say – in this letter?'

'I was brief and to the point. I said something like: Dear Professor Sage, (I rejected "Dear Daddy" as being too familiar!) Dear Professor Sage, (or did I say Howard Sage? I can't remember.) My name is Emerald Cartwright. My mother, Frances Delaney, was a student at Bristol University from 1971 to 1974 (that was right, wasn't it?) when you were a lecturer there. I have reason to believe that you are my father. And then I said something like: I would like to assure you that I have no wish to cause you any embarrassment or to make this relationship public. I just want you to be aware of my existence. I will leave it to you as to how we might proceed from here. Something succinct like that.'

Fran was finding Emer's jaunty attitude both a source of irritation and a cause for concern. There wasn't going to be a happy ending to this story, she could see. 'And . . .?' she said.

'And nothing. He didn't write back. Maybe he never got my letter, who knows? Anyway, I found out he was at Cambridge, so I wrote to him again there. The same letter more or less. And this time he did write back.'

Emer flipped open the box folder and took out a letter. It was ready and waiting for her on top of the other contents, as if she had rehearsed this scene and had all her props ready to hand. She passed it to Fran.

Fran reached for her reading glasses. She opened the envelope and removed the folded piece of paper inside. There wasn't much written on it. *Dear Ms Cartwright,* she read silently, her heart beating fast. *It is not unusual for people like myself, who are in the public eye, to receive communications such as yours. I do not recall your mother* (the fucking bastard!) *but then it was many years ago. I certainly do not recall any relationship* (fucking, fucking bastard!) *and so I see no point in taking this correspondence any further.* Underneath this, taking up nearly as much space as the letter itself, was an indecipherable flourish of a signature.

Fran was breathless with fury. She removed her glasses and let them dangle from their chain round her neck. 'The fucking prat!' she said. 'I told you not to do this. I warned you what would happen, didn't I? The lying, fucking bastard. Why didn't you tell me about this before?'

Emer gave a mirthless laugh. 'Because I knew what you'd say. I told you so! You should've listened to me. Which is exactly what you've just said now.'

'Oh, Emer!' Fran murmured.

But Emer was on the defensive now. 'I think what's really upsetting you,' she said, 'is him saying he didn't remember you. The beautiful Frances Delaney! What a blow to your vanity that would be, if it were true.'

'Emer!'

'But you're right, of course – as usual. He was lying. He did remember you.'

'Go on.'

'Do you remember Laura Birch . . . she was in the sixth form with me? Well she was at Cambridge and so I went to visit her, and while I was there I went to see him. That's why I went, of course, I wasn't that bothered about seeing her. Anyway, as soon as he clapped eyes on me it was obvious that he did remember you. So I said something like: "Good morning Professor Sage, (or was it afternoon?) I'm Emerald Cartwright. I wrote to you about my mother, and I see you do remember her now." And he said something along the lines of: "My dear girl, recalling your mother proves nothing." And then he peered at me and said: "You do, indeed, bear a very strong resemblance to her, but I'm afraid I can't see any likeness at all to my good self." That's what he actually said – "my dear girl, my good self"!

'He was all supercilious and sneery. He just didn't want to know. I fucking hated him. So I told him I was glad I'd come because now that I'd actually met him I no longer wanted any sort of relationship with him. I told him that you'd always said he was a complete and utter arsehole, and now I could see why.'

'Oh Emer!' said Fran, shaking her head. She wanted to say something sympathetic but couldn't immediately think of an appropriate remark.

'OK,' said Emer after a moment's pause. 'I did want him to be interested in me. And he clearly wasn't. And that hurt. But it was years ago. I'm totally over it, so there's no need to start feeling sorry for me now.'

They sat in silence, sipping their wine.

'Well, at least I know now,' said Fran. 'I've always wondered.'

She was also wondering why it had taken her so long to extract this information from Emer, why she had never pushed her before. Circumspection wasn't her usual modus operandi.

'Shall I tell you what I've always wondered?' said Emer. 'What made you have a relationship with him in the first place – if you thought he was such a prat?'

Fran shrugged. 'He was very attractive? I was young and foolish?' she said lightheartedly. It was what she'd always said – and how she'd always said it – when talking about Howard Sage. (But she hadn't been young when she'd embarked on her affair with Neil Lord, had she?) 'I was foolish,' she said, amending her excuse and altering her tone. 'He was a married man. I shouldn't have done it.' She glanced across the table at Emer. 'Not, I hasten to add, that I've ever regretted having you. That goes without saying.'

'It sure does,' said Emer.

Fran cleared the plates away and brought in some cheese and biscuits.

'What else's in the box?' she asked.

'Like I said, memorabilia. Reviews, magazine articles – some by him, some about him. Stuff about Imogen Sage.' Emer pushed the box folder towards Fran. 'Here,' she said. 'I'll leave it with you. You can peruse it at your leisure – or not – as you wish.'

'What about Imogen Sage? Have you ever tried to

contact her?'

'I did want to – years ago. A famous half-sister and all that. Much more interesting than Charlotte. But I didn't. And then I grew out of the idea. Grew up, you could say.'

Fran wondered if a younger Emer had tried and been rejected there, too. Thinking about the magazine article she'd read (which might well be in the box folder), it seemed more than likely that Imogen Sage, too, would have repelled any advances made by a half-sibling. Poor Emer.

'I'm glad we've had this conversation,' she said. 'I do wish you'd told me before though. I always knew you were lying when you said you hadn't contacted him.'

After Emer had left Fran put her reading glasses back on, opened the box folder and began flicking through its contents. There were newspaper and magazine articles in it dating back to the early nineties. She removed some of these and spread them out so that the dining table became covered in images of Howard Sage. A double-page article, dated 1995, began with a short biography and was accompanied by a selection of photos ranging over his life. One of these was a wedding photo: Howard marries Esther in 1967. Another showed him standing on the Downs – Clifton Suspension Bridge in the background – with his two small children. It was entitled: As a young lecturer in Bristol – 1973.

Fran stared hard at this picture. The children – Imogen and a little boy whose name she didn't know – were bundled up in winter clothing. Some trees, just visible in the photo, were leafless. Autumn 1973! 'Bastard,' she said out loud. But she had known perfectly well at the time that Howard Sage was married, and she hadn't cared, so there was no point being hypocritical now.

'I'd just broken up with a long-standing boyfriend,' she'd told Jane, making it sound clean and casual. But the truth was, that boyfriend had broken her heart – and hurt her pride. Philip Armitage! She hadn't thought about him for a long time. There had been a childhood sweetheart in his past, and in spite of his best efforts to leave her behind (and in spite of having enjoyed the privilege of being Frances Delaney's lover for nearly two years) he had gone back to her. Were they still together now, Fran wondered? Did he ever think about her?

She had launched herself at Howard Sage because she had been hurting (and to re-assure herself that she still had the power to attract), but she had emerged from her brief affair with him hurting even more. When he, too, had let her slip out of his life in such a casual, careless way, she'd hidden her pain and confusion beneath a barrage of anger and scorn. And although the pain and confusion had long gone, the anger and scorn had remained constant.

Fran looked again at the photo of the happy, smiling Esther Sage. She hadn't known her personally; she hadn't considered her at all. But she had known Jane – and she hadn't given her a second thought either, when she'd embarked on her affair with Neil Lord. She'd been feeling resentful then, too, because Patrick, against her wishes, had gone ahead and applied for and accepted the post in LA. So maybe this affair, too, had been an act of defiance and not just a bit of 'harmless fun'.

Although she was staring at the picture of Esther Sage, she was seeing another image – Jane, betrayed and full of rage, sitting on the bed at the cottage, pounding the mattress with her fist.

Ironically, Jane was the only person Fran had spoken to at length about Howard Sage. Nick Cartwright knew about him, of course, and Patrick, but only the basic facts. Jane, once she'd become Fran's confidante, had probed deeper. And although Fran always adopted a flippant attitude when talking about him, she knew that Jane was reading between her lines. And she liked that.

The next evening she rang Jane to tell her about her chat with Emer.

'It turns out she did contact him, years ago,' Fran said.

'She wrote to him first and then she went to see him at Cambridge. And, surprise, surprise, he didn't want to know! Just like I knew he wouldn't. He denied all knowledge of me – well, all carnal knowledge, anyway. Poor old Em! It must've been a blow to her at the time but she says she's not bothered now. I always said he was a prat.'

'Do you think that if you'd told him at the time that you were pregnant, he might've . . . you know . . . faced up to his responsibilities?' said Jane.

'And done what?'

'Supported you financially?'

Fran was dismissive. 'I doubt it,' she said. 'He was just a humble lecturer in those days. He wouldn't have been able to afford to. At least not without his wife finding out and . . .' She stopped. (Christ, what am I saying?)

'But how do you know he wouldn't have done something to help you, if you'd told him? OK, he might not have been able to set you up with regular payments and a weekend cottage, not at first anyway, but he might have done something.'

They seemed to be back on the subject of Neil. Fran wished that Jane would stop this constant analysing. 'Yeah, he would've tried to persuade me to have an abortion,' she said.

But Jane wasn't to be diverted. 'So, in your opinion, Howard Sage wasn't one of those men who would ever do the right thing?' she said. 'After they've gone and done the wrong thing, I mean!' She gave a strained little laugh, as though she'd just made a joke. 'That's what that Sylvia woman said about Neil. "He just wanted to do the right thing." But she was lucky, wasn't she? She chose the right man for her purposes.' She gave another hollow laugh. 'It's funny to think of Neil as being fit for purpose, isn't it? But you didn't think Howard Sage was like that? You thought you'd have been wasting your time telling him?'

'I'm not going to start soul-searching about that now,' Fran said. 'Not after all these years.'

'And you think Emer's all right?'

'I think so. She's a big girl now. And she's never tried to contact Imogen Sage – or at least she says she hasn't – although she did want to when she was younger.'

'Mmm. That's what Sarah wants to do – contact your young man. I know she's been searching for him on Facebook. But if she does, Lucy won't be too pleased. She's still adamant that she wants nothing to do with him.'

What a pity, Fran thought wryly, that Emer hadn't felt the same way about fucking Howard Sage and his offspring. But then, it shouldn't be Lucy she was comparing Emer to; it should be Mark – the illegitimate child who had let his grievances get the better of him.

CONSEQUENCES

1

Having – more or less – made the decision not to move, Jane had been immersing herself in home decorating magazines. (She didn't want Fran's house to be her only source of ideas and inspiration.) She had amassed an impressive collection of paint charts and was beginning to think that soon it would be time to invest in some tester pots. She hadn't told Lucy about any of this, though. And she wasn't going to until she was a hundred percent certain that she was going to stay put.

She had found a pleasing way to combine her interior design interests with her exercise programme. On her way home from her long walks in the park she had taken to calling into the John Lewis store in the town centre where she prowled round the furnishings and furniture departments, picking up leaflets and samples as she went. 'Can I help you, madam?' a salesman asked her one day. 'Not yet, thank you,' she'd replied. 'I'm only at the browsing stage.'

One Sunday afternoon, as she was emerging from the store into the Touchwood shopping centre, she ran into Kay who insisted that they go for a coffee.

'So . . . ,' said Kay, stirring her cappuccino, 'everything's been explained now, has it?'

'It would seem so,' said Jane. She hadn't spoken to Kay or Martin since the night she'd had dinner with them but they obviously knew about the recent developments. Perhaps the police had questioned Liz again – to ask her why she'd omitted Sylvia's name from the list of receptionists – and that's how they knew? Perhaps they had known all along? Or perhaps Sylvia had told them?

'Anyway, look,' said Kay, possibly sensing that Jane wasn't going to be any more forthcoming. 'It's Martin's sixtieth at the beginning of March. We're having a bit of a bash. I'll send you an invitation.'

Jane felt momentarily panic-stricken. A party! She couldn't go to a party on her own! And especially not to a party where loads of the people there would know about Neil and his other little family. Where Liz Hartley might be, for God's sake.

'It's Lucy's birthday at the beginning of March, too,' she said. 'I might be down in London.'

'When?'

'The second.'

'Oh good, Martin's party's on the eighth.'

'Right,' said Jane.

She had also been thinking about the future life she would lead in her transformed Solihull home. She would carry on with her job, of course. It was a pity she'd so readily abandoned the idea of becoming a full-blown teacher all those years ago but she was too old now to do anything about that. There was, however, nothing (or no-one) to stop her doing some other course. One of the women in her literature class had started a part-time degree in English Studies at Warwick last October, and she was older than Jane. She would make some preliminary enquiries.

And, if she were to do this while retaining her part-time job, she could easily justify keeping Bronia on for two days a week, for a very long time to come.

271

Sylvia – and son – were also very much on her mind. She kept wondering how they were coping with the uncertainty of their situation. Waiting was always difficult, but it wouldn't do Sylvia any harm to suffer for a change.

She rang Debbie Mason to ask if there was any news regarding Mark's prosecution but was told that it would take a while for the case to be reviewed. She thought about asking her for Sylvia's address or phone number, in case she ever did decide that she wanted to contact her, but she thought this might be considered inappropriate at this stage in the proceedings. She couldn't stop thinking about what John had said, though. Why had Sylvia told the police where Fran was? And why had she come to see Jane before Mark handed himself in? Was there something else she wanted?

Every time she opened her wardrobe door and saw the painting, she was reminded of these questions. She could use the painting as a pretext for contacting Sylvia. It wasn't such an outlandish idea, was it – returning it to its rightful owner? What possible harm could it do?

To do this, though, she needed an address or a phone number. She consulted the telephone directory, but there were several Ashworth, S's listed there and she had no idea where in Birmingham Sylvia lived. She wasn't going to ring every number on the off-chance that Sylvia would answer – or Mark, which would be even more embarrassing. 'Hello, this is your step-mother . . .'

She could ask Sarah if she had found Mark yet, but she decided not to. She didn't want to get involved in that little project right now. She wondered whether Sylvia herself might be on Facebook but when she looked – and what a lengthy job that was! – she couldn't find a Sylvia Ashworth whose photo or profile fitted the woman she was looking for. No, if she wanted to contact Sylvia she would have to ring the dental surgery and insist they give her an address or a phone number. Insisting might be hard over the phone, though; it would be much better if she went round in person.

The following Friday morning, on her way home from

her literature class, she found herself parking outside the surgery. It hadn't been her intention to come today – she hadn't sufficiently rehearsed what she was going to say – but, having made two rather pertinent contributions to the morning's discussion, she was feeling confident. She was in the vicinity; she would stop equivocating and just go ahead and do it.

Liz looked gratifyingly alarmed when she walked into the reception area.

'Jane!' she said.

'Liz!' Jane glanced at the other receptionist and nodded at her too.

'Do you want to speak to Martin?' Liz asked, her hand moving to one of the phones on the desk in front of her.

'No, it's you I've come to see.'

The two women stared at each other and Jane felt another surge of confidence. She smiled. 'I want to speak to Sylvia Ashworth,' she said, 'and I'd like you to give me her contact details. Her phone number or her email address, I don't mind which.'

Liz cleared her throat. 'I'm not sure . . .' she said.

'Not sure what? I know you're in touch with her so there's no point denying it.'

'I'm not sure that I can . . . that I should . . . give out personal information.'

Jane allowed her smile to widen. 'Oh, I think you should, Liz,' she said. 'You see . . .' She leaned across the counter and lowered her voice. This was so that the other receptionist wouldn't hear what she was saying, but it had the added (and rather thrilling) effect of making her sound menacing. 'I know you lied to the police. You withheld information from them. You wouldn't want me to make a fuss about that, now would you?'

She straightened up.

'I could pass your number on to her, if you like?' said Liz, also quietly. 'And she can contact you if she wants to.'

Jane shook her head. 'No. You'll pardon me if I don't

trust you to do that, all things considered,' she said. 'And it's what I want, not what she wants. I'd like her details now, please.'

Liz picked up a handbag from the floor by her feet and took her phone out of it. She reached for an appointment card and began writing on it.

'Thank you,' said Jane, taking it from her and checking to make sure she could read the mobile number scribbled across it. 'Tell Martin I said hello,' she said before turning and walking out.

Three impressive performances in one morning, she thought as she drove home. No doubt Liz would be straight on the phone to Sylvia. But she herself wouldn't be quite so speedy. She would keep Sylvia waiting. Let her wonder what it was that Jane wanted with her.

She let the weekend go by before deciding that the time was right. *Sylvia*, she texted. *I got your number from Liz H. I have your painting here and was wondering whether you would like it back? Jane Lord.*

Very shortly after sending this, a reply came back. *Thank you Jane, I would like that. I'll call round tomorrow about 5.30 to get it.*

Oh, will you? thought Jane as she read this. *I'll call round.* Not could I . . . or would it be all right to . . ? Just a statement of intent. One had to admire the woman's positiveness.

Jane brought the painting downstairs and propped it up on one of the worktops in the kitchen. She knew that she didn't have to invite Sylvia in when she came. She could just take the painting to the front door, hand it over, say goodbye and that would be that. But she wanted to talk to her.

She cast her eyes around the room. The whisky bottle had already been put away in a cupboard. Everything was in order. She filled the kettle, put some milk in a jug and shook some chocolate biscuits out of their packet and on to a plate.

Even though she was listening out for it, when the doorbell rang it made her jump.

'Come in,' she said, ushering Sylvia into the hall. 'Shall I take your coat?'

It was all uncannily like the first visit. The same camel coloured coat; the same charcoal trouser suit underneath it (a different blouse, though – a navy blue one this time). The same middle-aged, exceedingly plain woman.

Jane tried to imagine what Sylvia would have looked like twenty years ago. Obviously, she wouldn't have had grey hair then. Would she have worn glasses? Like the ones she was wearing now? She had a fleeting vision of a younger Sylvia, her long hair in a bun, her glasses firmly in place, sitting unnoticed, week after week, in her receptionist's chair, until one fateful evening, in true Hollywood fashion, when she'd let her hair down, whipped off her specs and made herself 'available' to an unsuspecting Neil.

Once in the kitchen, Sylvia sat down in the same place as she'd done before. Jane began to make the tea.

'Is there anything else still in the cottage that you would like to have . . . to have back?' she asked with a quick glance at the other woman.

Sylvia shook her head. 'I've already taken everything I wanted,' she said. 'Everything that was mine.'

Did that mean that she hadn't been bothered about the water colour, Jane wondered? If so, then why had she come to get it now? Perhaps because she, too, wanted to talk some more? 'Don't go getting too friendly with her,' Fran had said, and Jane had scoffed at the idea. 'I'd have to forgive her first and that's never going to happen, is it?' she'd said. But what if Sylvia were to say she was sorry for all the trouble she had caused, would Jane be prepared to forgive her? And if she did forgive her, would she also have to think about forgiving Neil? God! Now wasn't the time to be torturing herself with all this again!

And, anyway, how likely was it that Sylvia would say she was sorry? She had shown no signs of repentance so far. But as Jane was placing the tea things on the table, it occurred to her that this might be why she had invited the other woman round. To get her to apologise; to get her to show a smidgeon of remorse for the heartache she'd caused.

'So what's happening with the police now?' she asked, sitting down opposite Sylvia.

Sylvia gave her a brief account of what had already happened and what was likely to happen in the near future. She sounded hopeful. At best, no charges would be brought against Mark. At worst, he could expect a fairly light sentence. She was, she said, grateful to Frances for her fair and positive statement. They both were.

Jane found herself resenting all this optimism and orderliness.

'I've been thinking about things,' she said, 'and what I don't understand is why you called the police that night. You didn't have to. You said your son didn't want you to. He wanted to wait till the next morning and then dump Frances somewhere miles and miles away from the cottage. But you called the police and directed them to it. Why?'

Sylvia stared at the plate of biscuits on the table in front of her. 'I don't see why that matters now,' she said.

'I'm just curious, that's all. You present yourself as this caring, loving mother but then you go and do something like that. It doesn't make sense.' Sylvia's reaction to the scorn in her voice gave Jane a moment's satisfaction. 'It almost seems as though you wanted him to get caught.'

'No!' said Sylvia. 'I wanted to stop things getting any worse, which they might have done if your friend had stayed there another night. And I knew . . .'

'Yes . . . ?'

Sylvia shrugged and picked up her teacup. It seemed she had nothing more to say.

Jane was frustrated. Sylvia might want to leave things there but she didn't. 'You said, when you came here before, that your son . . . Mark . . . wanted to talk to me. What did he want to talk about?'

Sylvia put her cup down and ran a fingertip round her lips. 'He was angry,' she said. 'He wanted you to know that he existed. He wanted to . . . Oh I don't know . . . lay claim to his father or something like that.'

'Some financial claim?' said Jane.

Sylvia looked uncomfortable. 'I never made any financial demands on Neil,' she said. 'And I'm not making any now. I can see how you might be thinking otherwise but I can assure you I want nothing from you.' Her eyes travelled over to the painting on the worktop.

'Yes, but what about Mark? What does he want? Does he still want to talk to me?'

'I don't think that would be a good idea right now.'

'At some later date then?'

Jane thought that Sylvia wasn't going to reply to this but after a long silence she said: 'To be honest, I don't know what he wants. And when all this is sorted out I hope he'll just walk away and forget about it. But I don't know . . . He is who he is. I know you dislike me, but his position's different, isn't it? But I suppose we come as a package in your eyes.'

'I'm trying hard not to let that be the case,' said Jane. She sat back in her chair. 'It's difficult to be objective, though. You had an affair with my husband. You continued with it after Mark was born. You knew he was married. To me!' She jabbed her forefinger into her chest and was surprised by the loud thud it made. 'You didn't give a damn about me then. So why should I care about you now? Either of you?'

'I'm not asking you to.'

'I think I've been more than reasonable with you. And so, I might add, has Frances. I don't know how you have the nerve to make any more demands on us.'

'I'm not making any demands,' said Sylvia.

But Jane wasn't listening. 'It's me who should be making demands,' she said. 'I should be demanding an apology from you for what you've done to me and mine.' Sylvia, she noted, hadn't asked about Lucy and Sarah – about what they might be thinking now, about what their attitudes towards Mark might be.

'Look, I know you're the . . . injured party. I know that.

But how can I be sorry when I have a son who is the result of what happened. I'm sorry you had to find out. I always hoped you wouldn't. But that's the best I can say. And I can only repeat, I don't want anything from you. I only came here today because you asked me to. And as for your friend . . .'

Jane wished that Sylvia wouldn't keep referring to Fran in this way. 'Her name's Frances,' she said curtly.

'As for Frances . . .' Sylvia said in a rush, and then stopped, seeming to have changed her mind about what she was going to say.

Jane frowned. It wasn't the first time Sylvia had done this – made an oblique remark and then stopped. 'What about Frances?' she said.

There was a visible change in Sylvia's expression which Jane interpreted as a reaction to the hostile stare she was giving her.

'You asked me why I called the police that Monday night,' Sylvia said, her voice low and measured now.

Jane nodded.

'You think I did it so you would find out about the cottage, don't you?'

Jane thought about this for a moment. 'No, I don't think I do,' she said. 'If you'd wanted me to find out, you could have told me at any time. Although . . . once your son had gone and abducted Fran . . . perhaps . . .' It was hard to think this through. She shook her head, as much to try and clear it as to deny Sylvia's assertion. 'No, I just think it was a strange – an unnecessary – thing to do. And I've never bought your line that you were concerned about Frances spending another night there.'

'So you think I wanted Mark to get caught. Well I didn't. Of course I didn't.' She sounded defiant now. 'I knew he'd spent all that weekend bending over backwards to keep the cottage's location hidden. But I also knew . . . that he'd been wasting his time all along.'

Jane was confused. 'Sorry,' she said. 'I don't understand what you're saying.'

'He'd been wasting his time because your friend, your Frances, knew exactly where she was.'

'What do you mean? How could she have known?'

'Because she'd been there before.'

'What? No, you're mistaken. She couldn't have been there before.'

The room seemed to darken and all Jane could hear was Sylvia's voice in her ear: 'I don't know whether I was his first but I doubt if I was his last.' Her mind went blank for a moment, and then, slowly, a kaleidoscopic reaction began to take place. Fragmentary impressions, flashes of insight, phrases lodged in her memory, all started to swirl around, and just when it seemed as though they were about to settle into shape, they shifted and scattered into random pieces again. She folded her arms across her chest and began to rock gently to and fro, as if she thought she was sitting in the rocking chair.

'I'm sorry,' she could hear Sylvia saying, as if from a distance. 'I thought at first that you must've known. But when you said it was the police who'd told you the cottage was Neil's I knew then that she hadn't said anything. So, as it turns out, I needn't have done what I did. But at the time, I thought that when she was free she'd tell the police what she knew.'

Jane made an effort to concentrate on what Sylvia was saying.

'When I came to see you before, and I realised that you had no idea, I was going to tell you. But then I decided not to. I could see that she was a close friend. And I wouldn't have told you now, but for you going on about me being such an awful mother.'

'Yes, but how do you know? That she'd been there before?'

'I saw her. One Sunday. I went to the cottage to do some painting and when I got there I could see that Neil'd been there too. There was no-one in, but the fire was lit, there was food in the kitchen and . . . clothes in the bedroom.' Sylvia shrugged. 'It was obvious he had a woman with him. I locked up again and drove to the pub in the village. And his car was there in the car park. They were having lunch.' She glanced at Jane. 'An intimate lunch.'

'Yes but how can you be sure it was her you saw?'

'Oh, I'm sure. I wouldn't have rung the police that night if I hadn't been sure. I stayed and had a drink. He didn't see me but I wouldn't have been bothered if he had. It didn't matter to me that he was with another woman. I was just interested, that's all. And when she went to the Ladies I followed her to get a closer look. She was a very striking woman. So when I saw her picture on the telly, I knew straight away it was her.'

'When was this supposed to be?'

'Oh, I don't know. A few years ago. Spring, I remember, because I'd gone there to paint the wildflowers in the field behind the cottage . . .'

But Jane wasn't interested in this. 'How many years ago?' she interrupted.

'Four? Five?'

Four years, five. When would that have been? Jane couldn't think properly. In fact she couldn't think at all with Sylvia sitting there watching her.

'I think you should leave now,' she said, rising from her chair. She walked across the room and got the painting. 'I'm sorry but the frame's a bit damaged.' She opened a cupboard door, took out a handful of carrier bags and, selecting one, handed it to Sylvia. 'Here, you'll need something to carry it in.'

Sylvia stood up and slipped the painting into the bag. 'I'm sorry,' she said. 'Sorry I had to tell you this. I didn't come here with that intention.'

Jane closed the door behind Sylvia and, although it had only just gone six, double locked it and put the chain on. For a few moments she stood still, listening to the hollow, echoing beats of her heart. As she turned round, she caught sight of the green cagoule hanging by the door and a great surge of anger swept over her. But it was silly to start getting upset, she told herself. It couldn't be true, what Sylvia had told her. It didn't make sense. She needed to stay calm; to think.

She went back into the kitchen and began to tidy up. She couldn't begin to think with all this mess everywhere. She stuffed the carrier bags back into the cupboard and cleared the table. The biscuits, which she'd bought specially, hadn't been touched. She swiped them off the plate and into the bin. She put the cups and saucers into the dishwasher and emptied the teapot down the sink. As the tea leaves disappeared down the plughole, she felt a deep sense of impending disaster. This was a foolish way to dispose of them, she knew that – especially when there was no man in the house to deal with any potential blockage. And no friend now, with whom to rant and joke about it, were it to happen.

But it couldn't be true. Sylvia must have made a mistake. 'I wouldn't have rung the police that night if I hadn't been sure,' she'd said. Yes, but how sure could anyone be after four or five years? The woman she'd seen with Neil must have been someone who'd looked like Fran. 'She was a very striking woman.' Well, Fran wasn't the only striking woman in the world, was she? The only middle-aged, red-haired, striking looking woman . . ? Even so . . . it couldn't have been Fran. She should just get on the phone right now and tell her what this Sylvia woman had said. Then they could have a good laugh about it. It was such a ridiculous contention. Fran had never liked Neil; he had never liked her.

She couldn't help remembering, though, what Fran kept saying about Howard Sage. 'He was a bit of a prat, but he was very attractive.' She might have thought the same about Neil. But Fran had been young then. And she hadn't known Howard Sage's wife. She was a grown woman now and Jane was her friend. She wouldn't have done such a thing.

But . . . there was no getting away from the fact that she had been an adulteress. At least once, but there could have been other times, too. 'Does your mother have any other . . .

relationships?' DS Hooper had asked. And Emer had said: 'Who knows? It's not unthinkable, is it?' Maybe it wasn't unthinkable. Maybe nothing was unthinkable any more.

So when was this supposed to have happened? Four or five years ago, Sylvia had said, in the springtime? Was that possible? She tried to remember what had been going on in their lives then. Maybe the 'Frances Delaney' folder in her email account could help here.

She sat down at the computer and scrolled down to the spring months of 2003. No, it couldn't have been then. Fran's mother had still been alive and she had spent nearly all her weekends traipsing up to Lancashire and back. Nearly all . . . No! Not even Fran would . . . Good God, what had she just said? Not even Fran! So she did think that Fran was capable of . . . ? Well yes, she was capable of a lot of things, but surely not something as unforgiveable as this?

Jane turned her attention to spring 2004. But already she knew what she was going to find there. It'd only been a few weeks since she'd last looked. February 2004 was when Fran had come back from her trip to New Zealand. There had been no emails in March, April or May that year. Why not?

She stared at the computer screen. There had been nothing until June. *Here I am at last. I've been in such a whirl since I came back from NZ.*

Yes, I bet you have, thought Jane.

Patrick is working in LA now. He's been there since just after Easter. He wanted/still wants me to join him but after a lot of thought I've decided not to.

So Patrick had gone to LA and Fran had jumped into bed with Neil. Were they still sleeping together when she'd written this email, she wondered?

There's lots to talk about, not least my son and your daughter! How about that? We'll be related!

Oh, yes! There certainly would be lots to talk about the next time she saw Fran. She was close to tears now, but she was damned if she was going to cry. 'No!' she said out loud. 'No!' she repeated, shouting now. How could Fran have done this to her?

But it had always been an unequal friendship. She could see this clearly now. A friendship initiated by Jane and perpetuated by the marriage of their children. A friendship she had wanted far more than Fran ever had. 'You invest too much in her,' Neil had said. And he'd been right. But she'd always believed that it'd been an investment worth making. Until now.

She walked away from the computer and poured herself a glass of whisky. She wasn't going to let herself cry. If this were true, Fran wasn't worth crying over. But it was true. She knew it was.

Her mind went into overdrive, darting from one memory to another, from one lacerating self-judgement to the next. How could she have been so blind? Not just briefly, but for all those years? How could she have got Fran so wrong? What a fool she'd been. When all that stuff about the cottage had come to light, and then all the Sylvia business, she'd poured her heart and soul out to her. And all the time . . .

How had it happened? Had Fran seduced Neil like Sylvia had done? Made herself 'available'? And why had she done it? Because Patrick had gone to America? Because she could? 'I set myself the challenge and he rose to it.' That's what she'd said about Howard Sage. But had she stopped for one moment to think about Jane? Obviously not. Neither of them had. Jane couldn't be bothered to think about Neil's transgressions right now. He'd strayed way beyond the pale as far as she was concerned. But Fran! How could Fran have done this? After all the little acts of kindness Jane had shown her over the years?

Powerless now to stop herself, she lay down on the sofa and wept.

When the phone rang, two hours later, she was sitting in the kitchen drinking her third glass of whisky. She hadn't eaten since lunchtime. Her edges should have been dulled to oblivion by now, but they weren't. She walked unsteadily into the hall and grabbed the receiver. It was Fran. She held the phone in her hand and let it ring. When it stopped she put it down and returned to her rocking chair. A few minutes later, her mobile rang. She didn't answer that either.

She had school in the morning; she should go to bed now. Forgetting that she'd already done so hours earlier, she went to lock the front door and caught sight of the green cagoule again. 'You should've thrown it out years ago,' Lucy had said. 'Oh, should I?' she'd replied. 'And then none of this would have happened, I suppose.' But her sarcasm seemed misplaced now. None of this would have happened, if she'd thrown it out. Fran wouldn't have been abducted; she might never have found out about the cottage, or about Sylvia and Mark. And she would never have found out about Fran and Neil.

She snatched the cagoule off its hook and began trying to tear it into pieces. But it resisted her efforts. If she really wanted to render it unwearable, she would need scissors. With a howl of frustration she flung it across the hall.

2

The next morning, feeling slightly ashamed of the previous night's histrionics, Jane snatched the cagoule from the floor and hung it up in the alcove again, underneath one of her other coats.

She forced herself into school and struggled through the day. That evening Fran rang again, but she didn't answer. And when, after a further attempt, Fran left a voicemail message: 'Where are you? Ring me,' Jane ignored that too.

Not long after this Lucy rang to see if she was all right. 'Fran's worrying about you,' she said. 'You've not been answering her calls.'

'I've been out. There's nothing to worry about. I'm fine.'

'Well just ring her then.'

'I will,' said Jane. But not yet, she thought. She had an awful lot of thinking to do before she could trust herself to speak to Fran.

'Anyway,' Lucy was saying. 'I've sent you the links for a couple of houses you might be interested in, so have a look at them and see what you think.'

'Right,' said Jane. At this moment, she had no intention of entering into a discussion with Lucy about it, but she was one hundred percent certain now that she wouldn't be moving to London.

She spent the next few days and nights going over, again and again, all the details of the past few years, remembering how much pleasure her developing friendship with Fran had given her and how triumphant she'd felt in the face of Neil's scepticism. And now it turned out that all the while, behind her back, they'd been keeping their dirty little secret. And she hadn't suspected a thing. Just like she hadn't suspected anything during all the Sylvia and Mark years before that. How could she have been so blind? What was the matter with her?

The questions began piling up. Why had they done it; they had never liked each other? She thought she knew when it had started – when Fran came back from New Zealand – but when had it ended? Or perhaps it hadn't; perhaps it had been going on right until . . . No! That really was unthinkable! Fran hadn't seemed that upset by Neil's death. No, it must have ended long before then. It must have.

And had Fran known, all along, about Sylvia? Was that why she'd been so favourably disposed towards Mark – she'd known who he was and why he'd done what he did? But she'd seemed so shocked when the policewomen had told them that the cottage was Neil's. Was that all an act?

What hurt most – and what was so embarrassing to think about now – was how much she'd confided in Fran since Neil's death. Fran had been the one person she'd been able to talk freely to. The one person whom, in Neil's absence, she'd come to rely on. And when the whole cottage business had come to light . . . Jane couldn't bear to think of some of the things she'd said to Fran then. She'd ranted on about her sham marriage. She'd let Fran see how hurt she'd been by Sylvia's revelations. And then, just a few weeks ago, she'd sat on that bed at the cottage – the bed Neil had slept in with Sylvia, and the one she now knew he had slept in with Fran, too – she'd sat there and given Fran a privileged, close-up view of her anger and pain! It was absolutely mortifying.

She wondered how much more she could bear, and whether it was humanly possible to feel any angrier than she did now. Almost all of this anger was directed at Fran. She was done agonising over Neil, she told herself. What was the point? He was beyond reach; beyond retribution. Whereas Fran . . .

On Friday morning she made herself attend her class, but this week she had nothing to say about the new novel they were studying. She hadn't even finished reading it yet, the tortuous preoccupations of the book's protagonist being no match for her own. The Saturday of its title was the day of the Anti-War demonstration in March 2003 – the demonstration she had nearly gone on with Fran. The one she should have gone on had her courage not failed her.

Neil had gone to a football match that day. Allegedly. Although Mark would've been . . . what? . . . sixteen, so it would've been unlikely that he'd gone to the cottage instead. She hoped that Mark had refused to go with him. She really did.

That afternoon, as she sat in the lounge trying to read a bit more of the novel, her mind wandered off again. She remembered how Neil and Fran had argued over Iraq, neither of them attempting to hide the antipathy they felt towards each other. Or at least that was how she'd interpreted it at the time. Now she couldn't help but see it as some kind of sexual foreplay.

Who had made the first move, she wondered? And how? She certainly hadn't seen anything of Fran at the time she thought the affair must have started, so one of them must have gone out of their way to get things going.

She put the book aside and curled up on the sofa. She didn't want to dwell on the sex; it was so humiliating to think of them in bed together. Whenever she thought about Neil and Sylvia, the sex was always run of the mill and functional. He was being obliging; she, for the most part, was on a procreating mission. So nothing too adventurous. But Neil and Fran . . . She kept telling herself she couldn't imagine what they had got up to, but, of course, it was impossible not to try. Both of them, she felt certain, would have been showing off. God! It really didn't bear thinking about!

From time to time, since Neil's death, she had wondered what it would be like to have another man in her life. One thing she knew though – it wouldn't be easy making that first (metaphorical) leap into bed with someone else. But she couldn't imagine Fran feeling like that. Oh no. She'd have been so sure of herself. And Neil? Would he have had any doubts about his (decidedly middle-aged) prowess? Well, thought Jane, sitting up and thumping the cushion into shape, he ought to have had.

And then, to come home afterwards and compare her to Fran, as she felt sure he must have done. How dare he!

On the following Sunday afternoon, Jane had just returned from one of her long walks in the park when Fran rang again. She stood in the hall and stared at the phone until it stopped ringing, and then, acting on impulse, picked it up and rang back.

'Sorr-ee, I was just walking through the door when you rang off,' she said, impressed by her careless tone.

'I was beginning to think you'd gone into hibernation,' Fran said.

They had a short conversation during the course of which Fran didn't seem to notice anything untoward. Jane decided that this was how she would proceed. She wouldn't make any calls herself, but she would answer Fran's. She would be cool but civil. The confrontation, when it came, would be face to face. But only when she was good and ready, when she'd got all the weeping and wailing and self pity out of her system. The memory of the scene in the bedroom at the cottage was still raw; she vowed that Fran would never see her like that again.

She would also take her time deciding who else – if anyone – she was going to tell. It would do Lucy good, she thought, to see her wonderful mother-in-law in a new light, but poor John didn't deserve the fall-out from this, nor the embarrassment he himself would feel. There was also Patrick to consider. If he were to find out, it might mean the end of his and Fran's marriage. But is that my problem, Jane thought, her anger flaring up again? Did Fran worry about my marriage when she slept with my husband?

For all she knew, though, Patrick might take it with equanimity. It might be something he'd experienced before. Like Emer, he might feel that it was perfectly thinkable and 'so typical' of Fran.

'Won't you find it strange having Patrick home, after all this time?' she said in one of her next phone conversations with Fran. She didn't wait for an answer. 'Do you think he's ever been unfaithful while he's been away?'

'The thought has crossed my mind from time to time,' said Fran.

'If you found out that he had been, would it matter to you?'

The ensuing silence, while Fran thought about this, was short. 'Probably not,' she said. 'As long as it wasn't serious. And as long as it was over.'

How uncomplicated she made it seem. Why can't I apply those sentiments to my situation, Jane wondered? My husband and my best friend had an affair, but hey, it wasn't serious and it's over now!

'If you'd been unfaithful,' she said. 'Perish the thought, of course! Do you think he'd be just as understanding?'

This time the silence was longer.

'I don't see why not. If it meant nothing,' was the reply when it eventually came.

'And as long as it was over,' Jane said, repeating Fran's previous words. 'As long as it was all . . . dead and buried, so to speak.'

How easy it was to do this over the phone! And how surprisingly satisfying! It gave her such a feeling of power. She had been on the receiving end of so many shocks recently, but now she was in a position to start administering them. Whenever she wanted . . . If she wanted.

Lucy had been sending Jane the details of houses for sale on a regular basis. The time had come to tell her to stop house-hunting.

'Have you had a look at that last house I sent you?' Lucy

asked, almost before she and her mother had finished exchanging phone greetings.

That's one of the reasons I'm calling,' said Jane. 'I've been doing a lot of thinking lately and I've decided that I'm not going to move. I'm staying put – at least for the foreseeable future.'

'In Solihull?'

'Yes, in Solihull. And in this house.'

'But . . .'

'No buts, Lucy. I've made my mind up. I'm fine as I am here. And you should be concentrating on getting ready for this new baby instead of bothering about my living arrangements.'

When she'd finished talking to Lucy, she rang Sarah and had a brief conversation with her too. Sarah was as relieved as Lucy had been disappointed. Jane felt that neither was entirely disinterested. Changing the subject, she asked if Sarah had done anything about Mark. She had found him on Facebook, Sarah said, but hadn't contacted him yet. She was waiting to see whether or not he was going to be prosecuted. 'I'd definitely like to meet him,' she affirmed, 'but not in prison.'

'I don't think it'll come to that,' Jane said. 'We should hear soon, anyway.'

As she was locking up for the night, she caught her customary glimpse of the green cagoule, peeping out from beneath one of her coats. How silly it was to blame an article of clothing for all the things that had happened. Yes . . . *if* Fran hadn't been wearing it that night then some of this pain might have been avoided. There were so many *ifs* though. *If* it hadn't been raining; *if* she'd gone outside earlier – or later; *if* this and *if* that. But they were all incidental. The really fundamental ones were: *if* Neil had never had the affair with Sylvia; *if* he and Fran had resisted each other's charms. And these had nothing at all to do with the bloody cagoule. It was an innocent piece of clothing – which was more than could be said for the last person who had worn it.

She removed it from its hiding place and, like Bronia had done a few weeks earlier, hung it up again on a hook of its own.

3

The letter from the police station, informing Jane that the charges against Mark Ashworth had been dropped, arrived in the same post as the party invitation from Kay. Both caused her some agitation. Sarah would be contacting Mark now, and there were bound to be repercussions. As for the party invitation, she would probably turn it down. She didn't feel as though she could trust Martin anymore – or any of her and Neil's other mutual friends for that matter. But the sad fact was that without them she would be friendless. She had lots of acquaintances, who had never quite metamorphosed into friends, mainly because she'd never made enough effort with them. She'd never felt the need to.

Now, she told herself sternly, she would have to remedy this situation. The women in her literature class would be a good place to start. And if she were to do the part-time degree, there would be opportunities there too. It was absolutely ridiculous that she didn't have any friends that were exclusively hers.

Well, there had been Fran, of course. Until it turned out that she, too, had been a mutual friend.

What was she going to do about Fran? Have one almighty row with her . . . and then what? Tell everyone else before walking away from the friendship for ever? This would have such a damaging effect on the family and Jane wasn't sure she wanted to be responsible for that. So perhaps it would be best to just have the row but not tell anyone. And not walk away either? Seeing that she'd already decided – before this latest revelation – that she was going to be less dependent on Fran in the future, there was a good chance that any change in their relationship would be seen as circumstantial rather than fundamental. Perhaps only she and Fran need know that the friendship was well and truly over. But could she be so . . . forgiving? Because that's what this partial letting off the hook would be, a kind of forgiveness.

She found herself thinking about Nick Cartwright. He'd stood by Fran all those years ago when she'd been a young, single mother. He'd married her and adopted her daughter; he'd been a good husband and father; and then, when he'd outlived his usefulness, he'd been cast aside in favour of Patrick. Yet he was still friends with Fran. Somewhere along the line he'd been prepared to forgive and forget. To forgive, anyway, because Jane didn't believe that anyone could ever forget all that heartache and pain.

Perhaps he'd been too forgiving. Fran didn't deserve him. She'd never deserved him. And she doesn't deserve me, either, Jane thought. No, she was damned if she was going to become another Nick Cartwright. She would have to think this through again.

'I've been to see Mark,' Sarah said, a week later, standing in the hall with a small rucksack slung over her shoulder. It was nearly nine o'clock in the evening.

'Oh, have you?' said Jane, annoyed at being taken by surprise like this. 'Why didn't you tell me you were coming home?'

'Because I didn't know myself. I was going to go straight back to Sheffield tonight after I'd seen him but . . . I changed my mind.'

'Have you eaten?'

Sarah nodded.

They went into the lounge which was looking rather bare without the bookcases and occasional tables that, along with the furniture in the dining-room, Jane had sold to a second-hand emporium in Knowle only a few days before. Sarah glanced round but made no comment.

'So . . . how was it then, your meeting?'

'Good. He's nice. You'd like him. And so would Lucy if she gave him a chance. He's really sorry for what he did. He said to tell you that.'

Jane studied her daughter carefully. She seemed rather subdued. 'So what's the problem then? You don't seem very happy,' she said.

'No, I am. It went well. Better than I thought it would. It was strange though. He looks a bit like me – a bit like Dad, I suppose.'

'Where did you meet him?'

'In Birmingham, in one of those pubs down by the canal.'

'And what did you talk about?'

'Just ordinary things. What he does, what we all do, that sort of thing.'

'And what does he do – apart from abducting people, I mean?'

'He's a painter and decorator.'

'Really?' said Jane, casting her eye over the wall opposite her. (But no, that would be too weird!) 'And are you going to see him again?'

'I hope so. You don't mind, do you?'

'No, I don't think so. He's your brother, it's only natural you want to get to know him.' She paused. 'Are you going to tell Lucy you've seen him?'

Sarah smiled. 'Oh, yes! I can't wait to have that little conversation.' And then, replacing the smile with a look of concern, she said: 'Anyway, how are you?'

'Me? I'm fine.'

'Mark told me his mother came to see you again. What was that about?'

Jane stiffened. 'Oh . . . she came to collect something she'd left at the cottage, that was all,' she said. Had Mark told Sarah anything else, she wondered uneasily?

But it would seem not. Sarah had moved on. 'You've

been busy,' she said, indicating the empty spaces in the room.

'Yes I have. I'm going to redecorate and everything. I'm about to acquire some new furniture, and someone's coming tomorrow to measure the windows for some of those louvred shutters.' (Fran, she'd decided, didn't have a monopoly on these.)

'Wow!' Sarah said without any obvious enthusiasm. She hesitated. 'I'm really glad you've decided not to move to London.'

Jane nodded. 'I'm better off where I am,' she said.

'Yes, you are,' said Sarah.

Lying awake that night, Jane's thoughts turned to Mark. He had wanted them – her, Lucy and Sarah – to know of his existence. He had wanted – how had Sylvia put it? – 'to lay claim to his father'. Well, he'd done that now – with Sarah's help.

Jane had said that she didn't mind. But was this true, if it meant he would be hovering on the periphery of their lives now, perhaps for ever? 'He's nice . . . you'd like him,' Sarah had said. And perhaps she would, because leaving aside the fact that he'd kidnapped Fran (who probably deserved it anyway), he was blameless in all this. She thought about the football duvet at the cottage, and the little boy who had only seen his father in the gaps and spaces of his other 'real' life. And an idea began to form in her mind.

According to her solicitor she would be in a position to put the cottage on the market soon. She'd been feeling, though, that it wasn't really hers to sell – which was silly because she didn't feel like that about all the other things she'd been selling recently. And what else could she do with it, anyway? She certainly wasn't going to keep it. Or hand it over to Sylvia. Not to Sylvia who kept insisting that she wanted nothing from Jane. But what about Mark? Neil had kept the cottage for his benefit. He was Neil's son. She could sell it . . . and? No, she couldn't give him all the proceeds, but she could divide them between all three of Neil's children.

This might be a very good idea, she thought. It might even be 'the right thing' to do.

'Anyway . . . it's my birthday in a couple of weeks,' Lucy said a few evenings later – after she'd told Jane exactly what she thought about Sarah going to meet him.

'So it is. Shall I come down for it?' said Jane as if the idea had just occurred to her, when, in fact, she'd been planning for some time to have her confrontation with Fran on or around this very date.

'Yeah, do that,' said Lucy. 'It's on a Monday but we can have a little celebration on the Sunday. It'll have to be a lunch one, though. I'm useless in the evenings now. Shall we say you, Fran, us – and Emer too, I suppose? And I'll ask Sarah, but I won't hold my breath there. She'll probably be too busy fraternising.'

When Fran heard that Jane was going to be in London for the birthday weekend she sounded pleased. 'Why don't you stay here?' she suggested. 'There's more room. And we can do other things as well while you're down.'

'Thank you, but I think I'll be needed at Lucy's,' Jane replied, marvelling, for the umpteenth time, at Fran's inability to notice the coolness in her manner these days.

Under different circumstances, she thought, a touch wistfully, it would have been nice to do those 'other things'. She was going to miss Fran's company; life would be less rich without her. But whose fault was that? What Fran had done was unforgiveable. And the loss would be hers too – assuming, of course, that it even registered with her.

Jane kept trying to imagine how their confrontation would play out. She would demand answers to the questions that had been torturing her, of course. How had Fran and Neil got together in the first place? How long had the affair lasted? And why, why had she done it? Fran would probably say what people always said in these situations: she didn't know why; it'd meant nothing; she hadn't been in love with Neil (as if Jane needed reassurance on that score!); she was sorry. But what consolation could there be for Jane in any of this? Unless Fran really was genuinely sorry? In which case, might it be possible to salvage something of the friendship?

Was this what she wanted now, she wondered? It wasn't what she'd wanted yesterday. And there was no guarantee it would be what she wanted tomorrow. Fortunately, there was still time till Lucy's birthday for things to become clearer in her mind.

4

Contrary to expectation, Sarah announced that she would be present at Lucy's birthday lunch, seeing that she and her relatively new – and as yet unseen – boyfriend would be in London that weekend anyway, staying at his parents' house in Wandsworth. 'You can bring him with you, if you want,' Lucy had said. But Sarah didn't want.

'It's just as well he's not coming,' Lucy said to Jane on the Saturday afternoon. 'We haven't got that much space.'

She'd also thought about asking John's dad, she said, but if he'd brought his partner there would've been eight round the table and that would've been a bit of a squash, so she'd decided not to.

'Right,' said Jane, feeling disappointed for a moment that Nick Cartwright wouldn't be there. His presence would have provided her with an ideal opportunity to observe forgiveness in action.

The Mediterranean Pork Casserole had been simmering in the oven for well over an hour, and six small, clingfilm covered ramekins, filled with Jane's special chocolate ambrosia were chilling in the fridge. She was a bit worried there might not be enough time for this dessert to set properly, but it was too late now to be wishing that she'd prepared it last night.

Lucy was upstairs getting dressed, John was setting the table in the dining-room and Daniel was crawling around on the kitchen floor, steering a large toy engine into inconvenient corners and getting under his grandmother's feet in the process. It was nearly time for the guests to start arriving and

Jane was trying hard to control her nerves. After all, she lectured herself as she fussed with the smoked salmon starter, she had rehearsed this meeting with Fran so many times in her mind. She needed to get a grip if she was going to be as calm and unemotional as her script demanded.

But when the doorbell rang, she gave a startled cry. 'Who's that?' she said to Daniel. She heard John opening the front door and then Fran's voice in the hallway complaining about the lack of nearby parking spaces. 'It's Grandma Fran!' she said, answering her own question. She took Daniel by the hand and began steering him out of the kitchen. 'Let's go and say hello.'

Lucy came lumbering down the stairs at the same moment and the narrow hall was full to capacity. They filed into the lounge and sat down. Jane cast a critical eye over Fran who was looking as attractive as ever – in a different league altogether to Sylvia. And she thought back to the many times she'd commented on Fran's looks to Neil, and to how he'd always put on a show of indifference, as if to imply that Fran's beauty was in the eye of Jane's beholding, but not of his. The hypocritical bastard, she thought. But instead of feeling angry she felt strangely detached.

There was hardly time for any conversation before Sarah arrived bearing a birthday card and a bunch of flowers for Lucy. She seemed, to Jane, to be somewhat ill at ease – probably because Mark was an ongoing bone of contention between them. Daniel, however, was delighted to see her, and soon they were both playing with an impressive array of toy engines on the rug in front of the fireplace.

With a fixed smile on her face, Jane sat and listened to the chit chat going on around her. Everything was so familiar, so ordinary – as if nothing had changed. As if Fran's betrayal had never taken place. Or, to be more accurate, as if Jane had never found out about it. And it occurred to her that there was another option open to her. If she so wished, she could choose to perpetuate rather than shatter this illusion. She could say nothing – to Fran, or anyone else. Ever. She could guard her secret, as others had guarded theirs. Why not? she thought. This too might be the 'right thing' to do.

Well yes, for everyone else, maybe. But for her?

She rose to her feet. 'I'll just check the casserole,' she said, feeling the need to remove herself from Fran's presence for a few minutes.

But Fran followed her into the kitchen. 'Anything I can do to help?' she asked.

Jane looked around, as though checking. 'No,' she said. 'I think I've got everything under control.'

There wasn't much room in the kitchen and their close proximity was disturbing her. Trying to appear purposeful, she donned a pair of oven gloves and opened the oven door.

Fran perched on a stool and watched her lift the large red casserole dish out of the oven. 'Why don't you come back with me for a bit, after this?' she said. Stay for dinner, and we can have a proper natter.'

Jane lifted the lid off the dish. 'I don't think we'll need much dinner, after all this,' she said, giving its contents an unnecessarily vigorous stir.

She put the lid back on and, bending down awkwardly, put the dish back in the oven. She straightened up and removed the gloves. She should just come right out with it now and say something like: 'But I'll come anyway, and we can have a nice long chat . . . about you and Neil.' Her heart began beating faster and faster, louder and louder. Yes, that's what she should say. But: 'Let's just see how things go,' she said instead.

John came into the kitchen to prepare Daniel's lunch. 'Emer shouldn't be long,' he said. 'We'll eat as soon as this young man's gone down for his nap.'

'I'll put the rice on then,' said Jane, busying herself with a pan.

Sarah brought Daniel in and the kitchen was overcrowded.

'If there's nothing I can do, I'll get out of the way,' said Fran, leaving the room.

Emer was later than expected.

'Sorry!' she said, standing in the kitchen doorway, re-arranging her multicoloured-scarf round her neck. 'I had a late one last night, but I'm here now.' She greeted Jane warmly and then turned to Sarah. 'Nice to see you again. How are you?'

'I'm good, thank you,' said Sarah. 'And you?'

'Me? I'm starving. When are we eating?'

'As soon as this slowcoach has finished and gone for a sleep,' said John.

But with so many of Daniel's favourite people there to distract him, progress was slow.

'Come on, Danny. Eat up. Auntie Em's fading away here,' Emer urged him.

Jane smiled. There was nothing fading or faded about Emer.

As soon as he'd finished eating, Daniel was whisked away, but it took a while longer before he consented to lie down quietly and go to sleep.

'Thank goodness for that!' said Emer when John finally came creeping down the stairs.

It was time for the birthday lunch.

The dining-room was very small and the table, which had been moved into the centre, took up nearly all the space. Lucy sat at the end near the door, where there was more leg and bump room, and John sat opposite her at the other end. Jane was on Lucy's right – in the most convenient place for going to and from the kitchen, as and when necessary.

John opened a bottle of champagne and filled everyone's glasses, Lucy's included since it was a special occasion. Before they started eating, he proposed a birthday toast: 'To Lucy! Happy birthday!'

'Well isn't this cosy?' said Emer, smiling across the table at Jane and Sarah.

After everyone had made the obligatory comments in praise of the smoked salmon starter, Lucy said to Fran: 'I see that house at the end of your road has been sold.'

'How interesting!' said Emer.

'It is to some of us,' said Lucy. 'Mum was thinking of buying it.'

'Were you?' Emer looked surprised.

'No, I wasn't,' said Jane, glancing at Fran. 'Lucy just got carried away with the idea of me moving down here.'

'Why would you do that? You've got a lovely house where you are.'

'Which, by the way, is getting a massive makeover,' said Sarah.

'Is it?' said Lucy, turning to her mother. 'You didn't tell me that.'

'You didn't tell me either,' said Fran, her fork halfway to her mouth.

'Didn't I?' said Jane. 'Oh dear! I thought I had. But yes, I'm going to redecorate everywhere, and have new furniture and everything. I've already sold loads of the old stuff.' She smiled at Lucy. 'You won't recognise the place by the time I've finished with it.'

'Wooo!' said Fran.

(But you won't be coming to see it, so don't go getting too excited.)

'And . . .' Jane looked round the table to see how her next piece of news would be received, 'I've also applied to do a degree course at Warwick.'

There was a buzz of surprise and interest.

'A degree?' said Lucy. 'In what?'

'English Studies. Part-time because I'll carry on with my little job while I'm doing it. That's if I get accepted, of course.'

'You will,' said Sarah.

'And how long will that take you?' asked Lucy.

'Oh . . . years and years, I expect.'

'Well good for you!' said John.

'Yeah, good for you!' said Fran, raising her glass.

Jane lowered her eyes to her plate, slightly unnerved by Fran's approving response.

'Well! You've been keeping a lot of things quiet, haven't you?' said Lucy.

Jane smiled. Haven't I just, she thought. She collected the empty plates together and invited Sarah to go with her to the kitchen to get the main course.

'Mum . . . ?' Sarah began as she transferred the rice from the colander to a serving bowl.

'Yes?' said Jane abstractedly. She had just removed the heavy casserole dish from the oven and didn't want to hang around with it in her hands.

But before Sarah could say anything more, John came in to get another bottle of wine. 'Emer's being awkward and wants red,' he said.

They went back to the dining-room where Jane dished up the casserole and John poured wine for everyone – but not for Lucy this time. As they ate and drank, the conversation drifted on to the topic of the new baby. How would Daniel react to it, they wondered? And had Lucy and John decided on any names yet?

'Well, if it's a boy,' said Lucy, 'I really like the name Joshua. But John's not too keen on it.'

'I'm a tad more than "not too keen",' said John. He turned to Fran. 'Do you remember that Joshua kid at primary school, the one I loathed and detested?'

Fran took a major part in the lively discussion that followed, keeping them all entertained with her anecdotes about this particular child. Abandoning her cool reserve for a moment, Jane joined in the laughter. Saying nothing would be so easy, she thought. And she'd always known that Fran wasn't perfect . . .

'But it's such a lovely name,' Lucy lamented. 'You shouldn't let some obnoxious little boy turn you against it.'

'And if it's a girl?' said Sarah.

'Well, we're doing a bit better there. At the moment, Imogen is top of both our lists.' Lucy looked round the table. 'So I hope none of you know any horrible Imogens.'

Jane glanced first at Emer, who had her head down and

was tucking into her pork and rice, and then at Fran who, catching Jane's eye, raised an eyebrow.

'No, Imogen's good,' said Sarah.

Fran raised both eyebrows and cleared her throat.

Her apparent amusement and rather conspiratorial manner irked Jane. No, she decided, she absolutely wouldn't keep quiet; she would speak to Fran that evening. She leaned forward and peered into the casserole dish. 'There's quite a bit left,' she said. 'Does anyone want any more? John?'

'Yes please,' said Emer, holding out her plate.

Second helpings were served and a renewed bout of eating followed.

A few mouthfuls later, Emer looked up from her plate and addressed Sarah across the table. 'I hear you've had a meeting with my mother's abductor,' she said in a slightly louder tone than was necessary.

The abruptness of the question took everyone by surprise.

'Er . . . yes, I have,' said Sarah, looking embarrassed.

'And?'

'And he seems very . . . nice.'

'And have you met him, too?' Emer asked Jane.

'Me? No. Not yet.'

Lucy put her fork down with a clatter. 'What do you mean, "not yet"?' she said, staring at her mother.

Jane shook her head. She wasn't quite sure what she meant. But this probably wasn't the moment to say anything about what she was planning to do with the proceeds from the sale of the cottage.

'For Christ's sake,' Lucy went on. 'Sarah seems to think he's her bloody twin or something. And now you! I honestly don't understand why you're both so obsessed with him.'

Jane shook her head again. Mark, she reflected, was pretty low down on the list of things she'd been obsessed with lately.

'He's your brother,' said Sarah. 'And he'd like to meet you.'

'I don't care who he is. I don't want anything to do with him.'

'Aren't you even the teeniest bit curious?' Emer said. 'I know *I* was . . .' She paused for effect. '*I* was really curious when I found out I had another sister and a brother.'

Jane glanced at Fran again.

'Oh, for Christ's sake!' said Lucy. 'What are you on about now?'

'Nick's not my real father,' said Emer. 'Someone else is – isn't that right, mother dear? And I've got another sister and brother, that's all.'

Lucy looked accusingly at John. 'Tell me you didn't know about this,' she said.

John stood up to refill glasses.

'Anyway . . . the point is,' said Emer before Lucy could say anything else. 'I *really, really* wanted to meet them.'

'And did you?' asked Sarah.

'No. But my circumstances were different to yours.'

'In what way?'

'Do we really need to go into this now?' said Fran.

'They didn't know that I existed,' said Emer, ignoring this. 'They still don't.'

'I wish I didn't know that *he* existed,' said Lucy.

'But you do,' said Jane. 'You can't pretend you don't.'

'I've always regretted never meeting them,' said Emer, 'and I think you will too, if you persist with this attitude.'

'What fucking attitude?'

Emer smiled and held up her hands in a gesture of surrender.

'You're blaming Mark for what Dad did,' said Sarah, 'and that's not fair. It's not his fault he's who he is.'

'That's not true! I'm blaming him for what he did to Fran. Have you forgotten about that?'

'No! But he's sorry for that.'

'And I've forgiven him, remember,' said Fran.

Of course you have, thought Jane. But then, some things were easier to forgive than others. What was a bit of benign abduction compared to the betrayal of a friend?'

'Well I haven't,' said Lucy. 'I can't forget what he put us through that weekend.'

'He told me all about that weekend,' said Sarah, half turning towards Jane.

Jane frowned, remembering her earlier misgivings. Had Mark told Sarah why his mother had contacted the police that night? Did she know about Fran? Was this what she was trying to tell her now?

Fran sighed loudly. 'I wish we could all forget about that bloody weekend,' she said.

'Yes, I'm sure you do,' murmured Sarah.

Yes, she knows, Jane thought. But does she also know that I know? Did Mark tell her that, too? It was difficult to think properly. She was beginning to feel quite claustrophobic. She sat further back in her chair to put a bit of distance between herself and the rest of the people round the table.

'Look Lucy,' said John, 'if you don't want to meet him that's up to you. But Sarah's right. He's your brother and if you refuse to have anything to do with him you might come to regret it.'

'Erm!' Emer coughed. 'It was me who said that, thank you.'

'OK, I can see you all think I'm being unreasonable.' Lucy turned to Fran. 'Do you think I should agree to meet him?'

'Excuse me! Why are you asking her?' said Emer.

'*Erm!* Because I value her opinion,' said Lucy.

'That's very flattering,' said Fran, 'but I'm not sure I'm the person you should be asking.'

'No, I'd say you're the last person she should be asking,' said Sarah, her tone unmistakeably hostile. All eyes were on her now. 'I'm sorry, I don't mean to be rude, but . . .'

'But what?' Lucy demanded.

Sarah turned to her mother and hesitated, as though seeking permission to continue. Jane's heart was beating so noisily, she could hardly hear herself think. She held her breath and let the moment pass. She wasn't going to stop Sarah from speaking out now. Why should she, when all her own silly little dilemmas were about to be resolved?

'I know all about you and my father,' Sarah said to Fran.

It was out of Jane's hands now. A wave of elation swept over her, leaving in its wake the feeling of cold calmness she'd been striving for all along. In the puzzled silence that followed Sarah's remark, she readied herself for action.

Lucy was the first to speak. 'What the hell does that mean?'

Jane put a restraining hand on Sarah's arm. She would take charge now; she was well rehearsed. 'It would seem she knows your little secret,' she said, smiling at Fran. 'And so, may I add, do I.'

Fran put both hands to her face. 'Christ!' she said softly, through her fingers.

'What are you talking about?' Lucy said.

Jane looked down the length of the table and spoke directly to John: 'Do you remember how puzzled you were about Mark's mother calling the police that night? You said it didn't make sense, directing them to the cottage like that. Well, I'm afraid it did. She called the police because she knew that Fran had been there before.' She transferred her attention to Lucy. 'With your father.'

'Oh, shit!' said Emer.

Fran looked up and stared at Jane in disbelief. 'How on earth did she know that?' she said.

'She saw you there. Well, she saw you in the pub actually, but she knew you were staying at the cottage. She used to go there on her own sometimes and she just happened to go there once when you were there too.' Jane gave a wry smile. 'How's that for a coincidence, eh?' she said, her gaze travelling round the table before coming back to rest on Fran. 'She went upstairs. She saw your things. Then she went to the pub and saw you together. She got a good look at you, so when she saw your photo on the television she knew who you were. And when she found out that Mark was responsible for your disappearance she thought there was no point trying to conceal the location of the cottage any longer because you knew where you were.'

It was a long speech, well delivered. So far, so satisfactory, she thought.

'And you believe that?' Lucy said. 'No! It's not true, is it Fran? . . . Oh my God!'

'How long have you known?' Fran said to Jane.

'For weeks.'

Fran shook her head. 'I knew something was wrong,' she said.

'How very perceptive of you.' (So she had noticed that things between them had changed!)

'Why didn't you say something before?'

'What, over the phone? I don't think so.'

'You were having an affair with my dad,' said Lucy. 'When?'

'It was years ago, for Christ's sake,' said Fran. 'Before you two got married. It was nothing . . . nothing.'

'I don't believe this!'

'Don't you?' said Emer. 'Why not? I mean it's not the first time she's had an affair with a married man, is it?'

'For fuck's sake, Emer,' said Fran. 'You make it sound as though I'm in the habit of . . .'

'Oh? And aren't you?' interrupted Jane. 'Or was it just my bad luck that you made an exception for my husband? Because that's what he was, Fran, my sodding husband. And you! You were supposed to be my friend.' The cold calmness was beginning to desert her. She could feel herself getting upset and angry all over again.

Fran shook her head. 'I don't know what to say,' she said.

'How about sorry?' said Emer.

'Keep out of this,' John said to her.

'Were you in love with him?' said Lucy.

Emer gave a scornful laugh. 'Oh, *please!*

'No, of course I wasn't,' said Fran.

'That's all right then,' said Jane. She turned to Lucy. 'It's funny, isn't it? Your father doesn't seem to have been that lovable. Sylvia wasn't in love with him either.'

'Was he in love with you?' Lucy persisted.

Fran didn't bother to answer.

Sounds of wakefulness could be heard coming from upstairs. They all stopped talking to listen. When a series of preliminary whimpers gave way to some forceful yelling, John stood up and began easing his way out of the room.

'Don't bring him in here,' said Lucy. 'I don't want him hearing all this.'

The silence continued until Daniel's crying subsided, and then Fran said: 'Look. It was years ago, it meant nothing . . .'

'Well not to you, maybe,' said Jane. 'Tell me, which of you made the first move?'

'Mum, don't,' said Sarah.

'I need to know,' Jane insisted. But Sarah was right. It was unseemly to do this in public. This should be between her and Fran.

Sarah stood up. 'I'm going to go now,' she said.

No-one said anything to dissuade her.

Jane followed her into the hall. 'Why didn't you tell me you knew?' she said.

'I was going to, that night I came home,' said Sarah, struggling into her coat, 'but you didn't tell me either and I didn't want to upset you. And I didn't know whether you'd said anything to Fran or not.' She looked stricken. 'Oh, God! I'm really sorry. I didn't come here to do this, but she's so up herself and Lucy's so bloody all over her it makes me sick. Please tell me you were going to say something yourself.'

'I was – this evening,' said Jane. 'In private, though,' she added, allowing herself a little smile. 'But it's all right. It's probably better this way.' She gave Sarah a hug. 'I'm glad you came.'

After Sarah had left, she stood in the hall for a few moments gathering her thoughts. Yes, it was better this way.

All she had to do now was have it out with Fran and then matters would take their course without any need for further decisions on her part. She checked her appearance in the large mirror – there to create an illusion of space – before going back into the small dining-room where the atmosphere could no longer be described as 'cosy'. She wondered what had been said in her absence.

'Why don't you go and have a lie down,' she said to Lucy. 'I'd like to talk to Fran alone.'

She remained standing until Lucy and Emer had left the room. It was quite dark now. She switched on the main light and sat down. Fran, she thought, looked older all of a sudden, and no longer quite so 'up herself'.

'Well?'

'Look,' Fran held up her hands, palms outward, 'all I can say is, I'm sorry.'

'No, that's not all you can say!' said Jane. 'You can tell me why you did it, for a start.'

'I don't know why,' said Fran. 'It was stupid. And you know me, I do stupid things. It was when . . .'

'I know when it was. It was when you came back from New Zealand, wasn't it? Just after Patrick had gone to America? But what I can't work out is how the two of you got together. Because I certainly didn't see anything of you at that time. So who did make the first move?'

'Well it wasn't me . . .' Fran said and then stopped, possibly realising how childish this sounded. 'Neil was in London for some conference thing,' she went on. 'He rang and invited me out for lunch.'

'He rang?'

'He texted first and . . .'

'Texted! How did he know your number?'

Fran shrugged.

'He must've got it off my phone!' Jane leaned back in her chair and folded her arms. She gave a strained little laugh. 'I've been imagining something like the Sylvia scenario,' she said. 'You know – you making yourself "available" and him being unable to resist. But this time, you're saying, it was the other way round.'

Fran said nothing.

'So, go on. He texted you, out of the blue, and you thought . . . Hey, I'll have an affair with him.'

'I agreed to have lunch with him. I was . . . intrigued. I didn't know what to think. And then . . . OK, I should've just left it at lunch, but I hardly knew you then and . . .'

Jane gave an outraged cry. 'What do you mean, you hardly knew me? For God's sake, Fran! You knew me well enough!'

'I'm sorry. What I meant was, I didn't know you then like I know you now. I shouldn't have done it. But at the time it just seemed like a bit of fun . . .'

'Fun! Oh yes, it must've been great fun. I know just how much you and Neil enjoyed each other's company.' Jane paused. 'What you mean is, it was just sex.'

'It didn't last long.'

'What? The sex or the affair?'

Fran sighed and shook her head.

'How long did it last, as a matter of interest – the affair?'

'Not long. A few weeks. When we heard that John and Lucy . . . But it wouldn't have lasted anyway. It was never serious.'

'Things never are with you, are they?' Jane picked up her paper napkin from the table and began screwing it into a ball. 'Did either of you stop to consider me in all this? No, scrub that "either", I'm damned if I'm going to get all upset about Neil again. Been there, done that, t-shirt, etc. Did *you* ever think about me?'

'We never meant to hurt you,' Fran said quietly. 'Neither of us. (OK, sorry! I won't speak for Neil.) But you were never meant to find out.' Her voice rose. 'And if it hadn't been for that stupid woman, you never would have.' She shook her head. 'I wish now that it'd never happened, I really do. What else can I say? I'm sorry.'

'It's not just the initial betrayal that hurts, you know.'

Jane tossed the screwed up napkin into the casserole dish. 'It's everything that came after. All those family occasions when we were all together and I never noticed that things had changed between the two of you. And then, when he died . . . I trusted you and confided in you, and all the time . . . And then when I found out about the cottage, and about Sylvia and Mark, all that fake sympathy and advice you gave me. Did you know about them already? And about the cottage? God, I feel as though you've made a complete fool of me!'

'No! No! It wasn't like that. I knew nothing about his other life. And I didn't know the cottage was his either, honestly I didn't. I was just as surprised as you were when that policewoman told us. He said he'd borrowed it for the weekend from some friends.'

'How many times did you go there then?'

'Only that once.'

'For the whole weekend? That's a fair bit of fun. And the rest of the time?'

'A couple of hotels – just for the night.'

There was a long silence.

'Look Jane,' said Fran, leaning across the table. 'I know you're hurt and angry. Of course you are. But I hope we can get over this.'

'You want me to forgive you?' Jane said with a forced laugh. She studied Fran's face. How much of what she could see there was repentance, she wondered, and how much was anxiety? Because she must be worried about the various consequences she would have to face now. 'You want me to *let it go* and *move on* do you? Is that what you're hoping Lucy's going to do too? And Patrick, when he gets to hear about this, because he will now, won't he?' She shrugged. 'Well, maybe they will,' she said, thinking of Nick Cartwright, 'but I don't think I can.'

She picked up another napkin and tore it in two. To forgive or not to forgive? It brought into play those old favourites of hers again – deception and betrayal. Fran had been deceiving her for years, but, humiliating as this was, she could see why it had been necessary. (It was like Neil still owning the cottage.) So she might be able to forgive her for the deception. But the initial betrayal! Surely that was essentially unforgiveable.

In time, she supposed, the anger she was feeling now would abate (in fact, it might already have started to do so.) But that didn't mean that forgiveness would follow. And what would forgiveness amount to, anyway, if she could never forget what Fran had done to her? No, however she might come to feel about Fran in the future, one thing was certain; the way she had felt about her in the past was gone. Lost for ever.

She stood up.

'Jane, please . . .'

'I don't think there's anything more to be said.'

She walked out of the room, leaving the door open behind her. She could hear John and Emer talking in the lounge. She crept upstairs and sat on the edge of the bed in the spare room. Her suitcase was open on the floor. While she was trying to decide what to do next, she heard voices in the hall. Fran and Emer were leaving.

She went into Daniel's tiny bedroom at the front of the house and stood looking out of the window. She watched Emer set off on foot in one direction and Fran go in search of her parked car in the other. The sound of the front door opening and closing must have roused Lucy who she could hear moving around in the other front bedroom. Trying not to make any noise, Jane went back to the spare room and began packing her case. This done, she wheeled it on to the landing and knocked on Lucy's door. Lucy was standing by the window and when she turned round Jane could see that she'd been crying.

'I'm going to go home now,' she said, holding up a hand to silence her daughter's protests. 'It'll be better all round if I do.'

She carried her case down the stairs and deposited it in the hall. John was in the kitchen loading the dishwasher.

'Do you think you could call me a taxi?' Jane asked him. She looked at her watch. 'To Marylebone, in about half an hour. I've decided to go home this evening.'

'Oh! Are you sure?' John said, looking concerned.

'Quite sure,' she nodded.

Lucy came into the kitchen. 'Don't go like this,' she said.

Jane smiled. 'I'm not storming off or anything. I just need to go home.' She turned to John. 'None of this is your fault,' she said. 'And don't go worrying about me. I'm fine. I've had weeks to process all this, remember. Now you two need some time to get your heads round things.' She reached for the kettle. 'I'll have a cup of tea before I go, though. I'll make a pot, shall I?'

John stepped into the hall to call the cab and Lucy leaned against the worktop looking miserable. 'I can't believe this,' she said.

But Jane wasn't going to be drawn. Let them sort themselves out, she thought. All of them. It wasn't her problem anymore. All she wanted to do now was go home and concentrate on her own future.

She went to the fridge to get the milk. 'Oh dear,' she said looking at the row of desserts sitting neatly on one of the shelves. 'We haven't had these. Do you want yours now?'

Lucy shook her head. 'I'll have it later,' she sniffed.

'OK,' said Jane. She poured three cups of tea.

'The cab'll be here in twenty minutes,' said John coming back into the kitchen.

'Thank you.'

Jane handed him his tea and he took it with him into the lounge where Daniel was playing. She went back to the fridge and took out one of the ramekins.

'That just gives me time to have mine,' she said to Lucy, removing the cling film and dipping a spoon into the chocolate ambrosia.

The End of the Road

ABOUT THE AUTHOR

Rosaline Riley was born and grew up in Lancashire. She now lives near Streatham Common in South London.

For many years she was a literature tutor in the Lifelong Learning Department at the University of Warwick where she specialised in teaching 20th century and contemporary novels.

The End Of The Road is her first published novel.

Website: http://thecommonreadercommonwriter.pathline.co.uk/

10285320R00178

Printed in Great Britain
by Amazon.co.uk, Ltd.,
Marston Gate.